The Last Van Gogh

Will Ottinger

Black Rose Writing | Texas

© 2019 by Will Ottinger
All rights reserved. No part of this book may be reproduced, stored in a retrieval system or transmitted in any form or by any means without the prior written permission of the publishers, except by a reviewer who may quote brief passages in a review to be printed in a newspaper, magazine or journal.

The author grants the final approval for this literary material.

First printing

This is a work of fiction. Names, characters, businesses, places, events, and incidents are either the products of the author's imagination or used in a fictitious manner. Any resemblance to actual persons, living or dead, or actual events is purely coincidental.

ISBN: 978-1-68433-193-2
PUBLISHED BY BLACK ROSE WRITING
www.blackrosewriting.com

Printed in the United States of America
Suggested Retail Price (SRP) $19.95

The Last Van Gogh is printed in Garamond

To my wife Sandra - always there.

Acknowledgements

Special thanks to my beta readers, Joe Berton and Jon Harbuck, and to my Houston writers group, *Scribblers Ink*. Their advice and insights were catalysts that pushed me back to the keyboard on impossible days.

A heartfelt thanks also to Gloria Groom, author, Senior Curator, and Chair of European Painting and Sculpture at The Art Institute of Chicago. Gloria was kind enough to take time from her extremely busy schedule to read the manuscript and offer advice on Van Gogh's life. Thanks also to my editor, Ron Seybold, who opened new paths. And I'd be especially remiss if I didn't mention the excellent biography of Van Gogh by Steve Naifeh and Gregory White Smith: *Van Gogh – A Life*.

And last but first in my heart, to my wife Sandra, the world's most voracious mystery reader. She never hesitated to read and reread my efforts, always with a sharp eye and encouraging word.

The Last Van Gogh

August 1887 South of Eindhoven Holland

The red-bearded man stopped and snatched off his battered straw hat, glowering at the ducks alongside the dike. He picked up a stone and hurled it at the birds, scattering the family of mallards that left a trail of pinfeathers on the water's surface. Jamming the hat on his close-cropped skull he wiped sweat from his blue eyes and hoisted the wooden paint box, wincing as its leather straps chafed his shoulders. He'd seen no one for the past hour, not a wagon or fellow traveler, only sea water and clusters of mindless ducks. Abetted by the heat, pain suddenly gripped his lower extremities as the painting swam before his eyes and voices whispered it was all for nothing.

Damn the doctors, he thought, all of them. Pulling a small medicine vial from his trouser pocket he flung it after the ducks and watched bubbles rise to the surface. Worthless, he thought. The fools did little to ease his suffering, mouthing dire predictions to justify their inability to cure him. Commissioned for the painting several months earlier, he fell ill at Eindhoven's train station, his body failing him again. His pastor father, dead these past four years, would have died sooner had he known the cause of his son's affliction. His generous patron never asked about the embarrassing ailment acquired from some forgotten prostitute. But if ever there was good fortune in sickness, the man provided ample proof. His host had been kind, even solicitous of his recovery, but then, the fellow was a Frenchman far from home, not a pious Dutchman strangled by ecclesiastical guilt.

Willing each foot forward, he listened to the mournful creak of windmill sails in the distance. Hunched against the sun's glare, he shrugged at the box's weight and shifted the patterned carpetbag to his left hand, the threadbare satchel containing his only change of clothes. Each step intensified the misery in his groin, rekindling memories of agonizing days spent on his savior's spare bed. He'd endured this one last pilgrimage to a country populated by Christian zealots and dull conformists, people who regurgitated Biblical warnings and catastrophic predictions. Even the dust stirred by his feet appeared frightened to blemish weeds along the causeway. As a younger man, he'd tilted at religion before swearing never to cross another church doorway.

Thirsty and foot-weary, he ran a hand over his bristly beard and patted the pouch secured inside his waistband. His benefactor and caretaker had paid well for the painting, saying he wanted companionship and would keep her away from prying eyes. No doubt the strange man possessed means, but where had he acquired such a swath of good canvas? Its sheer size compelled him to construct a makeshift easel. Most likely the contraption was kindling now, but his host had paid in gold coin, so the girl and easel were his to do with as he pleased. With the money he earned, he'd shake Holland's dirt from his brogans and take the first train to Antwerp, then back to Paris. He'd find artists who understood the need to see the world in a new light and together they'd form an enlightened colony to revolutionize art.

    The sun rained fiery nails through the crown of the old hat as he plodded forward, the heat jumbling his thoughts. Unbidden, the girl's image reappeared and he smiled, repainting her again and again in his mind: A fulsome young woman standing alone in a field of wind-swept wheat. God in heaven, how he loved women! Peasant women and prostitutes and shop girls, young and middle-aged, fetching and plain. For months, her image haunted his half-sleep, taunting him until he was forced to paint her. The life-sized young woman had leapt off his brushes, quite possibly his very best work, but if no one ever saw her, it wouldn't matter. She'd been a grand experiment, one that had allowed free rein to his boldest brush strokes, an erotic indulgence. When he printed 'Vincent' at the bottom left corner, he apologized to her for the small intrusion into her world. He regretted leaving her behind, an exile like himself in this godforsaken country. No matter, he thought. She would live as long as he remembered her.

    The unforgiving orb reached its apex as he walked over his shadow, perspiration in his eyes. The persistent heat stirred his sullenness and he decided there was no loss if his critics never saw her. Exposed to the world, she might disappear into oblivion—or be cut apart, her dissected remnants painted over by incompetent drudges. He pushed aside his anger and dismissed the heresy that he'd abandoned her. After all, she didn't belong to him and better times beckoned. He would return to Paris and study harder. The best was yet to come, a fresh start. He regretted his few friends would never see the girl, but the disappointment was unavoidable like most things in life.

    Ignoring the sun, he lengthened his stride along the embankment. No matter those closest to him believed him quite mad. Life was good again and the girl would live forever within him.

Vienna August 1936

Louis Dejean stroked the lapels of his new suit and allowed the doorman to admire his tailor's ability. Short and well-proportioned, Dejean presented a dapper figure accentuated by a precisely trimmed black moustache and dark tonsured hair. After a moment, he sighed and accepted the fact the embassy attendant existed only to open doors for his betters. But the man's failure to appreciate his appearance was secondary. What was more important was the telephone call that provided time away from his dreary cubbyhole of an office.

Affecting the air of a diplomat on an errand of national importance, he smoothed the material again. Arranging his face in a distracted manner that befitted the Senior Assistant to the Auxiliary French Ambassador, he caressed the cane's silver handle, a thoughtfully surprising gift from dear Charles.

Charles, he sighed. My fabulous brute.

The attendant tipped his cap and hurried down the embassy steps to hail a taxi. Dejean descended and climbed into the rear seat, wiping his face with a handkerchief and wrinkling his nose at the car's interior that smelled as though dipped in wet cigar ash. The image of Charles mercifully returned and Dejean pushed aside an intoxicating fantasy.

"Where?" the driver grunted without removing the cheap cigar from his mouth.

Dejean gave him an address on The Graben and the driver let out the clutch with a jerk. The car, a top-heavy Steyr, hurtled along the spacious boulevard, the driver honking at traffic and pedestrians who ventured near the heavy automobile. Dejean grasped the passenger strap above the door, thrown to one side as driver swerved around a traffic policeman, ignoring the startled cop's indignant whistle.

Humidity oozed into the Steyr's interior, the air stifling after several blocks. Dejean stared out the window at awnings of dark clouds above the rooftops, his diminutive figure almost lost from view inside the car. Sweltering on the seat's foul-smelling fabric, he wiped his forehead with the handkerchief, longing for the office's circulating fans. He ran his index finger inside his collar, his fingertip tip slick with perspiration and warm hair oil. For a man acutely aware of his body, Dejean long ago accepted his propensity to sweat, the crass humor of some distant creator who punished him with overactive glands. But the deity also provided a sensitive face with a slender nose that smelled the slightest opportunity, a virtue for those without wealthy fathers or special talents.

Outside the automobile window, Austrians scurried toward their drab lives. He'd learned to live among his former enemies, but more and more shop windows displayed ugly swastika flags, reminding passersby that their stolid world was tottering again. Thus far, there was no blood in the streets. Not yet, he thought.

The Austrian driver scratched his neck and lifted his eyes to the rear mirror, examining Dejean. "You work in that embassy?" he asked, his rural accent thick.

"Yes."

"You a Frenchie?"

"I am French," Dejean said, irritated at the man's loutish nature.

"*Scheisse*, I thought so." The driver spat the nauseous cigar stub out the window. "Must be nice to have a cozy job. Sitting in a fancy office and dolling out orders to people, while good Austrians are lucky to find a job."

Dejean started to tell him few people listened to orders given by a mid-grade subordinate but decided he owed no explanation, especially to a foul-mouthed taxi driver.

The taxi swung onto the Graben and slowed, halting in front of a presentable four-story apartment building. Dejean, anxious to flee the toxic conveyance, stepped out and removed several bills from his wallet, counting out the fare, plus a tip against his better judgement. The driver reached through the open window for the money and Dejean saw the small swastika lapel pin.

The driver followed his eyes and looked up at Dejean with an officious smile. "Our ranks are growing. The time is coming when Austria and Germany will no longer be France's puppet. Soon I will ride in the back and you will drive me wherever I desire. We won't be cheated out of victory by Jews and Communists next time."

Dejean straightened. "I fought in the trenches for three years," he said. "France didn't need either to defeat you."

"It will be different this time."

Dejean jabbed his finger against the enamel pin. "Not if you follow that twisted little spider."

The two men stared at one another, the taxi idling. The driver was young, his long face sallow and unlined except for creases at the corners of his thin lips. A shiver ran through Dejean followed by a flash of anger. Was this the future, this puffed-up oaf?

A blue mailbox sat a few feet away. Dejean looked down at the outstretched hand with its grimy fingernails and pocketed the gratuity, laying the exact fare on top of the box. The driver yelled but Dejean strode up the steps without looking back. Behind him, he heard the taxi door open. He turned and braced himself but the driver snatched the money off the box, shouting another oath as the taxi roared away.

Dejean caught his breath, surprised at his courage at facing down the younger man. He hadn't experienced such exhilaration since the first days of the War.

A column of brass card holders aligned beside a heavy oak door included the name he sought: Claude Bernard - Number One. The caller had been insistent to the point of hysteria—'*D'une importance cruciale*'—but the building stood in a pleasant enough section of Vienna and he would be dealing with a fellow countryman. Bored with paperwork and unattractive workmates, Dejean had gladly accepted the mundane assignment. Café Emile was a mere three blocks away and one could only consume so much strudel and dumplings. Whatever the reason for the frantic call, he would do his duty, then walk to the famous French restaurant.

He let a lion head door knocker fall three times and heard a muffled curse. A man in sock feet and shirtsleeves yanked open the door. Backlit by a long hallway, a daunting figure inspected him as though Dejean was peddling newspapers. He guessed the man past sixty, his baggy trousers stained with past meals and wrinkled from neglect. Pulling loose braces over his impressive shoulders, his would-be host's agitation mounted.

"What do you want?"

Dejean took a half-step back and graced him with a slight bow. "Monsieur Bernard? I am Louis Dejean from the embassy. You called and we spoke."

An ingratiating smile. "Of course, of course, my apologies," the man stammered. "Come in. Some wine and cheese, perhaps?"

"No, thank you." Dejean shuddered at what would surely be the cheapest

Riesling in the city. "My time's at a premium as I'm sure you can appreciate," he said, following his host down the uncarpeted hallway. He tasted Emile's Roquefort crepes and hoped his unshaven host wasn't prepared to pour out a prolonged tale of woe.

The apartment was cooler than the street but reeked of cheap cigarettes and grease. A bay window faced the street, curtains cinched against the morning heat. Dejean's footsteps echoed on the bare floor as the man indicated a disreputable sofa. Dejean hung the cane over one arm of the couch, wrinkling his nose at the dreary apartment that offered few signs of civility. He looked at his host and saw the worried figure was close to tears as he dragged a chair from the dining room and sat facing him.

Best to get right to it, Dejean thought, shaken by the emotional display. "You said there was a matter of some urgency, Monsieur Bernard."

Despite his distress, Bernard's voice firmed. "Yes, a dead man and a girl."

Dejean retained his composure. "Have you contacted the police?"

Bernard edged his chair closer. "You are an art lover, are you not, Monsieur Dejean."

"Yes," Dejean replied, his discomfort intensifying. "I have a small collection. Secondary artists mostly," he added, although several museums coveted his small Corot.

Bernard nodded. "My research revealed as much."

"Research?"

"There are biographies of all embassy staff members at the library," Bernard said. "Yours was most interesting. Your collection and reputation. You're what one terms a novice expert."

Dejean acknowledged his status with a nod but he had not spent embassy funds to discuss his modest collection. Resisting the temptation to consult his watch, he forced himself to remain a humble servant of France a few minutes longer despite the man's confused state of mind. "May I ask what prompted your call and personal investigation of my background?"

Bernard held up a hand and walked to the dining room where his shoes sat beneath the table. He dropped into a protesting chair and slipped on one shoe, lacing it. "I apologize for my appearance. I never wear shoes or my boots inside. The neighbors complain about the slightest noise. Too many would like my apartment for their married children." He grunted and tied the other shoe. "If they knew about the girl..." He sat back and wrung his square hands as though angry neighbors might burst through the door. "But she is the reason I called you. We must make plans."

A woman, Dejean thought. In all likelihood, a messy affair of some sort, or a mistress with a lost passport. But he'd also mentioned a dead man and that didn't bode well. The approaching lunch hour produced a faint rumble beneath his belt buckle but he forced his face to remain neutral.

"Plans, you said."

Wiping his hands on his grimy trousers, Bernard paced to the window. "Surely you see what is happening around us. Less than twenty years after the War and the Austrians are smiling at Germany again. My neighbors brag that Germany's resident madman is an Austrian."

Dejean decided to say nothing about his arrogant taxi driver. What need was there? The signs were everywhere a sane man cared to look.

"And what do you propose we do about this situation, you and I?"

"You must help me avoid the worst for her."

"And this dead man?"

"He is no longer of any consequence."

Most likely a deceased rival for the woman's affections, Dejean thought. Oh well, such things occurred with distressing regularity in Vienna. "Does this woman require asylum?"

Bernard flapped his hand, started to speak and stopped, frowning at Dejean. "*Non. Non.* The embassy cannot be involved. It risks too much." Tears formed again. "I have no family, Monsieur Dejean, no funds, no one to rescue her. I have no choice but to trust you."

Dejean hid his smile. A lover to be protected, just as he thought.

"Our government in Paris is comprised of fools," Bernard continued. He spat the accusation as though the fact was published in the morning paper. He lit a Gauloise of cheap Turkish tobaccos. "I cannot bear her falling into barbarian hands. France is her only fitting home, but I fear she may not be safe even there." He closed his eyes as if doing so would magically transport the woman in question to safety. "We must save her."

Dejean fidgeted and Bernard hurried on.

"Yes, yes, I know. You are a busy man. You are owed an explanation," he said. Forearms on his knees, he stubbed out the cigarette on his shoe sole and rubbed his palms together. "I am a Jew, you see. Does that matter to you? No? Good. I was born in Alsace to Antoine and Miriam Bernard. I served in the War. 21st Chasseurs, if you care to look it up. Afterwards, I dabbled in fine paintings until the venture bankrupted me. I had little money and less patience to deal with thieves and second-rate artists." He grunted at the memory. "That also can be verified." He went to the window again and edged the draperies apart.

"In 1929 I traveled to Holland, to assess a small collection of Impressionist oils. They were authentic but few of any consequence. The owner was an ancient Frenchman who lived in an oversized house outside Eindhoven. He never married and claimed he'd outlived his family." Bernard let the curtain fall and returned to the chair. "While we were discussing terms of a sale, he had a stroke. Keeled over right in front of me."

Bernard lit another cigarette and Dejean's image of warm crepes grew fainter. I can always fill a sack with pastries from Demel's on Kohlmarkt, he thought, worrying that his new suit was already ruined by the couch's soiled cushions.

"I got the old fellow into bed and tried to quiet him," Bernard continued. "but he kept pointing at a closed door. When I ignored him, he became agitated and produced a key from a chain around his neck. With his final breaths, he told me he'd commissioned a painting in 1887. That the artist fell ill and he'd had nursed him back to health. The painter had admitted the work was like nothing he ever attempted, created for their eyes alone. He said the man even visited the painting years later, claiming he needed to add more color, to breath more life into the image. The old fellow said he hid the painting from the world, afraid it would be stolen from him."

First a woman, now a painting, Dejean thought. He'd allow Bernard a few more minutes before hunger overrode good manners. "And what did you find in this locked room?"

Bernard walked back to the dining room. "No one other than myself has seen her since that day." He opened a cellar door. "Come."

Wooden steps descended into blackness. Hesitating on the first step, Dejean smelled coal, ancient timbers, and rotted paper. The dining room light revealed a banister on his left and he clung to it as he descended the stairs behind the broad back. Eyes fixed on the narrow steps, he feared for his new suit should he slip. At the bottom, Bernard pulled a beaded chain and a string of electric lights blazed overhead like a carnival midway. A bulbous black furnace squatted in one corner, the cracked cement floor swept surprisingly clean. Bernard walked to a wooden contrivance that leaned against the far wall. How had he maneuvered such a massive box into the cellar, Dejean wondered?

"The furnace keeps her warm in winter," Bernard said.

A tarpaulin covered the shipping container. Three meters high and over four meters long, a panel had been removed from one end of the huge crate. Bernard reached both arms inside and slid a massive gilt frame onto a strip of threadbare carpet, balancing what he'd birthed upright. He steadied the oversized frame and carefully removed layers of packing paper.

The painting was life-size. A young woman stood in a field of ripe wheat as though preparing to step from the canvas, swaying grain around her burnished by an overhead sun. The dazzling orb burned into a cobalt blue sky as if threatening to dissolve the heavens. Arms bare, the girl's simple beltless dress was a swirl of brilliant blue, strands of flaxen hair tousled by a gentle breeze. Her direct gaze challenged Dejean to join her, to walk from the cellar's colorless world into the lush field. Thick impasto brushstrokes defined her youthful body with a lover's embrace, moving unashamedly across and around and beneath the dress's gossamer-like cloth. It was an artist's love affair on canvas, and only one artist could have created her.

Tears coursed down Bernard's gray-stubbled cheeks as he stepped back and laid his fingertips against a burst of yellow sunlight trapped in one corner of canvas, the touch so feathery it bordered on reverence.

"*La femme*," he said.

Stunned, Dejean dared a whisper. "She is alive."

September 1, 1939 Paris

Robert Everham Barrow frowned at his gold Patek. Nine-thirty. Louis Dejean was late again. Seated at the restaurant window, Barrow sighed and took a swallow of his third morning scotch. The American embassy would function one more morning without me, he thought, relishing the smoky flow of the whiskey over his tongue. Breakfast with the fastidious little Frenchman would no doubt start office tongues wagging again. For months, associates at the embassy ragged him about their friendship, reminding him that Dejean was a known poof who lusted after his young body. Barrow ignored the jibes. Dejean was loyal to his paramour, a massive auto mechanic named Charles—*mon divin Charles* Dejean called him. Barrow sipped his scotch. What the hell was the man's last name?

Not that it mattered. The lone passion Barrow and Dejean shared was love of early Impressionist painters. Robert Barrow was twenty-two, almost fifteen years younger than Dejean. He'd met the minor French diplomat six months earlier at the Galleries National du Jeu de Paume, a dreary American reception marred by watery cocktails and a quartet of mediocre musicians. He apologized to Dejean, who only laughed and said Paris's finest collection of Impressionist work compensated the lack of amenities. They cemented an artistic friendship, Robert young and fair skinned with ginger hair, his swarthy counterpart shorter by half a foot, both of them entranced by the French masters. That first night, the impeccable little Frenchman had ignored disapproving glances from his superiors as they strolled the length of the hall, Dejean swinging a silver-handled cane and extolling the color and composition of various works, oblivious of his assigned duty to inspire confidence in the Maginot Line and France's military capabilities. A week later, they met again at another reception, the bond progressing to lunches and eventually a rare introduction to the burly and painfully shy Charles, Dejean's lover.

A morning breeze found the restaurant's open doorway and stirred the edges of the tablecloth as Barrow checked his watch again. The soft fall air was pleasant.

He inhaled succulent aromas from the kitchen and forgave his friend's tardiness, accustomed now to Parisian time. Emptying his scotch, he raised the glass toward the waiter for a refill.

I should know better than to indulge my weakness so early, Barrow thought. It would only spawn another bout of desk-bound ennui, but he reasoned a double order of sautéed chicken livers with his eggs would mitigate the alcohol's effects. The scotch simply represented retaliation against the humdrum of clerical work awaiting his return. The waiter brought the drink just as Dejean appeared at the cafe door. He spotted Barrow and walked briskly to the table, collapsing in the chair opposite him.

"*Bonjour, bonjour,*" Dejean gasped. Perspiration coated his forehead and he offered no apology, flapping the napkin into his lap.

"Poland!" he exploded.

"What's happened?" Barrow asked.

"You haven't heard? Where do your embassy experts stick their heads?"

"I didn't go to the office this morning."

"*Le Boche* invaded Poland," Dejean said. "England's demanded withdrawal."

"War." Barrow's delightful tenure in Paris was fast coming to an end.

"A war France cannot win, my friend." Dejean hailed a waiter, "Not this time. The doddering fools at the War Ministry are still fighting the last one." Scowling at Robert's scotch, Dejean ordered a bottle of the restaurant's most costly champagne. "A perfect day to toast my country's ineptness."

Barrow held up a hand. "I hope you don't think we'll split that. I can't return drunk again."

Dejean laughed. "Did I say I planned to share?" He twisted a croissant in half, scattering crumbs as he slathered the roll with butter. "But I will be generous today. The world has gone mad and you will need fortification for what you'll see after lunch." He dusted crumbs from his hands with a brusque motion. "You must call in sick for the rest of the day."

Accustomed to two-hour lunches and impromptu tours of museums and galleries, the possibility of a leisurely afternoon eroded with Dejean's news. Panic would rule the American embassy in the wake of Germany's invasion.

Barrow shook his head. "Can't do it. They'll expect me to show up today. Sober for a change."

The champagne arrived with two glasses. The waiter poured and Dejean quaffed his wine in a single swallow. "Nonsense. Nothing any of us can do now." He refilled his glass and touched Barrow's flute. "To the end of peace and Europe."

Barrow gave in. "*Salut*, and damn 'em all."

They drank in silence until Dejean said, "A quick breakfast, then we're off. We have work to do." He broke off another chunk of the bread and pretended to study the menu as several men walked past the table. He interlaced his fingers on the tablecloth and assessed the young face across from him. So young to take on such responsibility, he thought, but he had only his instincts to guide him now. He pushed aside the champagne.

"I need your help, my friend," Dejean said dolefully. "I have a *probleme*, to employ the mildest term."

Barrow started to protest but Dejean plunged ahead. "If your embassy functions as ours, you can ship large items from France without the authorities delving too deeply into the contents or reason." The infectious smile reappeared. "To use an American idiom, there are ways to skate around any problem... if you grease the blades with money. I'm not a rich man, but I will supply whatever funds I can. You must help me."

The young American refilled his glass from the dark green bottle, the scotch happily greeting the onrush of good champagne. What the hell, Barrow thought, nothing wrong with a little intrigue. The civilized world's disintegrating and my brief diplomatic career's about over. They'll sack me for sure now. Cut loose a drunk and needless expense. He emptied his glass, removed his suit coat, and slung it over the back of his chair, smiling as the world softened around him.

"What do you want me to do?"

Chapter One

Saturday Night February 2018 Chicago

Winter rain crystalized into sleet as the police cruiser eased past my gallery's front window. The black and white turned the corner onto Huron and I relaxed. The Adam Barrow Gallery was having a good night and the last thing I needed were flashing red lights reflecting off Vasily Sorokin's paintings.

The police cruiser combined protection and a curse. I'd located my gallery four blocks from what was once Cabrini Green, Lyndon Johnson's failed public housing experiment turned ghetto. Tucked into a block of five attached businesses, my small contribution included what developers generously termed 'gentrified renewal'. Freshened with track lighting and an upgraded interior, first-rate contemporary realism filled inviting alcoves strategically arranged throughout the gallery. I'd accepted the hazards of locating near the city's slums, a part of the city that blended felons with artsy risk-takers. It was a gamble but I found the rich and adventurous got a perverse thrill from occasional slumming.

The crowd appeared in good spirits as I stood by the door, estimating the room's combined net worth, relieved the late afternoon storm off Lake Michigan hadn't dented eagerness to view Vasily's dazzling work. Persistent shards of sleet pinged against the front window as my assistant Sally, attired in the obligatory black cocktail dress, worked the room with her bubbly charm, her cropped blond hair bobbing among the crowd. Our star Vasily slipped among flashy singles and older couples, playing up his Russian accent, the show his largest exhibit to date.

An overfed contented-looking man wandered up and lifted his wine glass toward me. Harry Helms was middle management down to his brown wingtips, his eyes claiming indirect ownership of all he saw around him.

"Good crowd, Adam."

I shook my banker's hand. "Guarantees next month's payment, Harry."

My eyes followed his. The convivial crowds enjoying Vasily' paintings produced simultaneous smiles. Like most borrowers, my feelings for Harry swung between grateful and an urge to tell him to go screw himself. Owing people money does that to you.

"Nice to see you doing well," he said.

"No choice. You drive a tough bargain."

The banker laughed. "Good wine too. Goes with the crowd from what I can see."

"Your check's in the mail."

He grinned and wandered back to the browsers, looking at the walls as if he owned them, which, in fact, he did. I'd been fortunate in locating a small new bank. Desperate for deposits and loans they gambled on my dream. Unlike many competitors, my gallery was not wound around a mommy-and-daddy bank account. Maybe it was the lure of an art gallery as a client, but the bank bet on a desperate thirty two-year old, binding my future to the loan agreement in their files. It was a risk on both our parts, but I knew what I wanted. I wanted headlines that read "Deprived Boy Makes Good" or, "Thief's Son Overcomes Horrific Childhood." Hell, on the worst days, I'd settle for "Struggling Art Dealer Makes a Buck." Despite my unbalanced balance sheet, things were looking up. I'd finally gotten what I wanted, and while I might be slightly damaged goods, I was beating back the past.

My gamble on the talented young Russian artist produced my first major break. Half a dozen major critics agreed with my assessment and I smelled success. I smiled at Sally who winked and surreptitiously rubbed her thumb and forefinger together. Profit was in the air, and even the industrial pungency of newly-installed carpet grew less noticeable. I'd selected better Chardonnays and Pinots for the festivities, foregoing cleverly labeled vinegar that one endured at most openings. Better yet, I'd counted four pieces with red 'sold' tags. So far, so good.

I started toward Vasily when a disheveled figure bumped against the door and slid to the sidewalk, sleet bouncing off his outstretched legs. Unfortunate but not unusual, I thought with a frown. This wasn't Mr. Rogers neighborhood. When I looked more closely at the new arrival, the evening began to slip away.

My brother had arrived in all his glory.

Of all the chaotic nights in my life, I didn't need a besotted Wes appearing like some mythical Greek god bent on destruction. His back against the glass door, slumped beneath a partially collapsed umbrella, a thin khaki raincoat buttoned to his chin, his ratty tennis shoes scuffed sponges. I tried to signal Damon, my door-minder, but he was engaged in a hand-waving discussion with the caterer.

My brother's arrival caused the rain to fall harder and I envisioned the storm following him inside. He folded a broken umbrella with more care than it deserved and removed the high-topped shoes, slinging away water and grime as if the act might dry them. He slipped them back on and struggled to his feet. He pushed open the door and our eyes connected like first-round boxers assessing weaknesses.

The gust of lakefront wind ruffled expensive hairdos, their owners glowering at us as though the gallery was being raided. His soiled Nikes squished onto my pristine maroon carpet and I opened my mouth to suggest a retreat back into the rain, but something in his face chopped off the rebuke. Only moderately drunk for a change, Wes flashed his patented disarming smile.

"I'm looking for my brother, Adam Barrow."

"Hello, Wesley," I said, aware more eyes had shifted from Vasily's paintings to the confrontation.

Soaked to his underwear, his face sallow and lined, Wes seemed to have aged a decade since I'd last seen him sprawled on a tavern floor, but tonight he appeared more vulnerable in out-of-season clothes and a three-day growth of beard. Smiling at the crowd without the usual anger of most street people, he stepped back and theatrically surveyed my Boss blazer, gray slacks, and black silk tee. His sardonic smile confirmed I'd deserted the ranks of the proletariat.

"Bohemian or California cool?"

"Don't be an ass, Wes. What're you doing here?"

"Not the most brotherly greeting," he said with a tired grin. He swayed slightly, a damp stain spreading beneath his shoes. A tipsy brother and evening devoted to coaxing money from wealthy clients did not mix.

"Again, Wes, what do you want?"

"Sorry to ruin your soiree." He glanced down at the carpet, swaying. "And your floor." He smirked at the paintings around us and nodded as though confirming his worst fears. "You finally got what you wanted."

"You mean I didn't become a drunk like you and dad." I regretted the words the moment they left my mouth, but they were true. My brother and I didn't exactly live enchanted childhoods, constantly surrounded by the clink of shot glasses and whiskey bottles. Which was how we'd grown up. I eventually deserted the war zone, while Wes used my father's disease as an excuse to roll downhill.

"Does Barbara know where you are?" I asked.

Wes hesitated, then nodded as though remembering he was married. "Yeah, no problem. I got my pass signed tonight."

Twelve years older than me, my brother barely topped five foot nine. I stood four inches taller and had inherited my father's English genes, while Wes reflected the darker complexion of our Italian mother. My dark brown hair evaded the onset of age, while his was streaked dull gray, any distinguished appearance ruined by defeated eyes and loose skin that resembled spoiled veal. Whatever prompted his arrival, I suddenly regretted relegating my carpet's survival above my only brother. I maneuvered him past disapproving buyers, managing a smile as though a long-lost fraternity brother had stumbled in from the storm. Sally frowned and gestured at a black Lincoln Town Car that pulled to the curb across the street, the hopeful harbinger of more disposable income.

With no time to babysit Wes, I guided him into the work area where art storage bins rose to the ceiling and caterers tended tables laden with food and wine. Tuxedo-attired servers, another extravagance, stared at us. Wes collapsed onto a metal chair and I tossed hors d'oeuvres onto a rented china plate and handed it to him. I needed to get back to the waiting checkbooks.

"As you see, I'm in the middle of an opening," I said, ignoring the stares. Was Barbara roaming the streets looking for him? "Do you need a few dollars?" Wes had a reputation of borrowing from street sharks who added 20% interest a day.

He placed the untouched plate on the floor beside him and met my uneasy expression with the infuriating smile. "Actually, I do, but we need to talk about dad."

The mention of our father devalued the evening another notch. I was vaguely aware Damon and the catering supervisor stared at Wes with disgust. Beyond the door, I heard Vasily laugh, the chorus of cheerful voices pleading for my return. What was I supposed to do with an alcoholic brother on the most critical night of my brief career?

"Our father's dead," I managed.

"Something's happened." The light in Wes's eyes was a phenomenon I'd not seen in years. "He left us something quite unexpected, little brother."

"Use my name." I'd always resented being viewed as the family baby. "The estate was settled a year ago. If you remember, we divvied up his junk."

He shrugged. "I just got around to sorting through my share."

Searching for a forgotten twenty squirreled away in a book, I thought. He shrugged out of his sodden coat and hung it over the back of the chair. His soiled shirt, once a button-down white oxford, was remarkably dry, a testament to the valiant raincoat. My brother wasn't going away.

Beaming again, he said, "I found something. You of all people will know if it's bullshit."

I had to get back to my eager clients. "If you found something, keep it as a remembrance."

Wes didn't need my approval for whatever he'd found, having looked after dad in his last days, earning anything he discovered among a lifelong accumulation of junk. I long ago gave up on our father, and time never fabricated maudlin redemption in my eyes.

"This goes back," Wes insisted, "before his world fell apart."

"Look, stay here, eat something. I'll talk to you later. "

He eyed a server with a tray of wine. Slouched in the chair, he jammed his hands in his trouser pockets. "Okay, I'll wait." He cleared his throat. "Maybe one glass of wine?"

I started to protest but the furnace kicked in with a thump and a wave of heat washed over us from overhead vents. He closed his eyes as though a benevolent presence dispensed warmth on the needy.

I should have known better but I said, "All right, one glass, but I may be awhile."

"I can wait."

I pointed at the plate of food and headed back into the swirl of contented murmurs of praise for Vasily's sumptuous oils. The young Russian artist beckoned me toward an older couple who stood before the show's largest painting. Vasily flung an arm around my shoulder and grinned at the man and wife impeccably dressed in formal evening attire.

"Best goddamn gallery owner in city," he boomed at me, thickening his Russian for their benefit.

The wife blanched and her husband ignored Vasily's zeal. I noticed Mister GQ Magazine's diamond pinky ring and heavy Oyster Rolex as he edged back from the five-by-five canvas and grimaced at his bejeweled spouse. She held his stare and he looked back to the painting, a $50,000 magnificent Russian woodland scene of pale blue snow and shadows cast by dying afternoon sunlight, a startling reincarnation of Repin, Monet, and Renoir. I still could barely believe I'd latched onto Vasily before the major players found him.

The husband compressed his lips and shot his cuffs. "Your best price."

It was a practiced gesture, a demand rather than negotiation. I didn't get many assholes in the gallery but this guy just made valedictorian. I made eye contact with Vasily, one of the best artist-salesmen in memory. We both knew a sale stood in front of us, whatever the price. Dressed in black with a small neatly-trimmed black beard, he presented the perfect rendition of a successful artist, and I let him close the sale. His accent intensified as he waved at the painting.

"Ah, this one?" he intoned innocuously. "Best work in last two years." He raised three fingers. "You are third—how you say—expert to ask about it tonight," he lied.

Concern crept over the wife's features, ownership slipping away. She glared at her husband and set her lips in a matching grimace. Conceding defeat, he salvaged his ego as though considering a larger Bentley.

"My wife likes it, but I never pay face value."

Vasily gave the barest smile. "I do not think Adam resists ten percent reduction."

I nodded and matched his smile. "A check's acceptable."

Handshakes and smiles as we turned back to the painting. A waiter appeared with good timing and chilled chardonnay and we toasted the couple's exceptional taste, the wife gushing about hanging the acquisition above their new Brunschwig & Fils sofa. Try as I might, I couldn't avoid the sinking feeling that the astounding piece of art had been purchased as a sofa decoration. Only an interior decorator arriving with a swatch of cloth in hand struck more disgust in the heart of any gallery owner who loved art above adornment. However, in all honesty, I shouldn't have cared, having just covered the next six months' rent.

I cut my eyes toward the storage area where Wes waited. He rarely wanted to talk with me except when I bailed him out of drunk tanks from Chicago to California, sometimes with borrowed money, reluctantly excelling in the role of the younger brother playing Good Samaritan.

I offered another round of congratulations to the couple as Vasily promised to attend the unveiling at their home. He excused himself and I followed him through two more rapid sales, the night humming with magic called a buying frenzy in less sophisticated circles. Halogen spots radiated soft light off his magnificent paintings, breathing life into landscapes and village scenes to the delight of well-heeled buyers. As much as I loved their money, I loved the gallery more, reveling in opening the door every morning to walls of luminous oils encased in golden frames, my link to artists who painted their souls onto canvas and board.

Two hours later the last drinkers and dawdlers departed near midnight, the downpour having stopped, trading sleet for patches of ice along the streets. My calves ached after standing four hours in thin-soled Italian loafers, my smile cramping as I bid Sally and Vasily goodnight. Turning from the door, I faced the gallery, overwhelmed by the profusion of red dots indicating sales until I suddenly remembered Wes whom I'd left to the mercy of Damon and the snickering caterers. He'd kindled my curiosity with his claim of a supposed legacy from our father. Slinging my blazer over one shoulder I hurried into the work area. Two empty cabernet bottles sat beside the metal chair, Wes nowhere in sight.

I struggled to maintain my good mood. Angry but not surprised at being roped in by my brother again, I resolved to avoid him. Brother or no brother, I'd let him wallow in the gutter if he preferred life as a drunk. The thought killed my urge for a celebratory drink and I turned off the lights. I set the alarm system and locked up without a thought about the Lincoln still parked across the street.

Chapter Two

My phone rang at six-thirty next morning. I rolled over in the grey gloom and stretched my arm across the pillows before recalling I'd slept alone. Saturday mornings were not always so kind. Six girlfriends in four years left too many tangled sheets and tearful arguments. My last adventure, Cecilia, had morphed into a buy-me, take-me who consumed and then destroyed what I thought was a flourishing relationship. This morning, however, my bed and conscience remained intact after a profitable evening.

Rising onto one elbow, I fumbled with the insistent phone and fell back onto the pillow that preserved the aroma of the former queen of American Express.

"Hello," I said, hoarse from the previous night.

"Am I interrupting a tender moment?" Wes, always the wiseass.

"Only my sleep. Where the hell did you go last night?"

"Your wine selection was outstanding but my pride intruded. I got fed up with stares from minimum wage worker bees."

I sat up on the side of the bed, my previous evening's resolve fading as Starbucks asserted its addictive appeal. "You still want to talk?"

"I think we need to." The urgency I'd heard the night before resurfaced, and I wondered if it was a ploy to cajole another 'loan.' Barbara had forbidden more Johnny Walker handouts.

"There's a Starbucks around the corner on LaSalle," I said. "We met there a few months back, but you were pretty drunk."

"Too crowded. They jam coffee freaks in there like a Japanese commuter train."

Lingering elation from the previous night tempered my impatience. "Your call then."

"Dillon's for lunch. I'll save a booth in the rear. "

"Gee, an Irish pub. What a surprise."

"See you at noon."

He clicked off before I could suggest a quiet restaurant. I liked Dillon's, but bars represented luxury suites in hell with VIP elevators reserved for my brother.

I opened the gallery at ten, filled the empty spaces with new paintings, and left Sally with strict orders to sell the remainder. She successfully stifled her hilarity at my humor and I headed out into Chicago's alleged spring that ignored all calendars. Arctic wind, compliments of the lake, ricocheted off concrete and bricks, cutting through my black leather jacket and wool turtleneck like K-Mart cotton. My outfit was a holdover from my college days, an IRA conspirator off to bomb the Black and Tans.

The bar was six blocks from the gallery. Dillon's reluctantly tolerated Wes after an altercation with two Ivy League suits the previous month. The brawl came short of sparking a lawsuit, probably because he'd gotten his ass kicked, but there'd been previous episodes; alcohol acted as Wes's malfunctioning support system. If he was off his infrequent AA wagon, maybe I could head off the boilermakers.

Dillon's worked hard to replicate a Dublin pub. I opened the heavy glass door, greeted by Irish folk music, tall wooden booths, and a black tin ceiling. A sad string of wilted paper shamrocks left over from last St. Patrick's Day completed the ruse. Only a Colonel Blimp type in tweeds and bleating sheep wandering between tables were missing from the Auld Sod.

The portly Irish bartender lumbered to the end of the bar, a wet wooden match between his teeth. The sole authentic Gaelic fixture in the place, he leaned on the bar and inclined his head toward the rear.

"In the back booth," he said. "Any hint of a dust-up and you're both out of here."

I made my way past hunched backs along the bar, a few tables filled with early regulars from the neighborhood. Wes sat in a high-backed booth, head bowed, a pyramid of five shot glasses stacked in front of him. How much head start had he stolen on me? He raised the sixth glass in greeting.

"Welcome, little brother."

His navy windbreaker and khakis were relatively clean, his words not yet slurred. Like most serious drinkers Wes pushed hard to get drunk. The booths on either side were empty, the bar twenty feet away. I slid over the marbled green plastic seat and pointed at the triangle of glasses.

"Good to see you're taking AA seriously," I said.

"A temporary reversal. I wanted to show you and the sanctimonious bastards I can turn it on and off. Not everyone fits their theories."

"That kind of thinking does so much to show your superiority. Barbara must be proud to have married a man with an iron will."

Wes flushed. Either the whiskey kicked in or my observation found its mark.

"She understands," he muttered. "Really, she does."

"She's a saint, Wes. She should've bailed on you years ago."

"Thank you for the assessment of my marriage." Whiskey mangled the last word and I wondered how long he'd been here.

I leaned back and stared at him, aware of all the purported reasons for his drinking. Chief among them was being a failed caregiver for our father. Barbara's income as a top paralegal kept them afloat, while Wes's sales resume shrank to dated excuses followed by failed interviews. He un-stacked the glass pyramid and lined up his treasures in a row, his face close to the table to check the alignment. I watched and waited.

"You have a successful night with your Russian genius?" he asked, squinting at his handiwork.

"We made money," I replied. "I'll find a spot for you if you clean up your act."

Wes managed a crooked grin. "My act," he said without looking up. After a moment, he straightened and downed his shot. "I don't know shit about art. Except how to scam people. Our father was an expert teacher."

I ignored the truth and tossed him a lifeline. "You know people and you can sell, better than me. I can teach you about art and our artists."

"I didn't ask for a job."

"It's there for you if you'll grow up." I had a knack for stepping in it where Wes was concerned.

He managed a short laugh. "Thanks for the vote of confidence."

Same old conversation, I thought. Same barriers erected before I moved out of our house above Santa Monica. Baggage now for both of us, but fresh as the morning TV news in Wes's mind. We'd already reached the stage where I normally stormed off or escalated the quarrel. Instead, I raised my hand at the waitress and ordered a beer. Wes glanced at her but said nothing. I was mildly impressed with his restraint, despite the regiment of empty glasses. I pitied him. Maybe the previous night's success had mellowed me.

"You had something you wanted to show me," I said, anxious to get back to the gallery.

"I'm flattered you remembered in the midst of your triumph." Wes's voice rose. "Nothing like making money to fuel a little generosity."

The bartender glanced our way and turned up the music. Wes's last drink had hit home but I avoided the challenge. He tapped his fingers on the tabletop to the backbeat and waited for our usual argument to begin. When I didn't rise to the offering, he spoke slowly, careful keep his words from slurring.

"You want to know what I found, or you want to lecture me? If it's the latter, I'll find another bar."

"If it concerns dad, I want to hear it," I said patiently. A partial lie.

He drummed the table harder, a challenge in his eyes. "Sure, you do. A deserter's remorse."

"God damn it, Wes..."

"What? All your education didn't teach you to be honest with yourself?" He tilted his head back and drained the few drops remaining in his glass. "A deserter always pretends regret, claiming lost faith in the cause. You ran to Los Angeles and became a college boy, and I stayed with dad."

"Okay." I'd long ago accepted the truth that added to Wes's downfall. "I was an immature bastard if that's how you want to remember it. I lived with my mistake but I grew up." If there were a way to go back in time, I'd grab it. Reach back through the muck and mire and do what most of us desired: alter every bad decision we thought had been beyond our control. I wanted to compare the choices he'd made to my own, but something in his face stopped me.

"You still have a choice," I said. Damn it, I loved him despite his inability to overcome a shitty childhood.

The waitress plopped down my beer. Wes ordered another Bushmills and I didn't try to stop him. An Irish tenor sang about life's unfairness and I wondered if the man knew our family. Wes killed half his whiskey when it arrived and I studied my beer without lifting the mug. Drunk or not, his memory was accurate. We grew up in a battered bungalow in the hills above the Pacific, the small house built in the days before real estate prices became California's gold standard. It was the only house we ever knew and my father's affection for it never waned. Robert and Helena Barrow built the house before Wes and I were born and our mother loved it, the ocean view her one joy as my father emptied liquor bottles. She died the year I arrived.

Wes nursed him from a wheelchair to the bed from which he never rose. Living off my father's meager government pension and Social Security checks, Wes surrendered the prime years of his life, changing sheets and emptying bedpans. I ploughed through UCLA and the Chicago School of Art, my father living his dreams through me and my sporadic letters, as his love of art drifted away along with his mind. Per his will, Wes and I retained joint title to the property. In his last days, our father probably knew Wes would need a landing pad. The house was the single asset of any value he left us; not a piece of art remained on the walls, long ago pawned off for more liquor. When he died Wes couldn't move out fast enough. He grabbed his half share of the meager estate and tested his freedom up and down the California coast with a string of failed jobs. He justified his drinking by using my decision to leave him as a caretaker. He married Barbara and they lived in the old place for a year until its memories squirmed into his brain and he climbed deeper into the bottle. My role expanded to scraping together bail money and pleading with her not to change the locks.

I'd deserted Wes and my father, but what did I prove? I had an art education and a mortgaged gallery skirting the edge of financial disaster. Had I matured into something superior to Wes? Like the shopworn joke, Webster's had my photo next to the definition of mediocrity.

"You think you're a modern Phoenix?" Wes asked bitterly. "Some kind of martyr majestically rising from the ashes of dad's foul ups?"

I sipped my beer and didn't rise to the bait. Wes listened to another baleful Irish ballad, but the singer had nothing on us. I accepted there was no magic left in the world, no manna tumbling from heaven into your breadbox. Hell, not even working your guts out accomplished much of anything most of the time. Rehashing our boyhood didn't help, a shopworn exercise that ultimately collapsed into tedium because it spun round and round with no resolution or agreement.

"We're brothers, Wes."

"Barely," he scoffed and we laughed together.

We'd been late creations. Medical journals should have written up our father as a sexual marvel. Thank God, he married a younger woman, but when cancer took her, he loaded up with guilt and tried to survive without the woman he loved. Wes glared into his glass, then regained the spark I'd seen the night before. I couldn't tell if it was the alcohol or some new scheme he could borrow against. Unzipping his windbreaker, he withdrew a folded manila envelope. The front bore our names in our father's shaky handwriting. Wes tilted the envelope and dumped the contents onto a dry portion of the table.

"I'm not sure what the hell these mean, but I figured you'd know." Wes signaled the waitress with a raised finger. "Dad wrote one of them when I was in junior high. The other's a name I remember from his ramblings near the end."

The envelope bore a faint blue Par Avion stamp in one corner. The paper was tissue thin and had been mailed to our childhood home. I picked up the envelope with a stamp depicting a bullfighter flourishing a cape. The faded postmark read *Madrid, 24 Noviembre, 1941.*

"Read that one first," Wes said.

There was no return address and the gossamer paper appeared it might dissolve if I dropped it in my beer.

My dear Robert,

I pray this letter reaches you. I asked an old embassy friend to mail it from Spain if he succeeds in crossing the border. He knows nothing of our little venture, but I sleep soundly knowing the girl is safe. From a house outside Eindhoven to America. I shudder to think if she had been left to the kind mercies of Vienna, or even our beloved Paris. The German cochons are stealing everything, but you and I, we outsmarted them, so the girl eludes their grasp, thanks to whatever gods watch over us.

My advice to you is this: If you have her, do nothing for now. Keep her safe for the moment. War is not the proper time to reveal her existence to the world. Great minds who can appreciate her are scattered, and the remaining pigmies will not honor what they see. Vincent would desire she be given proper adulation, do you not agree? I fear what will happen if the Vichy collaborators discover we smuggled her out of France. Sadly, America remains neutral, and no one knows what your bureaucrats might do if they discover we liberated her.

I fear there's little time left for my kind. Charles is safe for now but the Boche confiscated my collection and are rounding up those of us they see as undesirables. My predilection is well-known and I'm certain they've included me in their orderly card catalog as socially objectionable.

Take care, my friend, and if the fates decide in my favor, we will share our ill-gotten but well-meaning gains.

Louis

I folded the flimsy and returned it to the envelope, confused. "Dad and this man Louis smuggled a woman out of France?"

Wes laughed as if he'd beaten me at my own game. He shoved a folded sheet of paper across the table. "Now read this."

Dad's full name was embossed in raised letters at the top of the stationary, the inked text uneven as though he'd written it in the dark. There was no date.

Wesley and Adam,
As they say, you'll probably find this when I'm dead.
I'm afraid I'm more than a little drunk as I write this, but that will come as no surprise. Forgive me this one time because I've found gin more effective than all the damned pain killers.

The next line was blotted out where his fountain pen had leaked as if he'd pressed down too hard.

The important thing now is the Van Gogh's safety. I've hidden it away and saved it for the two of you. The enclosed letter explains the one good deed I performed for art. My friend Louis Dejean and I did the right thing. Poor Louis. Murdered by the Nazis because he was a homosexual. Worse, I imagine some fool may one day claim we stole the painting, but there was no one left to steal it from, so we did nothing wrong. This time, I'm truly innocent.

Each time I gazed at her I found no words. After all these years I still cannot believe I possess it. The sheer scope of what the crazy bastard painted will boggle minds. In case you're wondering what the hell I'm raving about, the canvas measures an enormous six feet by 10 feet, maybe larger. Bigger than anything Vincent Van Gogh ever attempted to my knowledge. Nothing in any museum in the world can approach it.

Imagine me owning such a work. I can't tell you how many times I sat before her and fell in love all over again.

The writing became shakier as if he'd gripped the pen too hard.

Your mother understood that I couldn't bring myself to sell her. The girl is mine, one of two women I ever loved. She doesn't belong on an auction block with dollar signs spinning around some fool's head, or museum idiots arguing where to hang her to bring in paying crowds. She's safe for now and I commit her into your hands.

Typical drama of the kind good old dad preferred when he was drowning in his cups. The next line was scratched out, unreadable, the ink smeared by a drop of sweat or gin. Then, the last line:

32 *The Last Van Gogh*

Tired and thirsty now. I'll finish this tomorrow.

The remainder of the page was blank, but my eyes returned to two words.

Van Gogh.

I stared at the iconic name, realizing how Columbus felt when the New World appeared over the Santa Maria's bow. The sensation lasted just long enough for reality to reassert itself. An immense Van Gogh owned by our father?

Wes beamed. "Well?"

"Wes..."

He shook his head, ignoring the drink the waitress placed in front of him. "Look, he died before finishing the letter. I know what you're thinking, but why would he create a fantasy when he knew he was dying?" He lowered his voice. "Death bed confessions are admissible evidence in court. I know. I looked it up. And this Dejean backs his claim. We've got to find it, little brother."

If nothing else, my hard-won education served as a warning not to spend my life scouring attics for lost masterpieces; that's how people ended up junk dealers on the seedier side of town. I gently placed my hand on Wes's sleeve.

"C'mon, man. No one ever catalogued a Van Gogh like that. A wall-sized masterpiece that just disappeared? Did dad also keep a unicorn in the attic and bury a box of artifacts from Atlantis?" I tried to control my disbelief from edging into ridicule. "Look, all art comes to market because of the four D's: death, debt, divorce and disinterest. Only a few miracles ever pop up. I'm busting my butt to survive. I can't chase some fantasy dad dreamed up. Huge Van Goghs don't materialize out of thin air after a hundred years."

Despite my diatribe the buzz persisted inside my head. Our father claimed he owned an outlandish Van Gogh! I picked up Dejean's envelope, trying to construct a logical connection. The two letters failed to compute, another outlandish castle in the sky. A sixty-square foot Van Gogh was a phantasm spawned by my father's occasional experiments with LSD or patented five-day binges. There was no priceless Van Gogh whisked out of France before World War Two, then stashed away for 50 years. My studies of Impressionism never revealed attempts by Van Gogh to create a monumental canvas.

Wes lifted the letter from my fingers and reverently returned it to the manila envelope. A young couple took the booth behind us and he lowered his voice again. "If it existed," he persisted, "it would be worth millions, right?"

"It never existed except in dad's imagination," I insisted.

"But if it did, how much?"

I opened my mouth but refused to venture a number, partly because I couldn't imagine one. Millions wouldn't begin the cover its value. Off the charts. Wes had no idea what a massive undiscovered Van Gogh would be worth, and giving him a number would only inflame his eagerness. His excitement was tangible across the table, a shot at reparations for his bankrupt life—if the two letters' claims were true. Wes remained at war with our dead father, seeking a payday for his lost years.

On my side of the table, I harbored a guilty daydream of my own, seeking improbable ways to make amends for Robert Everham Barrow who cheated collectors and sold fake works of art with a winning smile that Wes inherited. His death never erased my guilt when someone connected our last name. Vasily's rise to fame was partially redeeming the Barrow name and I couldn't endanger it with two old letters. Somewhere above the smoke-filled barroom, dad's familiar chuckle rained down from the ceiling as he watched us argue over his pipedream. Dillon's was an appropriate setting to enjoy his last little joke. Wes had to see there was no reward in pursuing a fantasy.

"Don't get treasure fever," I said. "Even the painting's sheer size makes no sense. You and I crawled all over that house as kids. A canvas of those dimensions wasn't tucked away in a closet. Besides, Van Gogh didn't paint large. There's no evidence something like that ever existed, and if it did, it couldn't simply disappear without a record of its existence. The only proof is these letters you found. Even if good ol' dad discovered the Holy Grail, he neglected to tell us where he hid the damned thing."

Wes downed the last of his whiskey and stared into the glass as though the amber whiskey repaired the past. "Were we bad people? You and me and dad?"

"Not bad, just wounded," I said. "We got caught in his crossfire while we were trying to grow up."

Wes waved at the waitress again. The bartender intercepted the signal and shook his head at the girl. She hesitated, then walked behind the bar and pretended to count her tips. Wes refolded the manila envelope and tucked it into his jacket pocket. He started to rise when I caught his arm again.

"I was serious about a job," I said. "Come to the gallery after we close and we'll talk."

His mouth flirted with a smirk and I waited for the inevitable wisecrack. Instead, he surveyed dedicated afternoon drinkers at the bar and patted the envelope inside his jacket. "Maybe," he said, zipping up his jacket. "I'll check my appointment calendar."

"Your decision, Wes, but there's a job waiting if you want it."

Chapter Three

Wes didn't show and by six o'clock the last browsers made nice noises, bought nothing, and left before darkness covered the sins along Huron Street.

I straightened stacks of brochures and wandered among the alcoves, warmed by the paintings and graceful figurative bronzes, trying to rekindle the previous night's glow of sales. Vasily's few remaining paintings ruled the walls, lording supremacy over my other offerings. The impetuous Russian represented my salvation. I loved the business to the point of an irrational fixation despite my father's lifelong attempts to steal his fellow art lovers blind.

After Sally bid me goodnight I locked the front door behind her, checking the street for Wes one last time. In all likelihood he'd found a new bar to indulge his self-pity. I didn't want to totally write him off as a lost cause, but that moment was drawing closer.

Streetlights popped on as cars headed toward restaurants and the theater district. Standing at the window I watched the traffic and decided to walk to the aptly-named Viagra Triangle clustered between State and Rush Streets. Following my breakup with Cecilia I was in no mood to test Chicago's agreeable waters, but I could now afford a steak and a couple of Manhattans at Barlows. I started to turn off the lights when Wes knocked on the front door. I let him in and he looked around the gallery as if seeing it for the first time.

"OK," he said. "I'll give it a try."

I detected no hint of a Bushmills extravaganza or hangover. He'd gotten a haircut and upgraded to a blazer and pressed khakis, wearing black wingtips that were rundown at the heels but presentable. Mildly impressed, I sat behind the desk and indicated a chair as though interviewing a stranger, uncertain how badly he wanted to abandon his career as a street person.

"Alright, then," I said. "We'll forget about chasing Van Gogh's ghost and make some money." I glanced at my watch. "Vasily and his uncle are due in a few minutes, so here's the deal. I'll take you on if you stay sober. Big damn if, Wes. No second chance."

"I can do that."

"You begin by crating work to be shipped. Meanwhile, I'll teach you the business."

He grinned. "I'll try to forget everything dad taught us."

A heavy ring rapped on the front door.

Vasily, flanked by two older men, grinned at me through the window. I opened the door and his companions followed him inside. Vasily locked my upper arms in a bear hug, his neatly-trimmed beard rough against my face, warm vodka fumes washing over me.

"Adam, my friend!"

The heavier man with dead eyes walked past us to the rear door, testing the bottom panel with a steel-toed boot.

"Is okay, Arby," Viktor Krushenko called out to him, his grammar careless after six years in the United States. "I apologize for Arby," he said, shrugging. "Is his job."

Viktor Krushenko was older, Vasily's uncle, uncontested ruler of Chicago's Russian mob. Gambling. Prostitution. Loan sharking. Extortion. An occasional killing when required. Red-faced from the cold, he wore no hat and carried himself as though he owned Chicago's winter wind. Well into his late sixties, the Russian sported a brown cashmere overcoat worth more than all the suits in my closet. Balding and slow-moving, a village blacksmith who'd wandered into the city—only his muscles came with intelligence and few scruples.

The other man, Dimitri Bolkov, was Viktor's bodyguard and enforcer, a thirtyish skinhead with stunted ears and pitted face. Dressed in a short black leather coat and watch cap, Viktor and Vasily called him Arby for reasons never explained to me. A Coke machine on legs, he lumbered to the front door and checked the street. Heavily in my favor was the fact my star artist had no known connection to the pack of Russian thieves and murderers, an innocent family bystander.

I introduced Wes and Vasily grinned nervously as Wes and I lugged chairs from Sally's office. Ignoring the proffered chair, Arby remained stationed at the front door, scrutinizing the street and our little group of art lovers. Wes stared at the two Russian mobsters as though they'd parachuted in from the Urals. Standing behind Viktor, Vasily bit his lip and tried to smile as his uncle laid his scarred hands atop my desk. With a bemused air, he stirred the air with his thick index finger.

"You are cheating Vasily," he said.

Vasily hung his head, avoiding my eyes.

"The money is wrong," Viktor said. "Vasily paints beautiful pictures and you steal from him."

Vasily sidled closer to him. "No, Uncle. This is way business is conducted here. Adam and I are friends."

"A friend does not steal from a friend," Viktor said.

Shocked, I caught my breath. "We have a mutually beneficial agreement. Galleries accept work on consignment with a 60/40 percent split on all sales. The artist receives 60 percent, the gallery 40 percent." Vasily nodded and rested a tentative hand on his uncle's shoulder. "My business agreement with Vasily is more generous," I continued. "His work sells easily, so we came to a 70/30 arrangement. That's more than fair to him."

Viktor was wagging his finger again before I finished.

Vasily gripped his uncle's shoulder. "Uncle Viktor, Adam was first to show my paintings," he said. "Since then, I am represented in New York and Los Angeles, but they are very large galleries and pay me less money. My first loyalty is to Adam."

"No," Viktor said, laying his hands on the desk again. "We make new deal."

Wes's face swung back and forth between us, probably rethinking his decision to enter the art business. I forced myself to maintain eye contact with Viktor, wondering at the same time if a staring match with a Russian crime boss was a viable strategy. Viktor glanced at Arby, who left his post at the front door and stood behind me. After a moment, Viktor removed a gold cigarette case from his coat, lit up, and exhaled.

"He is my nephew," he said. "I promise sister I look after him but he is young. His heart rules his mind." Arby stood close enough for me to smell his stale clothing. Viktor slapped his palms on the desk.

"After tonight, you take twenty-five percent, give him seventy-five percent. This is better."

"I can't do that," I heard myself say. I could tell Wes wanted to move his chair to avoid being splattered with my blood. "I have to earn a profit. My overhead..."

Vasily probably saved my life or at least a useful limb. "He must pay his rent, Uncle, turn on lights, pay employees. He cannot exist to enrich me."

Seconds passed and I was aware of Arby's heavy breathing. Viktor stood and jerked his head at Arby who slouched back to the front door. He patted Vasily's cheek with a heavy hand. "He grows into a man, this one." His eyes fell on me again. "Alright, I let him decide for now. We talk again sometime, you and me."

We shook hands and I remembered where the custom originated: an ancient strategy to make certain the other hand didn't conceal a knife. Viktor took Vasily aside and said something to him Russian, then left with Arby in tow. I sat down heavily and waited for my breathing to slow.

Wes stared at me. "Can I rethink our employment agreement?"

"Is okay now," Vasily said, returning to the desk. "My uncle will not bother you again."

I stood with one hand on the chair for support. "I need a drink."

"We all go." Vasily's white teeth glistened and he threw his arm around my shoulder. "You must let me buy. An apology for my uncle who does not understand American business." He threw his other arm around Wes's shoulder. "I know where there is best Ukrainian vodka, better than Russian swill. The prettiest girls will sit with us. We celebrate last night, the three of us!"

I didn't argue. I switched off the banks of lights, locked up again, and we walked outside. The same black Lincoln Town Car from the previous night idled at the opposite curb, a pall of gray exhaust smoke collecting under the yellowish street light. I turned to Wes to suggest Barlows when the driver's window slid down and the gallery window exploded behind us.

Wes groaned and fell against me. The Lincoln sped away and I grabbed Wes as he slumped onto shards of broken glass, his back against the building, his eyes squeezed shut. I knelt beside him and saw blood on his left trouser leg. He opened his eyes and managed a half-smile, confused.

"Adam?"

Beside him, Vasily lay on his back and stared at the night sky with unblinking eyes.

Chapter Four

The ambulance bearing Wes disappeared around the corner onto Wells Street, siren moaning as traffic pulled to the curb to let Chicago's latest casualty pass. They'd removed Vasily's body after a flurry of police photographs, dispersing the gawkers until only a few drunks remained as rain began to fall again, washing away the blood.

The storm whipped gray curtains of rain off Lake Michigan. Red and blue strobes atop police cars illuminated my gallery like a roadside strip club. Inside the shattered window, a desecrated painting hung askew on the nearest wall, frame splintered, the canvas holed by bullets. Beneath the destroyed Expressionist nude, crumbled wallboard fragments littered my proud new carpet.

I raised my coat collar and retreated beneath the awning followed by a bored Chicago police sergeant, glass crunching under our shoes. The cop was a street veteran down to a scarred chin and wary eyes, his belly encroaching on his belt buckle. He removed his brimmed hat and brushed rainwater from the clear plastic covering, wiping the checkered band with a thick thumb before he tugged it back on with a street-weary sigh.

"Looks like you and your brother dodged a bullet," he said with a caustic half-smile. Discomfited by my expression, he said, "Well, he didn't actually dodge it. The EMT's said the bullet nicked the back of his calf without finding bone. Some blood loss but no permanent damage."

"I've got to call his wife," I said.

"Sure, in a minute. First, you wanna tell me what happened?"

Across the rain-slicked street, the space sat empty where the Lincoln had waited for us. "We walked out and someone started shooting from a car parked across the street."

The cop contemplated my shattered window. "I don't figure the boys from the projects, but you never know about those crazy bastards."

I shook my head, recalling the tinted window sliding down. Maybe a loan shark fed up with Wes's late payments? "The car was a black stretch Lincoln, the kind limo owners drive."

The cop took a cheap spiral notebook from his yellow raincoat and made a note. "But it could be gang bangers the projects. They like to cruise the streets at night," he said. "Lot of random shootings. The worst call themselves the Deuce's Disciples." He kicked at the glass shards around our feet. "I think this here was a screw-up. Mistaken identity or a drug deal gone bad."

I didn't say so but the cop's reasoning didn't feel right, a bunch of brainless bangers shooting up an art gallery. Glad to be out of the rain, the cop made another note and took on the jaded expression of investigating endless mayhem. Another Saturday night shooting and one more bewildered citizen he was supposed to protect.

"The dead guy," he asked. "Customer?"

"One of my artists." I almost told him about Vasily's uncle and decided against it. The police would find out soon enough, and a whole new avenue of investigation would begin, including my association with Viktor Krushenko. I didn't want to think about it.

The sergeant closed the notebook. "Okay. The detectives will want to talk with you tomorrow." He frowned at the rain blowing through my broken window. "Lousy fucking weather. Better get something over that hole. We'll keep a man here until you leave."

He ambled back to the circus parade of flashing lights and I went inside, wondering where in hell I'd find someone to board up a window on Saturday night. I'd lugged the exposed paintings to the work area, too disheartened to touch the ruined painting. I thought about Viktor and knew I should call him, but I put it off. Viktor would know about the attack soon enough and I tried not to think about what might follow. Vasily was dead, gunned down beside me, and that would bring repercussions for someone. Possibly me.

I called Barbara and got her calmed down after a few minutes, explaining Wes was basically okay. She kept asking me why Wes had been shot but I had no answer. I gave her the name of the hospital where they'd taken him and told her I'd meet her there. Hanging up, I stared at the jagged hole where my front window once existed. I waved to the cop stationed at the door and went to my office. Thumbing my iPhone for repair companies I located one open 24/7. The answering service claimed they'd be on their way within the hour and I almost believed the voice. Bundled in raincoat I walked outside and told the patrolman to go home, that I'd wait until the hole was boarded up.

I pulled up a chair by the front door as the adrenaline ebbed away, watching as cars slowed to ogle the damage. Gusts of rain gleefully destroyed my new carpet and I tried not to calculate replacement cost, wondering if my insurance covered gunfire. To my surprise a panel truck arrived half an hour later. Two workmen hammered up plywood sheeting, the rough wooden patch blighting the front of my beautiful gallery.

Not owning a car in a city where parking was a mixture of fate and voodoo, I called Uber to take me to the hospital. During the ride, it occurred to me the gunshots had been oddly muffled. I hadn't told the cop, but the recollection increased my uneasiness. Why would underage gangsters or a shyster bother with a silencer?

***

Wes had been discharged by the time I reached the hospital. A young black intern assured me the injury wasn't serious enough to keep him overnight. In the midst of usual Saturday night mayhem and need for beds, they'd bound the wound and released him with a supply of pain killers.

It was still raining as I called Uber again and headed for his apartment. Barbara let me in and I found Wes with a glass in his hand, leg propped on an ottoman, his eyes glassy.

"Hey, this Vicodin is great stuff," he said as if he'd discovered the solution to world peace.

Barbara sat on the arm of his chair and shook her head at me with less than fawning eyes. She inclined her head at the glass in his hand.

"Water," she informed me.

Maybe the shooting would prove a respite for him. Provide an enforced vacation from the lounges and liquor stores. Barbara sure as hell wasn't going to let him mix painkillers with booze. I pulled up a straight-backed chair from the dining room and tried to smile.

"You OK?" I asked.

"Is Vasily dead?"

I nodded.

"Damn. He seemed like a great guy."

"He was."

Wes shifted his weight and winced as his leg rolled to one side. I looked around. The apartment was sparser than I remembered, and Barbara appeared five years older. She was a lean woman who never worried about her weight, a great wife to Wes but not my biggest fan. She believed I enabled him with loans and bail money, short term solutions to his deeper issues. But what was I supposed to do? Leave him to the mercy of the drunk tank? She loved him in her own patient way that allowed me to overlook her faults, mainly her dislike of me.

She hovered over Wes, curly auburn hair and blouse damp from the rain, her face wet with tears. "This is quite a night," she snapped, her voice trembling as she brushed away a limp strand of hair. "Our home gets broken into, then you call to tell me Wes has been shot."

"You got robbed?" was all I could think to say.

"Never imagined the art business was this violent," Wes laughed, his eyes swimming with the Vicodin. "Russian gangsters and artists murdered in the street."

"You sure you're okay?"

He held up the glass of water. "I'm fine, but I never needed a drink more in my life. What the hell happened?"

"The cops aren't sure."

"Great location you picked, Adam" Barbara said over her shoulder as she strode to the kitchen. "A trendy neighborhood. You serve Sneaky Pete wine at your gala last night?"

"C'mon, Barbara," Wes croaked.

I resented her criticism. I hadn't envisioned a shooting gallery when I selected the location. "You're clear on the other side of town and *you* got robbed," I reminded her, although the sparse apartment didn't appear a likely target.

"We need to talk about what happened," Wes said.

"I'll talk with detectives tomorrow. The cop told me..."

"Not about the shooting," Wes said. "The break-in."

"Wes," Barbara called from the kitchen, "don't start again."

"He needs to know."

"Know what?" I asked.

Will Ottinger 43

Barbara sat on Wes's chair arm again and lightly ran her fingers through his hair. "He's not making a lot of sense, what with the pills and all," she said. "Something about a Van Gogh painting your father claimed to have owned."

"He told me about that, but what am I missing here?"

"The letters are gone," Wes said. "We checked but they're not here. Nothing else was taken."

"You sure the letters were here?"

"I changed clothes before I came to the gallery. They were in my jacket." He looked on the verge of bursting into tears. "Our one link to the painting."

"You're *sure* they were stolen."

"I'm a recovering drunk, not a moron," Wes snapped, his eyes half-closed as the pills worked their magic.

Barbara shot me a look hovering between 'help me' and 'get the hell out of here.' It was obvious there'd already had a conversation about a fictional masterpiece that would solve all their problems.

Wes bent forward and winced. "Dammit, Barbara, it's real."

She searched his haggard face, her own reflecting defeat fostered by years of disappointment. She started to reply but only shook her head.

"Okay, our old man was crazy," Wes admitted, "but he had no reason to lie. No money in lying. If he owned a forgery, why didn't he pawn it off on somebody years ago? God knows he always needed money."

"This is crazy," Barbara said. "What about us? You're putting this fantasy before everything we're trying to do. You're in no shape to run around looking for some painting. In case you haven't noticed, we're almost broke. Where do you think we'll find money to search for your Eldorado? You have a portfolio or bank account I don't know about?"

"Maybe we can find a backer." Wes insisted. I'd heard the same desperation when he discovered a liquor bottle was empty. He looked up at me. "What about your gangster friend?"

"Viktor Krushenko is not my friend."

"He was Vasily's uncle. He could help us."

"Wes, do you have any idea who these people are? Where their money comes from? It's possible Viktor was trying to get rid of me after our argument. The bastard's crazy, you saw that. You heard how unhappy he was about the split Vasily was getting. Maybe he meant the shooting as an object lesson to me and he screwed up. Either way, he won't be a happy Boy Scout when he finds out Vasily's dead."

"We need to find a way," Wes said, his optimism bolstered by the pain killers.

Barbara turned away and I was out of arguments. Our dead father was ripping our lives apart again, his sons lost in his dysfunctional shadow.

Chapter Five

The next afternoon, I was pitching a husband and wife on a small painting when Arthur Jennings strolled into the gallery.

    A thinner version of Elton John, Jennings christened himself a Los Angeles art broker. He wore a white Gucci polo shirt beneath what I guessed to be a $4,000 cream-colored suit. A blue Dodgers baseball cap topped the incongruous ensemble, his dyed blond hair falling almost to his shoulders in a sartorial anthem to the seventies. He smiled, smirking at my prospects over outdated hexagonal glasses as he skirted the galley perimeter. Pretending interest in what hung on my walls, he fingered a thick gold chain around his neck, thumbing a heavy crucifix. He leaned closer to peer at a small painting, pretending the pastoral scene appealed to him. When the couple left without buying, he walked up and we shook hands, his cold grip limp.

    "Mommy and daddy not ready to pop for a landscape with cows?"

    "Hello, Arthur. This your day to slum?"

    Jennings had lived less than a mile from us in Santa Monica, making a hand-to-mouth living selling the latest trends in cheap polyester clothes. He and my father had been drinking companions, hatching schemes to fleece victims with more disposable income than brains. I wondered how many skinny deals he and my father concocted, drinks in hand on our little terrace overlooking the Pacific. After I bolted, Arthur moved on to a higher clientele, selling whatever currently passed for art to Hollywood's coke and Lamborghini crowd, my father forgotten. He didn't own a gallery, and his phone wasn't listed online or in the LA directory. Not for the first time I suspected he harbored a long list of clients who lived at the edge of California's court system.

    He sighed and assembled a look of regret. "Sorry to hear about Sorokin. Is Wes okay?"

    "He's alright."

"The police have any idea what happened?"

"No," I said, eager for him walk back out the door.

He grinned. "Well, you're on the edge of a shooting gallery."

"What do you want, Arthur?"

"Hey, I'm in the city for a symposium. Dinner with clients got in the way of Sorokin's show. I wanted one more crack at making all three of us a shit load of money. Like I told you last week, no matter what you think of me, a few of my clients saw Sorokin's potential for appreciation. They would have paid major bucks compared to the schmucks that wander in here." He screwed up his face as if I'd cut him out of my will. "Too bad. There's no market for dead young artists who can't produce anything else. No one will remember his name in two years."

I couldn't resist sinking the needle. "Or maybe he was so good he'll be the next James Dean of dead icons. An art legend you missed."

He waved his hand and pulled off his ball cap, running his fingers through his long locks. "Maybe so, but you missed a profitable gig. One that cost both of us money."

"He didn't need you."

"He'll never find out now, and neither will you, right?"

"I do alright for a Midwestern cow town."

Jennings laughed and tugged on the ball cap. "Give my regards to Wes. And let me know if you stumble across another winner. The big sellers are out there, but they're hard to find, right?"

I watched him leave, hating to admit he was right. In all likelihood, we could have jacked up Vasily's prices, but dealing with a scumbag like Arthur Jennings wasn't worth the extra profit. I couldn't kick the feeling that had I worked with him, I'd be right back in the grubby little bungalow perched on the California cliff.

***

Vasily's funeral was a spartan affair.

I made the short walk from the gallery to the L-station, then took a cab to the little cemetery in Lombard west of the city. Rows of chipped granite angels and weather-worn crosses highlighted the morose little setting. I tried not to notice the parked Cadillacs and Mercedes—or the FBI agents in off-the-rack suits taking telephoto snapshots of every mourner from an almost respectful distance.

Congratulations, Adam, I thought. You just made the rogue's gallery in Washington.

A few women in black stood like statues next to impassive men as though observing an execution. An orthodox priest, conspicuous in an ornate green robe among the funeral suits, mumbled prayers in Russian I couldn't hear, much less comprehend. I almost didn't recognize Viktor dressed in a tailored suit and wearing a broad-brimmed fedora. Arby stood at his back clad in his trademark leather coat, the only mourner without a tie. Half-hidden behind large sprays of fast-dying flowers, Viktor gazed at the coffin, while Arby scanned the pack of Russian mourners. For the briefest moment, his eyes rested on me before seeking other targets.

After the service, I hurried out the cemetery's front gate. Icy wind numbed my cheeks as I punched up Uber, already dreading the frigid wait on the train platform. Shivering and watching for the car, a black Ford Expedition slowed and stopped beside me. The heavily-tinted passenger window hummed down.

Viktor inclined his head toward the rear door as Arby stared through the windshield. "We give you a ride."

A ride. Was Michael Corleone waiting in the back seat?

Hot air from the car's heater beckoned through the open window. What the hell, I was already on record with the FBI. Why not shoot the works and be marked as a full-fledged member of the Siberian fraternity? I opened the door and got in.

"You can drop me at the gallery," I said.

Viktor half-turned in the front seat. "First, we go to my house. Talk about what happened."

The outsized SUV swung west, away from the sad little cemetery. We rode in silence for ten minutes as the car bullied through light traffic, me strapped in the back seat like a truant child. We drove to Wheaton and turned onto a quiet street lined with overgrown oaks and single-story homes built before World War Two. The SUV slowed and turned into the drive of a nondescript house of white siding with a small porch. An attached garage huddled at the rear, the street empty. My condo seemed a continent away.

Viktor's house brought back memories of my grandmother's simple home in

Modesto, a cookie-cutter house from the thirties. It's Chicago counterpart bore dark window curtains and a wreath on the front door. Plastic sheeting protected the shrubbery against the cold, a roll of the stuff standing on the front porch. Arby wheeled the SUV into the garage and got out. Exhaust fumes and stale oil thickened as Viktor opened my door.

When I didn't move, he grinned and said, "Come, we only talk."

A stout woman in her sixties met us at the front door, a dark blue bandanna restraining frizzy gray hair. Not bothering to acknowledge us, she glanced at Viktor and marched to the rear of the house. Viktor waved his hand in the direction where she disappeared.

"My wife," he muttered.

Arby followed us into a tiny living room and leaned against the wall beside the front door, apparently his assigned station at all locations. The cramped living and dining room reeked of cigarette smoke and years of Russian cooking. A scarred coffee table sagged under the weight of oversized art books in front of a sofa with mismatched cushions; Viktor obviously had not spent his nefarious profits on an interior designer. Topping off the splendor was an ugly Tokarev automatic pistol atop one arm of a vinyl recliner facing a television slightly little smaller than a bedsheet. The closed curtains raised my level of claustrophobia as muted classical music played somewhere in the rear of the house

Viktor eased into the recliner and indicated the sofa. He opened the old-fashioned gold cigarette case, an elastic strip securing the cigarettes. I sank into the sofa and he lit up, fixing me with a tired expression as though I was an ostracized relative who had showed up at the funeral service.

"A sad day," he said.

I nodded, Vasily's murder made more distressing by the cramped room and automatic pistol by Viktor's hand. "He shouldn't have died like that," I said, "not with his life ahead of him."

Viktor inhaled deeply and exhaled smoke through his nostrils. "He should not have died at all, but I make certain is same for some other sonabitch." He stubbed out his cigarette in an ash tray filled with butts as his eyes bore into me. "Your brother. He is alright?"

"A minor wound. He was lucky."

Viktor's features remained carved from the same granite I'd seen at the cemetery. "And you, you were not shot. Just Vasily and brother." A declaration, not a question. Arby shifted behind me. Had anyone seen me get into the SUV?

"Only Vasily and Wes," I said.

Viktor's expression did not change. "Why you think Vasily is killed?"

I was tempted to ask if Vasily's death was connected to Viktor's chosen trade. Had Vasily played a role in Viktor's empire, one he'd never mentioned?

"Tell me why you were not shot," Viktor said. A feral smile revealed small even teeth. "Don't be frightened. Is only a question."

"Poor shooting, I guess." I gathered my courage and asked what needed to be asked. "Did Vasily make enemies among your... competitors?"

Viktor looked at me as though I'd asked if his dead nephew occupied a corner office in his empire. "He was not involved in business. I did not allow it."

"Then his murder makes no sense," I said. "He was a wonderful artist."

"Yes." Viktor drummed thick fingers on the Tokarev and glanced at Arby. Borodin's opera lilted from the rear of the house, strains of the symphony at odds with the mood in the room. "He was brave boy." He squinted at me as though pondering a puzzle. "You argue with me in gallery. Maybe you are also brave. Or only foolish."

I met his gaze. "Vasily was my best artist. I depended on him. More than that, we were friends."

"I know. He tells me."

"Then you know I had nothing to do with his death."

"I think is not Vasily someone wants to kill," Viktor said.

I blinked.

"Maybe someone try kill you and your brother."

The music died away as his words struck home. No, I thought. That made no sense. The shootings had been random, a screw-up by wannabe gangsters or someone Wes pissed off.

"The police think it was mistaken identity," I said. "Kids or drug dealers in a drive-by."

Viktor shook his head. "I hear expensive car wait for you to come out of gallery."

He had good sources. The car had been parked at the curb for two nights. I recalled the driver window sliding down, the abrupt stuttering of muffled shots and breaking glass. But why us? Viktor watched closely as I reran the scene in my mind.

50 The Last Van Gogh

"Your brother," he said finally. "He calls me."

My fear returned in a rush. "Wes?"

"You have other brother?"

"What did he want?" I asked, knowing the answer before he spoke.

"What you think?" Viktor said, raising his hands as though the answer was obvious. "He want my money." He opened a thick volume on the coffee table, thumbed several pages, and pushed the open book toward me. A spray of dazzling sunflowers lighted the room.

"Your brother is chasing Van Gogh painting like this. Only much bigger."

Damn you, Wes, I thought. I'm sitting in a Russian don's fetid little house admiring a picture because you decided to chase our father's delusions.

Viktor's gaze wandered back to the flowers, light coming up in his eyes. "Vasily, he shows me this painting many times," he said. His square thumb pressed hard on the glossy flowers. "Someday, he wants to be this famous."

"Van Gogh is very famous," I said feebly, knowing what came next.

"How much money this painting sells for, these flowers?"

I recalled the recent London auction that made headlines. "Almost $40 million."

Viktor turned two pages and dented another illustration with his thumbnail. More flowers bloomed in vivid color. "And this one?"

The purple blooms against green shoots and leaves were titled *Irises*, painted in 1889 at Saint-Remy, sold by Sotheby's several years earlier.

"$54 million."

"Two little paintings." Viktor stared at the illustration but heard only the numbers.

The amounts staggered me as well. Almost $100 million paid for two painting several years ago. What would they bring in today's seller market?

Viktor smoothed the crease left by his thumb and gestured at the four walls. "Your brother, he says there is bigger Van Gogh painting, one that fills this room."

I damned Wes again for ringing up dollar signs in the eyes of the frightening figure hunched over the book. Wes's careless mouth had guaranteed the attention of a Russian thug—and someone else who tried to kill us. I sat back. It made no sense. No one killed for a rumor.

Viktor's thick fingers massaged his fleshy scalp and looked closely at me.

Will Ottinger 51

"Your brother. He tells me two letters prove painting is real."

I wanted to yell at him, tell him my father was a drunk, that no such painting existed. If he ever mentioned a Van Gogh, I would have remembered. Instead, I said, "My brother believes our father's delusions. There's no missing Van Gogh."

His heavy eyebrows shot up as though I'd missed the obvious. "Then why someone steal his letters?"

When I didn't reply, Viktor pushed harder. "If painting is real, how much money?"

There it was. The same question Wes asked me. The letters cast tentacles, dragging along Wes who considered Viktor a savior, or worse, a potential partner. I shook my head, struggling to come up with an almost impossible number. Viktor had to see no such painting ever existed, that no undiscovered massive Van Gogh remained in the world. Putting a number on it would whet his appetite. I guessed he'd already done the math and tried for a convincing shrug. "Only an expert could tell you that."

Arby bumped the back of my chair.

"You are expert," Viktor said. "Give me a number."

Viktor watched as I closed the book and sat back. Arby had not moved. I tried to imagine a wall-sized Van Gogh. A sixty-square foot painting of an unknown girl by the premier Impressionist master. The most stupendous art find of the century. I knew my next words would seal mine and Wes's fate.

"Quarter billion dollars, possibly more."

"Ah," Viktor softly exclaimed.

"But it doesn't exist," I insisted. "Our father was a drunk and con man. This is nothing but another of his schemes to cheat someone. Who or how, I don't know, but the painting isn't real, Viktor."

He didn't hear me. "If we do not find it, some Jew will get his hands on it. It would be sacrilege to let them own such a painting. You cannot allow this to happen."

Arby grunted in agreement as though waiting for the order to burn down every synagogue in Chicago. When had the Jewish race become part of the discussion, I wondered? Vasily had been a carefree soul but I guessed old Russian prejudices died hard with men like Viktor and Arby.

The comment lingered as if they were waiting for me to agree. Somewhere in the house, a piano crescendo rose to match the tension.

"But to hell with the Jews," Viktor said after a moment. "Your brother understands what is involved." He rarely used Wes's name. Or mine. We were little more than inanimate devices to be clicked on and off at his pleasure. "He finds this painting and his wife love him forever. He keeps her safe and you are a rich hero."

My heart sank. Wes had told him about Barbara. I could hear him pour out his life. The booze. His struggling marriage, anything to gain Viktor's financial backing for the fantasy he'd created. Hell, Wes would have related his erotic dreams in explicit detail if he thought they would convince Viktor to finance his trip to Shangri-La.

"I wouldn't know where to begin," I said.

Viktor chose not to hear me. "I think is good idea you look for this painting. You are expert. You have art education, you know art people. You will find it." It was a simple statement. My role had been decided before I climbed in the SUV, and Viktor's decisions did not require a majority vote.

"I pay all bills, buy whatever is needed," he continued. "You find painting and we are 50/50 partners, you and me." 50/50? I swallowed my doubts, settling for a chance to walk away if he got his painting.

"And if it doesn't exist, what then?"

"We find a way you pay me back. I am a generous man, am I not, Arby?"

Arby grinned and I realized I'd never heard him speak.

"I have a gallery to run," I began. "I can't..."

Viktor waved his hand. "Your brother will run gallery. Arby looks after him."

I gazed down at the book cover, the colors shifting in the low wattage light as I contemplated the next few months, chasing something I knew did not exist. Had never existed except in my father's addled brain. I could run, I thought, try to disappear. Leave Wes with the gallery and bank note. I'd find a beach in Mexico and sit in a thatch-roofed bar until my money ran out. Maybe latch onto a wealthy widow and let nature take its course without looking back. But I couldn't leave Wes to Viktor's compassion, much as I disliked him at the moment. No one ever accused me of being a coward, but valor acknowledges its limits—if one envisions a long life.

Viktor stood, my visit at an end. He removed a silver money clip from his trouser pocket and spread a fan of hundred-dollar bills on the table. "Tell me when more is needed." He clapped me on the arm as though we'd completed a sale. "Do what is necessary. We will be very rich men, you, me, and brother."

If Wes and I lived.

Chapter Six

Next morning, I maneuvered Barbara's Subaru through Michigan Avenue traffic lights, doing battle with Chicago's morning commuters. Earlier at their apartment, she and Wes engaged in a heated argument. She threw her car keys at him and stormed out of the apartment, mumbling about taking a cab to Skokie where she worked.

Wes leaned back against the headrest as I swore at a Metro bus that swerved into our lane. "I'm glad my eyes are closed," he said.

"We should have taken the bus and let Barbara have the car."

He shrugged.

"Now we have to pay for parking," I said.

Wes grinned. "Our new partner and fellow art lover can pay for it."

"You think that's funny?"

He was enjoying my discomfort. "Let's toss the parking receipt and claim it cost twice as much."

"You can explain that to Arby," I said.

We parked in a subterranean lot below Michigan Avenue. Wes got out gingerly, favoring his leg, and we took the garage elevator to street level. Several blocks away the European Fine Art League occupied a 1920's building, the entrance door brandishing etched glass and scrolled wrought iron, the understated façade fronting a magnificent collection.

The advent of the League had surprised Chicago's art world. Financed five years earlier by the well-heeled Trevor Foundation, the venerable Art Institute of Chicago with its 125-year pedigree derided the competition, but wiser men pointed out the old and established became rusty and dented over time, losing out to pools of new money. How else to explain vast collections of western art in Japan, and French masterpieces decorating the walls of Las Vegas casinos?

Brushed off when I contacted the Institute, I called the League that expressed immediate interest in an unnamed Impressionist painting after I dropped the word 'donation' into the conversation. Its high priestess, Mary Barnum-Gordon, was chief curator of Impressionist Art, a Van Gogh authority with three books to her credit on the subject. A long shot, but her expert opinion might quell Viktor's lust for a lost Van Gogh.

We pushed through the elegant door and I felt a rush, aware of the superb collections beyond the walls. I presented my card and assured a young woman behind the reception desk that we had an appointment. She scrutinized my card and directed us to the administrative offices on the third floor.

"Let's get this over with," I said to Wes. He ignored his wound and gamely climbed the marble stairs behind me, clutching the handrail. We turned left at the small landing, confronted by an empty hall and electronic entry door. As we stared at the key pad, a young man pushed a cart past us loaded with wire-bound folders. He stopped at the keypad, brushed a card over the reader, and we held the door open for him, following the cart. At the first desk, we were directed past glass-front cubicles, the League's plush pile making my carpet resemble indoor-outdoor. Wes's appearance drew a few stares until we stopped outside a highly varnished wooded door. A plaque informed us we'd arrived at the domain of the Director of European Paintings and Fine Art Objects.

"Let me do the talking," I said to Wes,

I presented my card to the gate keeper who got to her feet, staring at the card. She knocked on the door and opened it a few inches as though we might charge past her.

"Miss Gordon? Two gentlemen claim they have an appointment with you?"

The Director condescended to see us and we entered the office where a superbly tailored woman commanded an oversized desk stacked with folders like those we'd seen on the cart. Her taut face, smoothed by Botox or expensive surgery, presented an unblemished brow and tolerant expression to the world.

"I'm Adam Barrow." I inclined my head toward Wes. "My brother, Wesley. I believe you're expecting us."

Mary Barnum-Gordon assessed us as though we were selling whole life. She didn't rise or offer her hand. Tapping a Mont Blanc pen on the glossy desktop she consulted her leather-bound desk calendar and indicated two chairs in front of the desk, foregoing the comfortable seating area beside her floor-to-ceiling window. "Have a seat, please."

The woman, an anemic, Pilates enthusiast, or gym junkie, was trim to the point of flirting with malnutrition. Her severe gray pants suit was courtesy of Armani, and she filled it with what I estimated to be less than five percent body fat. Every inch her hyphenated name, the ash blond hair stylishly clipped in disciplined disarray.

"Yes, a painting," she said, checking her calendar again. "You're interested in making a donation?"

"That will depend," I said. "We first need more information. An expert valuation in writing after you inspect the painting, of course. Your level of interest. Valuation for tax purposes. And whether the League intends to display it to the public or allow it to disappear into your storage vaults."

She regarded me with heightened respect. "Of course, that would depend on the artist and quality," she replied evenly. "Not every painting has the same degree of significance that it holds for its owner."

"This is a Van Gogh." I said, enjoying her effort to maintain her detachment.

"Really," she drawled.

"Really."

Mary Barnum-Gordon blinked and opened a writing pad, her lips firming. "I know the owners and locations of all Van Gogh works," she said with professional pride. Her eyes narrowed. "Your name again?"

"Adam Remington Barrow. The middle name's not an affectation. My father had an affinity for American Western art." My father, in fact, detested cows and cowboys.

Supremely unimpressed with my pedigree, her marble-smooth forehead conjured up a wrinkle. "And this—Van Gogh." She enunciated the name as though we shared a joke about art. "May I ask its provenance."

"An inheritance from our father."

"And its size?"

"Quite large. In fact, enormous is a more accurate description."

She restrained a smile. "The subject?"

"I'd rather not say at this point," I said. Although I didn't employ the inherited talent very often, being Robert Everham Barrow's son possessed advantages, such as how to be evasive to the point of lying when it suited the situation.

She remained composed with visible effort and said, "You're not giving me much, Mr. Barrow. Why not bring in your painting so we can inspect it."

"It's not in our possession at the moment," I said.

Much as she tried to remain polite, her cynicism reasserted itself. She leaned back in her chair, tapping the fat pen with her polished nails. She glanced at Wes and fixed me with a withering look.

"And the date of this mysterious work?"

"I don't know."

"But can I assume you have a verified path of ownership?"

"In a manner. The previous owners' names are known only to my brother and me."

Mary Barnum-Gordon patience was fast dwindling. "As I'm certain you know, there are multiple catalogues raisonne of Van Gogh's works. Untold papers have researched his life. I myself wrote a biography and two other books on his work. I'm not aware of a large missing Van Gogh. I'm certain you own a forgery."

Wes shifted in his chair. He was living a fantasy and the woman was tearing it apart. I imagined how much he yearned for a drink, and in that moment, I bonded with him.

"Is there someone else we could talk to?" I asked, resenting her desire to be rid of us.

"No." She stood and I imagined her trying to recall Security's extension.

Wes and I didn't speak until we were on the street again. He limped beside me toward the garage elevator, hands jammed in his pockets, unwilling to concede defeat. I honored the silence, aware we'd made fools of ourselves. Hopefully, Ms. Barnum-Gordon would never connect my name to the gallery.

"She's wrong," Wes said when we reached the car. "She doesn't know everything."

"More than us," I said.

"It's real, Adam. Dad left us a legacy to make up for all his crap."

I couldn't help but laugh. "A *legacy*? Really?"

"Why not? I believe he once owned something he valued above everything else, even you and me. At the end I think he realized that wanted to make amends."

I laughed. "By leaving two cryptic letters about a vanished painting?"

"He would have told us if he'd finished his letter."

"You're rationalizing now."

Poor Wes. His damaged memories far exceeded mine, but he'd created this new illusion of a repentant father. He wanted to believe in the Van Gogh's existence and the fact it might redeem our father and Oliver Twist childhoods. Tempted to point out the flaws of his logic, I kept my mouth shut. The past week had emptied me of circular arguments, but walking away was no longer an alternative, not with the smell of a fortune in Viktor Krushenko's nostrils.

Chapter Seven

Mary Barnum-Gordon was still fondling the pen when her phone rang. Surprised when she saw the caller ID, she got up and doubled-checked that her office door was closed. Had her caller watched the Barrows' arrival and departure?

"Learn anything?" the voice asked.

"They believe the painting exists," she said. "Which is more than I believe at this point."

"You've never doubted my judgment before."

"You've always been right until now."

"I forgot you know everything."

She tossed the pen on her desk pad. "I do when it concerns Van Gogh."

"No indication where they might begin their search?" the man asked.

"I'd tell you if they said anything of value."

A harsh laugh. "Of course, you would."

She bristled at the insinuation. "Just remember our arrangement. You locate it and the League will gather funds to purchase it. As long as we receive clear title without complications. We can't afford a scandal."

"You're sure you have donors willing to cough up that kind of money?" the man asked. "This isn't some little Pissarro sketch."

The Director flushed. "Are you positive the painting exists?"

"I have written proof. What concerns me is your ability as a fund raiser."

"There are resources you know nothing about," she said as though correcting an unruly child. "I don't need the League involved in anything nefarious."

Her caller laughed. "My goodness, Mary. Nefarious covers so much ground in our little world."

"Just be sure."

"Have I ever embarrassed you or your museum, Mary dear?"

"Not yet." For a moment, she thought he'd hung up until he laughed again.

"I assure you I never will," he said. "And let's not forget your private little commission. Losing it would be such a shame."

She started to reply but heard the dial tone.

Chapter Eight

Paris February 1888

Paris was a pariah, a succession of slaps in the face.

Two years in Theo's rue Lepic apartment had grown intolerable, a place where endless arguments with his brother festered until an irrevocable breaking point loomed. Conflicts varied from listening to Theo's unrequited love for Johanna Bonger, to his brother's inability to sell his paintings. Even forays to Tanguy's shop to purchase paints descended into heated arguments with Julian, the owner, over Paul Cézanne's color choices. He endured the role of an outcast, quarreling with almost every painter in the city's insular art world, his uncontrolled rages triggered by criticism of his work. Younger artists privately sneered at his unkempt appearance, while the darlings of the latest exhibits crossed the street to avoid him. Nothing had gone right since he set foot in the city. Certainly not his unendurable hours at Cormon's atelier or his attempts to build friendships with the few painters who tolerated him.

In the midst of turmoil and resistance, and with the gentle guidance of Theo, his eyes reluctantly opened to the Impressionist movement he had relentlessly attacked. The approach offered free range to his experiments with color and light, and he began painting the environs beyond Montmartre, along the boulevards, creating river scenes and sprays of flowers, foregoing heavy impasto for the thinned applications of Monet and Degas, even experimenting with new approaches, copying fashionable Japanese prints and drawings.

All of it fell into nothing with a failed show at the cavernous Restaurant du Chalet. The exhibit was a disaster, the walls bare again after a few weeks of shrugs and disinterested diners who barely glanced up from their dinner plates. Anger and disappointment morphed into newfound resolution and he returned to his love of impasto like a rediscovered cure. He laid down thick shadowless color with a renewed vengeance, sunlight and contrast his gods. As he unleashed his brush with fresh intensity, the city bore down on him with its dirt and bohemian haunts, weighing on his need for light and more light. Disconnection with Theo intensified despite *his brother's patient kindness and loans of money. Meanwhile, Paris had dimmed, a prison. He would give wings to his contempt and flee its sewers and crooked torturous streets. His future waited outside the city and he decided to break away forever.*

But first, he must return to Holland to repaint the girl. A trip meant journeying into the heart of the native country again with its hidebound inhabitants and watery landscape, but in his mind's eye, he saw her more clearly now, clothed in the glory he could impart to her. Such an undertaking would take weeks away from new work and he abhorred the thought of returning to Holland. Counting out the little money remaining in his pocket, he left Theo's apartment and walked to the train station, his excitement growing at seeing her again.

Chapter Nine

Our meeting with the lovely Ms. Barnum-Gordon had been a downer but about what I expected. Wes dismissed her as an art snob, intent on believing a fortune awaited us. No matter my opinion of the woman, I thought she'd been truthful. God may have approved whatever my father's intentions were, but there was no mislaid Van Gogh. I only hoped her verdict dampened Viktor's enthusiasm.

The Chicago Trib and television news had covered Vasily's murder with the media's usual delight for mayhem, connecting Vasily to his uncle with breathless innuendo. Two Chicago police detectives interviewed me until finally convinced the killing was mistaken identity. Everything pointed to another drive-by shooting by Southside morons, the murder unrelated to the Russians. The incident wasn't their style, they said. The shooting faded from the front page, and no one other than Viktor and I seemed to care Vasily was dead. Fighting off pangs of guilt, I tried to pretend I hadn't lost my cash cow.

Sally and I spent the morning dragging out the best remaining work. We had a few of Vasily's paintings left and other saleable work, but nothing approaching the young Russian. After we sold the remainder, my reduced cash flow and past due bank payments would transform us into another struggling high-end retailer. We were hanging paintings when the phone rang. Sally answered and handed it to me.

"Adam Barrow," said a familiar voice, "Jack McInnis here."

I smiled, a rare event since Vasily's death. As a young man, Jack had been an associate of my father, almost a protégé until they parted company. He'd clawed his way off Brooklyn's mean streets as a boy and run to California where dad discovered his potential. Hard-working and devoted to my father, I knew him as Uncle Jack. At first, he worked as a gofer, a whipping boy running errands. Later, my father dressed him in high-end suits, converting him into a handsome partner who lent credibility to whatever scheme my father hyped to the unsuspecting. A legend now in art circles, Jack lived in New York and Geneva, a perennial subject of magazine photo shoots.

"I heard about the shooting," he said. "Wes okay?"

"Yeah, he was lucky," I said, not knowing what else to say. "Are you in town? Arthur Jennings dropped by yesterday, his personality charming as usual."

"I saw him," Jack said. "We're both attending a symposium at the Palmer House. I guess they're not choosy. Hell," he laughed, "they let me in."

Before I left for college, Jack disappeared when one of my father's deals soured. He and I parted with no hard feelings, and I liked him. In his sixties now, Jack kept his athletic build. Dressed by a personal tailor, he sent out the vibes of a trust fund baby or executive at the top of his game, a dealer in fine art who played at the far end of the spectrum from Arthur Jennings and even farther from my station in life. If there was money to be made, Jack McMinnis snatched it away while others held meetings or fumbled with their iPhones. He'd always laughed easily and once told me my father taught him how the real-world worked. Over the years we stayed in touch with an occasional lunch and drinks.

"I saw Sorokin's work and thought you and I could make arrangements for me to broker his work, here and overseas, but I got here too late," he said. "He was a talent."

"He was my best."

"What's on your scope now?"

"Prayer and extra hours."

"Maybe we can work out something. I'm always looking for smart people who know the business."

Taken aback, I thought, why not. The gallery's chances of succeeding plummeted with Vasily's death, and an association with Jack McMinnis meant rubbing shoulders with his upscale clientele. Serious money rubbed off on the lucky, and I had no qualms about traveling among wealthy art patrons.

"Are you free for lunch tomorrow?" I asked.

"Wish I could, but I'm due in Tokyo tomorrow night," he said. "Next trip maybe, or whenever you get to New York."

"I'd like that. It's been a long time since we've talked."

"We'll plan on it then. Ciao."

He hung up and I climbed back on the ladder, struggling with an oversized painting and wondering about the last time Jack McMinnis climbed a ladder. His call was an upper in my day. I loved my gallery but earning sustainable profits spiraled downward when Vasily bled out on the sidewalk. Jack offered a backdoor escape from reality.

The front door buzzed. Sally and I turned to see Arby staring at us. I nodded and she buzzed him in. He walked to the ladder, never glancing at the paintings, while I climbed down and Sally climbed up to adjust the frame. From Jack McMinnis to Arby Bolkov within five minutes.

"Viktor, he want to see you," Arby said, the first words I'd ever heard him utter. His voice was surprisingly high-pitched. "Now."

"I'm showing Vasily's remaining paintings to several clients in about an hour."

"We go now."

Sally clenched the hammer she held as he ogled her bare legs, measuring her body, his grin exposing the mouthful of steel-capped teeth.

"Viktor has something he want to show you," he said.

"Can you hold down everything till I get back?" I asked Sally.

She nodded, frozen in place on the ladder as Arby ran his eyes over her again. I got my coat and followed him to the Expedition double-parked at the curb. I climbed in the back seat and he again lost his ability to speak as we drove to Wheaton, my uneasiness growing. His reputation for cruelty exceeded lore about the Italian Mafia; even the city's worst black and Hispanic gangs avoided his crews. The Van Gogh did not exist, and I needed to change his mind to avoid being dragged into his sphere. Refusing his invitation, however, was not an option. Arby pushed the metallic dinosaur to eighty on the Interstate and I couldn't shake the thought that one of these rides would be my last.

Inside the drab house, glossy art books were scattered across the living room floor in a colorful mosaic. Viktor appeared from the grim little kitchen, a sandwich in one hand, an incongruous china cup of tea in the other. He wore workman's gloves, his shirtsleeves rolled to his elbows. A door next to an old gas oven stood open, the babushka wife nowhere in sight.

I hoped to cut the visit short. "Wes and I talked with a Van Gogh expert. She says there's no lost Van Gogh and believes the painting's a forgery if it exists."

"Let me show you something," he said.

Arby shoved me in the back toward his boss and I lost it. Wes's wounding. Vasily's death. The fear and threats., I whirled on him and clenched my fists, ready for a fight I knew I'd lose. Arby chuckled and squared himself, a look of anticipation in his narrowed eyes.

Viktor pushed the last of the sandwich into his mouth and shook his head at Arby. He put the teacup on a table and wiped his greasy maw with a gloved hand. "I show you, then we talk."

Arby followed close behind me to the open door and Viktor flicked on a light switch. I followed him down a set of wooden steps into the basement, the pine boards smelling of sap and freshly-cut wood. Behind me, Arby closed the door to the kitchen

The basement smelled of raw wood and fresh cement overlaid by the acrid odor of sheet plastic. The setting below my feet was film noir, low wattage bulbs casting colorless light over an oddly slick floor. My eyes adjusted and I saw wall-to-wall layers of sheet acrylic. Heavy noise control curtains that I'd last seen on summer construction jobs hung from the walls and ceiling. A tank crashing through the walls would never be heard outside the room.

The frigid air tasted like I was sucking on a penny as I halted on the bottom step. A single wooden chair sat in the center of the room, stained ropes dangling from its arms and legs. Beneath the chair a pool of coagulated blood appeared black in the dim light, splatters radiating across the plastic-covered floor. A loosely tied plastic bundle rested against the far wall.

Viktor walked to the chair, careful to avoid the glutinous puddle. "This is work area," he said with a touch of craftsman's pride. "We collect good information in this room."

When I didn't respond, he removed his gloves and rolled down his sleeves. Arby sat down on the steps behind me and Viktor nodded at him with something that passed for affection. "Like others, you wonder why he is named Arby." A chill seeped through my topcoat as Viktor buttoned his cuffs with a smile. "Is not Russian name." Arby barked a noise that resembled a laugh. "I give him that name," Viktor said.

He walked to the lump of vinyl and picked up a three-foot steel rod. In the grey light I saw one end was gummy with what I took to be clotted blood. A stack of identical rods stood in a corner. Victor studied the bar in his hand. "You know this?"

I nodded.

"Rebar," Viktor clenched his fist around the rod and thumped the bloody end against the roped lump of acrylic. "Very strong. Strengthens concrete. Is

Arby's favorite toy, so I call him R-B. Ar-be. Like the restaurant." He laughed at his cleverness. "No gun. No fingerprints for police. Nothing." He waved the steel bar in the frigid air as if conducting an orchestra. "Just throw in water or on junk pile. Gone!"

Arby shifted his weight behind me.

"Arby, he like his work," Viktor continued. "He is good at it." He raised his chin toward him. "Show Adam."

Arby brushed past me and walked to the bound bundle. He untied the rope and peeled back layers of plastic.

The corpse was shirtless and barefooted, the face unrecognizable. Most of the body had been reduced to raw meat, hands and feet pulped into hamburger, splintered bones protruding like white thorns. Nauseated, I turned away, unable to escape the air thickened with congealed blood and butcher shop stench. I had never fixated on death. We were all basically dying. Growing up around LA, I knew life didn't always end as we hoped. I loved the California coast but it never loved me back. If nothing else, the city imparted a toughness to live on my own, a strength I never lost. I had no problem with the concept of dying, but I was damn certain I didn't want my life terminated by a length of rusty steel.

Expressionless, Viktor looked at the body as though inspecting a dented fender. "We find this one and ask him questions after Vasily is killed. No Russian kill him. My competitors, they are too smart to provoke me. If they want to kill someone, they kill me."

I forced my eyes back to the mutilated corpse. "Then who was... this?"

"Not Russian." Viktor tossed the steel bar to Arby. "We check. This is piece of shit who is hired to kill you and brother. For the painting, he tells us."

I stared at the mangled corpse, the basement meat locker cold. What the hell was Viktor saying? That we'd been targeted for a non-existent painting?

"He is hired by someone who want you dead," Viktor said.

"How do you know?"

"He tells us. He did not want to, but Arby convince him."

"Who hired him?"

Viktor shrugged. "He tells us same man pay him to steal letters from brother's apartment."

"He didn't give you a name?"

"He did not know name. He says someone hire him. Pay him to steal letters, then kill you and brother, but he does poor job."

"You believed him?"

Viktor shot me a disbelieving look. "After five minutes, he tell us anything. Even where mother lives if we want to know."

The two old letters yielded two dead men so far. Someone else wanted the Van Gogh and the killings only increased Viktor's hunger. It occurred to me that Arthur Jennings's visit might not have been connected to Vasily's work. That he might be connected to the Van Gogh and shooting. Had he heard the Van Gogh story? He was a conniving bastard but didn't seem the type to hire a contract killer. Still, who knew his boundaries with untold millions in the game. I'd lost track of him over the years, now realizing he was someone I'd possibly misread.

The crash of splintering wood jarred my thoughts. Arby was kicking the chair into kindling with his heavy shoes, tossing the scraps atop the body. He re-cinched the bundle with rope. Viktor scuffed the plastic sheeting on the floor with his toe and waved at the walls. "Get rid of plastic," he told Arby. "Burn everything. Kirill and Anatoly help you bury body. Throw away rebar some other place."

Glad to get away from the torture chamber, I stepped carefully around the crimson puddles, imagining my gallery carpet desecrated again by bloody footprints if and when I returned to the city. I followed Viktor's broad back up the steps, the sound of ripped vinyl assaulting my ears. Viktor closed the basement door on the horrors below and we sat, my eyes on the basement door, hoping Arby was haunted by the man's screams when the devil ushered both of them into hell.

Viktor waved at the art books scattered on the floor. "So, now you believe brother?"

"I don't know what to think."

He lit a Camel and waved it in the air. The smell of blood remained in my nostrils and I almost asked Viktor for a cigarette. I swallowed and from the expression of Viktor's face I guessed my thoughts were visible.

"Whatever you think, my friend, others believe what your father's letters say. They try to kill you but you will find this painting and then we get rich, you and me." He pushed one of the art books with the toe of his shoe and contemplated the colorful dust jacket. "Only now another man is also looking."

I nodded absently, trying to sort out the past week. How did I go from Vasily's opening to his murder and a mutilated corpse in an icy basement, a Russian mobster clinging to my back? Theft of the letters made sense now, but who else had Wes told about the painting? And why did they believe the fairy tale?

Viktor stood. "Arby drive you back to gallery. I must think what we do now."

Any thoughts I harbored about ignoring Wes's delusions vanished with the body in the basement. I'd worked hard to leave get-rich schemes, but life doesn't give a damn about your plans. Just when you think the road's been paved for you, someone's bulldozer rips it apart.

I waited for Viktor to say more but heard only sheet plastic being sliced apart.

***

The Contractor swallowed the last of his scotch and rattled the ice cubes to attract the bartender's attention. Other patrons in the hotel lounge saw a tall office dweller in a tailored gray three-piece Boss suit, an executive—unaware of the Browning automatic in a holster beneath his armpit, or the icepick nestled comfortably in its custom sheath strapped to his calf. Rail thin with engaging blue eyes and a thick lower lip, a patrician nose divided his narrow face. For the overly curious, he claimed he was Romanian, although his ancestors were renegade Armenians. Romania, however, deflected most people, particularly when he explained his ancestors came from the remote mountains of Transylvania. Visions of blood sucking bats and dirt-filled coffins stopped the nosiest bastards. Still, he regretted the genes from his ancestors. He would have preferred average white-bread physiognomy, advantages nature had denied him. His height and face made him memorable to witnesses who survived, but while his distinctive features were regrettable, he'd learned how to survive despite them.

He finished his expensive scotch and abandoned the idea of picking up the blond hooker at the far end of the hotel bar. Her gaze lingered on him several times with a brilliant smile. She was expertly coiffed and attired in designer fashions, obviously at the high-end of her trade. The man straightened his burgundy tie and returned the smile when she looked at him a second time, teasing her. He never liked paying for women. Better to find an appreciative secretary or lonely executive assistant who wondered why he disappeared after one night. He grinned at the blond, dropped several bills on the bar, and navigated the hotel lobby with an easy stride.

The penthouse suite on the 40th floor boasted wraparound windows, displaying Chicago's lakefront and skyline like giant movie screens. The Contractor surveyed the city's lights and kicked off his shoes without taking his eyes from the panorama. Still gazing at the glittering cityscape, he stripped off his tie and coat and hung them in the voluminous closet that could have accommodated the Chicago Bears starting offense. He stretched full-length on the king-sized bed before dialing his throwaway phone. A private line buzzed twice before a clipped voice answered.

"Talk."

"It's me," the Contractor said.

"I can read the number. What do you want?"

"To make sure you get value for your money," the Contractor said, hoping his confidence carried over the phone.

"That would be a welcome change. Your man killed some fucking Russian artist. That doesn't meet my definition of value."

"Not my fault."

"Your responsibility."

"The police think it was gangbangers."

"That doesn't change the fact you failed. Where's your inept associate now?"

The tall man deliberated for several seconds and decided on the truth. Their agreement was too lucrative to screw up. "Disappeared. Most likely, he panicked and bolted down some hole. I explained to him I don't tolerate failure. We'll never see him again."

"Could he identify you?"

"Arrangements were conducted through a third party. You can stop worrying."

"I was told you handled these matters with a certain efficiency," his employer said. "The older Barrow's wounded and his brother's probably wondering why. You should have taken care of this yourself."

"Too exposed and too many people around."

The phone went silent and the Contractor wondered if his employer had terminated the call. He'd received half the agreed amount and wondered if his benefactor was rethinking the contract in light of the failed hit. That was unacceptable in the Contractor's world, hoping the man realized the consequences. The Contractor pressed the phone closer to his ear and heard a faint sigh.

"It was a mistake on my part." The voice was measured now, failure relegated to the past.

The Contractor waited, studying the illuminated towers beyond the room's glass walls.

His employer spoke as though thinking aloud. "Adam Barrow's in the hunt now. His father may have been a drunk, but Barrow and his brother lived in the same house with him. They may know something they haven't realized yet. If so, it's possible the younger Barrow can lead us to the Van Gogh if you do as you're told."

The man said nothing, allowing his employer to lecture him. Following Barrow had a profitable ring. "You want me to stay with him?"

The edge returned. "You're sure you can do that?"

"If you keep your part of the bargain. You want your painting and I have expensive habits."

"I've learned that. Do your job and you'll be paid."

"And after he leads me to the painting?"

"Then you can correct your failure outside the gallery. I don't need loose ends."

"Don't go ballistic on me," the Contractor said. "There'll soon be nothing left for you to worry about."

The final click and the Contractor smiled as he laid the phone aside. He stretched his lanky body on the duvet and reached for the snuffbox on the bedside table. The oval art deco box was a long-time companion, almost a talisman. Its porcelain lid flaunted a 1930's nude languishing on four-poster bed, and unlike so many of his contemporaries, he'd selected the antique for its original purpose, foregoing its employment as a trendy vessel for cocaine. Snuff provided the momentary rush without cocaine's propensity to induce over-confidence, a trait he could ill afford.

Clicking open the box, he dismissed the phone conversation. The individual who enriched him was a moron, but that included almost every employer. Money aside, the job was the prize. The control, planning, improvisation, but best of all, the deception. He flowed into crowds of every social-economic persuasion, seamlessly transforming himself into one of them as his work demanded. It was the life he chose and only got better over the years.

Balancing the small mound of finely pulverized tobacco on his thumbnail, he lifted it to one nostril and inhaled. Savoring the bite, he rubbed his forefinger over the lid's image and wondered if the hooker was still at the bar.

Chapter Ten

The red-bearded man in threadbare clothes sat across from me at a sidewalk café. A bloody bandage covered his left ear. My father sat next to him drinking a martini, oblivious to blood coursing from the wound. People walked past us, laughing and pointing at the glistening bandage. When I yelled and pointed out the crimson splotches on the tablecloth, the stains swirled and morphed into a grotesque sunflower. Spongy yellow petals overlapped the table edges until they fell into my father's lap and inched up his body. Panicked, I leaped up, fear choking me as the fibrous blooms curled onto the sidewalk. I could not move, unable to struggle as the fibrous petals crawled up my legs...

I woke with a start.

The bedside digital clock read 6:15AM, which meant I'd lost sleep for the second night. In the darkness, the smells and image of the battered body in the raw basement returned. Shaken by the memory of the corpse, I bunched the blankets under my chin like a ten-year old, unable to generate the energy to face the cold room. How was an art dealer supposed to compete with people willing to employ lengths of rebar? I wasn't my brother's keeper or fictious super hero fashioned by an overpaid screenwriter. I never considered myself a coward and never shied away from a fair fight, enduring my share of brawls in high school and alcohol-induced brawls in college, but rapid-fire weapons were out of my league.

My cell phone vibrated on the night stand. I picked it up and wished I'd let it ring. Viktor's voice forced my head deeper into the pillows.

"Ah, Adam, you are awake early. That is good sign for my new partner." He was at his jovial best.

"Partner," I mumbled.

"You and me, we celebrate tonight. I take you to Tatiana. Best Russian restaurant in city." He groaned with mock anticipation and I imagined him licking his lips. "We sample flavored vodka Dorokhin makes. Very small glasses for Americans. He makes us a feast and we drink to making shitload of money."

"I told you, Viktor, there's no painting," I said, trying not to anger him.

He drew a deep breath. "Your brother, he believes the letters. You should also believe after what bastard tells Arby and me in basement."

"You want me to waste your money for a painting that doesn't exist?"

"Is okay if you do," he laughed. "We, how you say, spend money to make money, yes?"

"Viktor..."

"Tatiana Restaurant. Nine o'clock. I send car. No Wes, only you." He hung up.

The invitation, if you could call it that, convinced me I'd touched bottom but I was about to discover how wrong I was.

***

The night was freezing and Arby decided the SUV's heater was a decadent American luxury. The skies had cleared and millions of watts reflected off high-rise buildings along the lake as though electricity was a free commodity. Huddled in the car's backseat I tried to ignore the Golem in the driver's seat as Arby raced through yellow and red traffic lights, every car in his path an enemy. The stiff leather seat creaked as I braced my body against the chill and waited for the inevitable crash as we sped north on Lake Shore Drive.

Fifteen minutes later Arby swung into in a trendy business district off the lake. He braked the SUV beneath a striped canopy and waved off the parking attendant. A horn blared behind us. I got out with Arby who stood motionless by the car door and stared down the horn blower. The other driver assessed the specter in black and probably visualized an unplanned ride to the hospital. The other car backed up as the attendant hurried after it.

Tatiana was a red and black and faux gold Russian tea room seating a hundred diners. A smiling dwarf dressed in an ill-fitting gray suit dodged between tables, hurrying toward Arby and me. Wringing his pudgy hands, he jerked to a halt and I guessed the stunted little man to be Dorokhin.

"Mr. Bolkov, a pleasure as usual," he said, bowing as though a reincarnated Romanov graced the premises, his English better than Russian neighborhoods

72 *The Last Van Gogh*

along Chicago Avenue. He bowed again, his smile anxious. Flourishing his right arm toward a curtained glass door, he trotted ahead of us.

"Mr. Krushenko is waiting for you and his guest."

I tried to ignore diners' stares as Dorokhin led us to a private dining room. Arby and I entered and he shut the door, pulling heavy curtains closed before settling in a chair against one wall. A round table sat in the center of the room. Lit by a baroque chandelier, finely engraved silver and gold serving pieces accompanied three place settings of Sevres china, sparks dancing off an army of crystal glasses.

Viktor grinned at me but I looked past him at a spectacular woman dressed in black who occupied the chair beside him, smoking a thin cigarette, assessing me through the smoke. Far younger than Viktor and a half-head taller than her unlikely dinner companion, she wore an off-shoulder black dress, a simple black ribbon accentuating her faultless throat. Shoulder-length black hair, swept to one side onto a bare shoulder, glimmered black-purple in the overhead lights. High cheekbones defined her Slavic heritage as she tapped the cigarette on a sterling silver ashtray. Frowning as though I'd arrived with an overdue book, I decided horn-rimmed glasses and a severe hairdo could never transform her into the town librarian.

"Adam!" Viktor bellowed. "Welcome, my friend."

He indicated the empty chair beside him and I sat. Good job, Wes, I thought, taking stock of the approaching disaster. Thanks to my brother, I'd stepped into a freak show: a stone-cold killer, a ruthless Russian mob boss, and his girlfriend who stared unabashedly at me. I could walk out, but the strongest counter-argument leaned his chair against the wall beside the door.

A slender engraved bottle of vodka nestled in a sterling ice bucket beside Viktor, his bald pate shining with perspiration. He lifted the chilled bottle from its ice bed and half-filled my water tumbler. No ice, no lime, just straight vodka. His beguiling companion had not taken her eyes from me, and I marveled at Viktor's ability to attract such a creature—a superb example that money bought anything he desired. He did not introduce her and instead motioned to Arby who opened the door and crooked a finger at Dorokhin. The diminutive owner instantly appeared, hands clasped in anticipation as Arby closed the door behind him.

"We eat now," Viktor said. "Show my guest why you are best in city." He waved the empty vodka bottle at Dorokhin. "And bring more."

A minute later, white-jacketed servers rolled three linen-draped carts into the room. One of the waiters removed the ice bucket and replaced it with another containing a fresh bottle of vodka, Russia's finest according to Viktor. The overhead lights sparkled on the silver-domed platters, providing the illusion of embedded stars as waiters removed the covers with a flourish. Viktor waved them out and explained each dish. Dressed herring. Veal Orlov. Pelmeni. Pirozhki pies. Dorokhin hovered behind Krushenko, anticipating praise or reproach. Viktor ignored him and lifted the newly arrived bottle toward me.

"Hetman. Is best Ukrainian vodka in world." He topped off my glass although I hadn't touched it. He raised his glass and we touched rims as the woman watched.

"To partnership," Viktor grinned.

Not accustomed to drinking straight vodka from a water glass, we clinked again and I hesitantly took a swallow. Viktor hadn't lied; the iced Ukrainian vodka was superior. Viktor continued to ignore the woman although I detected an unspoken intimacy between them.

"Now bring flavored vodka," Viktor ordered Dorokhin. "Cinnamon, lemon, strawberry."

I speared a bliny pancake and sliced it apart, realizing I needed to eat to survive the night on my feet. Two minutes later the first shots of flavored vodka appeared in rime-coated aperitif glasses. I inwardly groaned, aware tomorrow morning would arrive at a heavy price.

Dorokhin placed the delicate glass in front of me and leaned close. "Cinnamon," he whispered. "Made by my hands. Not the commercial junk sold in liquor stores."

Viktor and the woman downed the shots without blinking and I followed suit. The freezing combination of rich cinnamon and fine vodka slipped smoothly down my throat and I nodded at Dorokhin, wondering when the vodka rodeo would end. Viktor wiped his mouth with one finger and nodded at the owner who smiled with relief. Belching, Viktor dragged more food from two platters onto his plate. Dorokhin returned with the second round of frozen glasses arranged on a serving tray draped in red velvet. I quickly consumed half a pancake as he presented the second shot.

"Lemon," he announced.

74 *The Last Van Gogh*

The overhead lights took on a gentler glow as I knocked back the delicious concoction, grateful Wes was exempted from the vodka fest. I turned to compliment Dorokhin but he'd already disappeared for the next temptation.

"You like?" Viktor asked.

"Very much."

"Is Dorokhin's best."

I added pickles onto my plate and consumed another bliny. Viktor, his mouth half-full, glanced at the woman as if remembering her presence. He washed down the food with vodka and pointed his fork at her.

"Katia Veranova, my associate." He finger-wiped his lips again. "She is good Russian girl. Good companion. After tonight, she is also your companion."

I looked at the woman as faint strains of a violin drifted into the room from a live quartet in the main salon. She ignored me, pushing uneaten food around her plate.

"My companion," I managed. "Why do I need a companion to find the painting?"

Viktor continued eating as though he hadn't heard me, eyes shining like a peasant. He took a generous swallow of vodka. "To protect my investment."

"If you don't trust me..." I began.

"Not you, my friend. Bastards who try to kill you."

I nodded at his companion. "Then why expose her?"

Viktor closed his eyes in joy as he swallowed an overloaded forkful of shashlik, washing the seasoned cabbage down with more vodka. "Best food outside of Moscow," he declared, raising a forkful of food covered in sour cream.

"Not to worry," he added between mouthfuls of food. "She is good partner for you, make sure you do not spend my money on brandy and whores." He shot an amused look at Arby. "She is good..." He waved his fork, stumbling for a word. "Associate. She is associate who will help you."

Katia said nothing. Why in hell did I need one of his women to watch over me? Had she known her paramour would place a new demand on her? I avoided her dark eyes and wondered if she spoke English. Whatever her skills, I didn't need a female Sancho Panza tagging along on a pointless quest. I didn't want or need her but I couldn't take my eyes from her. Not wanting to appear obvious and risk a close encounter with a length of rebar, I looked at Viktor.

"I don't need her. Wes will be with me."

Will Ottinger

Viktor cut a slice of meat pie and shook his head. "No. Brother runs gallery while you are gone."

Dorokhin arrived with the third shot. "Strawberry," he announced, ignoring the tension in the room. "Pureed fresh this morning."

I shot the aperitif and blinked, my thoughts wooly as the vodka kicked in. Had Wes just been tagged as a hostage?

"He must heal from his wound," Viktor added. "Is lucky bullet did not cripple him. Now, he learns gallery business. Is good for him. I help him find customers in Russian community. My countrymen will buy pictures if I make recommendation." He pointed his fork at me. "All settled." I translated Viktor's edicts to mean nothing would happen to Wes unless I did something stupid.

Katia spoke for the first time. "It will be alright."

Her voice was husky from cigarettes and vodka but there was no trace of Russian. She shifted her eyes to Viktor who continued eating as though she'd not spoken. She downed the strawberry shot and gave me the barest of smiles.

What in hell was happening, I wondered?

I turned back to Viktor. "Why can't I take Arby with me?"

"Arby is mine," he said. "He stays here. Protects your brother. Makes sure nothing happens to him after you leave country."

"Leave the country?"

Viktor tossed his fork onto his plate and belched. "Your brother tell me painter is from Holland long time ago, that this Van Gogh also is working in France when he is alive. Then painting comes to America." Viktor leaned close to me, eyes shining again. "We find it, you and me."

Knowing the battle was lost, I pushed my luck. "There's nothing but two ancient letters. If the Van Gogh existed, there's not even a hint what happened to it. My father was a drunk, Viktor. His letter wasn't dated, so he may have sold it to someone who's been afraid to reveal its existence, afraid the American or French government will claim it. Even if it's real, no one knows what happened to it. You never knew my father. He suffered delusions when he got older. He..."

Viktor stabbed the tablecloth with a thick forefinger. "You do not tell me family history. Your father was maybe a drunk but your brother tells me painting is real. That your father hides it somewhere. I believe him."

"You wouldn't if you'd known our father."

A soft knock interrupted us and Dorokhin stuck his head in. Viktor waved him away. When the door closed, he snapped his fingers at Arby who handed him a thick envelope. Viktor removed a wad of hundred-dollar bills and spread them beside my plate.

"Travel money," he said. "Tomorrow, Katia buys tickets to Amsterdam. Go and ask about this painting." He shoved the money closer and tapped his bulbous nose. "Use your nose. Is Van Gogh's country. Someone know something."

"And if it's a dead end?"

"Then you and Katia go to Paris. Find this Dejean. If he still lives."

I stared at her and imagined traveling to Europe with this inscrutable woman who was probably anticipating the Paris shops. The painting *had* to be a myth and taking her along complicated an already impossible situation. Still, Wes had almost been killed and I couldn't desert him despite the impossible situation he'd blundered into.

Arby walked behind me as I stared at the bills. Viktor waited for me to pick them up. Russian folk music drifted past the heavy curtains, and in spite of my penchant for self-preservation, I made no move toward the money. Accepting it meant reviving the past. My father failed Wes and me and we shared his genes, Wes toppling after him, using a weak man's failures to justify the lure of bars and taverns. I had escaped and submerged myself in art, earning earned two degrees and starting a business. Picking up the money meant chasing Wes's dream, extending our line of family disasters.

Despite the warnings, the Hetman and vodka shots whispered that finding a lost masterpiece would expunge my role as a deserter and convert my father's legacy from alcoholic thief to modern-day miracle worker—if I lived. That was a major 'if', but I owed Wes and myself that much.

I picked up his money and Arby opened the door for me, flashing his dental work. The woman lit another cigarette, her face impassive.

Viktor drained his glass and grinned. "Go find my painting."

Chapter Eleven

I unlocked the gallery early next morning, the conversation at Tatiana playing in my head like balalaika missing half its strings. The furnace hummed and I heard hammering in back. Wes limped out and sat in front of my desk, appearing calmer than I'd seen him in months. There was no sign of a hangover, unlike the evil trolls trying to jackhammer their way out of my skull.

"How's the leg?"

"It hurts but I'm mobile," he said.

"I never took you for an early bird."

"The bars aren't open yet."

"I hope you're kidding."

He flashed the infectious smile and I detected no residue of a bender.

"I'm glad you're here before Sally," I said. "The two of you are going to be running the gallery for a while. Any problem with that?"

"No, I like her. No artsy bullshit."

"I could be gone a couple of weeks," I said, wondering if that was optimistic.

"Where are you going?"

"Viktor's sending me to Amsterdam and Paris, thanks to the letters you showed him."

Wes either overlooked the comment. "Art dealer to world traveler in a single leap,"

"Don't get excited," I said. "Your Van Gogh's a wild goose chase."

"And I'm not invited."

"Victor wants you to stay here and learn the gallery business."

"You mean stay out of your way."

"Wes—"

"Oh, hell, I don't care as long as you find the painting."

I thought about Katia and tried to imagine Barbara's reaction if Wes flew off to Paris with a beautiful woman. "Anyway, I'm not going alone," I admitted. "Viktor's sending a watchdog with me."

"The delightful and sophisticated Arby?"

"A Russian woman."

"Good looking?"

The question cut deeper than he knew. "What the hell does it matter?"

He grinned. "It doesn't. But Barbara would have kittens if I ran off to Europe with some Russian chick. Anyway, I hope this one's a cut above your other conquests. Barbara thinks you need serious counseling in your choice of women. Said you'd be better off finding a Bryn Mawr grad or Midwestern farm girl."

"Or shooting myself."

Wes grinned. "I didn't say I agreed."

He gingerly propped his damaged leg on the corner of my desk, then eased it to the floor when I shot him a disapproving look. One doesn't sprawl in the art business.

"Okay, is she a stripper or an escort?"

"Whatever she is, she's Viktor's property."

"Hot?" Wes persisted.

I hesitated and said, "Yeah, yeah, she's attractive, but don't forget who we're dealing with here. I'm not about to jump between the sheets with Viktor's girlfriend."

Wes conceded the point and I plunged ahead. Too many fences remained between us and he deserved an explanation why I'd agreed to chase his dream. Even if Wes derided my explanation, I needed to say it aloud for my benefit as well as his.

"There's another reason I agreed to all this. If by some improbable chance we find this mislaid Van Gogh, we'll have closure with dad," I said. "At least I will. Then we can both let him go."

"I don't owe him anything," Wes said bitterly. "My involuntary servitude as his bartender and nursemaid was paid in full the day I walked out of that damned house."

I couldn't argue with him. "We're covering old ground again. You were the good son but I bailed out. I owe both of you."

The front door opened before he could reply and Sally joined us. If there was ever a walking portrayal of perky, she fit the definition as she wiggled her fingers at us. I dreaded the day some executive took a second look at her looks and talents and offered her more than a retail life. Tossing her handbag on a chair she caught our expressions. "What? I miss something?"

"No, everything's fine." I'd already informed Sally I'd be away from the gallery for a while. "I just told Wes I was leaving. He's under your tutelage until I get back."

"No problem." She grinned at him. "So long as he doesn't drink Rush Street dry, I won't try to be the boss." She glanced at the notepad on my desk and back to Wes. "Did you tell him about the phone call?"

Wes shook his head. "You took the call, boss."

Sally grinned and flipped him off. They would get along fine without me. "A woman from the League called," she said. "Said you talked with her a couple days ago. I told her you'd be out of the country for a while and she asked where you were going. I told her and she said 'Lucky him' and hung up. She didn't leave a message. Did I screw up telling her about your trip?"

I wondered why the affable Mary Barnum-Gordon was interested where I went. Had she learned something about the Van Gogh? I picked up the phone, called her office, and was informed she was meeting with donors in New York.

Hanging up, I thought for a moment, then shook my head at Sally. "No problem telling her." I looked at Wes whom I could tell was wondering about the call as well. Pushing it aside, I pulled Viktor's envelope from my coat pocket and counted out three thousand dollars.

Sally ogled the pile of cash. "Is that my long-deserved bonus as your top employee?

I returned the rest of the money to the envelope. "That ought to keep the doors open, but let's play it safe and not tell anyone else where I've gone."

"What the hell are you guys doing?" Sally asked.

Wes counted the stack of hundreds and grinned at me. "Viktor?"

I nodded. My toes were on the edge of a high dive board with shallow water below, chasing two phantoms: The Van Gogh and remission of family sins. I gave Wes a fatalistic shrug. In for a penny, in for a pound of dirty money.

Chapter Twelve

The Contractor's cell rang on the car's passenger seat. He pulled the rental off the highway and shut off the engine. The temperature inside the Toyota plummeted as bitter wind off the lake invaded the interior. Hoping the balky heater would cooperate when he restarted the engine, he checked the rearview mirror and opened the console beneath his right arm where the long-barreled 9mm Browning rested out of sight. Recognizing the caller's ID, he punched the answer button.

"Are you alone?" the voice asked.

"I wouldn't have answered if I wasn't."

Paper rustled at the other end. "You're leaving on a trip."

A passing car slowed and the Contractor laid his hand on the pistol. "Where?"

"Amsterdam to start. Barrow's going after the painting."

The Contractor knew Europe well, and traveling would be a welcome diversion after the failed hit and endless surveillance. Impressed with his employer's access to information, he said, "You do have good resources, don't you?"

"Retaining high-tech geeks in the right places is a good investment. The woman's computer proved simple to hack."

"And, of course, you know where they're staying in Amsterdam."

The man gave him the hotel name and the Contractor said, "And how does all this help me find your Van Gogh?"

"If you can't do it, I'll find others who'll find you and get my money back."

For all his wealth, his employer lacked understanding how these things worked. While the role reversal of being he hunted was intriguing, he wouldn't allow that to happen. He had rules, a protocol he devised as a college student. One of the rules ensured no one posed a danger to him, no matter the cost.

He'd run out of money during his last semester. Sick of working two night jobs, he was kicked out of his dorm when he failed to pay his tuition. None of the bright young faces he passed every day cared what happened to him, money magically appearing in their campus mail box each month. His first robbery proved an unexpected windfall, a clueless messenger carrying a company payroll. The man's carelessness cost him his life, the Contractor only briefly regretting the killing. He drank heavily that night and woke up next morning with the mother of all headaches but the guilt had vanished in the night. The second robbery was easier, the second killing guaranteeing his safety. The police never suspected a college student of the sting of robberies and killings, and he realized he found a calling. After that, money became his opioid.

He became known and found people who needed his talents, splurging on a red MG, a sleek little machine. He loved the car, regretting the necessity of burning it after he used it in a hit-and-run to dispose of an inept embezzler who cheated the wrong hedge fund manager. Word spread in the right circles and larger contracts came his way despite his youth. It surprised him how easily he rationalized the work, his bank account growing simply because he did what others feared or refused to do. He quickly perfected his vocation, paydays growing larger with a string of unsolved crimes in his wake. He was careful and he was good, realizing there was serious money in high-profile hits and, like many with specialized skills, he abandoned college to hone his talent.

"I'm disappointed," he said to his benefactor. "Are we down to threats so soon in our friendship?"

"Don't get above yourself. You're hired help."

"Now my feelings are truly hurt, but I assume you called for reasons other than insulting me." An eighteen-wheeler growled past and the Contractor jammed the phone hard against his ear.

"Barrow and the woman leave on Friday," the voice continued. "I'll leave travel money in the usual place. Stay with them in Amsterdam."

"Is our friend also traveling with his brother?"

"No, the woman bought only two tickets."

"Who's the woman?"

"Katia Veranova. Mean anything to you?"

"She sounds Russian, which I don't like."

"Why?"

"I followed Barrow to a Russian restaurant," the Contractor said. "He had dinner with Viktor Krushenko."

"Who in hell is Viktor Krushenko?"

"The uncle of the artist who was killed. Krushenko runs Chicago's Russian mafia. Controls drugs, prostitution, anything illegal that makes money. He gained control by eliminating the tacos, blacks and dagos. No one with any brains crosses him."

"So?"

"So, if Krushenko's involved, I'll require more money. I didn't count on the Russians."

"I was led to believe you didn't worry about competition. You want out?"

The Contractor ignored the implication. His feet growing numb, he started the car, and kicked on the heat to beat back the cold. He tucked the phone against his shoulder and rubbed his hands together.

The voice at the other end grew animated. "Barrow's *got* to believe the painting's real. Neither he nor his rum-dumb brother has money to chase castles in the sky. You think this Krushenko's paying Barrow to find the painting?"

The Contractor heard the flicker of alarm and suppressed a laugh. "If it's worth what you claim, he'll have his dirty finger in the pie."

"I don't like the Russians in this."

"You think I do? These bastards will kill you for stepping on their foot."

"Nothing to be done about it now. We'll just have to beat them to the painting."

The Contractor smelled opportunity. "It'll get more expensive if Krushenko's involved. You're competing with a warehouse of money. You can't expect..."

"Just find the goddamn painting. I'll pay whatever's required."

"I want another $25,000 for expenses. And to keep my body out of Lake Michigan. I didn't figure on dealing with these people." No reply. "Or you can find someone else," the Contractor said. "Start over and take your chances." Making demands was risky, but the stakes had risen with the Russians in the game and there were always other clients.

"All right, you'll get your money."

"I knew you'd see the light. Are we friends again?" he asked, but the connection was already broken.

Chapter Thirteen

Arby drove us to O'Hare before dawn. Katia and I had First Class seats on the early United flight to Amsterdam. The ride to the airport wasn't bursting with convivial conversation, but at least the SUV heater functioned, a courtesy, I guessed, to Viktor's playmate.

The pre-dawn temperature teased 20 degrees. Dressed in woolen navy-blue slacks that clung to long legs, Katia stepped from the car like a runway model. A short ermine jacket enveloped her plain white sweater, turning male and female heads as we checked our luggage. I didn't look forward to the long overseas flight. Katia Veranova was a distraction I didn't need. Strapped in an airline seat provided too much time to ponder a hopeless chase and reopen family wounds. The likelihood of finding the Van Gogh was too small to seriously contemplate, but the possibility gnawed at me. What if our father once played the hero?

Walking to the gate Katia indicated she'd sit one row behind mine and across the aisle.

"Shouldn't we sit together?" I said. "Make plans for Amsterdam?"

"We have time."

Great attitude. "I guess you'll be shopping while I scramble after Viktor's Van Gogh?"

Her expression didn't change. "My job is to protect you."

"And Viktor's money."

"If that's what you wish to believe."

Tired of bouncing off a glacier wall, I shut up. She stopped at a newsstand and bought half a dozen fashion magazines. My anger edged up another notch when she waved me ahead of her in the passenger line, hanging back among our fellow travelers. After a few minutes she walked to concourse window and watched the conveyor belt load luggage into the bay of the Boeing 747. What next? Check the pilot and crew ratings? She appeared calm enough but maybe the self-assured woman was a white-knuckle flyer.

On board, a First-Class flight attendant took Katia's fur and my pride and joy, a heavy Andrew Marc leather jacket. I occupied a spacious window seat and ordered a drink, telling the young woman to bring another when we were airborne. Why not? It was going to be a long flight.

The Boeing leveled at 35,000 feet and Katia unsnapped her seat belt. My eyes followed her as she made two trips to the rear of the aircraft. Several male heads leaned into the aisle to enjoy the rear view as she made eye contact with each passenger before returning to her seat. Nonplussed when the flight attendant informed her there were separate restrooms for First Class passengers, she nodded and closed her eyes.

I cradled my second scotch and water and resisted looking back at her. The last thing I needed was a female watchdog. I'd been given no choice, not the way Viktor explained things. I was throwing darts in the dark, searching for a painting that took on mythical proportions in his mind. Adding to the disaster Wes had created, I had an appendage I didn't need: the girlfriend of the most vicious man in Chicago.

I drained the scotch and peered out the window in boyish wonder. I never set foot inside an airplane until I was nineteen years old. This flight launched me toward what sensitive people saw as closure, whatever in hell that meant. I'd abandoned a dying father and floundering brother and run away to… what? If there was the faintest chance the Van Gogh was real, I might salvage self-respect and slam shut a chapter of my roller coaster life. Whatever the result, I accepted penance came at a price that included mollifying our new master.

After a third scotch, I dozed and dreamed of the red-bearded man again. We were arguing about our fathers when I awoke with a start, having missed two meals, the free slippers, and supply of unlimited drinks. I'd slept most of the flight, sparing myself endless recriminations about a dysfunctional childhood.

Stretching, I turned and found Katia staring at me. I smiled but she buried her face in her *Vogue*. Struck again by her aloof beauty, I accepted that whatever happened on our little European jaunt, an erotic escapade was not on the program.

We landed at Schiphol Airport in late afternoon beneath a canopy of earth-hugging clouds. Amsterdam's main airport greeted us with icy wind born on the North Sea, rocking the aircraft as we taxied to the terminal, snow flurries smacking against the window. Katia donned a white ski cap as we deplaned and cleared customs, met outside by a private limousine, courtesy of Viktor's money. Wrapped in our thoughts we maintained an uneasy truce as the car maneuvered along the historic city's boulevards and cramped side streets.

The Banks Mansion, a venerable old five-story hotel, occupied a busy street corner, one side staring straight down into an ancient canal. The traditional European exterior was contradicted by sleek furnishings and amenities, including complementary tourist bicycles. We checked into adjoining rooms, and I received a questioning look from the bellman when Katia ordered him to put her luggage in the separate bedroom. I ignored his smirk, aware cynics believed hotels spawned separate moral universes—large buildings filled with beds, a playground liberating guests from vows and promises.

I tipped the bellman and he quietly closed my room door. Katia bolted the door behind him and checked the connecting door between our rooms. For an awkward moment, we faced one another until I gave up suppressing a yawn.

"I plan on sleeping an hour before dinner," I said.

"We should talk about tomorrow."

"Too late. You had your chance on the plane. Go shop or whatever you want. I'm taking a siesta unless you'd enjoy watching me fall in the canal."

She shrugged, double-checked that both doors to the hall were locked, and went to her room, leaving the connecting door open. Heedless of my modesty, I stripped to my briefs and fell face down on the bed, asleep in a minute.

***

The reliable alarm inside my head woke me a little before eight. I sat up in the darkness with a start. Katia sat on the window seat at the foot of my bed, smoking a cigarette, her outline barely visible in the darkened room. Still dressed in her travel clothes, she sat without moving, contemplating the canal below. I padded to the closet in my shorts, grabbed a hotel robe, and headed for the bathroom.

"Are you up for dinner?" I yelled from the bathroom.

"Whenever you are ready."

After showering, my room was empty, the door to her room open. I dressed in fresh slacks and a crewneck sweater over a button-down white oxford. Brushing my hair before the bath mirror, I studied my reflection when Katia came into view in the mirror. My hand froze in mid-air. She stood with her back to me, naked except for a black thong. Mesmerized by the flawless curve of her spine and long athletic legs, I watched her balance on one foot and step into a forest green skirt. She disappeared from my line of sight and I stared into my mirrored eyes, seized by adolescent guilt and raw yearning. Improbable as it seemed, I wondered if she purposely gave me a show.

The hotel concierge recommended Vinkeles, a restaurant located in another hotel, assuring us it was a short walk. After a few blocks I realized the concierge's directions took us through an old section of the city. Narrow brick streets imitated dim tunnels, most of the shops darkened. Half-hearted streetlights left pools of shadows but I pushed aside my uneasiness. Amsterdam had one of the lowest crime rates in the Netherlands.

I turned to say something to Katia when a figure emerged from a doorway and shoved me off the curb. I stumbled and landed on my ass in the cobblestone street. Our assailant grabbed for Katia's purse and her elbow connected with his chin. She stomped a stiletto heel onto the top of his foot, the crunch distinct. The man howled, swapping greed for pain as he lurched backward. Katia rammed a knotted fist into his solar plexus and he dropped to his knees. Getting to my feet, I watched her grab his hair and punch him in the temple. He toppled onto his side without a sound, twitching once. The fight, if you could call it that, was over.

She bent and retrieved her purse.

"Are you all right?"

"Are *you* okay?" I managed.

"A sneak thief," she said, stepping close enough for me to smell her perfume. She smoothed my jacket lapels, avoiding my eyes as she looked down at the groaning figure. "Not a very good one."

There'd been no time to react to the assault. Not that she needed me.

"Where did you learn to take care of yourself?"

"Such people are no danger," she said, "unless they have a knife or gun."

Chagrined, I dusted myself off and tried to reassemble my manhood. "I feel pretty useless about now."

"He was just closer to me," she said. "No harm done."

"Yeah."

She looped her arm through mine, the intimacy surprising me. "Come. You said you were hungry."

Vinkeles, like many chic restaurants, boasted overflowing ferns, etched glass, and scrubbed brick walls, the interior illuminated by art deco sconces and table candles. Katia requested a table away from the windows with a view of the street. I looked over the wine list and attempted to link her actions with the elegant back I'd seen in my mirror.

She lighted a cigarette and scanned our fellow diners as though nothing had happened. I knew we'd truly arrived in Europe when no one screamed or called the police as her smoke drifted over nearby tables.

Looking back at me, she said, "Since we will be together for some time, you must call me Kat."

Kat. Could any name be more appropriate for the exotic violent creature studying me in the candlelight?

"Alright, but we flew four thousand miles together and I just watched you destroy a man twice your size. All I know is you're Viktor's girlfriend and I'm to call you Kat."

"Girlfriend." An amused smile, the first crack in the wall. "You think I am one of his wide-eyed strippers?"

I changed the subject. "Does he think I'll blow his money unless you watch over me?"

She took a long drag on her cigarette. "No, he thinks you may die, and if that happens, he won't get his painting."

"And you'll make certain I don't get killed."

The wall rose again. "Yes."

I ordered wine and a bearded waiter filled our glasses, his eyes devouring Kat. "With all due respect to your talents, I'd rather have Arby tagging along with me."

"Viktor needs him," she said. "Arby knows Viktor's enemies."

"And you'll know *my* enemies—in a country of strangers." Kat returned my look, candlelight failing to soften her expression. "And if someone attempts to kill me, exactly what are you expected to do?"

"Protect you."

I picked up the menu and pretended to study it. If Viktor wanted to guard his investment, why send a martial arts model? Laying aside the pricey bill of fare, I leaned toward her as she scrutinized our fellow diners again before she folded her hands atop her menu.

"Timing is the danger," she said.

"Timing?"

"Whoever tried to kill you did not find what they needed in the letters stolen from your brother. Viktor doesn't believe they'll harm you or your brother until the painting's located, but we don't know when that might happen. These people believe you may find it. If they find the painting first, they'll kill you and your brother," she said as though explaining a complex business transaction. "Viktor believes they will follow us to see what we find. Until then, these people need you."

"So, I'm disposable once it's found."

Kat took the smallest sip of her wine and lifted her slender shoulder. "You and your brother can cause ownership problems. That's why they must kill both of you."

That was blunt enough. "And you can prevent that?"

Her head came up and met my eyes with a feral look. "Yes."

"How do you know all this?"

"I can protect you. You do not need to know anything else."

The waiter refilled our wine glasses and asked for dinner orders. I motioned him away and ordered a second bottle of wine. I fought off jet lag and took stock in my situation, deciding alcohol was the best remedy while I hunted down a painting with a beautiful woman who casually demolished muggers. I poured more wine for both of us, pushing the point.

"Not good enough. Tell me who you are."

"You cannot..."

I lowered my voice. "I appreciate what you did just now, but my brother's life is in danger, maybe mine too. Viktor or no Viktor, I'll fly back to Chicago tomorrow unless I know why he sent you instead of Arby."

"You should be thinking differently," she said. "I just explained that letting you remain alive is a problem if the painting *is* real. You and your brother will claim ownership, of course. Whoever these other people are, they cannot then allow either of you to live. I can prevent that from happening."

This wasn't what I'd bargained for. "I need to know how in hell you're supposed to do that."

She refolded her napkin and lowered her voice. "You ask me to tell you something that is not pleasant," she said.

Will Ottinger 89

"Tell me."

"My name is not Katia Veranova. I was born Svetlana Kosdrenkov. Before I came to America, I was what your CIA calls an operative. I worked for the KGB."

For a moment I was uncertain whether to laugh or bolt from the restaurant. All I knew of the KGB was what I saw in movies where people were yanked from their beds in the middle of the night. She'd thrown a switch and a trace of her Russian accent reappeared. "The *Komitet* now calls itself the FSB."

As though revealing a plot from a spy novel, she said Viktor operated many businesses in Moscow, none legal in a city where crime ruled the streets abetted by highest echelons of power and influence. She'd met him during a sting operation and discovered he had more power and influence than her handlers imagined. Quietly and over time she and Viktor formed a symbiotic alliance, a member of the KGB and a criminal. She crushed out her cigarette and gave me a look that said she didn't care if I believed her or not.

"For the first time, I enjoyed nice things that had always been denied me. I helped him and he helped me. We worked together in the Black Market but Viktor made mistakes and angered the worst criminals in Moscow," she said, "including well-placed officials in the government. Those in power marked him for death."

There was more. Illegal visas, currency swaps, passports. Together with Viktor and Arby, she ran. "I thought conditions changed in Russia after the Wall fell," I said.

Kat made a small noise. "Little changed after the Wall came down. To become an officer in my section, I was ordered to get close to a young dissident, make him my lover. Obtain names of his movement's leaders, then dispose of him."

"Kill him." Who was this lovely woman behind the wine glass?

She ignored me. "A simple operation but I could not do it." She shrugged. "So, I escaped with Viktor." She looked at me with renewed intensity. "I *escaped*. I did not defect. I am not a traitor."

We ordered dinner and she told me her story as though relating a normal life, the explanation contradictory to the beautiful woman across from me. She possessed the appeal to lure a man into bed and then murder him, but I couldn't wrap my mind around the possibility. I didn't claim to be a saint but I couldn't imagine the world she claimed to have inhabited.

She exhaled as though exhausted from a long race. "As I said, I am not a defector like those who run to your government for protection in exchange for information." She gave a resigned smile. "But my former associates do not believe that. They will always look for me."

"So, you became this Veranova person." I was a struggling gallery owner now collaborating with a trained assassin, her tale the stuff of Le Carré novels. "What do you do now? When you're not protecting Viktor and coerced art dealers."

She'd barely touched her wine, examining the stemmed glass with a distracted smile. "I help Viktor. At first, he tried to make me his mistress. When I refused, he accepted that I had a more practical value. After we came to Chicago, Viktor did whatever was required and I became more valuable to him, an Arby no one sees." She fell silent, then wiped her lips and raised her hand at the waiter. "If you and I were different people, I would share more wine with you and possibly something more," she said, "but I'm your only protection and tomorrow will be a long day."

The waiter arrived with an expectant grin. Kat cancelled my second bottle of wine and asked for the check. Neither of us spoke in the taxi back to the hotel, our silences becoming standard fare. I could think of nothing to say after her revelations, and it wasn't until weeks later that either of us recalled the tall blue-eyed man beside the hotel entrance. By then, it was too late.

Chapter Fourteen

At that moment on a Moscow street, Anatoli Tasso trudged across a city covered with white frosting. Early afternoon sunlight fought its perennial war with swirling snow that stung his face, a halo of white vapor escaping his mouth. Nondescript as a lamppost, Tasso was easily overlooked. His closely-cropped black beard showed streaks of gray through its brittle coating of ice, passersby seeing an actuary or assistant store manager if they bothered to look twice at him. Heavily bundled, his head lowered against the wind, he focused on the ice encrusted sidewalk, avoiding the monstrosity that waited across the square. Grey hair escaped beneath his sable fur cap and he did not look into the windows of Dyetsky Mir, Russia's largest toy shop, the obscene dichotomy not lost on him that a store for bright-eyed children shared Lubyanka Square.

Eyes averted, he hurried past the shop toward the Neo-Baroque building. Known simply as Lubyanka, the four-story block of yellow sandstone squatted like a swollen toad in the cold sunlight. Russians claimed Lubyanka was the tallest building in Moscow, that you could see Siberia and the gulags from its basement cells. His breath a white fog of regret, he sighed, aware he and the building's occupants had dishonored Russia.

Crossing the square, Tasso drew a deep breath that bit into his lungs, remembering a boyhood prayer as he pushed through Lubyanka's outer doors, removing his fur hat and brushing ice from his beard. No matter how many times he entered the soulless building, he never overcame the sensation he might never walk out. His footsteps echoed across the cavernous lobby, the polished parquet floor laid down before the Bolshevik revolution. As always, he was taken aback by the high ceilings and ornamental appointments that gleamed in utter contrast to what lay beneath his feet: A basement with slanted tile corridors that allowed blood to flow into open grates. Filthy cells where life was prolonged to inflict pain and more suffering. This had been Nikita Khrushchev's playground when he headed the NKVD, where a walk down its darkened corridors ended with *genickschuss*, the Nazi's term for a bullet in the back of the neck. Tasso glanced around the lobby and saw the building's gift shop was closed, a nod to some minor official's sense of shame.

A small directory beside the bank of elevators indicated the Federal Security Services now occupied third floor where Colonel Aleki Gusov waited for him. Tasso stared at the Bureau's new identify. Whitewash over rotting wood, he thought, stepping into the elevator. The lift hummed and Tasso unbuttoned his overcoat, allowing a rare smile at the KGB's grandiose title. Vladimir Putin preferred the less terrifying connotation, a bland label designed to sooth the consciences of his Western counterparts.

The elevator doors opened and he showed his identification to an army captain behind a metal desk facing the elevators. The officer recognized him and pointed down the grey-carpeted hallway to a familiar reinforced door. The thick pile carpet swallowed his footsteps and he paused outside the door, removing his cap and overcoat to reveal a nondescript business suit and cheap tie. The usual wave of anxiety assailed him as he turned the handle and stepped inside.

A tall man in full uniform stood behind a carved antique desk holding a china cup of steaming Brazilian coffee. Tightly swaged drapes cast the room in shadows as though anxious to conceal its true function and connection to the squalid cells four stories below. The room exuded bureaucratic privilege, its furnishings and appointments dishonoring the abject homes of most Russian workers. Even the aroma of fresh coffee seemed a sacrilege.

Hand extended, his blue eyes illuminated by two Imperial table lamps, Gusov strode to his visitor, soft high-top boots crafted in the style of a Czarist cavalry officer, the Order of Lenin pinned to his tunic. Tasso kept his own medal in a cardboard box in his apartment closet.

"Anatoli Gregoryevich Tasso!" The colonel's rumbling voice belied his skeletal frame as the two men shook hands. "My clock chimes one o'clock and you walk in the door. I admire an awareness of time, but then, I admire your effectiveness in all things."

"Colonel." Tasso leaned into a small bow.

Gusov indicated the rigid chair in front of his desk, foregoing four overstuffed chairs and an engraved silver samovar in one corner. So, Tasso thought, this was to be purely business. He had not seen Gusov in six months, not since Putin's private dinner party at the Kremlin where Tasso had sat at the far end of the table among lesser party notables.

"Would you care for coffee?" Gusov asked, making no move toward to samovar.

The coffee's aroma tempted but Tasso thought it best to learn why he'd been summoned. "Thank you, no."

Gusov eased into his chair and picked a letter opener, a miniature replica of a bayonet. He swiveled the chair and scanned the desktop computer behind him, pointing the small knife at the screen. Tasso made out unreadable lines of text as Gusov worked the mouse, appearing older as he studied the monitor, the first silver streaks evident in his sleek black hair.

"So many weaklings have forgotten our goals," he muttered without turning.

The tantalizing fragrance of the coffee wafted around his chair and Tasso regretted not asking for a cup of his own; so much of his life had been spent waiting on orders from men like Gusov, listening to fools and the brilliant alike. The colonel swung back to face him and Tasso confirmed that the man had indeed aged.

"Vladimir… President Putin… is concerned we have become lax since Gorbachev's failures." Gusov suppressed a grin like a hockey player who sees an opponent in pain. "Our president subscribes to Stalin's maxim: No man, no problem. And so, dangerous enemies in London like Glushkov and Litvinenko have been removed without incident. Others unknown to you also met the fate they deserved. The Western press gnashed its teeth for several months but soon found other dogs to chase." Gusov tossed the letter opener on the table and frowned.

"Regrettably, the president now finds himself treading unknown waters.
 he said. "As ex-KGB, he is careful to assess his enemies before acting. This new American president is thus far unreadable, an unknown quantity. Vladimir's own father, you remember, was NKVD, a strong man who understood what was required. I tell you this so you understand that until he has this president's measure, there can be no disruption, no untoward incident, especially on American soil. Do you understand?"

Tasso duly nodded and knuckled his beard with his forefinger, his foreboding excavating a raw pit in his stomach. Gusov's warning hung in the room and Tasso imagined the words settling like ravens on the desk.

Gusov picked up a light brown file folder with a blood red tab. He ran a finger down one edge, measuring the finely-honed instrument who sat across from him.

"How old are you, Anatoli Gregoryevich?"

"Fifty-one." Tasso wondered if the file contained his dismissal papers and Gulag destination. A tap on the button beside Gusov's hand and soldiers would instantly appear to take away a servant no longer useful to his masters.

"You've kept yourself trim," Gusov said. "A good example for those of us engaged in shuffling paper and committee meetings."

"I try, sir." A compliment before the axe fell?

Gusov opened the folder and handed him a typed sheet. A black and white bureau photo of an attractive young woman was paperclipped in the upper right corner. "Do you know her?"

Tasso studied the photograph a full ten seconds. He'd honed a memory for faces, a skill that saved his life more than once. He handed back the sheet.

"No."

"Not surprising. She's much younger than you. The president himself hand-picked her when he sought recruits from the International Affairs section at Leningrad State University. She was a special project, an orphan, not a university student, but rather someone who fit the mold he was seeking. Unusually good material that could be shaped into an effective operative."

"She's very pretty," Tasso ventured. "A Red Sparrow?"

Gusov laughed. "Much too young and succulent for you, Anatoli." He looked almost wistfully at the photo. "Svetlana Kosdrenkov. Quite a little songbird but not one you'd want for a pet. What the Americans label a Honey Pot, but efficient when elimination was required. Three successful assignments involved very high-profile individuals." Gusov laid the photo aside. "She was traveling in Holland earlier this week with a male companion. Why, we don't know but our man there lost her."

"Then she's definitely alive."

Gusov frowned. "Oh, yes. Very much alive. She defected four years ago with a petty criminal named Krushenko. Slipped into the United States with him and disappeared. We traced her to Chicago a week ago. Living under another name, we assume."

Two ravens flapped onto Tasso's shoulders, carrion breaths warm on his cheeks.

"Your English is excellent and you've been in America a dozen times," Gusov said. "You are highly convincing as an exchange expert in economic matters, and if I recall correctly, an excellent recruiter of several Americans who share our dreams. We've never asked you to risk yourself there in more dangerous matters. As a result, you've stayed beneath American radar, which makes you the best choice now."

Tasso inclined his head at the folder. "So, I am to rectify this problem."

Gusov nodded. "From all we can ascertain, the woman has thus far kept quiet, but if she's discovered to be in the country illegally, there is old history Vladimir wishes to avoid." He gave a dismissive laugh. "The Americans are currently twisted in knots over illegal aliens, and she could be used as an example. In such an event, she might decide to trade her knowledge for immunity. We cannot afford that." He stared at Tasso who waited, broad hands folded in his lap. Gusov picked up the small bayonet and ran a finger down one edge. "Fifty-one," he mused. "You are certain you can still perform what's required?"

"Yes."

"Many grandfathers are younger but your age provides good cover. A seemingly harmless addition to our embassy staff in Washington. The Americans will see only another pencil wielder nearing the end of his career." He smiled benignly at Tasso who shrugged off the implication and maintained his composure.

Another assignment, Tasso thought. Was he surprised or disappointed? Better than a minor desk job in the building's bowels. Or worse. If the years of names, dates, and disappearances cataloged in his memory banks were seen as a liability, he might never leave the building alive.

Gusov looked down at the folder before raising his chin at Tasso, pushing the folder across the table with a bony index finger. "Quietly, Anatoli," he warned. "Nothing to lift even a single eyebrow. Not in Washington or the Kremlin."

Gusov remained seated as his visitor picked up the folder and left. He stared at the door and resisted rethinking his decision. He'd seen something behind Tasso's eyes. The light dimming, perhaps, the old war horse growing old. Still, the current matter required the master's touch, even though Tasso would soon have to be put down.

Chapter Fifteen

I awoke next morning with bright ribbons of sunlight painted across my bed. The connecting door was open and I heard the shower's hiss from Kat's room. I padded to the window, pushed open the casement, and peered down at the canal bank where patches of snow clung to the stone embankment. February was the coldest month in Amsterdam, but the morning sun promised a reprieve from Chicago's glacial disdain for humans. Wind stung my bare skin and I pulled the window closed, looking around. Sometime during the night, Kat had slipped into my room and jammed a chair under the doorknob that led into the hotel hall.

Dressing, I recalled the previous night and her confession. She might keep me alive, but why had she worked for something as loathsome as the KGB? I knew it was an age-old human weakness, equating appearance with what lay in someone's heart. Whatever the reason, there was little doubt she'd lived in the heart of darkness.

The Rijksmuseum was a short taxi ride from the hotel. I'd read that Amsterdam retained Old World charm, a contradiction of old and new where shops sold weed-laced chocolate confections, and prostitutes openly displayed their wares in shop windows. Van Gogh's difficulties in finding female models would be non-existent today.

I'd been granted a brief appointment with the Rijksmuseum director. The vast repository of Dutch art was not known for its Van Gogh collection, but the dowager queen of Holland's museums housed 800 years of Dutch paintings and knowledge. The archives might contain a rumor about a lost Van Gogh.

In the taxi, the prior night widened the gap between Kat and me. I was the first to break the uneasy truce. "Okay, here's our story," I said. "You're my assistant and we're researching my new book on Van Gogh. I'm reaching for crumbs here, but maybe there's a link or information we overlooked. I didn't have any luck getting an appointment at the Van Gogh Museum, so if we find nothing here, we'll head to Eindhoven."

Kat took a map from her purse and located Eindhoven. "An hour's drive. I'll have a car pick us up at the hotel."

Ten minutes later, four imposing stone towers filled the taxi's windshield. The six-story museum fronted a vast reflecting pool sheltered by trees, the reflection serving to double the building's scale. Arches had dominated its architect's imagination and I was reminded more an English university than a museum, expecting any moment to encounter dons in black robes wandering the grounds. Inside, the grandiose space resembled a medieval church with soaring arches, vaulted ceilings, and stained-glass windows that inspired reverence among the small morning crowds wandering the display halls. Immediately struck by the scale of Rembrandt's paintings displayed on the first floor, I quietly perused the final resting place of the old boy's patrons and friends whom he'd painted centuries ago.

"Over 150 rooms and two hundred years of Dutch art," I told Kat as she gazed up at the vast skylight illuminating the gallery. It wasn't the vast warehouse of priceless art one saw in St. Petersburg but the masterpieces and magnificent gallery sufficed to overwhelm the senses.

The tap of her heels on marble floors magnified our sense of unbounded space as we approached the information desk, sufficiently awed as though penitents seeking absolution. A serious young woman directed us to the museum offices and picked up a phone to alert *Herr Directeur*.

Fabian Bakker was a public relations poster boy. Youthful and blond, he greeted us effusively and indicated a pair of chrome and leather chairs in front of an ostentatious desk, appraising Kat. Taking his seat behind the desk, he wasted a single perfunctory glance at me, his gaze fixed on Kat who smiled and crossed her legs, revealing an impressive expanse of thigh. A faceless instructor in the KGB had trained her well in using her attributes to full advantage.

"So, another book on Van Gogh?" he said.

I smiled. "Always room for one more."

"I'm happy to repay a debt to my counterpart in Chicago," he said with an unctuous smile. "He was kind enough to indulge one of our young researchers last year."

Kat returned his smile and I knew we wouldn't be given the bum's rush as long as her abbreviated skirt did its duty. I introduced her as my associate, giving him a few more moments to mentally undress her. A luscious bodyguard had its advantages.

I interrupted his fantasies. "We appreciate your time, *Herr* Bakker. We know you're very busy."

He steepled his fingers beneath his chin and upped his glossy smile a notch. "How can I assist you?"

I described an imaginary Van Gogh book outline and our plan to collect original source material. He listened with polite boredom. I tossed in a casual reference to a lost Van Gogh, indicating it might provide an interesting footnote in my work.

"The rumor indicates an extremely large picture depicted a young woman. Do you know any tales about a woman in Amsterdam or Eindhoven whom he might have painted?"

Bakker laughed. "As I'm sure you're aware, most women in his life were prostitutes. Why do you ask?"

I shrugged with all the innocence I could muster and decided to cut closer to the truth, adding, "If such an outsized Van Gogh exists, you must admit it would be the find of the century."

"You are welcome to search our archives although I doubt you'll uncover anything useful. We deal in reality."

"You never heard any tales about a painting that might have gone missing? A painting unaccounted for or lost? A rumor that hung around the edges?"

Bakker had perfected the tolerant smile he turned on me. "Mr. Barrow, this is the Rijksmuseum, the space informed us. We don't deal in… rumors. If there is a missing Van Gogh out there, we would surely be aware of it. After all, you *are* in the Netherlands."

He tolerated my fantasy about a book a few minutes longer, an excuse, I thought, to indulge his erotic fantasies about Kat. I found myself oddly jealous and fed him my tale about needing to meet with his research department.

"Of course," he said smoothly. "But I do hope you're not squandering your research time pursuing this wild story. If you'd care to discuss your proposed work in more detail, I suggest dinner at one of Amsterdam's restaurants." He smiled at Kat. "A private dining room," he said. "For one or both of you."

Kat manufactured a blush and returned his smile. "Possibly on my next visit."

Judging the time ripe, I asked, "Would it be possible, *Herr* Bakker, to arrange an appointment for us at the Van Gogh Museum? It might save time if we had your recommendation."

Bakker ran his hand down his Ferragamo tie, anxious to impress Kat. "Of course." He buzzed his secretary and asked her to alert his counterpart at the Van Gogh.

I thanked him and we stood. He came around the desk, buttoning his suit jacket. He handed Kat an embossed card and kissed her hand. "Until your next trip."

We exited through the museum's massive arched doors and strolled past the reflecting pool, the placid surface unruffled. I regretted not having time to explore the museum's magnificent collection, but Viktor hadn't included tourism as part of our expense account. Kat dropped Bakker's business card in a trash receptacle and we headed to our appointment, winding our way through Amsterdam's Museum Quarter as morning sunlight cut the edge off the cold.

***

Located among the lush acres of Willempark, the Van Gogh Museum boasted a modern building that reminded me of a coffee can chopped in two: one half pale stone, the other half encased in wraparound glass. Several other buildings exhibited efficient use of industrial concrete that contrasted sharply with the Rijksmuseum's splendor. A small park of sunflowers assured us we'd found the master's palace that housed more than 500 examples of the Dutchman's work,

Immediately struck by the interior's contrast to the Rijksmuseum, the design informed us we'd left the outdated world of dark varnished canvases and entered the age of Impressionism. I couldn't resist a quick stroll through the galleries, overwhelmed by the sheer volume of Van Gogh's work. Self-portraits. Flowers and forest scenes. Peasants. Nighttime skies. But not one single painting approached the scale of the work described in my father's letter.

Kat and I were directed to the second floor where a neatly-dressed woman informed us the Director was unavailable, but that the Deputy Director was expecting us. Would we be kind enough to wait while she fetched him? She led us through a warren of functional cubicles and ushered us into a meeting room dominated by an immense clear glass table resting on four granite plinths. She indicated a tray of coffee and left. Two minutes later a slender man in his sixties entered and shook hands with us.

"Jorn Van Beek," he said, his English perfect. "Bakker said to expect you."

Short and dressed in nondescript brown suit and blue wool tie, he was the mirror opposite of Bakker. Older and feminine prim, he paused and peered curiously at me through horn-rimmed glasses. I felt my shields clank into place.

"*Herr* Bakker indicated we might be of assistance to you." He scanned my face more intently.

"I'm Adam Barrow and this is my associate, Miss Veranova.".

Van Beek continued to scrutinize me as if my face occupied a wanted poster in the post office. He offered coffee and we declined. He poured a cup for himself and settled in a chair across the table, his eyes on me I tried to maintain my composure. The tall window backlit the unsmiling austere figure as he interlaced his fingers over his vest in a professorial manner and gestured at his cup.

"My major weakness," he said without picking up the cup. Then, "May I inquire why you're here?"

I repeated my tale about researching a book. He sipped his coffee and I slipped in several vague details about a lost Van Gogh. His eyes assumed new life, but unlike Bakker, Kat had ceased to exist as Van Beek peered at me over the cup's rim, his tone wary.

"A lost Van Gogh," he said, settling cup in its saucer. "I take it you wish to establish this picture is factual."

"Not at all," I quickly added. "We simply want to include references to all his work, real and rumored, cover all possibilities, if you will."

"Where did you get your information about such a picture?"

"An obscure reference," I said.

"Do you have a description?"

"Like I said, it's an unsubstantiated rumor."

Van Beek pulled off his glasses and tossed them on the glass tabletop with a sharp click. "But you must know its subject," he persisted.

"It depicts a young girl."

"You've seen it then?"

I hesitated, "Not actually."

Van Beek picked up the glasses and squared them on his face. Pushing away the cup and saucer with a curt gesture, he looked at Kat, then back to me. "I don't believe you," he said. "I think you are frauds."

He overrode my protest, a tremor in his voice. "I remembered the name and saw the resemblance immediately," he said bitterly. "Even after all these years, I recognized you, *Herr* Barrow." His hands trembling, he pulled the rimless spectacles closer. "My father was an art dealer. I was only a boy doing odd jobs in his gallery, but I remember his excitement when Robert Barrow sold him what he purported to be a Whistler. My father used most of his capital to purchase it, and never recovered from the ridicule when the painting proved to be a fake. His gallery failed and he never recovered a cent." His voice wrapped in disgust, he said, "You *are* Robert Barrow's son, are you not?"

I felt Kat's eyes on me as I held his glare.

"Yes."

"Are you attempting to establish provenance for another forgery, *Herr* Barrow? Follow in your father's footsteps to cheat others of their life savings?"

"I am not my father," I said, humiliated my father's legacy extended fifty years and 3,000 miles.

Van Beek stood, his face flushed. "I must ask you to leave."

Kat was on her feet before I could reply. "Thank you for your time, Herr Van Beek," she said. "We won't intrude on your memories any longer."

Van Beek did not move as we walked from the room. My face burning, I hurried down the broad steps, Kat trailing behind me. Wes would have taken pleasure in my panicked retreat from the truth. Kat said nothing as we escaped the sterile building. I hailed a taxi, resisting the impulse to tell the driver to drive faster.

Back in the hotel room I threw off my coat and dropped into a chair by the window. Kat took the window seat and lighted a cigarette. She'd been honest with me and deserved the same.

"Van Beek told the truth," I said. "My father was a liar and con man. He was also an alcoholic who sold fakes of the art he loved."

Kat lit a cigarette. "Your father was a criminal?"

"He was never caught."

"A professional."

That hurt but I didn't correct her. If such a career existed, my father worked his way up to a professional level. The past was dead but I'd been sentenced to relive it, given Wes's discovery

"Wes and I didn't grow up like other kids," I said. "My mother died the year I was born and our father drank away his life. He drank and schemed how to cheat people like Van Beek's father. There must be a million other stories like the one you just heard. Nothing very complicated. My father was a thief who happened to love art."

Kat turned her head and blew a stream of smoke. "And you believe you are damaged because your mother died and your father was a thief."

"You don't think those are good reasons?"

"You know nothing about damage."

Subdued and aware how pathetic I sounded, a door opened cracked open inside me, but I slammed it shut. You don't toss away a lifetime of feeling sorry for yourself because someone had it worse. Feeling sorry for yourself was the world's second-best sport.

"I've never seen your version," I said.

"Pray to God you never do."

"So, the KGB didn't allow sorrow?"

"The KGB allowed anything so long as it benefited the state."

We'd landed only twenty-four hours earlier but I was ready to head home. An encounter with one of my father's victims will do that to you. There was also the small matter of my companion casually destroying the mugger and the memory of Vasily lying in a pool of his blood. I hadn't wanted a crusade to prove my father's tale and, attractive as Kat was, I wanted nothing to do with the KGB or Russian mafia. My brother climbed to a new pinnacle of folly, only this time he dragged me along. Not for the first time, I imagined what an animal experienced with its leg caught in a steel trap, the only choices being to chew off the limb or wait to die.

"Look, I'm not making comparisons. I'm only was trying to explain what my father was."

Kat crushed out her cigarette. "People do what they must do."

Chapter Sixteen

Amsterdam succeeded admirably in reviving the Barrow family's sordid past. Alive or dead, my father was an unforgotten millstone. One museum bigwig had restrained from laughing us off the premises because our host wanted a shot at Kat, while the other dismissed us as criminals. The only positive thus far was spending Viktor's money rather than my own.

Kat made two phone calls and we checked out. The hotel restaurant offered a simple menu but my appetite died in the two museums.

"I arranged for a car," she said as our food arrived, her eyes fixed on the door. "It will be here in thirty minutes."

Ignoring the food, I rubbed my face with both hands. "Amsterdam was a waste."

"Not a waste," she said, nibbling at her salad. "No one disproved the painting's existence."

"No one believes it exists either."

I ate without tasting my sandwich, while she watched the entrance and kitchen doors. I couldn't keep my eyes off her. No matter her past, she was an intriguing woman who unexpectedly appeared outside the realm of my pathetic love life. Catching myself in a daydream, I remembered I was her responsibility, nothing more.

An unshaven man in workman's clothes appeared in the restaurant doorway, his rough dress more suitable for the delivery entrance. He waved away the hostess who approached him and scanned the restaurant. Kat raised her chin almost imperceptibly and he walked to our table.

"Miss Englestot?" he asked, his Dutch accent strained.

"*Ja?*"

He handed her a brown paper sack and bowed. "*Uw cadeau Van de tante.*" Without acknowledging me, he walked past the hostess before she remembered to admonish him.

Kat dropped the sack into her carry bag without looking inside and returned to her salad. "A birthday gift from my aunt," she said.

A birthday gift delivered by a stranger in Holland during lunch in a restaurant we'd never seen. It seemed Viktor's network extended further than I imagined. Either that, or Kat knew more than she was telling me.

"You want to tell me what just happened, *Miss Englestot?*"

She wiped her lips. "My aunt always remembers me on my birthday." She raised her hand for the check. "The man delivered something from her, that's all."

"Nice to have Russian relatives in Holland who remember your birthday."

I paid the bill and we left. A 4-door silver Mercedes sedan pulled to the curb and a young man in a Beatles t-shirt and jeans jumped from the car almost before it stopped. He scanned the street before coming around the automobile to open the back door for Kat. I walked to the other side and got in.

"This is Yuri," Kat said as we settled into deep leather seats. "We were associates in Moscow."

Associate. The label Viktor attached to her in Chicago. I tried not to imagine what the appelation might include.

Fifteen minutes later the rearview mirror reflected Amsterdam's disappearing outskirts. Yuri set the cruise control at a staid 100kph and raised a smoked glass partition between the front and rear seats as we headed south onto the A2 Expressway. The powerful engine settled into a quiet hum, an engineering waste in Holland where they enforced speed limits, unlike the insane German autobahns. It started to drizzle and escalated into a downpour, creating an intimate setting in the rear seat. Fat rain drops thumped the rooftop and the car's smoked windows. Kat settled in her corner, her large carry bag at her feet as she stared at the blurred landscape. Despite her confession, I couldn't take my eyes from her.

Dressed in cream tapered slacks and a ribbed green sweater, she picked up the carry bag and placed it on the seat between us, withdrawing the sack that contained a cloth bundle. Inside was a blue steel automatic pistol. She racked back the slide and dropped the empty magazine into her palm before shoving it back into the pistol grip with a satisfying click. Why was I not surprised this was her 'birthday present'?

"Walther PPK," she said, "the .32 caliber model with an eight-round magazine." She dumped a handful of shells from the sack onto the cloth and inspected each brass-jacketed bullet. Popping out the magazine again, she thumbed eight shells into it, cocked the pistol, engaged the safety. She transferred the Walther to her leather purse and dropped the spare shells into the sack. Her past life and familiarity with firearms served to dampen any lascivious dreams.

"James Bond's favorite weapon," I said with a feeble smile.

"It's small, easy to conceal."

"Quite a thoughtful gift from your old aunt."

She smiled at me, enjoying my discomfort. "She's concerned about my safety."

"Mine too, I hope."

She started to reply but turned away to gaze out the car window, the mask in place again. I watched the rain-hazed Dutch landscape stream past, clearly out of my depth. Handling the pistol had returned her to another world, and I had no problem with that so long as she knew what she was doing. The entire trip was a colossal blunder, not to mention a waste of Viktor's money that I was spending like a Silicon Valley tycoon. My best strategy would be to convince him I'd made a valiant effort to locate the painting, hoping Kat substantiated my diligence.

It was still raining as we reached Eindhoven's residential outskirts. A thriving town in Van Gogh's day, the city mingled antique and modern, stone windmills reflected in shop windows. I tried to imagine cobbled streets where Van Gogh had walked, buying his paints and engaging prostitutes.

Kat checked us into a gabled hotel in the center of town. I examined a tourist brochure in the lobby and confirmed the hotel was surrounded by a cluster of art galleries. Judging by one glossy ad, Gallery Gölitz appeared the most prestigious, specializing in works by 17th and 18th century Dutch artists. The understated color advertisement screamed exclusive and expensive, listing Piet Vinck as the owner.

Leaving our luggage with a bellman, Kat motioned for me to wait beside the hotel door as she stepped onto the rainy sidewalk. She pretended to search her purse, examining the area as she transferred the PPK to her raincoat pocket, a precaution I found reassuring when I recalled Vasily's lifeless body sprawled on another rain-slicked sidewalk. Clouds hovered over the rooftops, the air crisp with winter. I flipped up my coat collar and we traipsed to yet another unlikely destination where I anticipated one more chilly reception.

Gallery Gölitz was located in a fashionable district, small streets marked by galleries and expensive boutiques. We mounted six steps and a bell jangled as we stepped into a heated interior that smelled of money and black credit cards. An elderly man in a three-piece suit emerged from the rear, a younger man at a Queen Anne desk half-hidden behind a computer monitor.

The old gentleman briskly marched to us with a warm smile. "*Welkom. Ik ben Piet Vinck.*" He bowed and flourished an arm at the selection of richly-framed paintings as if introducing his family. His good-humored greeting was a respite from the condescension and suspicion we'd encountered in Amsterdam.

"We're Americans," I said. "We hoped you might spare us a few minutes."

The smile broadened, his English very good. "I am the owner, Piet Vinck. It would be my pleasure to assist you." Real or feigned, I commiserated with the owner's enthusiasm, understanding every walk-in represented a potential sale if something irresistible was discovered on the walls.

I introduced myself and Kat and wondered where to begin. Notwithstanding the man's cheerful manner, walking into an up-scale gallery and expecting the owner to waste time listening to a tale about a missing Van Gogh story was asking a lot, particularly since I didn't believe it myself. Why should Vinck believe a wild rumor about one of his country's most revered artists? He'd no doubt endured endless stories about alleged masterpieces discovered in grandma's dusty trunk, or magically appearing in a country cottage. I decided to be straightforward, hopeful we'd at least get a sympathetic hearing before we slinked away.

"We're seeking information about a lost Van Gogh," I said. His open expression did not change and I plunged ahead.

"My brother and I uncovered evidence that an immense Van Gogh was smuggled out of France at the beginning of World War II." Embarrassed, I glanced at the employee who ignored us, hunched over his keyboard. "According to two old letters, the painting was never seen again. I believe it may have been painted in or around Eindhoven. One letter mentioned an old house that may have existed in the last century. I know it sounds crazy, but we're trying to verify the painting's existence."

Vinck pursed his lips, and I couldn't tell if his eyes reflected pity or amusement. "You talked with museums in Amsterdam?" he asked.

"Yesterday. The Rijksmuseum and Van Gogh Museum."

"And what did they tell you?"

Hell, I thought, why not tell him the truth. "They said we're chasing a phantom. That we're fools or thieves or imposters, or all three."

To my surprise Vinck tossed back his head and laughed. "Yes," he said, "they would say exactly that. Their educations bled all curiosity out of them. They believe only what they tell one another at their conferences." He chuckled. "Hopelessly stale gatherings where they present impossibly dry papers. They are already fossilized, no matter their ages." Mary Barnum-Gordon's face floated to mind.

Kat laughed and Vinck shot her an appreciative grin, unaware he'd witnessed a rare phenomenon. So far, there wasn't much to dislike about him.

He crooked a finger at us and we followed him to a spacious office in the rear, walking past oils painted by celebrated Dutch artists in the 17th and 18th centuries. He closed the office door and indicated two comfortable armchairs, removing his coat. An exquisite Van Ruisdael landscape occupied the wall behind his desk, the only painting in the room. Sporting a snug vest and bright red tie, Vinck pulled open a desk drawer and propped his shoe on the edge, observing Kat and me.

"I'll be honest," I began, "Eindhoven's our last hope. We're stumbling around your country with only two letters to guide us."

Vinck's grin returned. "You are explorers then, you and the lady."

Taken aback, I feared I'd played the fool again. Vinck patiently folded his hands on the cluttered desk, his smile still in place. "No, really. Without people like you, the world is boring. We become stagnant and self-satisfied. Nothing new or exciting is discovered. Worse, we stop searching for what is hidden or concealed from us." Vinck took a pipe from a desk drawer, filled it, and thumbed a butane lighter. Pausing in mid-light he raised his considerable snowy eyebrows at Kat. "Do you object?"

"I love the smell," she said.

Vinck got the briar going, filling the office with sweet tobacco smoke that reminded me of scorched cherries. "My grandfather possessed very little of value as a young man," he began, examining the glowing pipe bowl, "but like you, he was a searcher, a dreamer. He went house to house, inquiring about old paintings no one wanted." He turned and gestured at the Van Ruisdael behind him. "This was one of his discoveries, one I'd never sell." He paused, enjoying the tobacco and memory. "Gölitz Gallery has existed for almost ninety years because he too was an explorer."

"Can you help us?" I asked.

He chewed the pipe stem and hummed as though coming to a decision. Despite his friendliness, I sat without moving, waiting for the polite refusal and explanation that he had better things to do than listen to two foolish strangers.

"You mentioned a house," he said. "Do you know where it was located?"

I shook my head. "I realize the last war destroyed much of the area around Eindhoven. The house may be gone."

Vinck drew on the old pipe. "You set your sights very high, *Herr* Barrow. It might even be said you are seeking a ghost. The odds against you and the young lady finding a Van Gogh are outrageous. I'm not a naive man but I too am a dreamer at times, so I see no harm in your search. If you discover nothing, nothing is lost."

He thumbed an old-fashioned Rolodex. "There is someone who roams our countryside. A painter, a good one in my estimation. She knows which houses survived the war." He lifted the phone and dialed. "It would provide a great deal of pleasure if I had a small part in proving you right."

Vinck smiled as a voice answered. "Ah, good morning, Juliette. Piet here." He winked at us. "I have two people in my office whom you might help. They're Americans looking for old houses near the city, those more than a hundred years old." He nodded at us. "Good, good, I knew you'd be your usual helpful self. If today's convenient for you, I'll have them meet you at the Kastel Inn. In about an hour?" He raised his eyebrows at us and we nodded. "Good. Thank you, dear Juliette. See you soon, I hope."

He hung up and wrote down her full name and the inn's address in Bremfeldt. The bell jangled over the front door and he rose, shaking our hands. "Now I must try to make money from the living," he said. "I wish you luck in recovering the past."

I thanked him, grateful people like Piet Vinck existed in a world where a lost Van Gogh was nothing more than a fantasy. Vinck offered the first ray of hope. The timid sun dodged behind an approaching storm and I smelled rain. Kat signaled our driver and five minutes later we headed for the Kastel Inn as the skies threatened to burst open.

Chapter Seventeen

The Mercedes slowed, dodging bicycle riders as we eased into the picture book village of Bremfeldt. The Kastel Inn was a half-timbered public house wedged between two 19th century shops. A survivor from the late 1800's, the brick-red tiled roof sloped steeply toward the street. Yuri parked several doors from the entrance and leaned against the front fender as Kat and I walked back and entered the tavern.

A stout middle-aged woman rose from a table and approached us without hesitation. Raw-boned and square-set, she wore a woolen cap and sturdy farmer's boots, dressed for the field in a khaki hunting jacket and a man's baggy trousers. Her stubby nails were crusty rainbows of dried oil paint, her bulky jacket smelling of turpentine. She wouldn't have shocked me had she lit a cigar.

"I'm Juliette," she said in passable English, shaking our hands with a firm grip. Her eyes, blue and inquisitive, were set deep in a wind-chapped face. "You are the Americans Piet called about?"

I nodded. "We're looking for old houses built before 1900. Whoever once lived there may have a connection to Van Gogh. I wish I could be more specific, but that's all the information we have."

Juliette's expression didn't change as though accustomed to hundred-year old house searches. She removed the red watch cap to reveal short-cropped gray hair. "Come have a beer with me."

She led us to a planked table and held up three fingers at the barkeep, marking her as a regular. We were the sole patrons in the tiny *hoffbrau* that smelled of fermented hops and cigarettes. Kat declined the beer and Juliette smiled at her. "You'll miss something special. De Molen's our best beer." She turned back to me. "Tell me what you know about this house."

I explained that an old letter placed the house south of Eindhoven. She rubbed her calloused palms together, most likely anticipating the beer's arrival.

The mugs arrived and I raised mine. "Cheers."

"*Proost*!" Juliette took a satisfied swallow and wiped her mouth with her hand, closely observing us. I was glad we had come with Piet Vinck's recommendation.

"I know this town, the whole area," she said. "My family has lived here since the first idiot built a dike to keep the ocean away." She took another swallow. "It would have been better if the fool had traveled east until his feet found dry land."

I smiled. "But then we might have missed Rembrandt and your windmills and tulips."

Juliette returned my grin. "We Dutch are very obliging despite being poor judges of land." She wrapped her hands around her mug and made a face. "Only a few old houses in this area survived the war. The Germans used many as strong points. After the war, developers demolished others." She drained her beer and gave off a healthy belch behind her chapped hand. "A few of the older ones were spared. Maybe half a dozen houses remain today. I can show you those that escaped the Germans and bulldozers."

"Are they occupied?" Kat asked.

"Some. Most are empty. I like to paint the abandoned ones."

"If you'll show us, we have a car," I said.

"I have a truck," Juliette countered. "You can follow me."

Gloomy skies leached color from Bremfeldt's streets. Kat waved the Mercedes forward and we got in. A mud-spattered old Ford F-150 came around the corner and Juliette waved. We followed the American relic from the village, turning off the highway onto a narrow dirt track.

The first house was a burnt-out shell, half a charred chimney its tombstone. If this was our house, it was long past leaving any clues. The second dwelling was little more than a tenant cottage where collapsed pig sties littered the overgrown yard.

Undeterred, Juliette climbed back in her truck and we followed her back to the highway. Up and over a slight rise, she turned off onto another dirt road. Seagulls rode currents, fleeing the approaching storm, protesting our intrusion as we halted near a deserted structure that had once been an imposing house.

The exterior sagged, grey and brown boards molting faded scraps of paint as though the house was a corpse in the final stages of decay. Juliette tromped toward the dilapidated hulk that ruled the barren countryside; a slab-sided barn huddled behind the sprawling ruin. Nearby, an ancient windmill stood guard over the bleak countryside, ragged sails frozen in time. Kat instructed Yuri to wait, her words lifted away by the wind as the squall rolled closer.

"I've painted this one several times," Juliette said softly as though the house demanded respect. "It's the largest, deserted years before I was born. I tried to get the owner's permission to come onto their land, but there's no record who owns it today. The war destroyed all such records. Not even a name survived."

The pile of boards listed to the left as though the years had leaned on it. I stepped through knee-high grass, feeling I was treading on a grave. The elements had wreaked revenge on the house, gap-toothed holes in its walls where windows had been smashed by storms or man, the empty spaces condemning our trespass with hollow eyes. Only a set of rusting hinges remained where the front door once existed.

"My grandmother told me stories about this place," Juliette said as we stepped through the door. "Claimed it was haunted by an old Frenchman who lived here alone, never marrying or venturing into town. She said he stayed on the property as though there was an invisible fence he could never climb."

Overcome with rot and mildew, the interior had been stripped bare. No furniture or fixtures. Areas of the floor had disintegrated, leaving black pits in what had once been the main living area. A large fireplace was partially collapsed into rubble of blackened stones, and a charred corner marked where an intruder chose to build a small fire. Gusts of wind swirled through the open windows as we followed Juliette. I eventually stopped counting the rooms, stepping over empty liquor bottles and soiled rags. Nothing indicated a painting had ever graced the ruins, much less a red-bearded ghost. Only a suffering house waiting to be put out of its misery.

I went back outside and circled the house. Except for the barn and distant windmill, no landmarks disturbed the featureless landscape that stretched to the horizon. Nothing in the brown and gray earth tones hinted Van Gogh once found his gods of light and color where we stood. The rest of the afternoon promised more of the same as I watched the storm edge closer. I longed for the warmth of my gallery, cursing Wes again for stirring Viktor's greed, getting himself shot in the process. Any hope of identifying a fictional house in Holland appeared a humorless joke.

Hands in my pockets I contemplated the derelict barn. The decaying structure complemented the terminal house, dying brothers-in-arms. A splatter of raindrops found me as Kat and Juliette walked into the yard and we watched sheets of rain race past the windmill toward us. The barn was closer than the car so we made a dash for it. Kat lost her shoes, the deluge at our heels as we sprinted through the weeds. With Juliette's help, I shouldered open the warped barn doors and we ducked inside just as rain assaulted the roof.

Inside the gloom, deserted animal stalls sat along two walls. Water poured through a gaping hole in the roof, transforming the dirt floor into a circle of mud, rekindling the stench of dried manure and long-departed animals. A single door stood open at the far end. Edging around the morass, we found a cramped storage room, its single window miraculously intact.

The room held a menagerie of broken farm implements, old lumber stacked in one corner. Rain pounded the roof and my melancholy swelled as I surveyed still more decay. I started to walk out and stopped. Weak light from the rain-smudged window drew my eyes back to the boards. Leaning against them was a manmade rectangle festooned with a rainbow of yellows and blues, reds and greens. Three stout planks were hinged to the upper beam. Braces of some kind. Someone had constructed supports to keep the crude contrivance upright. Intrigued, I walked closer and with Kat's and Juliette's help, I dragged the contraption away from the wall onto the dirt floor and extended the hinged struts.

I stepped back, my heart hammering. The colors decorating its wooden edges were richer and brighter in the center of the tiny room. Measuring more than six feet by ten feet, the dimensions matched my father's description of the painting. The storm's roar faded as I realized what I was looking at.

"An easel," I murmured. "A damned easel."

Kat looked at the tottering contrivance. "You're seeing what you want to see. That's a pile of old boards nailed together."

I shook my head, exasperated she couldn't see what stood before us. Thunder shook the barn and the rotting frame trembled as though taking its first breath in more than a century.

Kat toed my discovery with her bare foot. "Whatever this is, it proves nothing. Viktor expects you to find his painting."

"My painting," I said, exasperated. "It belongs to Wes and me if it exists."

Juliette ran a hand down one edge and grinned at me. "A painting? It must have been some painting."

She dug her thumbnail into a calcified lump of yellow paint, then rolled the crumbling bits between her fingers and held them beneath her nose.

"Oil paint." She wiped her hands on her trousers and contemplated the huge easel. "I wonder what the artist painted."

I took a coin bearing the profile of Queen Beatrix from my pocket and turned to Kat. "Do you have an envelope?"

She opened her purse and removed our airline tickets. Juliette eyed the pistol but said nothing. I braced one edge of the frame and pried off half a dozen chips of desiccated paint, dropping them inside the envelope. Reluctant to remove my hand, I stared at the spattered wooden rectangle. Was it an easel Van Gogh constructed to support an enormous canvas? The supposition was a stretch, but what other purpose could the framework have served in this desolate setting? For all my father's lies and travails, I might be touching a relic that verified his outlandish claim. Not quite an epiphany, but a tentative step out of the purgatory where I'd lived most of my life. For my sake and Wes's, I needed the old easel to be genuine.

"What now?" Kat asked.

The rain beat harder. I ran my hand up and down the length of rotting lumber, reluctant to walk away. Had we found proof, or stumbled upon a chimera that would propel us deeper into a fool's quest? I slipped the envelope with the paint chips inside my jacket. Juliette said nothing, obviously trying to decipher what she heard and saw. I reverently collapsed the supports and returned the makeshift contraption to the wall, covering it with the remains of a moldy tarp.

"Where do we go now?" Kat asked.

"Paris," I said. "Louis Dejean is our only remaining link. If we can resurrect him, he'll tell us what to do next."

Chapter Eighteen

April 1888 Provence France

The night sky over Arles swam with an ocean of stars, their brightness untainted by the dim streetlights. He set up his easel next to the awning of a closed tavern, blocking the narrow sidewalk and causing a drunken night owl to detour into the street. Star-lit heavens were one of his few pleasant memories of Nuenen where he'd strolled as a child with his father and sister on starry nights. He clung to the memory, frantic to recreate the sky on canvas, a remedy for his embittered childhood.

He removed the paint-smeared brush from his mouth and spat in the gutter, squinting at the canvas. *No one attempts this*, he thought, straining to see in the darkness, *but what would life be if we had no courage to attempt anything?*

Two years in Paris had been a failure. Filled with loathing for those interested only in the slavish dictates of other painters, he had seen little hope of success if he stayed among such Philistines. Adding brighter hues and shades to his palette he moved toward a new realm of color. The stunted Toulouse-Lautrec dismissed his paint-heavy strokes and pressed him for more accurate anatomy, but he now saw what a few others like Seurat and Signac had discovered.

Disheartened by failures to sell his work, he tired of watching his brother hawk his paintings and drawings to disinterested dealers and magazines, eking out an existence in his brother's apartment. Even the few second-rate dealers who reluctantly accepted his work on commission showed the paintings only out of respect for his brother. Mocked by young artists in Cormon's atelier, he packed his meager belongings and fled to the country, glad to be free of half-wits and second-rate painters who saw him as unworthy to kiss their rings. Fed up with endless arguments about theory and 'artistic revolution,' he'd taken the train to Marseilles in February to be closer to Monticelli, the painter he most admired. Stepping from the unheated rail carriage during a stop at Arles, he ignored the bitter wind, entranced by the countryside, imagining the fields with the promise of spring only a few weeks away. Cashing in his remaining ticket, he trudged to the town's solitary hotel and found new life.

A drunk staggered against to the easel, almost tipping it over. The derelict yelled at him without looking back and weaved up the cobbled street. The painter detested the louts in Arles—but her fields and meadows! The land reduced all else to mere specks of dust. Casting out bitter memories of Paris, he wiped his oily lips on a smock sleeve and leaned back to study the canvas. He was so close but the canvas failed. Disgusted, he smeared the oils with a swipe of his hand and snatched the ruined attempt from the easel.

If the world is blind, he thought, I will learn to create light from darkness.

Chapter Nineteen

The weather cleared and Yuri made Paris in less than four hours. Early evening descended as we reached the suburbs, traffic in the world's most beautiful city, frenzied as ever. Kat tapped a cigarette from her pack and lit up, cracking the car window to admit a stream of cold air. An ex-smoker, I sucked in the second-hand smoke without a trace of guilt. To its credit, Europe remained unconvinced that tobacco was the devil's henchman.

Streetlamps came up in the city of lights and I recalled the old easel and chips of dried paint—if that's what we'd found in the barn. The more miles we placed between us and the paint-splattered boards, the less certain my discovery seemed. Viewed from a distance, logic insisted there was no legitimate connection between the easel and Vincent Van Gogh.

Kat had booked reservations and we checked into the Hôtel L'Enfant d'Or, an appropriate name for lost children like us. With shoes and cuffs still caked in Dutch mud, I looked like an unruly child admitted into the parlor, hotel guests lowering their newspapers to stare at me. As in Amsterdam, Kat circled the lobby, noting entrances and exits, while I signed the register. At her insistence, I chose adjoining oms on the second floor located away from the elevator and stairwells.

In my room, I called Sally's apartment to make certain the gallery was still standing. Envious I was calling from Paris, she said Wes was a charm, that he was still limping but that he'd sold three paintings—and would I let her tag along on my next trip to Europe?

"Your friend Arthur Jennings dropped by yesterday," she added.

"What did he want?"

"You," she said. "He's not a nice person."

"I knew I hired you for your powers of observation."

"He stayed all of two minutes and left when I told him I didn't know when you'd be back. He may be your friend, but I think he's a creep."

"Your radar's working," I said. "Avoid him if you can."

"I won't buzz him in next time."

"Good decision."

Hanging up, I spent the next fifteen minutes under a steaming shower leaning against the tiled wall, wondering what Jennings wanted. I guessed the adage was true about bad pennies showing up. With Vasily out of the picture, there was no reason for him to put in another appearance.

Wrapped in my robe, I knocked on Kat's door and suggested we dine early. I called the maître de who suggested a nearby spot for an early dinner. I'm sure he expected nothing less from Americans, but the early hour assured us a reservation in Paris.

We left the hotel and Kat shook her head at Yuri who waited behind the wheel of the Mercedes. We walked to the restaurant, the car slowly following us.

The wine and dinner were excellent. Kat had no qualms about spending Viktor's money, ordering a Domaine de la Romanée-Conti, red elegance in a bottle. Its cost would have covered our hotel rooms for a week. Most of the people around us were tourists. A camera flashed accompanied by light applause. A family's laughter overrode an operetta softly playing over the sound system. The excellent Burgundy eliminated my reluctance to pry further into Kat's world as I added wine to her glass.

"What about your life before the KGB, before Viktor?"

"I had no life as you call it," she said. "I was born in Minsk. I was two years old when a car hauled away my parents in the middle of the night. No one ever told me what they were charged with and I never found any record of what happened to them. My grandmother took me in. I remember nothing about my mother or father except a photograph my grandmother showed me." She took a sip of wine. "They may as well have been strangers on the street."

"And later?"

She tapped the rim of her glass with a fingernail. "My grandmother died when I was five and I was placed in a state orphanage." She drained the remainder of her wine and didn't protest when I replenished her glass. As if remembering her duty, she surveyed the restaurant and refocused on me. "It was a hellhole where you fought or you died. The strongest did anything to survive the staff and predators among the inmates. Do you wish to hear more?"

"Whatever you want to tell me."

"I did whatever was required to survive, Even the older children learned to avoid me. When I was eleven I killed a guard with a sharpened spike I made from a spoon. Those in charge couldn't prove I did it, but those around me knew and left me alone. Fear and reputation were weapons. I learned to use both."

I waited for the rest.

"One day, two men came to the orphanage. I remember looking out my window when a black GAZ braked at the entrance. We rarely had visitors in business suits who drove new cars." I added wine to her glass. She could have been drinking water for all the effect it had on her. "An hour later, a matron came to my room with a paper sack and told me to collect my belongings."

"How old were you?"

"Fourteen."

I shook my head, struggling to imagine an environment so far removed from my school days where I begged a dollar to go to the movies.

"Our visitors were KGB. Frightened my parents' sins caught up to me, I later learned the Bureau conscripted 'talent' from orphanages, selecting the smartest trouble makers." She shrugged. "The staff agreed I qualified."

"What happened?"

"They drove me to Leningrad without speaking a word. A plane took me to Moscow that night." She smiled at the memory. "I was scared out of my wits. Not of the two men, but the airplane. I rarely saw one except miles above the orphanage."

"Did anyone take advantage of you?" I asked, afraid of the answer.

"No, that came later. Training was more important. Sex with recruits was reserved for higher-ups in the Party after we were assigned to a Bureau section. The most appealing girls were taught how to dress, how to approach men, how to use their bodies. Better-looking boys underwent the same training. Your agencies call us 'sparrows' and 'honey traps.' We were directed to diplomats, scientists, military personnel vulnerable to blackmail."

"They selected you for this?"

"I thought so at first," she said, "but when I turned seventeen, I was one of two girls transferred to the Directorate of Special Tasks. We attended classes day and night on everything from languages to weapons. We received better food, a Moscow apartment, spending money, everything. We attained status above other recruits. Those of us in the 13th Department were trained for assassination, what the services call liquid affairs. Your CIA calls it wet work."

I swirled my wine, remembering her assignment to eliminate the young dissident. She'd given me everything but one essential element. "Why didn't you run away?"

Kat stared at me as though the burgundy had softened my brain. "You talk as though I was given a choice. There was nothing for me outside the KGB. I'd have been put on the street, a non-person. In my case, vodka and a life of prostitution. The authorities allowed me to re-create myself. But as with all good things, there was a price to pay. You're not the only one who's being hunted."

"You're free now. Viktor will protect you."

She emptied her glass. "You know nothing about such things."

Our food arrived and she kept her eyes on her plate. I couldn't decide if she was angry or embarrassed. Had my questions opened old wounds and pinned her to a board like a damaged butterfly? I ordered coffee and she cradled the cup when it arrived, peering at me over the rim with envy or longing. At least that's what I told myself. Lowering the cup, she ran her fingers through her long hair in a languid gesture that aroused my hunger for her until I recalled what she'd once been.

After coffee she lit a cigarette and said, "Are you shocked?"

"Not a nice story, but you're free now. Why work for Viktor? You can become anyone."

Kat tapped an ash in the ashtray. "Viktor is…" she paused. "Viktor is more complicated than you believe. He can be generous or unforgiving. He is not always the savage you see. When I first told him of my early life, he built a private orphanage outside Moscow without telling me, one unconnected to the state. There was no profit in it for him and it cost a great deal of money. I don't know if he did it to please me or get me into his bed. I can never fully explain many things he does."

"But you can start a new life, go anywhere you like. If he's as understanding as you claim, he'd let you go."

"I need Viktor," she said, "even in America. The KGB has a new name, but it never forgets or forgives. As you Americans are fond of saying, same old, same old. To them, I am a turncoat, a traitor. There is a price on my head, Adam."

She'd used my name for the first time. A hint of vulnerability, a frightened five-year old dumped in an orphanage?

"You are the first man other than Viktor to hear all this," she said. "I never wanted to tell another person." She reached across the table and took my hand. "Together, I think we will find this painting if it exists."

She paid the check without another word. Outside, Yuri pulled to the curb, but she waved him off and we walked back to the hotel, her body against mine. Her face hidden behind her raised coat collar, she took my hand.

***

Half asleep, I didn't hear her footsteps.

My blanket stirred and Kat slipped beneath the covers, her arm around my chest, her naked body against my back. I faced her but she pushed me onto my back and mounted me, covering my mouth with hers.

Our joining wasn't an act of love. She imprisoned my body beneath hers, any thought of foreplay forgotten. Her breath tasted faintly of wine and cigarettes, our mutual desire consummated in a single rush, her incantations vehement and unintelligible, her insistent pleas dissolving into muttered Russian. I could only utter her name, surrendering my body until we collapsed, her damp flesh enveloping me. A river of perfumed hair brushed my face as she rolled onto her back.

"You are my first in two years," she murmured.

Struggling to recover, I turned her face to me and smiled. "You're my first Russian."

I couldn't make out her features in the darkness but her voice was playful, more human since I'd seen her glowering at me in Tatiana.

"Who were the others?" she teased. "Whores in the Loop? Clean-cut American girls and hungry housewives? Does this make you an international man of the world?"

"A happy man."

She swung out of bed. Naked, she padded to her room and returned with an ashtray and pack of cigarettes. She leaned back against the headboard and I studied her profile in the dim light that edged past the closed drapes. A sheen of perspiration clung to her face as she stared across the room, drawing deeply at the cigarette, retreating into her armor.

"How could I be anything but happy?" I said.

She stubbed out the cigarette and glanced at the bedside clock, drawing the sheet over us. A siren wailed along the boulevard and she kissed me.

"It's midnight," she said. "If you are man enough, we have hours to increase your happiness. And mine."

Chapter Twenty

Three thousand miles from Paris, a phone rang in a mahogany paneled den illuminated by a Tiffany lamp. A man in a silk smoking jacket rose from a wingchair, cradling a brandy snifter in one hand. He walked to a burled walnut desk and picked up the black Lucite phone receiver, an antique from the 1950's.

"I followed them to Paris," the Contractor said.

The man sat behind the desk and scrutinized the gilded liquid in the bulbous crystal glass. "What are they doing in Paris?"

"My guess is they're looking for this Dejean mentioned in the letters."

"Where are you now?"

"Across the street from their hotel."

"Have they spotted you?"

A grunt. "Driving the ugliest rental car in Europe?"

"What happened in Holland?"

"They went to two Amsterdam museums and a gallery in Eindhoven. They met a Dutch woman in a hick town outside Eindhoven and drove to three old houses. They stayed about an hour at the last one. I checked the place when they left. A wreck. Nothing there."

The man sipped the cognac. He leaned back in the leather chair, rolling the snifter stem between his fingers. "Stay with them. Anything they uncover may save us a lot of trouble."

"Why not let me take the woman somewhere quiet? In an hour, she'll tell me everything."

The man started to slam the snifter down on the desk pad and caught himself. "Damn it, I told you. Nothing that attracts attention. Follow them and we'll find the painting. After that, you can do whatever you like."

Chapter Twenty-One

Next morning, the bed beside me was empty. Sheets and blankets were scattered on the floor and I heard movement in Kat's room.

I rolled over, shivering. Last night was not a dream. She'd given me her body, a desperate gift. An incontrollable desire or demand, I wondered? My ego preferred the former but I knew better. Before we left Chicago, I'd consulted a Russian-English dictionary and discovered Katia meant chaste or pure, her new name obviously a KGB attempt at humor.

After I showered and slipped into a hotel robe, she came to my room. She turned her cheek when I attempted to kiss her. If there was such a thing as a KGB face, Katia or Svetlana, or whoever she was, wore it in the light of day. I didn't push the issue.

Paris still believed in phonebooks and there was a slew of listings for Dejean, eighty-four of them. Kat spent the morning calling each one, using her excellent French to good effect. None sounded as if they were ninety or a hundred years old, and no one knew a relative who collected Impressionist Art before World War II. A check of her laptop revealed the same dead end.

We sat at the small table in my room and stared at the phone book, waiting for an epiphany. Any answers that Dejean's family might have provided would remain a mystery, since we couldn't call every listing in France. Kat smoked the day's first cigarette as I enjoyed my second cup of good French coffee, an idea surfacing.

"There's one more possibility," I said. "Dejean's letter mentioned his collection. If it included major artists, there's a chance a record exists."

"That's possible," she said, "but where would we look?"

"There were so many paintings and sculptures looted by the Nazis that a registry was established after the war to recover stolen art. If I remember my art history, their main office is in London. I can call them."

She yawned. "Later. Last night created an appetite."

At least she remembered. "You read my mind. Dejean can wait another hour."

Fifteen minutes later Yuri dropped us at Cafe Zola, the busy restaurant's name embossed in rustic gold lettering on huge glass windows. The interior was warm, butter and garlic promises escaping the kitchen. Filled with locals and a few tourists, the ambiance was uniquely French. Dark wood. Vineyard wall posters, Wooden floors scuffed by a century of shoes and boots. Had we overlooked Toulouse Lautrec sketching by the front door?

Kat pointed to a table and a waiter seated her facing the door. Two dogs crouched beneath a nearby table and five feet away, an ancient wooden cage contained a green and yellow parrot plucking furiously at its plumage. The bird sidled back and forth on its perch, screeching epithets in French, none of which I guessed were wholesome or complimentary.

The service excellent as hordes of waiters and busboys swerved between closely-packed tables. Our food arrived and I attacked my flank steak and *pomme frites*. Grinning at Kat between mouthfuls, I teased her to tempt the parrot with a few questions. When she stopped responding I looked up from my plate.

Halfway across the restaurant, a man quickly raised a newspaper in front of his face. When he lowered the pages, he and Kat linked eyes before he looked away and carefully folded the paper. In his mid-forties, he was nondescript, dressed in a loose-fitting business suit. He lifted his index finger at a passing waiter who leaned down and pointed. The man placed the newspaper on his chair and stood.

Her eyes downcast, Kat spoke in a whisper. "*Чept!* Damn!"

"What?" I asked.

Without another look in our direction the diner skirted the tables and headed toward the rear of the restaurant. Kat pretended to tease the parrot, keeping the man at the edge of her vision until he disappeared through swinging doors marked *Publique Téléphone*.

She placed her napkin beside her plate and slipped on her overcoat. Leaning down, she kissed me on the mouth, blocking the view of other diners. She lifted the steak knife from my fingers and slipped it up her coat sleeve, gripping my shoulder.

"Leave money and wait outside," she whispered.

"What are you..."

"Do it now."

The serrated blade concealed, she picked up her purse and followed the man through the doors.

I dropped a wad of euros on the table. Affecting nonchalance, I weaved past the tables until I found myself on the sidewalk, blanching as the cold found me. Walking past stacked chairs and patio tables, I halted at a bookshop window and waved to the Mercedes. At the same moment, Kat hurried from the restaurant, her face averted as Yuri pulled to the curb. Without a backward glance, I followed her into the car as she snapped instructions to Yuri before the door closed. A glistening red dot marred her white blouse, her right hand and coat sleeve soaked in blood. What in hell…?

"Are you alright"

She didn't answer and the powerful sedan sped away, weaving through side streets, tossing me from side to side before it merged back into traffic along a busy boulevard. Skirting a slow-moving bus filled with Japanese tourists we swung into another narrow street and began evasion tactics again. A mile later, Kat checked the rear window. She touched Yuri's shoulder and said something in Russian. The Mercedes slowed and cruised past the Sorbonne along the Seine. We parked alongside the Quai de la Tournelle where Notre Dame Cathedral dominated the skyline above the water.

Kat got out and motioned me to follow. Hunched against the cold we dodged tourists and locked arms, leaning on the railing like first-time sightseers. After a few moments, she looked both ways along the sidewalk. Leaning over the metal railing as if scrutinizing the river, she dangled one arm toward the muddy surface. The knife slid from her sleeve and I watched bubbles disappear. Back inside the car, Yuri handed her several handkerchiefs and a plastic water bottle. She'd not spoken to me since we entered the car.

"What happened?" I asked.

She poured water over a handkerchief and furiously wiped her hands, the cloth turning pink. "The man with the newspaper. He was KGB. I remembered him from a raid." She scrubbed harder. "I think he recognized me and was calling his superiors for instructions."

"You *think* he recognized you? You aren't sure?"

Kat concentrated on wiping each finger clean, digging at the edges of her long nails. She dropped the bloody handkerchief on the floorboards and wet a second one, swiping her shoe tops.

"I cannot take chances," she said, her voice tight.

"Is he dead?"

She looked up at me without emotion. "I hope so."

"And you're not hurt?"

"No."

She struggled out of the designer coat and saw the red spot on her blouse. "Be a gentleman and give me your coat."

We drove to the hotel, Yuri checking his rearview mirrors after he made every turn. I couldn't keep my eyes from the bloody bundle on the floor. Draped in my coat, Kat slipped lower in the seat. Flushed, her mouth slightly open, she scanned the sidewalks and cars on each side of us. The lovely woman I'd made love to the previous night had just killed a stranger in a crowded Parisian restaurant. With a steak knife.

At the hotel, we hurried through the lobby, my coat over her shoulders. We didn't speak in the elevator and I followed her into my room where she dropped my coat on a chair. Without looking at me, she walked into her suite and closed the door. I heard her shower and sat on the side of my bed, absorbing what had happened. On top of everything, I was now complicit in a murder.

***

The Contractor sat alone at a green metal table outside the patisserie, only a few passing cars intruding on his surveillance of the hotel entrance. Dressed in frayed workman's trousers and a heavy winter coat, he wore heavy-framed glasses and a black beret. The driver of the Mercedes looked him over and went back to surveying the sidewalks.

Ignoring the chill, the Contractor punched a number into his cell phone and pressed the cold plastic to one ear, keeping his eyes on the silver car. He heard a series of clicks and faint ringing, blowing on his latté's foam and inhaling the steam. The milky blend was a woman's drink, an indulgence he occasionally enjoyed. Savoring the steam until his employer answered or his quarry emerged from the hotel, he wrapped his free hand around the scalding cup until there was a click at the other end.

"They were in a restaurant earlier today," he said. "A man's throat was cut." He took a tentative sip, hoping he'd interrupted his employer's sleep.

"A coincidence?"

"Barrow and the woman came out in a hurry and jumped in a car before I could follow them. I talked to a man in the crowd before the police got there and he described the woman. It was her."

The man on the other end cupped his hand over his receiver and told the naked woman beside him go into the bathroom and close the door. He waited until she complied, then sat up on the side of the bed. "What does that have to do with us?"

"I thought you'd want to know."

"Your point being?"

"The description on TV matches the woman traveling with Barrow."

The man ran his hand over the warm sheets beside him and heard the toilet flush in the bathroom. "And?"

"Maybe the murdered guy was connected to the painting."

"Maybe's a useless word. Facts would be a highly refreshing change."

The Mercedes had not moved and the Contractor stretched his long legs onto the sidewalk, enjoying the latté and his employer's distress. "If they're here looking for the painting, there has to be a connection. Why else kill some man in broad daylight? What else can it be?"

"Find the goddamn painting. I told you that's all that matters."

The Contractor drained the cup. A puff of wind cut around the corner and fluttered his frayed trouser cuffs. Fed up with orders, he lowered his voice. "I've got a bank account full of your money. If I walk away, I can enjoy Paris for a few weeks and you can hire someone else. How would that be?" He pictured the man's face. "Watching you scramble for your fucking painting might be worth whatever I'd lose."

"No, you're wrong," the man said. "Breaking our agreement wouldn't be worth a few nights in Paris. Even if I never find the painting, I'll find you. Money buys others with your skills and you wouldn't like the outcome."

The phone went dead and the Contractor slipped it into his overcoat pocket. His employer enjoyed threats. No harm if they were only words. He rotated the empty cup on its saucer. Threats frightened most people but his employer knew nothing about him. He could easily disappear but he didn't want a contract on his head. If the Van Gogh existed, he was close and he'd find it if he stuck to Barrow. Get the damned thing and collect the rest of his money. Then a vacation.

He wiped his lips with a paper napkin and stood, the insults ringing in her ears. No one earned the right to criticize him, particularly a rich prick living a life that others rarely glimpsed. He started across the street when an outrageous thought struck him. He skirted the Mercedes and headed away from the hotel, affecting a limp for the driver's benefit, the idea maturing.

What, he mused, if he found the painting—and his employer never saw it? He never broke a contract or harmed an employer, but he'd never been close to the kind of money the painting would bring. An accident was easy to arrange and getting rid of Barrow and his brother was a simple matter despite the botched attempt outside the Chicago gallery. The Van Gogh had to be worth several fortunes, enough to allow him to live among the beautiful people wherever he chose. He didn't know shit about art, but he could arrange a quiet sale if he got his hands on the painting. And wouldn't it be delicious to attend a highbrow soiree and have someone mention his employer and how terrible it was the poor dear died so tragically. The Contractor smiled and quickened his pace, imagining himself owner of the world's most valuable painting.

Chapter Twenty-Two

Kat didn't come to my bed that night. Her room was silent, her door was closed when I awoke. I'd slept only a few hours before the dawn's frail light inched into the room, failing to erase the memory of her blood-stained clothes. It had been so simple for her to approach the man's back and draw a knife across his exposed throat. I stood at the window and stared into the deserted street, recalling how deftly she'd concealed the knife beneath her sleeve. The KGB trained them well but no painting was worth the violent universe I'd stumbled into.

Slipping on my robe I sat on the bed, my hand on the phone to check return flights to Chicago. I picked up the receiver, stared at it, and dropped it back in its cradle. Wes had set the madness in motion, his decision fueled by Irish whiskey, spurred on like a jockey seeing the finish line. But there was no way I could leave him at Viktor's mercy. My brother saw the Van Gogh as an opportunity to impress Barbara and save his marriage, getting rich in the process. His impulse left me little choice but to find the painting or prove it existed only in our father's fermented brain.

A knock on the hall door. I peeked through the door's security hole. A bellman balanced a tray of pastries and silver carafe. I let him in and he placed the food on the table in the center of the room. He left and the connecting door opened, the PPK in Kat's hand. Dressed in a tailored pants suit of light gray wool, she wore thin gold hoop earrings, the loops drawing attention to her hair. She went straight to the coffee, poured a cup and settled beside the window, her long legs crossed at the ankles.

"I ordered room service," I said. "I thought we'd start early."

"Never open the door unless I'm in the room," she said.

I cinched the robe's belt and offered no comment about the previous day or her absence from my bed. Having led a somewhat conventional life with limited exposure to assassins, I only stared at her.

"Yesterday had nothing to do with you," she said. "My past reappeared and left me little choice." She shrugged as though we'd forgotten to make a dinner reservation. "I'm sorry to have involved you. It's important you believe that."

I poured myself a cup, unaccustomed to a woman who felt the need to kill in a public restaurant. *If* the man was KGB, and *if* he was calling Moscow to report her whereabouts, she'd had little choice, given her training, but necessity failed to sooth my conscience. If someone put my head in a noose, what would I do? Try to reason with him? I had no way of knowing. Drawn to her in spite of my dismay, I couldn't envision her past or the wasteland she'd fled. I accepted her as a bodyguard out of necessity, knowing now I'd also fallen in love with this strange woman, one capable of disposing of a human being with a steak knife.

Kat placed her cup on the table. "Yesterday was terrible," she said, "but you must understand I had no choice."

"What happened yesterday," I said bitterly, "is your business." What was I expected to say? Bad luck? I'm glad you had a knife?

She read my eyes. "Sleeping with me does not include the privilege of judging me," she said. "Survival is all that matters now. Not only yours but mine as well."

She was right. I could continue the search or walk away and take my chances with Viktor. Either way could have disastrous consequences for Wes and me. Maybe her as well.

She banked her anger and folded her hands in her lap like a schoolgirl. Remorse, I wondered, or a pose calculated to keep me in the search? Did her innocent posture reflect regret or professional training?

"You're right," I finally said. "Your life is none of my business."

She lighted a Virginia Slim and exhaled smoke at the ceiling, shaking her head. "The odds of him stumbling on me were phenomenal. Showing up in the same restaurant on the same day in Paris. This was a distraction I did not need."

I didn't consider cutting a man's throat a distraction. She waved her hand, relegating yesterday to an unfortunate incident, as though diners in the restaurant had criticized her table manners.

"That is behind us," Kat said. In spite of her dismissal, I saw again a young girl pretending to be brave, driven away from an orphanage in a black car.

I crossed the room and held out my hand. She dropped the cigarette in her coffee cup, hesitating a moment before accepting my peace offering. Paris morning traffic hummed below the closed window, the sounds muffled, and she didn't move as I leaned down and kissed her cheek. "Let's see if we can find what happened to Dejean's collection," I said. "It's a reach, but what else do we have to do except find a new restaurant?"

She picked up her bag and removed an ugly black pistol, new from its appearance. She set it on the table beside her chair and I guessed Yuri had acquired it for her.

"Yuri found the Glock for me," she said. "It's light and you now need a weapon with you at all times. You can handle an automatic pistol?"

I picked up the blockish weapon and tested its weight with an abashed smile. "I shot a .22 rifle when I was a kid."

Kat looked as though I'd never learned to eat with a fork. She pointed to a small lever on the left side. " This model holds 10 rounds. Move the safety down. One bullet's already in the chamber. Just point and pull the trigger."

She picked up her purse as I turned the gun in my hands. "Make your call and see what you can learn about Dejean," she said. She slipped on her coat, opened the room door, and checked the hall. "Lock this door after me and lock the connecting door."

"Where are you going?"

"I need to walk."

I slid the door chain in place behind her and looked at the pistol on the table. The door to her room was open and I peered inside, guilty at my voyeur temptations. Her bed was made, not a piece of clothing in sight, unlike my disastrous room with clothes on the floor, a dirty glass on the credenza. The maid's job, right? It appeared Kat retained the discipline instilled by the orphanage or KGB. Or had she just run away and not told me? I checked the closets, relieved when I found her clothes.

Resisting the urge to rummage through the dresser drawers, I tried to assign her a place among my past lovers, failing to find a niche. With Kat, I accepted there was more than the physical, far more than even the anticipation it would happen again. There was an element of sheltering her, a reversal of roles. No clever repartee or gamesmanship. She was my lover and shield, but she'd become more than that. Everything, even the frantic sex, pared down to survival of the fittest. My face warm from the memory, I locked the connecting door and walked back to the table where the matte black pistol contrasted with a colorful travel magazine. Glock seemed more a Doctor Seuss character than lethal weapon.

Point and pull the trigger.

I searched my notes and found the telephone number for the Art Loss Register in London. The organization was tasked with locating, identifying, and returning looted art after World War II. If any record existed of Dejean's collection, the organization might reveal living family members. The trail was probably cold but little else remained. I jotted down a few details about my story and made a list of questions before I dialed Great Britain.

After two transfers, a droll British voice answered. "Neville Durrant here. Can I be of assistance?"

"I'm an art dealer from the United States, Mr. Durrant," I began. "I'm seeking clarification on the origin of a painting that's come into my hands."

"You have reason to suspect its provenance?"

"It's European. I want to be certain it's clean."

"The subject?"

"A Mary Cassatt. Mother and small child." It was a safe lie. God knows how many such scenes Cassatt painted.

"Any information about its original owner?"

"My source mentioned a Louis Dejean, a Frenchman who died during the war. I'm in Paris at the moment and seem to have hit a dead end."

"Could you spell it, please?"

I spelled Dejean's name.

"Any idea when or how he died?" Durrant asked.

"My seller believes he died in one of the camps during the war."

"That's not much to go on, is it? Can you text me a photograph?"

"The painting's in Chicago and my gallery's closed for repairs at the moment."

"I see." The line went silent before he said, "Let me check and I'll ring you back, Mr..."

"Barrow. Adam Barrow of The Adam Barrow Gallery in Chicago." An unimpressive bit of information, but it lent credibility if he checked on me.

"Yes, well, we'll see what we can turn up."

I gave him my number and he clicked off. I went to window and checked the street below. The Mercedes was dutifully parked at the curb. Yuri leaned against the passenger door, smoking a cigarette. No sign of Kat. I ordered a second carafe of coffee from room service, staying close to the phone if Neville decided to humor me.

The phone rang an hour later. "Mr. Barrow? Neville Durrant here." I fell in love again with British reliability.

"I checked our French registry and found a reference to a man named Louis Dejean who possessed a small collection of Impressionist paintings. In 1943 the Nazis charged him with being a degenerate. He was murdered at Buchenwald later that year. Seems the collection was discovered in a small French town after the war. Another Frenchman claimed to be the rightful owner. Our file is spotty, but it appears the claim was contested by Dejean's daughter. The entire matter was quite untidy, but the man prevailed since he had a will signed by this Dejean who left everything to him."

"Who was the man?"

"A Charles Langlois."

Charles was the name in Dejean's letter.

"And Dejean's daughter? Any details about her?"

"Afraid not. As I said, we don't have a lot."

"Any idea how I might contact this Langlois?"

"The last address we show was in Bonnières-sur-Seine."

Monet country. Where an art lover might choose to live. "When was the dispute settled?"

Paper rustled. "1987."

"That long ago," I muttered, my hopes floundering again.

"He would be ancient now, Mr. Barrow. There's little chance he's still alive."

I did the math and agreed. In his nineties if he was a day. "Well, nothing ventured, nothing gained."

"There's no record he owned your Cassatt but so much work is still missing." Durrant drew a weary breath. "We're a long way from the end, but we're having increasingly good fortune returning stolen art to its rightful owners if we uncover proof of ownership. It's a lengthy process, but our work's exposed several Nazi war criminals in the process. The courts are realizing there's no statute of limitations on barbarism."

"One last question. Was there an address for the daughter?"

"Just her name, I'm afraid." He spelled it for me.

"Thank you again. You've given me a place to start."

I hung up. Durrant was right. Thirty years was a long time since Langlois surfaced. Almost eighty years had passed since Dejean was murdered in a concentration camp, a faceless man who may or may not have colluded with my father to save a Van Gogh.

A map in one of the room's magazines indicated Bonnières-sur-Seine was near Giverny. My French being barely passable, I hoped Kat had better luck in finding a listing for a Charles Langlois. Who the hell knew if he was even alive? Durrant had given me a starting place and old men didn't often change addresses.

A knock on the hotel door. I picked up the Glock and checked the spyhole. Kat was back, wearing a new coat and carrying a large shopping bag. I unlocked the door and she handed me the bag.

"A gift," she said.

I smiled. "You already gave me a pistol."

"Open it."

Beneath Burberry wrapping paper was an expensive khaki raincoat with a removable wool tartan lining. I hefted its weight in both hands. "Very nice. Did you buy it with your money or Viktor's?"

"Viktor's," she smiled.

I put it on. Deep pockets, the waist belted, the weight perfect for Paris or Chicago wet winters.

"This one is more fitting for an art dealer," she said.

"I'll wear it tomorrow. We're heading north."

"You found something?"

"Someone named Charles Langlois. A man named Charles was mentioned in Dejean's letter. The Art Register in London said Dejean left his collection to this Langlois. He was last listed as living in Bonnières-sur-Seine near Giverny. With my luck, he's probably been dead for twenty years."

Kat took a map from her purse. "Fifty kilometers. Population 4,000." She pulled up her laptop. "I'll see if there's a Langlois listed there. If not, someone may know a relative."

"Whatever happens, we can make a side trip to Monet's gardens."

Chapter Twenty-Three

"We missed her."

Tasso sat in Gusov's office, facing his harried superior who unfastened his tunic collar, a white tee shirt contrasting with the drab brown material. Shrouded in half-shadow, the two table lamps reflected the colonel's restless eyes. Tasso, forgotten for the moment, Gusov burrowed the tip of the letter opener into the desk blotter, digging at the soft cardboard. He scowled at Tasso as though his subordinate was responsible for what happened.

"By sheer luck, one of our agents spotted her in Paris but she killed him before he could act," Gusov tossed the opener aside. "Clever little bitch."

"We trained her to survive," Tasso said with a note of pride.

The colonel ignored him. "She left the city with the man we've since learned is an art dealer. We have no idea where she's gone. Sooner or later she'll return to the United States but I must give Vladimir weekly reports."

Fear clouded the colonel's face.

"Do you know what it's like to disappoint him?" Gusov said, his voice plaintive. "To tell him he must wait?" He rebuttoned his collar and refocused on the older man. "When are you scheduled to leave?"

"Three days."

Gusov waved a hand. "Leave tomorrow. I've notified our Washington Embassy you're to be given every assistance. Ignore the rabbits who run the embassy and do whatever is required. They live in daily fear of being expelled for some transgression, abandoning their fast food restaurants and mistresses. The idiots mean nothing to our mission."

Tasso realized Gusov no longer saw him, his eyes fixed on the pitted blotter. Tasso waited a moment longer and walked from the room without speaking.

Chapter Twenty-Four

Kat discovered a Langlois living in Bonnières-sur-Seine. I changed into woolen slacks and blue oxford shirt, shrugging into my new coat. I slipped the Glock into the deep right pocket and checked my reflection in the mirror. Behind me Kat removed the PPK from her purse and ejected the magazine to check it was loaded. Bonnie and Clyde, I thought. Well, my last name *was* Barrow - no relation to Clyde so far as I knew. All I needed was a fedora, a 1933 Ford roadster at the curb with the motor running, and Warren Beatty's face. In my dreams.

The drive on A10 took us north. Yuri maneuvered through surprisingly light traffic and Kat touched my sleeve once, looking at me with an expression impossible to decipher. Hope or despair or the memory of the man in the restaurant? Sitting beside a woman who shared my bed and cut a man's throat created questions about morals I'd always taken for granted.

The Seine wound through wintry countryside on our right, woods and fields concealing the emergence of spring. As we neared the town, clouds of chalky white smoke rose above the tree line from an industrial complex that fouled the river. Yuri turned off the highway and ten minutes later we drove into the center of an ancient village dominated by a modest church spire. A stone World War II memorial guarded Bonnières-sur Seine's main intersection, the circular remembrance cordoned off by knee-high chains, withered bouquets against the granite base.

Yuri followed Kat's directions until we stopped at a modest cottage. Dark green shutters, yellow flower boxes, an ancient chipped slate roof, indistinguishable from its neighbors. Wisps of smoke unfurled from twin chimneys at one end of the house.

A coffee-colored boy in his early twenties answered the door. Stick-limbed and over six feet tall, he wore a sleeveless black vest over a starched white shirt, his dark trousers sharply creased. He smiled, stared at the Mercedes and spoke with a lilting Caribbean accent.

"*Bonjour.*"

"*Bonjour*," Kat replied. "We are Americans. Do you speak English?"

The smile broadened. "Oh, yes. That is my first language. I come here from Jamaica to work for Mr. Charles."

"Charles Langlois?' I asked.

"Oh, yes. That is his name." The smile bloomed brighter. "I am Gerome, his helpmate."

"I'm Katia and this is Adam," Kat said. "We'd like to talk with him if we may."

The smile dimmed. "Today may be a good day. If you'll wait a moment, I'll see if Mr. Charles will sit down with you."

Kat and I took chairs in front of a shallow fireplace struggling to produce a semblance of warmth. The small heap of coal produced more smoke than warmth, smoldering fitfully. The furnishings were comfortably worn, wooden chairs and tables blackened with age. Nothing remarkable about the room until I looked at the nearest wall.

The paintings glowed beneath modern spotlights. I walked to them in a daze, recognizing the artists ten steps away: Corot and Vuillard. The dainty Corot depicted a boy and young girl sitting by a brook, the colors rendered with subtle touches. The Vuillard was larger, a woman seated beside a vase of flowers, a pensive expression on her face as she gazed out an open window, a pastoral scene in the distance. Neither was a print or giclée reproduction, both priceless originals, a small fortune sleeping in a smoky room, concealed in plain view.

I returned to my chair with a backward glance at the paintings.

"What is it?" Kat asked.

"Later."

We heard voices and Gerome pushed a vintage wheelchair into the room. Charles Langlois was skeletal, an old man bent forward above the oversized spoke wheels. He wore slippers and red plaid flannel shirt buttoned to his chin, large listless hands resting on a woolen blanket spread over his lap. The emaciated body gave the impression that all air and fluids had been vacuumed from his body, leaving a withered cocoon. Eyes closed, Langlois wheezed, dozing until Gerome touched his arm. The eyelids fluttered open and the cadaverous remains gazed at us with surprising intensity.

"Mr. Charles will speak with you now," the boy said, delighted as he proudly placed one hand on the stooped shoulder. "His mother was English, you know. He speaks English quite well."

The relic raised a hand in polite acknowledgement, his breath labored as cataract-clouded eyes shifted between Kat and me. I glanced at her. There was no need to prevaricate; Charles Langlois might desert the living before our eyes.

"Mr. Langlois," I began, "did you know Louis Dejean?"

He pulled back and craned his neck at me, the words slurred but defiant. "Louis left them to *me*. The paintings are mine!"

We'd found Charles Langlois.

"We know," I said. "We want to talk with you about a painting he owned."

His eyes flashed, spittle on his lips. "*Je m'en fous*. I proved I owned all the pictures. Louis wanted me to have them, not her." The bloodless lips constricted. "She cared nothing for him."

I guessed this was Dejean's daughter.

Hands locked behind her back, Kat leaned toward him as if extracting information in Lubyanka's depths. "Where are the paintings now?"

"I had the right to sell them," Langlois whined. "Poor Louis. The Germans overlooked me in their search for our kind." He gestured at the Corot and Vuillard. "I kept only these two as reminders of him. He wanted me to remember our love." The memory floated away and he looked up at Kat as though seeing her for the first time.

"You are quite lovely, my dear."

Kat graced him with a smile. "Thank you."

Langlois giggled and touched Gerome's arm. "Women were always a wonder to me," he said. "Charming creatures until they learned I was unavailable."

Gerome smiled, embarrassed or sympathetic.

"Did Louis Dejean ever show you a Van Gogh?" I asked.

"Only once." Langlois's face glowed, his memory retreating seventy years. "It was quite handsome, all color and light and…"

Kat stepped closer to the wheelchair. "You saw it?"

Langlois's chin dropped onto his chest with a sigh, asleep again.

"Mr. Charles cannot always control when he naps," the boy said. "If you care to wait, he will continue talking with you in a few moments."

Langlois's eyes sprang open, his narcoleptic nap evidently over.

"The Van Gogh," I prompted, afraid he'd drift away again. "Can you describe the Van Gogh to me?"

He nodded. "A woman, I think."

My mind raced. "How large was the picture?"

Langlois lifted his trembling hands two feet apart. "This big? I remember precisely where it hung in the Louvre. So many lovely paintings to see. I remember it was a rainy day," he said, Kat and I forgotten.

"Another Van Gogh," I prompted. "Was there another picture?"

Confusion. "Another?"

I sighed and looked at Kat.

"Was there another Van Gogh, a much larger one?" she insisted.

He opened his mouth but his head abruptly dropped again. Spittle dribbled onto his shirt and Gerome gently wiped it away.

"Oh," Gerome sighed, "he falls asleep many times each day. Another moment, if you please."

Kat and I looked at one another and waited. Coal embers softly popped in the fireplace as though fearing to wake the old man. The two paintings drew my eyes again. Disappointed that Langlois had no memory of an immense Van Gogh, I reconciled myself to facing Viktor. Gerome looked at us, then affectionately grasped Langlois's forearm.

"Sir?"

Langlois's head snapped up and Gerome smiled with pride. The old man blinked and found Kat again, his eyes dissecting her with an intelligence once acute.

"A large Van Gogh?" I said.

"There was a picture I never saw," he mumbled. "One Louis promised to his daughter."

The daughter. Thank God his synapses clicked in and out, his stuttering brain verging on full-blown Alzheimer's.

"A very large Van Gogh?" Kat asked.

"Louis told me it was large, that it would take care of his daughter in her old age." The left side of Langlois's ravaged face tightened with disgust. "She was such a bitch."

"What was her name?" I asked.

"I don't remember," Langlois whined. "So long ago…" The head tipped forward yet again accompanied by soft snoring.

Gerome looked at us apologetically. "I am so sorry again, sir. It appears he will now sleep the remainder of the day. Conversation tires him so."

So close, I thought. The London Register confirmed ownership was contested by a daughter, name unknown. Checking birth records would be a gamble with so many records destroyed during the war. What were the odds of finding her, assuming she was still alive? We'd been so close. Elusive as she might prove, she remained our sole lead.

"Perhaps we can come back tomorrow," I said.

"May I ask what time?" Gerome asked.

Catch the old guy before he tires, I thought. "Around ten?"

"That will be fine." Kat and I were halfway to the door when Gerome stopped us. "I'm certain he can tell you more about the lady. He does not like Miss Marguerite, but I think he may tell you more. He talks about her quite often."

We stopped and stared at the boy.

"Marguerite?" I said.

"Oh, yes. That is her name. Miss Marguerite Bouchet."

"Gerome, is she alive?"

"Oh, yes. She lives in New York City."

***

We stayed the night in a cramped B&B in Bonnières-sur-Seine. Kat returned to my bed and the lovemaking was gentler with a wary intimacy. I had no idea if she sensed the transformation, or if I misread my reaction. When we pulled apart, she reached for the proverbial cigarette and sat up against her pillow, her bare leg draped over mine. I wiped my face with a corner of the sheet and caught my breath.

She filled her lungs with smoke and stared at the ceiling. I didn't know where her thoughts took her, but mine danced around something I labelled as love. I'd seen her darker side but was beyond hurling draconian judgments. The KGB had infused her with predator's blood, a hawk that killed to stay alive. Distancing herself from Moscow hadn't yet stilled that instinct. I stared at her profile, recalling the serrated knife blade, unable to forget the spot of blood on her blouse.

Chapter Twenty-Five

Tasso awoke with a start. He'd dreamed of Lubyanka's basement, each filthy chamber filled with crying children and colorful toys. The odor of his rumpled shirt broke through his half-sleep as a metallic voice announced the Aeroflot Airbus A330 would land at Dulles in fifteen minutes.

Squinting at overcast morning skies outside the window, he ignored the seat belt sign and made his way to the restroom. His mouth tasted like a rusty sewer grate as he cupped his hand and drank from the small tap. Splashing water on his face, he wiped his beard dry with a small paper towel and re-knotted his tie. Finger-combing his hair, he stared in the mirror and frowned at the inevitable jowls and deep lines around his eyes, more grey seeming to have invaded his beard overnight. Gusov, he knew, had detected the same decay.

The embassy car waited outside the terminal. The car's window powered down.

"Doctor Brezenkov?"

The driver was clean-cut and too young in Tasso's estimation. He nodded and allowed the man to take his single suitcase, recalling the 26-mile car ride required to reach Washington. Settled in the rear seat he shunned the driver's attempts at conversation, content to watch Virginia's rolling countryside flow past the BMW's tinted windows. Blotches of snow dotted the fields along the expressway, and as always, Tasso marveled that capitalism flourished, the string of small towns and villages alight with neon and flush with businesses. The appearance of such prosperity reawakened old doubts, the endless strip malls and massive truck plazas jarring contrasts to the sparse landscape outside Moscow.

Forty minutes later, his pulse quickened as the car rolled into the vibrant city, capitol of his lifelong enemies. Washington mimicked Moscow's obsession with functionality, the government buildings designed to inspire solidity and confidence, but the American capitol lacked spires and domes and Russia's pre-

Revolution grandeur. Moscow's ancient beauty remained untrammeled by its stolid masters despite a hundred years of committee planning.

The car turned onto Wisconsin Avenue and Tasso saw the embassy a few blocks ahead. "How long has it been since you were last here, sir?" the driver asked.

"Four years."

The driver pointed over the hood. "Every day now, we must endure *that*."

Tasso saw the street sign.

"Nemtsov Street," the boy said. "The American generals and corrupt politicians renamed the street in front of our embassy. An insult designed to honor a counter-revolutionary."

Were the comments a required litany, or was the driver taking no chances with the stranger? Tasso didn't comment on the sign. The assassination of Boris Nemtsov had made headlines for a week. A democratic activist, Nemtsov was gunned down outside the Kremlin, the murder inexplicably blamed on five Chechens. Putin's government denied involvement and the incident faded from the newspapers.

A metal gate slid open and the car pulled into the embassy's rear courtyard. He showed his credentials to an armed guard at the door and the driver followed him inside with his cheap suitcase. Tasso was met by another dour-faced guard and shown to an office where the carpet and closed drapes smelled of cigarettes and nervous sweat. Settled in the seating area, he gathered his wits, familiar with the role he must now play. A staff member arrived with a platter of dark bread and sliced meats along with a carafe of coffee and bottle of Yamskaya vodka. A heavy crystal glass filled with ice cubes sat next to the vodka. Tasso dumped the ice in the coffee cup and poured vodka into the glass. He took a grateful swallow and thanked the heavyset man who took his station by the door without acknowledging him.

Tasso studied the familiar room. Little had changed since his last visit. There were now two framed photographs of Putin on the wall, another portrait gracing Ambassador Korinkin's desk. In its distinctly Russian style, the room replicated Gusov's office except the furniture and appointments were top American quality. Tasso took another swallow of vodka and closed his eyes, fighting off the effects of the interminable flight. He looked up as Korinkin strode into the room and waved away the guard.

"Ah, Brezenkov, you've come back to us." The ambassador projected good humor but Tasso knew the portly oaf detested him. Like many in the diplomatic service, Brezenkov could not be trusted, concealing his slyness behind a practiced front of jovial affability. Did his American counterparts mirror such dishonesty?

Tasso grasped the pudgy hand in a single perfunctory shake. "It's been awhile, Ambassador."

Korinkin resembled an aging basset hound with immense jowls and drooping rheumy eyes. The Ambassador poured himself a vodka and dropped heavily into a chair, his face flushed as though he'd jogged to the embassy from the Lincoln Memorial. His suit vest, straining to contain an ample belly, revealed his white shirt. In the past they tolerated one another in a mutual truce. Tasso considered Korinkin an overpaid servant who carried water and mucked out the stables, while others did the fighting. God knew what Korinkin thought of him, not that it mattered. Tasso swirled the vodka in the heavy glass and ignored the food.

"You have my orders?"

Korinkin walked to his desk and returned with a worn briefcase and sealed envelope. "I am to tell you the target is leaving Paris for New York tomorrow. The woman and a male friend are traveling together." He grinned. "I'm informed they are rarely apart."

Tasso ignored the leer. A companion, he thought. A complication but a minor one. He tore open the envelope and thumbed the contents. Money. Visa. Passport. Various up-to-date credentials identifying him as Dr. Anatoli Brezenkov, a logistics professor at the Moscow School of Economics. Someone had been careful enough to include a prepared speech on the World Bank that he would never present. Everything verified his usual identity, one he hoped American intelligence services had not penetrated. He dropped the envelope in his briefcase.

"We will provide whatever else is required," the ambassador continued. "Colonel Gusov made it clear you have top priority until your mission is completed. If you require a weapon, we can supply any number of choices, but of course, you cannot fly with a pistol on your person or in your luggage."

The buffoon must think me an idiot, Tasso thought. "Of course. Have someone meet me in New York with a Nagant and silencer."

Korinkin shook his head as though a wayward child had blundered into the room. He lit a cigarette and studied the vaulted ceiling. "I know you are what the

Americans call Old School, but there are more subtle methods now available to us. Almost undetectable. The new methods were most effective in London." He looked at Tasso. "Our technicians spend many hours developing efficient weapons. You should consider updating your arsenal."

Tasso placed his glass on the table with deliberate care. "Relics like me prefer the familiar. A simple Nagant revolver will do, Korinkin. With a silencer."

Chapter Twenty-Six

Next day in the car Kat and I handed our pistols to Yuri at Charles de Gaulle Airport before we passed through the screeners to board our flight to New York. Kat gave him a hug and we watched the Mercedes roll away, on our own again.

I had a First-Class window seat, Kat two rows behind me. As before, I watched her make her journey to the rear of the aircraft, inspecting each passenger. A tall man in the last row of Economy smiled at her.

I fought to stay awake, using the solitude to make sense of the past week, the proverbial plug pulled on my most of my doubts. Maybe my father told the truth once during his chaotic life. Or possibly the whole story remained nothing more than alcohol-induced fiction as we grabbed at smoke. In the unlikely event the letters were true, I held onto the possibility that I'd stumbled into an unlikely connection. I considered my lovemaking with Kat might have twisted my reasoning into wishful thinking but I'd seen what I suspected was an immense easel, then listened to senile ramblings about a painting bequeathed to an embittered daughter. Marguerite Bouchet, if she were alive, might add another piece of the puzzle to complement an unfinished letter and rotting boards in a Dutch barn. *Might* was a word rapidly wearing out its welcome.

We landed mid-afternoon. Unlike other enthusiasts, I never liked New York, a city where no one smiled other than drunks and wide-eyed tourists, where mounds of garbage blocked sidewalks. At least Chicago's planners showed sufficient foresight to include miles of alleys.

Kat and I inched through customs at JFK, wedged against impatient and irritable passengers. Outside, we pushed past the harried mob of cab seekers toward a black sedan. The car swerved in front of the lead cab at the taxi stand, two Pakistani cabbies yelling obscenities as we slipped into the rear seat and our Russian driver pulled away. Two brown paper sacks on the seat held another PPK and my new friend, the 9mm Glock. Kat arranged the smaller pistol in her purse and I slipped the Glock inside my raincoat pocket, almost accustomed to its weight. So far as I recalled, concealed carry was not included in Art 101.

Kat had booked us into the Baccarat on 53rd south of Central Park. Flaunting a mirrored lobby, Baccarat Maison was a hedonistic fantasyland for adults. Glass walls, soaring mirrors. A kowtowing staff hurried among the white décor that defined a theme park for the uber-rich. I knew the extravagant hotel by reputation and refused to consider what it was costing Viktor.

A solemn bellman led us to our lavish suite on the top floor, opened voluminous sheer curtains to admit sunlight into a bridal-white room, and padded out ten dollars richer. Hell, it wasn't my money and Kat had selected our lodgings. A tastefully-arranged silver tray flaunted a pyramid of tastefully arranged fruit. I selected an apple, guilty at ruining the artistic display. Walking to the window I gaped at the city skyline, while Kat powered up her laptop. I crunched into the apple and watched her long fingernails tap the keys.

"I can use a shower," I said.

Kat ignored me. "I found two Bouchets with the first initial M."

Technology was going to deny me a shower.

"What if she remarried?" I asked.

"Then we'll look elsewhere."

I tossed the apple core into the wastebasket and wondered where in hell 'elsewhere' might be. Fogged by jet lag, I visualized standing under a warm shower as Kat scrubbed my back. Oblivious to my fantasy, she checked business listings.

"Here's a commercial listing," she said. "'Madame Bouchet – Antique Treasures.'" She frowned. "Treasures?"

"My guess is they're European antiques," I said. "'European' automatically converts junk into treasures."

Kat checked her watch and dialed the number, putting the call on speaker phone. A recorded voice said the shop was open until 5 PM.

" French," she confirmed. "An older woman by the voice."

"Hope springs eternal."

My shower and fantasy would have to wait. Five minutes later we were in a cab. Bouchet's shop was located on Second Avenue in the heart of an antique district. Shops offered relics of all varieties, a few displaying dubious imitations. Kat and I peered through Bouchet's front window. The shop belonged in the Fifties, merchandise tilted toward the lower scale in terms of quality.

A brass bell over the door roused a tiny woman from a desk in the midst of old-fashioned wooden showcases. I guessed her to be in her eighties, her bleached face indicating she avoided sunlight. She wore an ankle-length black dress with a tattered hem, her hair arranged in a generous pile of gray. The pinched face had long ago surrendered to the passing years. She bustled toward us with a retailer's ever-hopeful smile.

"*Monsieur, madam,* you are seeking something special? A gift, perhaps?"

"We'd like to talk with Madame Bouchet."

"I am Madame Bouchet."

"Are you the daughter of Louis Dejean?"

The smile fell away as though I'd punched her in the stomach. Hands at her sides, she stepped back. "Why would you want to know such a thing?"

"We apologize for intruding on family matters, but if you're Marguerite Bouchet…"

"That is my name, but why do you want to know about my father? He's dead these seventy years."

"It concerns a painting he may have owned," I said.

She stiffened again. "Is that any of your business?"

"As I said, Miss Bouchet, we don't mean to pry into your life, but the painting is very valuable. A Van Gogh your father may have saved from the Germans."

Her thin lips set, she eyed me closely, struggling to assess what lay behind my questions.

"I know nothing about your family," I said, "but…"

"Family." The word snapped from her lips like an obscenity. "I had only a mother. I renounced my father when he deserted us."

We'd found her.

The old woman's tone grew vindictive as she prattled on. "Bouchet was my mother's name. I was a girl when we changed our name. It distanced us from *mon père* and his kind. Oh, I knew what he was even then, and I wanted nothing to do with him. My father was a degenerate just as the Germans claimed." She swung her gaze between Kat and me as if we emitted a disagreeable scent. "Why are you here?"

"We're looking for a painting," I said.

"So you said." She gave a spiteful laugh. "A painting? Look around you, *monsieur*. Do you see paintings on my walls? Paintings are a waste of hard-earned money. My father..." She flapped her hands. "My father. Oh, he loved his paintings, loved them more than my mother and me."

"I'm very sorry," I said, awash in her bitterness.

Kat rescued me. "We're seeking information on just one painting. One your father may have owned."

Marguerite Bouchet closed her eyes for a long moment before they returned to us. "I knew someone would come one day." Her forbearance at an end, she glared at Kat. "How do you know about my alleged legacy?"

"There was a letter from your father," I began. "In it he mentioned a very large Van Gogh, one my father may have owned. We talked with Charles Langlois…"

"Charles Langlois." She spat the name like an ancient curse and I feared she might expire at our feet. "He said my father intended me to have it, but I never touched it. The old pederast told me it disappeared." She flicked her fingers at the ceiling. "Most likely he sold it after my father was killed. Robbed me of my inheritance."

"Miss Bouchet," I said, "we don't know if the painting ever existed."

"Oh, it existed, monsieur. I assure you it was real."

An embittered delusion?

"Did you ever see it?" Kat asked.

"Oh, yes."

The second shoe fell.

"Where did you see it?" I asked her.

"In a photograph my father sent to me. Before they hauled him off."

"Where is the photo now?"

"In my office."

Marguerite Bouchet's office matched her stature. Undersized and untidy, dominated by a roll top desk and two wooden chairs on rollers. Unmarked cardboard boxes and questionable *objects d'art* cluttered the corners; true to her claim, there were no paintings. Kat and I pulled the chairs beside the desk, careful not to disturb the towers of boxes ready to topple onto trespassers.

The woman deftly wheeled her chair to her desk and opened a small drawer. Her hand trembling, she removed a yellowed envelope and slipped out an old-fashioned photograph with scalloped edges. Holding it close to her face, she studied the image as though debating whether to share the photo. She laid it on the corner of the desk.

"My legacy," she said as I picked up the small black and white photo.

A dapper middle-aged man stood beside an enormous canvas. Smiling, his hand rested atop an elaborately scrolled gold frame. I focused on the man for a microsecond, my eyes seeing only the immense canvas. The figure in the painting matched the man's height, a life-sized portrait of a young girl in a field of swaying wheat. The photograph was colorless, the details slightly out of focus but my heart began to race. The immense work might have been painted by anyone but the technique screamed Van Gogh and the dimensions matched my father's description. I turned it over and read the developer's date on the back: *3 Mars 1940*. Had my father taken the photograph?

I passed it to Kat who squinted slightly and brought it close to her face as Bouchet had done. Was her perfection blighted by far-sightedness?

The old woman plucked it from her fingers and lightly ran her index finger over the surface. "*That* was my father," she whispered. She stared at the photo, her voice lost in time. "Louis Dejean, damn his eyes."

Kat and I allowed Marguerite Bouchet her past as she glared at the snapshot. After a moment, she looked up, older and smaller. She replaced the photograph in the envelope and slammed the drawer shut.

"Charles Langlois sent that to me after the war, taunting me if I gauged him correctly. Somehow, he avoided the Germans, while my father died in one of the camps. How or exactly when, I don't know." She frowned at the drawer. "I fought Langlois in the courts and waited for years for the painting to appear. I myself believe it was lost in the war like so much else. No, monsieur, you should not be wasting your time chasing this thing"

For the first time since I'd read the two letters, the photo proved the Van Gogh's existence. The painting matched my father's description and the story he'd committed to paper in his final days. I had to believe it existed despite the Bouchet's doubts.

"May I copy the photo and return it to you?" I asked.

She brushed a hand across the desktop, her demeanor softening as though the photograph unleashed fonder memories. She wistfully wiped away the dust. "I have no other remembrances of my father," she said, her voice reflecting lost dreams. "Nothing. My father…" She raised her head apologetically, examining us before she touched the drawer again. "I do not know either of you. Surely you understand I cannot part with it although I despised him. Repulsive as he was, this is my only memory."

"Would you make us a copy? I'll gladly pay you for your time."

She dropped her hands to her lap and smoothed the threadbare dress. "Yes, I could do that. Come back in three days."

Three days. Marguerite Bouchet sat motionless until we bid her goodbye and left the shop.

"Three days?" I said outside. "What else does she have to do?"

"She's a lonely old woman," Kat said. "To make a copy she'll have to touch the photo again. Revive dead memories."

"You think she'll make a copy?"

Kat thought for a moment. "No. I don't think we'll ever see the photograph again."

"It's only a photo."

She looked at me. "More than I have."

Marguerite Bouchet's acrimony was beyond healing. A gust of gritty wind chased crushed coffee cups along the sidewalk as we searched for a cab. Neither spoke as the wind swirled Kat's dark hair across her face until she captured it in both hands and pushed the strands beneath her coat collar. Her ivory cheeks mottled by the cold, I marveled at her beauty and wondered what our nights together meant to her. She asked for nothing beyond the physical. No unspoken promises or professions of love. I remained her ward, her presence a favor to Viktor. The thought cut my pride like broken glass.

We jogged across Fourth Avenue, dodging traffic, finding only occupied cabs. I wondered if her thoughts remained in the cramped shop with the lonely woman. My own could not shake the little photo. All three of us had outlived our fathers, thrust into worlds beyond our control.

"You've never said how you feel about me," I said. A dumb thing to say, but I needed something, unable to put my feelings into nobler words.

Her gaze fixed on the sidewalk, she didn't look up until she pulled me into a dank alley filled with dumpsters. Decay collected in our throats and nostrils, and she dug a pack of cigarettes from her purse as though giving herself time to think about what I'd blurted out. Avoiding the wind, she lit one and blew smoke toward the garbage as though it might erase my words.

"What do you want from me?" she asked.

It was a fair question. My search had involved a Russian woman I couldn't have imagined a few weeks earlier. From Vasily to Victor to a quest that began as a gesture to placate my brother. Standing in the wind-swept alley, I tried and failed to picture the rest of my life without her.

"Just don't walk away without telling me," I said.

"Now's not the time to talk about such things," she said. "Attachments get you killed."

After a moment, she allowed me to take her hand and we headed back into the street, no closer to understanding what was happening to me.

***

Standing in a shop doorway across the street, Anatoli Tasso had watched the man and woman exit the antique store. Luck was with him as the afternoon crowds of shoppers thinned. Crossing the street, he signaled to the waiting car a block away that joined the flow of traffic. Trailing half block behind his target he watched the couple duck into an alley. It was indeed his lucky day. Picking up his pace he closed to twenty-five feet. Two quick muffled shots and he would disappear into the car.

The silenced Nagant revolver was half out of his pocket when a group of shoppers and gaggle of uniformed schoolgirls approached from the opposite direction. He dropped the pistol back into his pocket and walked past the alley, another stranger in the crowd. Another time, Tasso thought. He would wait.

Chapter Twenty-Seven

The Contractor waited between two parked cars until Barrow and the woman disappeared up the street. A single pedestrian followed them, the man seemingly intent in catching up to them but he stopped short and waited at the curb for a car that picked him up.

Heading north, the Contractor walked past the antique shop, glanced inside and continued another block before doubling back, pausing occasionally as though window shopping. Maybe it was a waste of time, but he'd run dry of information. Barrow's visit to the antique shop possibly meant nothing, but the shop *was* European although he saw no paintings inside. The connection was thin but a quiet talk with the owner might pay dividends.

The brass bell announced Bouchet's second customer within the hour. She scurried from her office, her eyes bright when a well-groomed man returned her hopeful smile. He was dark, a foreigner by his looks, the type who sought the obscure that larger shops overlooked. At the very least, the customer represented more promise than the strange couple who delved into her best-forgotten past.

"*Bonjour, bonjour,*" she said, frowning as the tall man opened a cabinet and removed a tiny Austrian bronze, the rarity depicting an African child clinging to the neck of a giraffe. The case was clearly marked 'Do not open,' but she brushed aside her annoyance and brightened her smile, willing to overlook the transgression should he discover something irresistible.

The Contractor weighed the miniature bronze in his palm, displaying perfect teeth as he held up the tiny figurine with a smile. "I like this one."

"Ah, a rare example with original paint. You collect bronzes?"

"I have a large collection. My preference is black pickaninnies," he said, his smile broadening. "Not politically correct in today's sensitive climate, but I see them as reality."

Madame Bouchet suppressed a second frown. She did not like such language, particularly from someone who dressed as though he was educated. She abhorred the racist depictions prevalent in older European pieces, but she reasoned they were reflections of a different era, and such pieces were becoming increasingly difficult to locate. At a more practical level, they demanded higher prices and sold well to serious collectors.

Sniffing a sale, she said, "I believe I have others that match your taste. I haven't put them out yet."

"Wonderful." The charming smile again. "I'd very much like to see them."

"I believe they're in my office. You may discover something to your liking."

The man replaced the piece and closed the cabinet door. "That would make my day, *Madame*."

The Contractor followed her to the chaotic office and closed the door behind them. He grimaced at the dirt as the woman stood beside a roll top desk and placed her index finger against her thin lips.

"Bronzes, bronzes." She inspected the office.

The Contractor removed his breast pocket handkerchief and swiped at a chair. He sat down and crossed his legs, tugging at his trouser crease.

"There is another item that interests me," he said as she sorted through a stack of small boxes.

The wizened eyes, certain of a sale now, crinkled with pleasure. "Tell me what you're seeking."

"More a concern than an interest, actually."

"I can assist you in locating any number of antiquities."

He nodded as though confiding in an old friend, having learned the value of sociability. "May I ask you a question, *Madame* Bouchet?"

She gathered the disreputable dress beneath her and sat behind the desk, her spine straight as her mother had taught her. "As I said, I'll be glad to help you, Mr.—?"

"Van Gogh."

Marguerite Bouchet recoiled and involuntarily glanced at the desk drawer. "You are fortunate to possess such a famous name," she managed. She had not lived 83 years to trust in coincidences.

"A very valuable name as it turns out," the customer said.

"What do you want?"

The smile again. "The delightful little bronze in the case. And information." She did not move.

"The couple who just left. What did they want?"

Van Gogh twice in a single day, as though her father sent messengers to taunt her. "My customers' business is their own. I have certain ethics."

The Contractor's was on his feet. His right hand gripped a sleeve of black material. "No, *madame*. Today, their business coincides with mine."

"You cannot..."

He slapped her face, a shock of gray hair falling over one eye.

"What did they want?" he grated, leaning closer.

She tasted blood in her dentures. The war had toughened her and provided contempt for barbarians, absently wondering how men of quality fell to such depths.

He slapped her again, harder, the open-handed blow loud in the confined space. "Again, *madame*, why were they here?"

Marguerite met his eyes and shook her head. Grimacing, her tongue pushed the dentures back in place. No, this was no gentleman. She wiped her lips with the back of her hand, surprised at the sight of her blood.

"They were looking for a lamp," she croaked. "A Regency lamp by..."

He struck her a third time and spots flashed before her tear-filled eyes. The Contractor placed his hands on the arms of her chair and leaned his face close. "I can keep this up all afternoon if you like."

Marguerite Bouchet inhaled his cologne, a delicate scent, memories of kitchen cinnamon and lilacs from her mother's garden. Too many such memories consumed her time as the years accumulated. She'd grown old beyond her allotted time, the dismal little shop her last refuge. After she gave it up, what then? The constant growing pain in her abdomen frightened her, and she feared what doctors' tests would reveal. What could this horrid man do other than hasten the inevitable? She would not end her life with cowardice. She would not betray the man and woman like her father had betrayed his wife and daughter. She stared into the confident eyes.

"A lamp," she said firmly.

The Contractor straightened. Either she was a fool or incredibly brave. A lamp made no sense. Barrow and the woman weren't man and wife on a shopping spree. Searching for a particular lamp swerved too far from their mission. The old woman was lying.

"If that's what you prefer," he said. He turned away and slipped the pistol from its holster, screwing the steel tube over the Browning's muzzle.

Gripping the arms of her chair, Marguerite Bouchet waited. Her fear slipped away as she glared at his back, her mouth numbed but no longer bleeding. What could be worse than her dingy apartment, a scruffy yellow cat her sole companion. A dear creature, the only thing left to love in her life. What might happen to it, she wondered, when she was no longer there to take care of it?

"My cat..." she began.

The Contractor turned and shot her an inch above her nose. Her arms wilted over the sides of the chair without a sound, her mouth open.

He did not move for a full minute, listening for the bell above the door. He removed the silencer and returned the automatic to its holster, smoothing his lapels. The old crone had lied, certain now she'd wasted his time. He checked a few dilapidated boxes for bronzes, found nothing, and swore. Adjusting his tie in a dust-laden mirror he started to leave when the desk drew his attention. If she possessed anything of value, the roll top was the most obvious hiding place.

He rolled the chair and body aside and shuffled through papers on the writing surface. The center drawer revealed bills of sale, two notices for past due taxes, and an empty tin box that once contained tea bags. He yanked open two smaller drawers and found what he sought in the second.

The black and white photograph was the sort produced by antiquated box cameras. The painting was larger than the Van Goghs he'd seen in museums, the date on the back of the photo confirming it was taken decades ago. He slipped to photo inside his jacket pocket. Had Barrow and his traveling companion seen the photograph? No matter, the old photo told them nothing about the painting's whereabouts unless the woman revealed its location. A few more minutes of pain might have revealed more information. He could live with the mistake, and his employer need not know he overlooked the opportunity. But the day hadn't been a waste. He imagined the man's excitement when he shoved the photo under his nose.

The Contractor wiped his fingerprints from the desk, chair arms and door knob. Walking rapidly past the shop's castoffs and junk, he stopped next to the front door. Opening the display case, he dropped the giraffe in his coat pocket. The bronze would take center place in his collection but he regretted again not being more patient with the old woman. A few more minutes might also have revealed information and other bronzes squirreled away in the dingy cubbyhole.

Opening the door, he turned up his collar and touched the photograph. The day wasn't a total waste. His oversight had been careless, but then again, perfection was such a taxing goal.

Chapter Twenty-Eight

December 1888 Arles France

Marooned inside the house, he prowled room to room, his eyes avoiding crushed paint tubes and half-finished canvases. The light and countryside around Arles offered an artist's paradise, every field and hillock pleading for paint. But no longer. Not for the past six contentious weeks. To venture outside was a senseless act unless one was willing to watch the wind whirl canvas and easel into the sky.

Bits of food clung to his beard and frayed sweater as he pressed one hand against a window pane, hoping to halt the persistent rattle. December was an unspeakable month. Nights like this were the worst, he thought, the cold mistral wind punishing everything in its path, stealing under doors, wedging dirt into every crevice of his beloved Yellow House. Almost 800 kilometers from Paris, he may as well have stood on the moon.

Nothing had worked out as planned. It had started well enough. Gauguin had arrived to share his plans for a new fraternity of artists and his hopes soared. The year began agreeably enough but disaster crept closer as their friendship fell away amidst niggling arguments. The unrelenting weather sharpened his own careless words, his outburst tonight driving Gauguin from the house. His pictured his companion rolling in the arms of some whore on the rue du Bout d'Arles, ready to depart for Paris or faraway Martinique again. Dreams of a new art community withered amidst their arguments, blown away like the infernal wind that loosed its fury on the French countryside.

Without sunlight and lush fields to divert him, the attack descended like locusts. The little house was his fortress, but not even medieval towers could deflect what doctors labeled 'mental epilepsy,' what others straightforwardly labeled as insanity. The latter likelihood heightened his fears he might end up a groveling idiot, confined and forgotten behind stone walls. Cooped up in the house, the relentless attacks intensified the specter of what awaited him, a black-cowled wraith that delighted in mocking his failures.

Outside, a loose shutter pounded the masonry walls. Placing both hands over his ears, he squeezed his eyes shut and staggered blindly around the room. Collapsing in a chair, he picked up a flask and gulped raw cheap cognac. Below the grimy window, children chased one another in the dark street, their laughter mocking the wind and night sky. Christmas was two days away, a time for joy and celebration. Hungry for morning sun, he gazed at unframed canvases filling the room: flowering orchards, fields of laborers, tortured groves of cypress trees. Worthless paintings no one desired. No Paris dealer, not even Theo, his industrious brother, found buyers, so they decorated the room's walls and corners like orphaned children pleading for homes.

He swallowed more cognac, oblivious to its coarse quality. Worthless, he thought, all worthless. Swirls and dabs of paint of no value to those who professed the ability to see into a painter's heart. Looking away from the legion of paintings, he pictured the huge canvas he'd abandoned in Holland. No salon in Paris would have appreciated that girl. Their small minds were content to ruin reputations and argue the latest trends and theories.

The girl.

The memory punched a hole in his chest like a lover gone astray. An outlandish sentiment. She'd existed only in his mind but he brought her to life. She was a rendering of passion he never shared with a true soulmate, a longing that consumed him until he created her. Was he wrong to leave her in the Frenchman's faraway house like a castoff lover, abandoned in a country populated by stiff-necked zealots with no appreciation of her beauty, lost forever to admiring eyes?

Outside, the wind rushed at the house, the tempest howling like a demented wolf seeking its mate. He nestled the flask in his lap and lowered his eyes, ashamed of his unkempt beard, the bristly thicket streaked with weeds of gray. A tear emerged and he stifled a sob. It was after midnight. Where was Gauguin?

He dropped the flask and wandered into Gauguin's bedroom, stopping before a small mirror mounted on the wall. The gas light reflected a stranger's face. Full lips, cracked and peeling, the wiry beard tangled with neglect. It was a face no woman could abide, much less lay claim to. If he erased the image...

Leaning toward the mirror, his fingers grazed the handle of Gauguin's straight razor. Later, he never recalled lifting the blade, or pinching the ear lobe between his thumb and forefinger. The man in the mirror slashed downward, the lower half of an ear appearing between his fingertips. Frightened by the torrent of blood, he screamed and staunched the flow with a dirty towel, and stumbling about the room, crashing into the few pieces of furniture. He tossed the saturated towel aside and pressed one of Gauguin's shirts against the mutilation, careening back to the other room. Gasping in pain, he collapsed in a chair and flung the grisly slice of cartilage on the table, the agony unbearable.

He fingered the bloody lump of flesh. A gift, he thought, for Gabrielle, the lovely 18-year old maid at his favorite brothel. His head swam but he forced away the waves of pain. He would then find Gauguin and show him this unassailable evidence of their friendship. With the shirt staunching the flow of blood, he ground his teeth and laid the offering on a sheet of newspaper. Using one hand he folded the page into a sodden red square and staggered into the night.

Chapter Twenty-Nine

Half-bottles of champagne and premium labels stocked the wood-paneled minibar in our room. Cocktail glasses and tall crystal flutes called my name from a sideboard. I removed a miniature bottle of Black Label and held it up to Kat who shook her head. Dressed in one of my dress shirts and panties, she stood at the window, consumed by her thoughts. I poured a straight-up scotch and dropped in a plush chair, closing my eyes. Our cocoon on the top floor sealed off frantic motorcycles and desperate sirens in the streets below, the white wonderland unsullied by noise and grime. If the rich lived like this, I vowed never again to criticize their indulgences. The only glitch was Viktor's money financed our sumptuous surroundings with no foreseeable return on his investment. I kicked off my loafers, pushing aside the consequences. Sunk in the chair, I stretched my sock feet onto the ottoman, uneasiness growing as I recalled Arby's hungry grin. We'd hit a wall and the prospect of failure rewound the image of bloody rebar.

"The damned painting could be anywhere," I said.

Kat ignored me and for an instant I regretted unearthing the photo, recalling Marguerite's grief as she gazed at the father who'd abandoned her. In our ignorance and haste, we'd unknowingly trampled her long-dead past.

"We saw the photo." Kat said as though reading my mind. "We will tell Viktor the painting is real."

I took a swallow of whiskey. "Great. Get him more excited about a painting we can't find. Maybe he'll forget about spending his money and let me move in with him."

"We'll go back to the shop tomorrow," she said. "The woman might recall something more important than the photograph."

She closed the drapes and I looked across the room at her body silhouetted against lights from Manhattan's skyline, my thoughts tumbling over one another as they'd done in the alley. I'd tried and failed to weave her into the odyssey where we found ourselves, my self-pity lumbering to a halt as I remembered the feel of her skin. Other than our lovemaking, Holland and France proved busts with the exception of what may have been a rotted easel. My friend at Northwestern University could perform an analysis of the paint chips, and if he confirmed their age, add weight to the theory that the unknown Van Gogh existed, but a few paint spatters got us no closer to finding the damn thing. We needed an ally, someone with insider knowledge and resources to point us in a new direction. Kat and I had played everything close to the vest, but we'd hit a wall. Dismayed, I halted in mid-groan, setting my drink on the glass-topped coffee table.

Jack McMinnis.

As a young man, Jack had worked for my father. He might shed new light on what we'd missed. Telling him about the painting was a risk but I'd run out of ideas.

"I have a friend here in New York," I said. "Jack McMinnis. He grew up here but he worked with my father when I was a boy. My father might have mentioned the painting when he was drunk. Maybe where he hid it." I picked up the glass, took a swallow, and weighed the risk. "McMinnis is rich with connections in the art world." Kat was frowning before I finished.

"What?" I asked. "You have a better idea? Listen, I don't consider Jack a competitor. I remember him disagreeing with my father about paintings. Even as a young man, Jack hated French Impressionism and that pissed off my father. Listening to them argue was part of my early education." Kat's expression did not change. "I'm just playing this by ear now. No disrespect to Van Gogh."

"You must not be so trusting," she said. "If this painting's as valuable as you claim, you cannot trust anyone, no matter what they profess. This kind of money…" She sat on the ottoman and touched my knee, her eyes searching mine with fierce intensity. After a moment she went to the mini bar and filled an Old-Fashioned glass with ice, bottled water, and a wedge of lime. She drank half and returned to where I sat, standing over me. "We are in this alone."

"No, we have Viktor and Arby as playmates."

She caressed the back of my neck. "Listen to me. You have no friends now. Not even your father's old ones. Viktor's interest makes this idea of yours all the more dangerous. Whoever else is searching for the painting will run out of patience at some point. If that happens, they will take better aim next time." She peered down at me. "You cannot involve this McMinnis. For all you know, this may get us killed."

She loomed over me like Nurse Ratchet, scrambling my thoughts. Frustration clouding my judgment. I stood and went to the window, staring down at cars and buses that scurried through the streets like disciplined beetles.

"You're the expert in killing." I said, regretting the words as they left my mouth.

She didn't reply. When I started to apologize she sat in my chair, gathering her arguments. Her bare legs across the ottoman she leaned her head back. There was so much about her I would never know. Nothing prepared me to cope with a woman who had lived with the threat of a bullet in the back of her head. But in the end, the painting belonged to Wes and me, and I'd make the decisions.

***

"Adam!"

Jack's voice on the phone was a balm from the past tinged with sporadic good memories. We chatted for a few minutes and he invited us for drinks at his townhouse. An hour later our taxi halted in the 1100 block of Park Avenue. Kat had said nothing during the ride and I let her indulge her suspicions. I paid the driver and peered up at the new high rise in one of the most expensive neighborhoods on earth.

A doorman admitted us into a lavish lobby where an unsmiling concierge phoned Jack after ascertaining we were not selling time shares or perpetual care plots. Behind what I took to be a bulletproof glass cage next to the elevator, a uniformed guard inspected us. Kat looked at the uniform and back to me. Young and hard-looking, the guard wasn't the typical retired cop making a few extra bucks. Conscious of our pistols, I hoped the building's security equipment didn't include a metal scanner. Bringing concealed guns into the building wouldn't be viewed like kids smuggling a half-pint into their parent's basement.

Jack's penthouse occupied the entire twenty-fifth floor. The mahogany-paneled elevator ascended like a soundless pneumatic tube with no sensation of movement. The doors opened onto a richly appointed hall of dark wood with more square footage than my condo. A solid door guarded one end of the hallway, a surveillance camera mounted above. I lifted a mermaid-shaped door knocker and let it fall twice. A swarthy reed-thin man with paper smooth skin wearing a white dinner jacket abruptly opened the door as though he anticipated my knock. He wore aviator dark glasses, his tone just condescending enough to be irritating.

"Mr. Barrow?" He frowned at Kat. "I am Kalil. Mr. McMinnis is expecting you in the solarium."

He took our coats without appearing to notice the weight in my pocket. Kat kept her purse. Our greeter ushered us into a spacious room that Warren Buffet might call home. Surrounding glass walls exposed a wraparound brick terrace offering a king's view of the city, the room easily accommodating a hundred guests. I surmised Jack's living quarters occupied the floor beneath us. Kalil resumed his station in the foyer and I almost didn't notice Jack until he moved away from a fireplace that dwarfed the elevator.

"Adam," he said, his hand outstretched before he reached us. "Too long, too long." He appeared little older than when I'd last seen him, still carrying his six feet without an extra pound. Intelligent eyes beamed at us from his angular face. A golden retriever rose from an Orvis dog bed beside the fireplace and padded beside Jack who stroked his head.

I gripped his hand and indicated Kat. "This is Katia Veranova, a friend."

Jack admired her with a knowing smile as though evaluating the merits of a thoroughbred race horse. "You've definitely come up in the world, son. No offense intended, Miss Veranova."

Kat measured him with a polite smile and I guessed she was estimating the cost of his white cashmere pullover and fashionably rumpled gray slacks. He led us past two Holbein originals on ornate easels, our footsteps muffled by Persian rugs that overlapped one another like sleeping manta rays. The fireplace blazed, four precisely-cut black rosewood logs giving off a flowery scent. A slight chill added a touch of the outdoors, the fire evidently the room's single source of heat. Jack was a bachelor but the furnishings allowed for a variety of tastes. Centered above the room, a twenty-foot round skylight focused moonlight on an immense onyx slab borne by stainless-steel supports, the polished surface adding a strange reflective warmth to the room. Kat and I sat on a leather sofa fit for a monarch as Jack settled in a matching chair, the retriever on its haunches beside him, inspecting us with soft intelligent eyes.

"And this is Goldilocks the Third," Jack said, scratching the dog's ears. "Helluva time housebreaking her but she's worth every minute."

"I like what you've done with the place," I said.

An indulgent smile. "Kalil, see what our guests would like to drink. Then take Goldie for her walk, if you will."

Kat requested water and I asked for scotch, guessing it would be top-end. I couldn't help but gape at our surroundings as Jack's man servant walked to the wet bar at the other end of the room. Jack leaned toward us.

"The dark glasses," he murmured. "Kalil has an unusual sensitivity to light. Quite the oddity for someone born in the Middle East. Twenty-five years ago, on one of my trips to Syria, I found him living on the street in Damascus, a filthy ten-year old. I guess I felt guilty about the money I was making and adopted him. Bribed the authorities, actually."

"Good for you," I said.

Kalil returned with the drinks, avoiding eye contact. Had he heard his history repeated to strangers? Clicking his fingers, he motioned to the dog that trotted to his side to be leashed and led out the door.

The 50-year-old scotch scarred my palate forever as I sat back and looked around the luxurious room. Life at the moment could be worse. "A high-rise Taj Mahal," I said. "I guess you're not running errands any longer."

Jack laughed. "Only if they're profitable, which brings us to your call. I hope you'll let me handle what remains of Sorokin's work and consider working for me."

I recalled his interest in Vasily's work and it occurred to me I never mentioned his employment offer to Kat. I avoided her eyes and took the plunge.

"I need your help with another matter."

Half an hour later I'd covered everything since Vasily's murder. Kat crossed her legs and let me talk as though listening to a confession in Lubyanka's depths. I left out Viktor's involvement, knowing it wouldn't make a strong selling point. Jack took a swallow of his drink and didn't interrupt, measuring us over the rim of his vodka and tonic with what I took to be amusement. I finished, aware of the hiss of burning logs. Jack centered his glass on a linen napkin

"Your father always told a good tale," he said. "And I remember the story about a huge Van Gogh. He told that one when he got truly hammered. I listened wide-eyed before I learned to separate fact from fiction. When he was in his cups, most of what he said was bullshit."

"Jack, I saw a photograph of the painting." Kat shot me a look.

He picked up the drink and frowned. "Do you have the photo?"

I glanced at Kat and hesitated. "No."

"A fake?" Jack asked.

"I don't think so."

"Can you get a copy of the photo?"

The question of the day. "It's very personal to the owner."

Jack held up his hand. "I won't pry," he said. "What are you planning to do now?"

"You know the market, Jack. People and resources we might have overlooked. Frankly, I'm out of ideas."

Jack settled back. "Well, you've joined a big club. Chasing lost masterpieces is a hobby with some people, but the world's full of kooks." He smiled at Kat. "Present company excepted, of course. But I'll admit an occasional piece shows up in places that would baffle Sherlock Holmes. Closets, storage lockers, garage sales, attics. If your painting exists, it could be rotting under someone's mattress."

"This just isn't just a painting, Jack. We're talking about a Van Gogh."

Jack gave a half-smile. "Crazy bastard. Splattered color everywhere. You'd have thought he owned a paint factory."

"I know you don't like him but there might be a lost Van Gogh out there."

He gave me a sharp look. "Based on a Robert Barrow drunken story and two old letters? I don't think so."

"My father was specific."

"Adam, your father should have worked for Disney or Spielberg. You never heard half the tales I listened to. Gordon's gin created fantasies both directors would have loved. He was a great guy in many ways, but a windfall was always around the next curve. Problem was, he never chased anything in a straight line. Too easy to devise a new scheme and take shortcuts at someone's expense, including mine. That's why I left him."

I'd heard the story before. Who could blame Jack if he took me for my father's son? I studied my drink and mentally shrugged. Jack had been worth a try. The dazzling room confirmed he dealt in certainties, not pipedreams. Contacting him was a long shot and I was back at square one with Viktor breathing down my neck.

Jack read my disappointment and softened his features. "Look, I'll ask around. A few discreet questions. See if anyone's heard of your missing Van Gogh."

"I'd appreciate it," I said, recognizing his courtesy as sympathy, knowing his offer emanated from our shared past. "Probably another of dad's daydreams."

He softly clapped his hands together. "Okay, enough about this mysterious Van Gogh. I can help you in a more rational fashion. If you'll let me broker Sorokin's paintings, we both make some money. I can get top dollar, and I'll give you 75 percent of the gross if that helps you. I have clients who'll appreciate his work. Maybe then we can talk about an arrangement to work together."

Overwhelmed, I downed my drink to cover my emotions. Despite Kat's wariness, old friends increase their value over time like fine wine. The Arthur Jennings types fell into the cardboard box variety. "You sure you want to do that?"

"I'm serious about both. I'll email the address where to ship the paintings. And if anything pops up on your Van Gogh, I'll call you. Just give me a shot if the damn thing surfaces."

We shook hands and Kalil let us out. In the elevator, Kat punched a button and halted us on the third-floor. I opened my mouth but she placed her finger against her lips and raised her eyes to the security camera buried in the elevator ceiling. The door opened and I followed her into a hall of doors. Another camera in the hall slowly swept its length. She pulled me beneath the swiveling glass eye, concealing us.

"Give me your weapon," she said.

I handed her my pistol and she ejected the magazine with a sharp click. The magazine was empty.

"Never leave your weapon with a stranger," she said.

"I told you. I've known Jack my whole life."

"And the Arab? You know him too?" She inserted the empty magazine back into the pistol grip and returned the pistol to me. "He's a bodyguard, Adam. Next time, keep the coat with you."

My crash course in KGB efficiency completed, I shut up and we descended to the lobby as I rethought my decision at bringing Jack into the game. We exited the elevator and Kat manufactured a dazzling smile for the young guard who relaxed his grimace and beamed at her.

In the street, we found myself back in the realm of the mundane. I'd come away from Jack's with nothing. I raised my face to sunlight reflecting off McMinnis' windows at the top of the building, an unattainable domain and one more dead-end.

Chapter Thirty

The Brighton Beach bar squatted two blocks from Lower New York Bay, having long ago surrendered its glory days, pride of ownership traded for dirt and trash flanking the front door. A fly-specked window framed a tired Budweiser sign, the stuttering neon enticing locals who cared nothing about the mislaid ambiance of Dominic's Bar and Grill.

Unshaven, clad in jeans and a denim work jacket, the Contractor hunched at the far end of the bar, a beer bottle beside his aluminum hard hat. He hated beer, but ordering a Manhattan would have tempted closer scrutiny, jogging memories if the meeting went south. He cradled the sweating beer bottle as though it was his only friend and endured the malt's bitterness.

Around him, tabletop jukeboxes and a beer-sodden wooden floor echoed his college days before he pursued finer things without the burden of study and tuition. He'd been fortunate since he walked away; no former college chums stopped him on the street to inquire about his post-campus employment.

He studied his reflection in the bar mirror. The jacket scratched his neck and reeked of fried food and someone else's sweat but he gladly endured the stink, a badge of honor to his way of thinking, one that separated him from competitors whose ego overrode professionalism. After a cursory glance from the regulars, he'd achieved invisibility, a construction worker hunched over a brew before heading home to the wife and kids. Removing the ornate box from his jacket pocket, he breathed in a dollop, the snuff's bite whetting his thirst.

A rush of cold air swept paper napkins and coasters off the bar. A well-dressed figure wearing leather gloves, an overcoat, and flat Kangol cap hesitated in the open door, the new arrival drawing curses and shouts. The man closed the door and walked past the wall booths, ignoring the glares. Everyone forgot about him when he took a seat two stools away from the Contractor. Pulling off the gloves, he ordered a rye on the rocks and studied his reflection in the bar mirror missing much of its original silvering. Rolling the ice cubes in his drink he waited until the bartender shuffled away.

"I told you we were never to meet," he muttered without moving his head.

The Contractor glanced in the mirror, curious about the employer he'd never seen. Staring back at him was a face without worry or want, typical of those who wanted unpleasant problems to disappear.

"This is a working-class neighborhood," the Contractor said. "You think anyone cares who you are?"

"Still too much risk," the man said.

The Contractor waggled his beer bottle. "Exceptions to every rule."

His employer grunted, his eyes roaming up and down the bar. "Nice place you picked. The cabbie didn't stick around."

"You prefer the Four Seasons where everyone knows you?"

"We agreed never to meet face-to-face."

Asshole, the Contractor thought. Too much money and too many pretensions of superiority generated cloak and dagger precautions. How satisfying would it be to forget the money and off him right here, he thought? In front of God and everybody. Walk out the door while everyone stared at the body on the floor. The cops would get nothing from the crowd who never really looked twice at a working man. He shoved the fantasy back in its box.

"As they say, rules are made to be ignored. You want to bitch or know what I found?"

"So, tell me what's so important that you broke my rule."

"I needed to give you something in person." The Contractor took a swallow of beer and dried the bar with a paper napkin. He waited until the bartender began an argument with a drunk at the far end of the bar and shoved a business envelope to his employer.

The man made no move to pick it up. "You could've mailed that to me."

"I went to too much trouble for some post office moron to lose it."

"Whatever you have better be worth the trip to this shithole."

"If you don't want it…"

His employer ran a finger along the rim of his glass. "What did you find?"

"Your dreams."

The Contractor almost enjoyed the man's clandestine crap. Secret agents swapping state secrets. Nothing wrong with being careful, but most clients

170 *The Last Van Gogh*

weren't so cautious if they got what they wanted. "You'll find this worth the ride down here."

The man picked up the envelope and removed the photograph.

"Is that what you envisioned?" the Contractor asked.

"Where'd you get this?"

"A delightful lady made me a gift of it."

Unable to take his eyes from the photo, the man could only stare. "A gift?"

"Of sorts."

"Is she aware of what this represents?"

"She isn't aware of anything now," the Contractor said. "Aren't you going to congratulate me?"

The man's eyes locked on the photo. The painting *was* enormous, he thought, far larger than he dared believe. Proof that every expense was worth the risk. Even lacking color, the small black and white image was astounding. Wavering wheat and sunlight enveloped a young woman who stared at the viewer from the enormous canvas. Van Gogh had outdone himself, raging against the huge swath of canvas to render a work of unimaginable beauty and proportions. Regaining control, he reverently returned the photo to the envelope and slipped it in his coat pocket. He moved onto the stool next to the Contractor.

"What about Barrow and the woman?"

"I followed them and found your photo."

"Did they see it?"

"I have no idea. The lady wasn't cooperative in answering my questions."

The man bit his lower lip and frowned.

Enjoying his employer's discomfort, the Contractor signaled the bartender. "This calls for another beer."

Remaining silent as the barkeep twisted the cap off his companion's beer, the man gently patted the envelope inside his coat and stared into his drink, ignoring the killer beside him. As effective as his hireling had proven, the arrogant bastard appreciated nothing about art or the magnitude of what they were chasing. His kind were sharp blades, nothing more. He rolled the whiskey glass between his fingertips and made a decision. Reaching inside his coat he returned the envelope.

"Make a copy," he said. "No, two copies. Send one to Barrow. So far, he's found nothing that helps us. The photo will keep him looking. I'll give the other to a lady friend at the League. She needs to know I'm getting close."

"A few hours in some out of the way place and I'll convince Barrow to move faster," the Contractor said.

"I told you. I can't take those kinds of risks."

The Contractor shrugged and returned the envelope to his pocket, patting it. "One more thing. The photo cost an old woman her life. I think an additional payment is needed to soothe my brittle conscience."

They looked at one another in the mirror until his employer turned away. Killing the old woman didn't concern the Contractor but it might produce more money. The more he stared in the smudged mirror, the more the Contractor hated every bastard who employed him to keep blood off their soft hands. But then again, they possessed a singular advantage—they paid better than branch banks and convenience store robberies.

"All right, there'll be a bonus," his employer said.

Neither looked away until the Contractor broke the impasse. "You look as though you're seeing someone beneath you. Remember, you hired me"

"Don't remind me."

"You need damaged goods like me. If you see something you don't like, live with the fact I perform a service you need." The jukebox clicked and Bobby Darrin sang about a man with a knife.

His employer finished his drink and stood. "The photograph means nothing. I want the fucking painting."

He walked out and the Contractor drummed his fingers on the bar, looking at the door. Definitely a thousand horsepower asshole, he thought. In all probability, the painting meant little more than an opportunity to get his name in the papers and ensure invites to uptown parties thrown by his peers. The Van Gogh was a rare bauble, unavailable to the unwashed masses. His employer would never sell it if he got his hands on it. Public acclaim was a mirror to preen for the benefit of other rich morons. The man already had all the money he would ever need. To own something to the exclusion of others; that was what mattered. The Contractor frowned and fidgeted with the bottle, regretting he the job required him to deal with those who considered themselves above him.

The bartender appeared, a chewed red swizzle stick between his teeth. "Another one, chief?"

The Contractor looked up at the slovenly man who would give a city health inspector serious pause.

"Chief?"

The man blanched. "No offense, mister. I thought you might be one of them Indians what works high steel on new skyscrapers. Hell, no way you'd get me up on one of those things. I ain't akin to heights myself."

The Contractor studied his bottle. No profit in making a scene that would be remembered later. If the ignorant bastard thought he was an Indian, all the better. He finished the beer and beckoned to the bartender closer with a crooked finger and lowered his voice

"I'm from Transylvania, not Oklahoma. That mean anything to a dumb shit like you?"

The man swallowed and shook head.

"You ever hear of Dracula?"

The bartender gave a sickly grin. "Sure," he said, hoping the customer at the end of the bar would signal him for a refill. "I seen all the Bella Lugosi movies when I was a kid."

"The real Dracula was a great uncle of mine. But it's daylight and I'm sitting here plain as day. Vampires don't come out in the daylight, but you see me, right?"

"Sure, mister, I see you just fine. I didn't mean nothing."

"You know, a lot of people don't know my people still drink blood."

The man paled and the Contractor laughed as he pushed off the stool and dropped a few bills beside the bottle. Leaning over the bar he patted the man's cheek.

"But hey, not today. Today, I was thirsty for a beer."

Chapter Thirty-One

The ivory-white telephone refused to shut up. Phones had developed the nasty habit of waking me and I rolled away, deciding to let Kat answer it until her hair dryer's howl returned me to reality. I picked up and heard Sally's voice, having forgotten I told her where we were staying.

"Adam?"

"Yeah."

"I received a phone call this morning from someone named Phillip Dansby." she said.

Phillip Dansby. Another phantom from my father's past.

"Very British or whatever they call themselves nowadays," she continued. "Anyway, he said you were old friends and heard you were in New York. He wants you to call him. I told him I'd contact you." When I said nothing, she hesitated and said, "I told him where you're staying. He was persuasive." She giggled. "Charming, actually. Did I screw up telling him where you were staying?"

I let her dangle for a few seconds in the noose she'd created. "It's okay. I know him. Give me his number."

I wrote down the local number and Sally updated me on the gallery I'd deserted. Viktor had been good as his word and sent buyers, so we were covering the rent. Wes hadn't missed a day. She said he was a quick study and gained several pounds, reading books on contemporary realism. If nothing else, Barbara owed me a modicum of forgiveness for working a minor miracle.

After I hung up. I started to dial Dansby and stopped. The Van Gogh was bringing out the big guns—if that was the reason for Dansby's call. I needed time to think about the august Phillip Dansby, late of Her Majesty's armed forces. Now living in New York, Dansby could buy and sell Jack McMinnis.

I got up and padded to the window. Opening the drapes, I stared at the skyscraper across the street until I realized I was naked. Modesty restored with a hotel robe, I was thinking about Sally's call when Kat walked from the bath, combing her hair, dressed in an identical white terry cloth robe.

"Who was on the phone?"

"You heard it over your chainsaw?"

"A morning requirement."

"Sally called to give me an update. Said the gallery's still intact, and Phillip Dansby tried to reach me."

"Should I recognize the name?" she asked.

"Not unless you subscribe to Sotheby catalogs, *The Economist*, and *Vanity Fair*."

"One of your American Renaissance Men?"

"An unbelievably wealthy one," I said, "but with a checkered history."

"And you know him."

"Another friend of my father. Wes and I knew him long before he bid on several islands and financed a space exploration company."

"You're joking."

"I'm not. Kings and presidents call him when they run out of money."

She stopped combing her hair. "The Van Gogh?"

"That's my guess."

"We should put an ad in the paper," she said. "Let everyone know what we're doing."

I ignored her. "God knows how he found out, but there's little in the realm of the art world that escapes him. He has the world's largest private repository of Impressionist Art. He brokers high-end work and keeps the best pieces for himself."

"You want to involve this man?"

"My guess is he's already involved whether we like it or not."

"You said a checkered history."

"Despite his public persona, rumor says he's something other than your typical hard-driving billionaire. In all probability, the stories are fueled by his competition, but several skirmishes made the grocery store tabloids. A few other incidents attracted the police, but he's never seen the inside of a courtroom."

"Who is he?" Kat asks.

I plopped in a chair, rubbing the bridge of my nose as I recalled his flamboyant history. "Major Phillip Dansby, formerly of Her Majesty's Coldstream

Guards. From what I remember, educated at Harrow and Sandhurst, then recruited by the SAS. He rose quickly through the ranks before he resigned his commission under a shadow. Since then, he's been involved in a number of art-related scandals. He broke away from my father years ago and I lost track of him."

"But he remembers you?"

I sighed and told her the rest of Dansby's known history. "Several years ago, he fell out with his partner. The man died two days later. A hit-and-run accident. No one was arrested. Before that, a former partner disappeared and was believed drowned, a suicide. Either he was involved with people who enjoyed very bad luck or he's not someone to cross."

Kat cocked her head and resumed combing her hair. "He sounds like Viktor."

"He was one of the few who visited my father during his last days, I'll give him that. He could be an ally or enemy."

She walked to the window, distracted by another wild card I'd tossed on our table. "And you're going to contact him?"

"I think he found me."

"You can call him later. We skipped breakfast and I'm hungry." She walked toward the bathroom. "Then we'll go see Madame Bouchet again."

I stepped in front of her and wrapped my arms around her waist, inhaling the scent of expensive soap and shampoo. Beneath the robe her bare breasts pressed against me. I pulled her closer. "I've got a better idea. Let's put an edge on our appetites."

She pulled back and studied me for a long moment. Was she angry at my cavalier attitude about Dansby? Two seconds later, her hesitancy ceased to matter as she stepped out of my embrace and let the robe fall to the floor. Viktor's clock was ticking but breakfast had just turned into a late lunch.

***

As we dressed, Kat flipped on the TV. I donned my best slacks, a button-down white shirt, and new navy blazer, completing my disguise as a respectable art dealer. At the least my attire wouldn't embarrass me if we bumped into Henry Kissinger in the lobby. I asked for Kat's opinion but she held up her hand, staring at the TV. A somber female reporter intoned a funereal announcement that surprised few New Yorkers anesthetized by daily mayhem.

"... was found this morning by a concerned neighbor who told police she heard the victim's cat meowing loudly for the second straight day. Police found the apartment empty but later discovered the elderly woman's body in her antique shop. She had been shot once but police said there were no signs of a robbery. Marguerite Bouchet was owner of European Treasures, a store on Second Avenue, and police are baffled about the motive."

Kat clicked off the set.

"Poor woman," I said.

"Too much of a coincidence."

A long-dead Dutch artist was proving a deadly ghost. Money aside, could the painting make up for lost lives and a lifetime of wrongdoing by my father? Did his approaching death frighten him into a lucid moment, leading me from a gory Chicago basement to Amsterdam and Paris, and now to an iconic hotel in the heart of New York? Vasily, the bludgeoned corpse beneath Viktor's house, and now Marguerite Bouchet. Three people dead for an expanse of old canvas swathed in oils. No picture was worth the price.

"You wanna bet the photo's gone?" I asked.

She considered the blank screen. "No way to know," she said, "but we can't get swept up in a police investigation."

We finished dressing and headed downstairs.

***

After lunch, we had coffee in the hotel bar, the lounge emblazoned with a black and white tile floor that complemented the decor. We were discussing Bouchet's murder when a tall man in his mid-sixties strode toward our table. Kat pulled her purse onto her lap and slipped her hand inside.

Impeccably dressed in a pin-striped black suit, Phillip Dansby wore a Coldstream navy and burgundy tie. His precisely trimmed moustache matched meticulously cropped gray hair. Even with the passing years, he looked more than fit to mount guard outside Buckingham Palace.

"Adam Barrow, it's been a long while," he said without offering his hand. He swept his arm around Baccarat's sumptuous bar. "Very chic but it's not Claridge's in London, is it? Still, you've come up in the world, dear boy."

"Phillip." I absently wondered if he was still entitled to wear the regimental tie. I introduced Kat and he joined us without an invitation. He grinned approvingly at Kat as he pulled a chair to our table and squinted at me, his head tilted back.

"Last time I enjoyed your company was that garish July Fourth party at your little house above Santa Monica," he said. "You were just a lad when I tried to explain the difference between a rebellion and a revolution to your father." He laughed. "As usual, old boy was too potted to see the distinction, but wasn't he always?"

I reined my anger, fighting off the feeling he belonged in the extravagant hotel, while I was an imposter.

"What do you want, Phillip?"

He ignored me and appraised Kat. "And your name, my dear?"

I leaned forward. "Phillip?"

"Don't be a boor, Adam," he said, his expression hardening. "I was only interested in your lovely companion's name. I need to discuss a business matter and your gallery staff was most helpful in locating you."

"Sally's too free with information."

He grinned at Kat. "It's the accent, dear boy. It proves quite irresistible in so many instances."

"I'm impressed." I never bought his manufactured charm, and money hadn't softened his conceit. Assuming a contrite look, he smiled at me.

"Touched a soft spot, did I? My apologies."

His tight-lipped smile annoyed me and I wondered if it was apparent Kat and I had made love an hour earlier. "You've never been one to renew old acquaintances."

"Depends on who they are, doesn't it?" Dansby's flourishes were overdone to the point of yelling, 'Look at me, I'm British.' He swiped at his lapel with the back of his hand as though the material offended him. "Even you must admit Robert Barrow drank himself into oblivion, and I understand your brother stumbled after him. You were the smarter one, running away like you did."

I bristled at the truth. "You only contacted my father once after he became ill."

"No, and I regret that to some degree," Dansby said. "I avoided a few petty schemes he brought to my attention. Your father always played small, I'm afraid.

Some men are cursed with less than mediocrity."

"What do you want? You didn't come here to reminisce over my father's failings."

"Straight to matters, is it?" The fabricated smile again. "So unlike your father who would have cheated the Pope out of his robe given half a chance. " He reached across the table and patted my forearm in a fatherly manner before settling back in his chair before he answered my question.

"The Van Gogh, my boy, the Van Gogh."

I pulled away my arm. I didn't need another player in the game. He sensed my anger and softened his demeanor.

"Would you share a cup of coffee with me as an apology for this little confrontation?" Before I could reply, he snapped his fingers at a passing waiter and ordered before turning back to Kat. "Note how well I've assimilated, my dear. The bean has replaced the leaf."

Coffee arrived in an ornamental carafe and he ordered the server to refill our cups, pouring half a cup for himself, filling the remainder with Dover cream. "I prefer the French variation," he said, topping his cup himself. "Cafe au lait. I suspect my former brothers-in-arms would consider me a traitor for such heresy. Banish me from the barracks or some such rot." For the briefest moment, his face took on a wistful reflection. He recovered and inspected Kat with a practiced eye.

"How do they prefer their coffee in Moscow, Miss… Veranova, is it?"

Kat had not uttered a word since he joined us. No name, not a word. Dansby's network reached farther than I'd imagined.

"Do give my regards to the charming Viktor Krushenko," he said to her. "Such a refined gentleman of the world."

Kat didn't reply and Dansby sat back, tapping his spoon on the white linen tablecloth, producing a brown smudge as he measured her reaction. "No need to look so shocked, my dear. I have Russian businessmen and officials as friends. Some are exceptionally well-informed, but your secret's safe with me. There's little meaningful money in such mundane affairs." He was enjoying himself, flaunting his control over the lives of lesser beings.

"I have sources in the Netherlands. People who keep me abreast of rumors concerning rare works on art. A few well-placed American dollars pays handsome dividends. One confidant tells me your Van Gogh's quite large. Just how large, may I ask?"

He knew and was definitely in the hunt now. No use denying the obvious. I pointed at the mirror behind the bar. "Twice that size, possibly larger."

His eyes shone. "Oh my."

When Kat and I remained silent, Dansby drummed his coffee spoon on the table like a metronome. "I hope this isn't another of your father's castles in the sky. Shame to see you carry on a disreputable family tradition." He continued tapping the spoon and looked at me with pity and amusement. "Whatever you think of me, I can help you if this painting exists."

Kat took the spoon from his fingers and spoke for the first time. "Blood in the water, Captain Dansby?"

"Major, my dear. Retired."

"Of course."

Dansby retrieved the spoon and tossed it onto his saucer. "I do apologize for sounding presumptuous, but I have resources beyond your imagination. You would find my help most useful."

"And if we don't need your help?" I said, tired of his cat and mouse charade.

He shrugged and gave a theatrical sigh, sipping his milky concoction. "Oh well, in that case, it seems I've become the bore." He waved his hand as though the matter was already forgotten.

"Let me make it up to you," he said. "I'm hosting a little soiree at the Plaza tonight. A fund-raising gala for autistic tots. Black tie, of course. I've assembled the most delightful collection of wines to make it endurable." He brushed a nonexistent crumb from his knee. "You'd have no obligation to stay for the dreary speeches. God knows I won't, even though I'm sponsoring the damn thing. Privilege of rank and all that." He unabashedly stared at Kat. "And you, my dear, you would be ravishing in the right dress. I keep an open account at a marvelous boutique a few blocks from where we're sitting. The latest Oscar De La Renta would be perfect, I think."

"We don't—" I began, but Kat cut me off.

"We'd be delighted, Major. I haven't done any shopping since we've been in New York."

"Splendid." Dansby removed a slender gold fountain pen from his suit coat and wrote down the shop's address on a card bearing his name in thin script. "All settled then. I'll call and tell them to expect you."

"And I suppose I'll have to rent a tux for your gala?"

"Nonsense," Dansby pulled back his head and measured me. "Size 40 regular, I would think. I'll have my man at your room within the hour. Have you tip-top before six."

"You assume a lot," I said.

"My prerogative as your evening's host." He smiled at Kat again. "I do hope you'll both join us, Miss Veranova." He shook my hand, bowed to Kat, and walked away. We stared after him and Kat returned her purse to the floor.

"He is Viktor in better clothes," she said.

"But he speaks better English," I teased, "and you accepted his offer of a dress."

Kat watched Dansby stride through the lobby. "Of course."

"Stay close to your enemies?"

"You are learning," she said. "It will be an expensive invitation for Major Dansby."

I pushed my jealousy aside, time slipping away from us. "I hope the bastard remembers my tux."

***

"Hello, Phillip."

Still thinking about the Van Gogh and Kat's legs, Dansby halted in mid-stride. The seated figure in Baccarat's lobby smiled up at him and a name surfaced.

"Brezenkov," he said without restraining his disdain. "What a pleasant surprise."

Tasso crushed out his American cigarette in a cut glass ashtray and rose to shake Dansby's hand. "It is a pleasure once again," he said, his English heavily weighted. "What has it been? Three years? The World Trade Conference in Boston, I think."

Dansby measured the bearded man's factory assembled suit and polyester tie. Was it the same suit the Russian had worn at the Harvard symposium? His own French cuff shirt from Chang's cost more than the man's entire ensemble, including the scuffed cheap shoes. Dansby recalled they'd shared a dinner table at the conference. Afterward, the Russian had offered a drink in the faculty lounge and Dansby had accepted out of curiosity. Ten minutes into the excellent malt, he knew he wasn't conversing with an obtuse economics consultant. Decades of dealing with the Russians taught him the difference between a business discussion and a KGB interview, the questions and answers going into Tasso's memory bank for later dissection and usefulness. Was Dansby perhaps a fellow traveler? Blackmail candidate? Bribable idiot? Nothing had come of the conversation and he'd forgotten about the Russian until today.

"I would very much appreciate a private talk with you," Tasso said. "In a more quiet setting."

"Not again," Dansby said. He remembered the clumsy attempt to recruit him in Boston, Bresenkov subtle as Howard Stern. He shifted his weight and stole a glance into the lounge where Adam and Kat were finishing their coffee. Two Russians in one day was a coincidence, and he long ago discarded the fallacy of coincidences where money and Russians were concerned. Still, it was unlikely Brezenkov or whatever his name might be, was connected to the Van Gogh. Dansby shot a cuff and looked pointedly at his Rolex.

"It's good to see you again," he said, "but I'm late just now. Maybe next time you're in New York."

Tasso manufactured a smile intended to elicit sympathy. "I need a favor."

"Same objective as before, Anatoli?" Dansby asked, but something in the Russian's tone prevented his walking away.

"I assure you it's quite different. It's personal this time."

Dansby sighed. "Are you staying here?"

"Here?" Tasso waved a dismissive hand around the lobby. "You must believe my country holds me in high regard."

Dansby realized they could be in the lens of American cameras, but he'd been the CIA's target more than once. Russian money flowed freely for those who knew where to look and Brezenkov might represent a fresh pipeline. He caught the Russian glancing into the bar where Kat and Adam were rising but let it go. He could spare the sad face an hour and he had to eat dinner somewhere.

"Meet me tomorrow night at Rinaldi's. Seven o'clock," he said. "The concierge can give you the address. I'll buy the drinks this time. But if you play recruiting sergeant again, I'll walk out and stick you with the bill which I doubt your state security forces will approve."

Chapter Thirty-Two

Kat and I stepped from the limousine Dansby sent to collect us. Above us, the Plaza Hotel's formidable entrance glowed in the beams of two searchlights. Kat wore a fitted dress, an ankle-length sheath of gold lamé that exposed her elegant back in a deep V past the lower regions of her spine. Despite five-inch heels, she floated up the stone steps beneath the overhead array of fluttering flags as though she owned the building, her face unreadable as befitted a countess or bored socialite. She ignored the appraisals and kept her eyes straight ahead as the admiring doorman ushered us into the ostentatious foyer.

I guessed the Hollywood spotlights were Dansby's contribution to the evening's festivities. The venerable old landmark needed no glitzy trappings to enhance its reputation, the staid edifice a reincarnation of Vienna in the early 1900's, a gilded New York icon for old and new money. Fronting South Central Park, the hotel formed the perfect stage for Kat who collected more stares.

"Your friend must enjoy quite a reputation," she murmured as we traversed the baroque lobby. "They kept the shop open for me past closing time. I heard the shop girls in the back arguing whether to treat me like royalty or a concubine."

I ran my eyes over her and wondered how she handled such things when Viktor paid the bills. "Whatever you endured, you've made my day," I said, running my hand over her bare back.

The sound of an orchestra filtered into the foyer decorated with huge sprays of fresh flowers. A man in white tie and tails indicated two long tables flanking massive doors guarding the ballroom. Our names were checked off a list by two blue-haired matrons who ignored me and measured Kat's unabashed display of flesh. Their disapproval clearly on display, the sentries granted us admittance with tight smiles.

Inside the Grand Ballroom the crowd spelled money and privilege. Recessed arches along the walls framed exotic gowns among the sea of black tuxedos, the dance floor a coral reef of color in motion. At the far end an orchestra played 'In the Mood,' band members dressed in wide-lapelled suits reminiscent of the 1940's. Trombone in hand, a smiling Glenn Miller lookalike directed the band, smiling at the dancers. Time discovered a way to backslide for serious old money in the room, but I figured even the ultra-wealthy deserved a shot at reliving their youth. Several celebrities and well-known television faces walked past us, a former UN ambassador escorting an adoring female news anchor firmly chained to his arm.

"Tell me again why we're subjecting ourselves to this," I muttered to Kat.

"A reconnaissance," she said lightly. "Plus, I get to play dress-up."

"You're becoming Americanized."

She graced me with a dazzling smile. "Isn't that a good thing?"

No one wasted a glance on me. Men forgot the drinks in their hands as she swept by, but my anonymity evaporated when Dansby broke away from a group and headed toward us. His fitted tux a male model exhibit, he halted a few steps from Kat and spread his arms, admiring her from heels to hair. Conversation around us dropped off a cliff as Dansby and Kat captured center stage.

"Ravishing, just as I imagined," he boomed. "Your taste is exquisite as I knew it would be." Disregarding inquisitive faces around us, he swept aside her river of black hair and leaned closer to one ear. "So much better than TSUM in Red Square, wouldn't you agree?"

Kat gave a wan smile as I lifted two champagne flutes from a passing tray and stepped closer to Dansby. "Whatever you may know, Phillip, this is not a subject for the rest of the room."

He clasped my arm like an old Harrow chum. "You're right, of course. No more allusions to the past, including yours and mine, dear boy." He graced those around us with a smile, nodding at people who caught his eye. "Here comes another old acquaintance," he said quietly, lifting his chin at Jack McMinnis who was making his way through the crowd.

"Well, you do find your way around," Jack said, shaking hands as he appraised Kat. "Miss Veranova, I had no idea you could light up an entire ballroom. You're a fortunate man, Adam."

"You've met?" Dansby said with feigned surprise.

"Only recently," Kat replied, smiling at Jack.

"I found them in the bar at Baccarat this afternoon," Dansby said. "Invited them to join us at this dreary affair."

I looked at Kat. "My father collected quite a menagerie of friends."

Dansby laughed and McMinnis polished off his drink. "Henchmen is a better description," Dansby said. "The old fraud had better taste in art than friends. No offense, Adam."

I restrained the impulse to defend Robert Everham Barrow. Whatever the evening's outcome, we might discover my father created the Van Gogh tale as an afternoon's amusement to spice up a dull day. A good laugh after dropping a little peyote washed down by a gin and tonic. A cosmic joke designed to punch holes in the lives of those closest to him. But I'd handled the easel and seen the photograph. There was something out there, dammit.

"Adam's on his way up," McMinnis said to Dansby. "An art dealer with a gallery in Chicago."

"I know," Dansby said as he surveyed the ballroom with thinly disguised contempt. "He's come to the right place to hawk his wares if he's so inclined. Crème de la crème of New York money. Tons of disposable income and guilty consciences with emphasis on the latter." He turned to McMinnis, their mutual dislike palpable. "I imagine your finer sensibilities compels you to attend these affairs."

"We little people do what we can to save the world," McMinnis replied.

Both men appeared wound too tightly for the alcohol-fueled gala, their mutual animosity obvious to anyone who looked closely. I wondered how much each man knew about the elephant lurking in the room and accepted I had little control over whatever transpired during the evening. A resurrected Vincent Van Gogh might as well have stood beside all of us, ogling the glittering crowd.

The band swung into 'Moonlight Serenade' and I grabbed Kat's hand. "I'll leave you two to sort out the problems of too much money."

I handed Dansby our drinks and pulled Kat onto the dance floor. She slipped into my arms and I was surprised to discover I was the better dancer. Moscow Central's charm school for assassins had failed to include ballroom dancing in its curriculum. She might possess deadly street smarts, but I trumped her on the dance floor. It was a long set and she slowly moved more gracefully, following my lead. My right hand stroked her exposed back and she tilted up her face. I kissed her, guessing it was a scandalous display in such company, but who the hell cared? I'd likely never see anyone in the crowd again unless my luck continued downhill.

The song ended and we started off the dance floor when Dansby slipped his arm around Kat's waist as the band launched into 'String of Pearls.' "Host's prerogative and all that," he said, stepping between us. He beamed at Kat. "As we said in more civilized times, may I have this dance, m'lady?"

Kat took his hand and smiled at me. "Go get another drink, Adam. I'm sure the Major's a wonderful dancer." She raised her arms toward him and I stepped away. Moving into the crush of dancers, Dansby moved without effort to the quicker beat, guiding Kat across the dance floor as though partners in past lives. She laughed at something Dansby said, and I wondered where she managed to conceal the PPK beneath the dress.

I made my way to the bar where McMinnis joined me and ordered a drink.

"Are you as bored as I am?" he asked, looking around. "I'm a regular at these things as it is, but two of my board members at the Animal Protection League trapped me into this one." He sipped his drink. "Goldilocks said I owed it to them."

"Then you had no choice."

Jack followed my eyes to the dance floor. "Playing both ends against the middle?" he asked, studying Kat and Dansby.

No believable lie popped into my mind. "Dansby somehow found out about the painting."

"Son of a bitch does have his contacts. You trust him?"

"God, no."

"Watch yourself. He's got more lines in the water than a charter boat captain." Jack tossed back his drink and ordered another. "Lots of people regret dealing with that Limey fraud." An older man beside him turned with a frown and started to speak until McMinnis placed his drink on the bar and faced him. Raised on the streets, the expensive tuxedo failed to temper Jack's Irish genes and the man walked away.

"Kat only just met Dansby and she called him a bastard," I said as his eyes followed the man.

"Smart girl."

On the ballroom floor, she gave no evidence of her earlier judgment. She swung her hair and laughed at something Dansby whispered to her. His lips lingered close to her ear as he fingered one of the spaghetti straps of her dress. I fought off the urge to push through the crowd. I'd look churlish if I cut in. She could take care of herself and I hoped the dance produced something other than his fingerprints on her back. She moved effortlessly in his arms and when the music ended, he dipped her to a smattering of applause. I lifted a finger at a waiter for another champagne, surprised at my jealousy.

Dansby and Kat remained at the crowd's edge, two brilliant koi in a flow of river carp. engaged in conversation as Jack lowered his voice.

"I made a few calls," he said, eying them, "No one's heard anything about a Van Gogh. But you may be on to something for all I know. The two letters you mentioned are a fact, right?" He tossed back his drink and stared at Dansby. "If you find it, it'll knock certain people on their ass."

"That's what Wes is hoping."

The fact that I stood at the epicenter of New York's elite, disguised as one of them, confirmed that it wasn't only Wes who wanted to find the painting. And Phillip Dansby hadn't invited us to his soiree out of fondness for me or my father. Someone had killed Vasily by mistake, and there was a good chance Marguerite Bouchet was murdered by same someone who believed the painting was real. Quarter of a billion dollars provides a warehouse of motive.

Jack placed his glass on the bar and winked at me. He walked to the dance floor and asked Kat for the next dance. Disappointed he'd beaten me to her, I watched as McMinnis took her in his arms. Jealousy was a new sensation after my string of round heels and one-night stands. But then, I'd always been sort of stingy.

Later, I danced with Kat and caught her looking over my shoulder at Dansby and McMinnis. Vaults of cash held more appeal than me at the moment. I might be the only man in the room who slept with her, but the knowledge offered little consolation. The bubbly kicked in and I felt like an impoverished relative asked to escort a wealthy cousin to the cotillion.

"See anything you like?" I said.

She leaned her head on my chest without replying. The dance ended and I grabbed another champagne flute. To hell with it all, I thought. I shoved my way through the crowd with Kat in tow and bid Dansby an abrupt goodnight. McMinnis had slipped away and I guessed his civility extended a limited distance toward his more famous rival.

At the hotel entrance the doorman directed us to the limousine Dansby had reserved for us, the driver refusing the tip I proffered. Settled in the seat facing me, Kat looked out the window as the cavalcade of city lights paraded past the limo. Ensconced in the beige leather seats, I lifted a fat bottle of iced Dom Perignon from the built-in bar and uncorked it, spilling champagne on the plush carpet.

"Son of a bitch," I muttered, slinging wine from my fingers. Kat pretended not to hear and I pushed the issue.

"You seemed to enjoy your dances."

"With you," she said. "And with your two friends."

"Especially with them." I poured champagne without offering her a glass, unable to control my mouth. "But I can understand that. They offer a helluva lot more than me."

"So?"

"So, you seemed to enjoy yourself a little too much."

"Don't be a child." She stroked her gold-encased thigh. "This dress is the nicest I ever owned. More expensive than anything Viktor bought me." She removed a crystal glass from the bar and filled it. "Chase your painting, Adam, and let me appreciate the evening a few minutes longer."

"Amazing what a boatload of money can do," I said, unable to let it go.

When she didn't reply, I said, "You like Dansby?"

She shrugged. "He's nice enough. He said I could keep the dress."

I drained my glass; the dress suddenly tawdry. "Lucky you." I know how stupid it sounded but I let the champagne rule my mouth.

"You need to grow up, Adam," she said. "Drink your free champagne and don't ruin the evening."

I sulked in my corner and poured myself more champagne, wondering where all this was leading us.

Chapter Thirty-Three

Rinaldi's was one of Dansby's favorites. Squeezed between Tiffanys and a Barclays office in upper Manhattan, the restaurant featured a Northern Italian menu and old-fashioned tile floors. The inauspicious décor belied its pricey bill of fare, reminding uptown diners that authenticity came at a price.

Arriving thirty minutes early, Dansby positioned his bodyguard at a separate table as dusk fell over the city. The precaution seemed ludicrously Sicilian but he never trusted the Russians, particularly an operative with a false name. Brezenkov or whatever his real name, had been insistent on the meeting, knowing it would be cut short if he attempted to use or turn him. Brezenkov's urgency, however, piqued Dansby's curiosity. There was something personal in the request, and one never overlooked an opportunity to make money, especially when modern-day Russia played the game. Ruled by thugs or not, Dansby had made more than his share of legal and illegal profits from Russia's new ruling class, including the billionaire cadre that ruled Moscow's streets. If his Russian guest could grease the rails, all the better.

Alone at the table, Dansby nodded at his protection at the other table and ordered a bottle of Poggio Amorelli, his favorite Tuscan wine, allowing the waiter to pour a single generous glass without waiting for his guest. Who the hell cared what the Russian thought about manners? Or if the duplicitous bastard was even aware of Emily Post's dictates. Dansby took a swallow of wine and corrected himself. The KGB or whatever it now called itself did not employ half-wits. Whoever and whatever else Brezenkov might be, he would be well trained in Western manners as well as the KGB's finer arts. His glass was half empty when the man he knew as Anatoli Brezenkov walked in wearing the same suit and shoes Dansby had seen at the hotel.

Tasso pulled out a chair and inhaled. When had he last enjoyed a four-star meal? He spotted the large man seated a few tables away.

"We are not beginning our meeting with trust," he said to Dansby.

Dansby removed his wallet and handed Tasso three one hundred-dollar bills. "Here. Buy yourself some decent shoes, for God's sake. Yours look as though you walked through a gravel pit on your way here."

Tasso stared at the money. When was the last time he could afford a fine pair of shoes? He had to admit that his were a giveaway to anyone who closely observed him, a subtle warning he might not be the college professor and economic specialist he claimed.

"I recommend the veal and *pesce* here," Dansby said, filling his guest's wine glass. "My treat so long as you avoid another fishing expedition."

Tasso pocketed the money and nodded at the third man again. "I requested a private meeting."

"Trust is a luxury," Dansby said. "You of all people know that."

Dansby waved away the waiter and looked at his watch. "You have an hour. That's quite enough time for whatever you have to say."

Tasso swirled his wine, no doubt an expensive selection but he preferred vodka for what came next. He'd made his decision before boarding the flight to Washington. Everything now hinged on Dansby's willingness to believe him.

"I want to leave Russia," he said. "Forever."

Caught unawares, Dansby kept his face neutral. "You don't need me for that. Walk into any American agency and declare asylum."

Tasso shook his head. "I don't wish to defect. No CIA or NSA. If I refuse to answer their questions, I might never leave a cell. If I play the role of a turncoat, what would remain after they squeezed me dry? Relocated in one of your desert towns with a new name and pittance that allowed me to buy your hamburgers? With no family left behind in Russia, I can escape without reprisals, but if I run, I must run to something better." He fell silent, the clink of silverware the only sound in the restaurant. "I want a new life, but not as a traitor."

Dansby was shaking his head before Tasso finished. "You expect me to believe you want to desert your masters and live in America? Use someone like me to help you disappear? I'm too old a dog to buy your tale of woe."

Tasso was playing the serf, hating the necessity to debase himself in front of an enemy. Dansby was no fool and Tasso recognized his past worked against him. He was bargaining from weakness, but what choice remained to him? Anything he said sounded like lines from a play intended to convince a hostile audience.

How could he ask for compassion when he'd devoted his life to destroying people like Dansby? He reached for the wine bottle and topped his glass, his plea sounding like a cheap spy novel.

"Do you want me to grovel? What would you have me say? That I want to live out my remaining years as a decadent bourgeois?" Tasso's smile failed. "Believe what you will, Phillip, but I am no longer fool enough to believe in Lenin's form of equality. Such equality means I will live out my life in a free one-bedroom apartment provided by the state. A few medals and no luxuries, nothing to show for my loyalty, waiting for a knock on my door if an official decides my brain holds too many secrets." He studied his glass. "You know nothing of such things."

"And you believed I would help you, let you compromise me?" Dansby scoffed. "I don't know who you are but I can guess. Your brand of Russian is the last I would ever trust."

Crushed by the truth, Tasso could no longer meet Dansby's eyes. Nothing he could say would explain forty years of servitude he could no longer justify. He half-turned in his chair and pointed at Madison Avenue outside the restaurant window.

"You take all this for granted, while I can only…" Tasso cursed his show of weakness. What was the matter with him? He'd always controlled his fear but now his future loomed all too clearly if he plodded forward like some bovine creature in the slaughter pens. The meetings with Gusov rotated a harsh light onto what awaited him. Tasso had lived his life like some subterranean canine, a Pavlovian hound responding to buttons pushed by men no better than him. But what was the use? There was no way Dansby would understand.

"What if I *were* to believe you, old boy?" Dansby asked. "What would you have me do? Adopt you?"

A sliver of light appeared. "You have many dealings in Russia." Tasso hurried on. "I know this. I also know many important people. People who seek a better life in Russia. I know where there are weaknesses and broken linkages, individuals willing to quietly invest money in the West without interference from Moscow. I could be the man behind the curtain as you Americans say."

"And what about your other talents, if we can call them that?"

Tasso shrugged. "If you have need of them." Dansby followed his glance at the bodyguard whose head was bent over a bowl of pasta. "Better for you there is someone more interested in your safety than his food."

"And if I buy this sob story of yours, what would you expect in return?"

"A taste of something better." There, thought Tasso. I said it. "A new identity with money to enjoy what your country offers. I assure you I can earn it many times over."

Dansby studied him. There was an element of temptation in what the old operative offered. Russia remained medieval and a guide through the totalitarian maze could keep him ahead of competitors. He would need to be very careful but the returns could be astronomical.

"Even so, they'll send people to look for you when you don't return," he said.

"With your assistance, I can avoid them."

"And if they find you?"

"Then I die and you lose nothing."

Dansby calculated the odds. The Russian could be useful if he was telling the truth. "What about the Russian woman you were watching at the Baccarat?"

"Ah." Tasso looked at him with renewed admiration. His host was either observant or well-informed. Either way, the woman was his problem—and possibly his salvation. If he carried out Gusov's mission and killed the woman, it might deflect those tempted to pursue him. Her elimination could become his shield, particularly if no one believed he was talking to the American intelligence agencies. Tasso might simply become a bird who flew past the hunters' guns and was never seen again.

Tasso shrugged. "The woman doesn't concern me."

"I hope not. She and her friend are assisting me in locating a very valuable painting. I wouldn't want anything to happen to her. Or the painting I'm looking for."

Tasso raised his hands from the tablecloth. "Paintings are playthings for rich men. I prefer the comfort your money would buy—warmth, taste, touch."

Dansby signaled to the waiter for menus. "Just so you understand I call the shots."

He'd done it, Tasso thought. He imagined chains snapping apart, the links clanking to the floor around his chair. "I won't do anything to displease you," Tasso replied evenly, wondering if he'd just lied to his newfound mentor.

Chapter Thirty-Four

Slouched on the bus stop bench, the Contractor watched Barrow's condo, the narrow brownstone walk-up fronted by a black wrought iron fence. The Contractor flexed his shoulders against the unyielding boards and rolled his neck. Arms stretched across the back of the bench, he yawned, enduring the early morning cold.

Clad in an army surplus camo jacket and distressed brown pants, he tugged down his plaid hunter's cap, the ridiculous ear flaps obscuring half his face. The brown paper sack beside him held a high-pint of ginger ale. The soda, replacing the whiskey, did nothing to fight the cold. Only two handwarmers concealed in his jacket pockets prevented his hands from numbing up. He unscrewed the bottle cap, swallowed several mouthfuls of the sticky-sweet liquid, and winced. Maybe it was thin blood or his regimen of a low carb diet, but he longed for a stretch of white sand scorched by round-the-clock warmth.

Watching the morning traffic, he convinced himself his decision was the right one. Barrow was an easy target but the assignment had dragged on too long. They'd skipped patience when his chromosomes coalesced, an attribute he endured but regretted. His employer would go ballistic but he'd deal with him if the necessity arose. Turned off by endless stalking, he was ready to enjoy his Swiss bank accounts and the money he'd already been paid. After he sold the painting, he'd soak up sun and good whisky thousands of miles away from his employer's vengeance and Chicago's cold.

A young couple approached, muffled to their chins against the cold. The Contractor tugged off a tattered glove and picked his nose. He sniffed loudly and wiped the residue on his sleeve. The man and woman hurried past him and turned the corner as he pulled on the glove. His fingers numb, he pressed both hands against the warmers in his pockets. Morning traffic sped along Wells Street. A taxi ran the yellow light and the Contractor checked his watch. Lounging back, he patted the jacket. The Browning nestled snugly in the shoulder holster, the silencer in his pocket. The weapon had proved its worth and he preferred its heavy steel construction to trendy composite weapons, the weight a pledge of reliability. The unfamiliar got you killed.

He dug the snuffbox out of his trouser pocket and inhaled finely-ground tobacco, stamping his feet as the tobacco burned his sinuses. He checked his watch again. If his employer knew what he was talking about, Barrow's flight landed over an hour ago. He rose from the bench, stretched his arms above his head, and removed the bottle, sliding the sack half way down the label. Taking a swallow, he stumbled into the alley behind the bench. Concealed in the shadows, he braced one shoulder against the brick wall and checked his sight line to the condo across the street. Removing the automatic he screwed the silencer in place. Pressing the safety off, he held the pistol behind his leg and closed his eyes. What was he doing, he wondered again? He'd never defaulted on a contract or failed to carry out his instructions.

A black Expedition slowed and stopped. The rear hatch popped up and Barrow stepped from the car. The Contractor retreated deeper into the shadows and removed his right glove. Steadying his right hand against the frozen wall, his bare index finger cupped the trigger. A single muffled shot, then a second to make certain. He waited for the adrenaline rush, shivering as the cold seeped into his disguise.

A hulking man got out of the driver's seat and removed a suitcase, dropping it on the sidewalk without speaking. One of the Russians, the Contractor guessed. Barrow watched the SUV pull away, a stark silhouette against the cream-colored building.

Finish it, the Contractor thought. He peered over the pistol's custom sights, took a breath, let half out… and lowered the Browning.

No.

Resting his head against the cold bricks, he rethought his decision. His employer might be an egotistical bastard but throwing away easy money grated on his better judgement. Killing Barrow in broad daylight on a public street was a rookie mistake that invited disaster. What if a patrol car appeared at the wrong moment, or a civilian got a clear look at him? Eliminating the art dealer would be simple enough at the right moment. But killing Barrow now struck a match to a stack of cash and left him peering over his shoulder if his vindictive employer hired some halfwit to come after him. There would be time enough to kill Barrow and steal the painting from under his employer's nose.

He engaged the pistol's safety, unscrewed the silencer, and returned the Browning to its holster. The wind funneled through the alley, anesthetizing his exposed ears and wrapping a sheet of sodden newspaper around one leg. The Contractor kicked it away and flipped up his jacket collar, satisfied he'd made the right decision. The additional money would extend his holiday and allow him time to recover the appetite for his work.

Tossing the stale soda in a garbage can, he watched Barrow lug his suitcase into the building.

Chapter Thirty-Five

I gave up on conversation from the airport. Kat and I hadn't exchanged ten sentences during the flight to Chicago. Arby let me out at my condo, the early morning street deserted except a street person slumped in the alley across the street.

The SUV disappeared up Wells Street and I watched it for several seconds, straining to see Kat through the tinted windows. I wondered if I'd misread her, that she wasn't the forgiving kind. Okay, I'd been an asshole in New York but some assholes deserved second chances. Flattering myself I fit the latter category, I swore at my stupidity and went inside. The Van Gogh might be an illusion, but Kat had become all too real.

I dug out the envelope of the paint chips and looked up the phone number of the chemistry department at Northwestern. Showered and dressed in fresh clothes, I indulged myself with Viktor's money and took a cab to the gallery,

Wes emerged from the office in what appeared to be a new blazer and tan golf shirt. Buffed penny loafers replaced the tired lace-ups. He'd gained weight and his eyes clear. Maybe my Mother Teresa impersonation was paying dividends.

He embraced me. "Welcome back, little brother."

My throat tightened and I returned the hug. Wes pushed us into shark-infested waters, but he was my brother and I still might salvage our lives—unless I screwed up and got us both killed.

I stepped away and regarded him. "How're you doing?"

"Working hard to overcome a guilt trip. A couple of bartenders called to tell me I'm starving their children."

Sally was at lunch, so I had time to update him. The trip. The easel. Meeting with what remained of Charles Langlois. I told him about the photograph and death of Marguerite Bouchet in New York. Also, about McMinnis and Dansby, leaving out my relationship with Kat as I showed him the envelope of paint chips.

"You remember I once told you about Aaron Dubinsky at Northwestern? He's a chemistry professor and full-blown forensics nut. Believes he should be directing episodes of CSI with a starring part. He can tell me if these chips are oil paint, and if so, how old."

Wes grinned. "The Van Gogh?"

"Maybe. I scraped them from something that may have been his easel. Could be house paint for all I know."

"Then I wasn't wrong to ask for Krushenko's help," Wes said.

"You have any idea the mistake you made, Wes? Who we're dealing with?"

"I know he's willing to help us."

I omitted Kat's deadly encounter in Paris. Wes had blundered into the world's underbelly and taken me with him, a universe where strangers were beaten into pulp with industrial steel and a beautiful woman was trained to slit a man's throat. My brother might be getting sober but he needed a touch of reality.

"You don't know anything," I said. "Viktor and Arby made sure I saw what remained of the man who shot Vasily. You needed to look hard to see what was once human. Maybe then you'd change your mind about of our benefactor."

He blinked. "What are you going to do?"

"Check out these chips and give Viktor a progress report, such as it is."

"And the woman who went with you?"

"What about her?"

"Viktor may want to know everything that happened."

It would require a long night to explain the last ten days. Sally walked in and saved me with my second hug of the day. "The tourist returns," she said.

I glanced around at the walls. "Everything here okay?"

She shot me a pained expression. "How could you even ask with the dynamic duo in charge?"

"That's all very comforting, but did you sell anything?"

"In fact, business picked up without you tramping around, straightening pictures and biting your nails. I think you'll like what the books tell you. Your Russian friend has quite a following of art lovers. I couldn't understand half of what they said, but they knew art. At least art appreciation was once taught in Mother Russia."

We talked shop for a few minutes and I gave them McMinnis's address. If Viktor handled Vasily's estate and I could convince him to let me work the deal with Jack, we'd both make money. I skipped the part about him offering me a job. Jack had thrown me a life preserver that might too good to pass up. I told Sally Wes and I were headed to Northwestern and would be back before closing.

***

Doctor Aaron Dubinsky's office was located on the first floor of an ivy-covered administrative building that looked like an advertisement for prestigious universities. Leaning back in his office chair, Dubinsky's shirt tail spilled over the chair. Buddha-round, he frowned as he dropped the graded papers on the floor beside his chair. A fleshy finger dug into one ear as he scrawled comments on the exams. Tiny feet propped on his desk, he saw me in the open doorway and shoved the paper aside as I introduced Wes.

Resettled in the distressed chair Dubinsky interlaced his fingers behind his balding head. "I assume you drove up here for a reason."

He listened to my story, growing more animated as I talked about the painting, stepping on students' papers as he came around the desk to inspect the chips. Eyes alight, his smile widened.

"Give me a day or two and I'll tell you their age, country of origin, and whether the painter was blond or brunette." I hoped for a red beard and mutilated ear.

I dropped Wes at his apartment on the way back and headed to the gallery—and wished I hadn't. Arthur Jennings sat across from Sally at my desk. An imposing block of African granite stood by his side dressed in an undersized plaid sport coat. One eye was milky white with no pupil or iris. Feet apart, massive hands crossed in a fig leaf pose, the remaining eye measured me with a lifeless expression, a capable offensive guard or interesting playmate for Arby.

Sally looked up gratefully, her professional smile collapsing in relief as she relinquished my chair. "Mr. Jennings and his associate have been waiting to see you."

Jennings pumped my hand like a shipwrecked sailor delivered from the sea, his bodyguard staring at me. Dressed in 60's bell-bottom trousers and a Guns and Roses tee-shirt, Jennings sported a silk Dodgers jacket and a jade pendant on a long gold chain. Even accompanied by the black juggernaut, he was either brave or stupid to flaunt such a bauble near the Projects.

"Hey, buddy," he said, "good to see you again. I heard you were back from vacation." He winked at the bodyguard. "Our boy's a world traveler now."

My flight had landed four hours earlier. He was well-informed about my schedule and I began wondering about the extent of his influence.

"I was just explaining to your delightful assistant that you were always the more resourceful arm of the family," he said. He tilted his head toward his companion. "I told Lamar you and I were old acquaintances. That we could come to an arrangement." He popped a cinnamon Tic Tac in his mouth and turned to Sally. "Honey, would you excuse us for a few minutes?"

Sally disappeared into the storage area, looking back like it might be the last time she'd see me intact.

"I told you. Vasily's paintings aren't going to California. They're being shipped to Jack McMinnis in New York."

Jennings toyed with the pendant. "Jack, always the entrepreneur. The man's a wonder, isn't he? Got his manicured nails in anything that makes a buck."

"That seems the case."

"But I'm no longer interested in a dead Russian's work."

"Then why the social call?"

He looked hurt. "Adam, can't we just discuss business?"

I gestured at Lamar. "So, what's the deal with him? You never walked around with a troglodyte covering you."

Bad choice of words. Lamar had no idea what I was talking about, but knew I'd categorized him as a lesser species. He took a step toward me, the good eye measuring his punch. Jennings placed a hand against the broad chest and shook his head.

"I'll tell you something," he said to me. "A lot of people misjudge Lamar. They look at him and don't like what they see, but after a few hours alone with him, they're best friends, you know? Let's just say it's better to stay on his good side."

"What do you want, Arthur?"

"The Van Gogh. Something like that brings more money than an eighteen-wheeler loaded with high grade weed. And that kind of money needs protection."

I tried not to react but he read my face. "Don't act so innocent," he said. "LA's not so big I don't hear things." When I didn't reply, he walked to the nearest wall and inspected a small oil portrait. Lamar didn't move or speak, and I wondered if he and Arby sprang from the same tribe of mutes. The profits from Arthur's ventures let him buy a lot of Lamars.

"I can help you," he said without turning from the painting. "Provide funds to look for the old boy's work. Find you a discreet buyer who doesn't want tax problems. Give you cover if you need it. Lamar's very good at assisting the needy."

"Arthur..."

He bent closer to the painting and inspected the frame. "A fucking Van Gogh," he sighed. "An auction house wet dream." He turned back to me. "We find it and you keep your Russian cupcake in style. Buy anything her little Bolshevik heart desires." He waved a hand around the gallery. "And this place becomes the largest gallery in the Mid-West, maybe the whole damn country. Fifty-fifty partners and nobody's the wiser, *capice*?

"I have a partner."

"Tell him you got a new one."

Despite the mountain looming beside him, I managed a smile. "You and your playmate won't convince him to go away. He doesn't like competition."

Jennings' face reddened. "You think I'm making a suggestion?"

"I think you're begging for more trouble than you can handle, Arthur."

He stepped so close I smelled the Tic Tac. "You sound like Cagney in an old gangster movie," he said, "but it doesn't work for you. Let me and Lamar worry about competition."

The doorbell chimed and I saw Kat looking through the glass front door. I hurried to the desk and buzzed her in. Wearing a white wool skirt and matching cashmere turtleneck, she appeared taller in black leather boots. The large purse she'd carried in Europe was slung over a short mink jacket. I kissed her cheek, more relieved to see her than I wanted to admit.

She glanced at Jennings and assessed Lamar. "You're in a meeting?"

Arthur took her hand, dragging hungry eyes over her body. "If you're the Russian girlfriend, the descriptions didn't do you justice." Kat reclaimed her hand and ignored him, her eyes fixed on Lamar whose single eye returned her stare.

"Your old man would have been impressed," Jennings said.

"People keep telling me that."

Kat opened her purse as if inspecting the contents, keeping Lamar in her line of vision. Jennings took one of my business cards from the desk and wrote 'Room 1720' on the back with a wink at Kat. He withdrew a plastic entry card from his jacket and handed both cards to me.

"Whitehall Hotel," he said and turned to Kat. "Me and him are going to be rich men." He and Lamar walked to the door and surveyed the street. Kat waited until they left.

"Your father collected interesting people," she said.

"Yeah, with Viktor dumped in the mix. A bunch of real winners."

She shrugged. "Some good, some not so good."

"Not a lot of good on my side. My father's buddies got what they wanted and left him like the guy at the circus who sweeps up elephant shit."

I flopped into Sally's chair and closed my eyes, the week catching up. We had four players in the game now, while someone else waited in the weeds. Someone not even Kat could see.

Chapter Thirty-Six

The Nagant revolver lay by the hotel window on a page of the New York Times. Beside it, seven 7.62mm rounds stood on end like a squad of dutiful soldiers. Drapes closed, Tasso's dilemma deepened as he repeatedly ran an oiled patch through bore and seven cylinders. Satisfied the revolver was in perfect working condition, he laid it aside and pulled open the drapes. Fifteen stories below, the maze of traffic amazed him as always.

Where had his self-respect gone, he wondered? He'd been the state's loyal servant for almost forty years, evolving from a young zealot to—what? An aging man longing for comfort? Gusov might allow him to live out his years, forgotten and unmolested. Why not dispose of the woman, collect another medal for the box in his closet, allow life go on as before?

Dansby hadn't contacted him and that worried Tasso. He didn't believe Dansby was the type to sell him to Moscow but one never really knew men's hearts. He hoped the Englishman was absorbed in chasing his painting, possibly with the aid of the Kosdrenkov woman, although Tasso could not imagine how such a woman could help Dansby find a valuable work of art. Tasso had made his deal with the devil and now must wait. Throwing in his lot with Dansby could not sever the past but it was a start. The decision had been simple enough. Leave his dysfunctional country for a world where basic needs were not luxuries. Nearing the time that he'd be seen as a liability, he recalled Gusov's thinly veiled taunts. Whatever the man's reasons, the churlish comments reinforced the truth. Tasso at most was two years from becoming a burden, a shadow who wouldn't be missed if one night there was a knock on his door.

Tasso contemplated the hotel room. How could his country's ideology explain the modern furniture, the clean linens on the king-sized bed, flat screen television on the wall showed whatever you liked? Everything his eyes touched shamed his Moscow apartment. But no matter how much he longed for what he saw in America, nothing would prepare him for the future he was making. If he held true to his resolve he must adapt to a foreign land, a fugitive among millions of strangers. Worse, he struggled to repel the blasphemous word: traitor. He stared at the streets below again, firming his resolve and accepting the dangers that accompanied his decision.

I will not betray my country, he thought. Not one word to American intelligence. He'd done everything asked of him by his handlers and everything he knew would die with him. But must he also die in the squalid apartment on Zhenko Street as a final duty to the motherland?

He wiped the oily patch over the revolver a final time and dried the grip with a washrag, hefting the pistol. The Nagant had been designed more than a century earlier but it never failed him, while newer automatics jammed at inconvenient moments. A favorite of the NKVD and commissars during the Great War, the Nagant was slender and lightweight but carried a lethal punch, the preferred weapon of Lubyanka's executioners. If he was successful in disappearing, Tasso decided he would leave behind everything he owned except the old pistol.

Screwing the tubular silencer onto the muzzle, he shook the blued frame, satisfied the fit was tight. He reloaded the revolver, wrapped it in a hotel towel, and returned it to his suitcase. Reluctantly, he picked up a bathroom glass of Stolichnaya and grimaced before taking a swallow. The American facsimile of Russian vodka was little better than acid piss, unworthy of its appellation. Somewhere in America there must liquor stores that sold good Russian and Ukrainian vodka. Otherwise, life might prove unendurable.

His cell phone rang and he looked at it for several moments before answering.

"Anatoli! You are enjoying your woman-hunting vacation?"

Tasso didn't reply. The man was insufferable.

"Not to worry," Korinkin laughed. "This is a secure line. The Americans are not the only experts in telecommunications." He giggled almost girlishly. "Have you met your date yet?"

"Say what you have to say, Korinkin. You have news for me?" Tasso kept his voice neutral in case the conversation was recorded for Gusov's benefit.

"What?" Korinkin jested. "You can't enjoy a few minutes with a fellow countryman?

"I am here on Colonel Gusov's orders, not for your amusement."

"All right, be a Moscow bore if you must. I thought since you were staying at a Holiday Inn, you might be enjoying an American holiday." Korinkin laughed at his joke.

"Why did you call me?"

"You are sitting in the wrong hotel."

"Explain."

"The woman's returned to Chicago." Korinkin chuckled. "You won't like Chicago. The land of Al Capone and American criminals. The city produces weather that rivals our own. Better to return to Moscow and pack your winter coat!"

The man was a fool. Tasso thought. Nonetheless, traveling to the midwestern city meant an unfamiliar environment, and changes produced complications.

"Do you have an address?"

"She keeps an apartment at 910 West Chestnut near the center of the city." Korinkin said. "Quite an expensive address. Her Russian pimp must keep her in style, but do not underestimate this Krushenko. Our records show he and his henchman are not nice people."

"Neither am I."

Chapter Thirty-Seven

May 1889 Saint-Rémy France

Outsiders described the grounds at Saint-Paul-de-Mausole as picturesque, a sprawling country village. In reality the asylum grounds were a former monastery, the stone buildings nestled in a mountain valley outside Saint-Rémy. A prior bastion of Catholicism, the complex now housed faithful and atheists alike, its current owners abstaining shackles and straightjackets, treating patients like eccentric guests.

Vincent's first impressions were encouraging. Doctor Peyron, the director, escorted him around the gardens as though the newest resident was a well-adjusted visitor. Overweight and bland, Peyron reminded Vincent of a gloomy train conductor compelled to exhibit good humor, but the man was pleasant enough and there were no bars on the windows. Most patients they encountered nodded and smiled, seemingly content with their lot. The surrounding hillsides teemed with trees and vegetation, a lush palette of muted colors. The asylum might well provide a place to free himself from the rages that rendered his life unlivable. Paid for by his brother Theo, the voluntary commitment created optimism that he might yet defeat his demons.

Arms linked with his sullen patient, Peyron forced his eyes away from the mangled stump that was once his ear. Walking the grounds, he pointed out well-maintained buildings and the absence of walls. The place not being what he expected, Vincent enjoyed a sense of relief, half-hearing the portly overseer who explained he was free to roam the grounds and beyond if he 'behaved.' Despite Theo's warnings about unpredictable outbursts of temper, Peyron said he could roam the property at will. He would even be allowed to paint outside the compound. Under supervision, of course. Surely, he explained, Vincent could understand there must be eyes on him for his own safety. It was the institution's duty.

Yes, this would do, Vincent thought. In his cramped room, he unpacked canvases and his few belongings. Assurances about the civilized setting were plainly truthful with no intent to shackle him in a cellar or steal Theo's money with false promises. Peace in such a setting might bring freedom from the attacks, a fresh beginning but with the understanding he could not remain here forever. Theo could ill afford that, not with a new wife and a baby on the way. So much depended on regaining control but he acknowledged his debt to Theo. The realization rekindled seeds of doubt, old fears bubbling to the surface in spite of his initial optimism. Sitting on the narrow bed, he pushed the thoughts away. If he dwelt on past breakdowns, he would fail his brother and tumble into the pit again. Good Theo had taken on a tremendous burden, and he must prove himself worthy of his brother's faith and expenditure.

In the days that followed he painted and painted well, recapturing control of his brushes and finding Saint-Paul's rhythms. Two-hour baths in deep stone tubs provided solitude and produced a calming effect. The food was much better than he was accustomed to with sufficient amenities to justify Theo's outlay of funds. Taking his easel and armful of stretched canvases on day trips into the countryside, Vincent hardly noticed the staff member who dutifully tagged along. His keeper maintained a respectful distance, the valley and hills rejuvenating his lust to paint: pines, laurel, olive groves, gardens of irises, wind-carved cypresses tempted his brush at every turn.

In early June he dragged his easel and paint box outside near midnight. A brush clamped between his teeth, unaware of the oily handle, he wielded a second brush in frantic strokes, his face turned upward to the night sky as he again sought to capture silver pinpoints in the blue-black sky he'd laid down on his canvas. Pleased with the painting, he slept well. Saint-Paul provided his first peace in years with only the demented cries of a few howlers at night to disturb the tranquility.

The attack came in July without warning. One morning after a trip into Saint-Rémy, the staff discovered him eating dirt in the courtyard. Three men forcibly restrained him and dragged him screaming to his room. The descent was steep, blacker than past forays into the familiar abyss. He tumbled into its depths, lacking the will to claw his way out. The next day they caught him consuming pigment from paint tubes. Mouth smeared with a rainbow of color, his eyes wavered between blank and wild. Peyron removed his paints and quarantined him in his room, a chair, bed, and chamber pot his only companions. Pretty as she was, he barely noticed the young girl who brought his meals, and further outings were forbidden, the room's single window admitting sunlight only in the mornings.

The madness clawed him for a month until he awoke one morning to find the beast had crawled away. Terrified now of a recurrence and suspicious of Peyron, he decided to leave before another attack struck. His paints were still forbidden to him and the lengthy 'healing sessions' with Peyron yielded nothing but talk and more talk. He had to hold a brush in his fingers. Recapture the urgency that drove him to paint canvasses no one wanted. It mattered little that Paris preferred the trendy dabblers who labeled themselves meaningful artists.

By May the next year, he was better and Theo would understand the necessity to get free of Peyron whose interminable lectures did nothing but crush his artistic spirit. He would take the train to Auvers, a bucolic little town north of Paris. It offered a quiet setting to calm his soul. Surely Doctor Gachet, who had shown him many kindnesses in the past, would provide a bed until he found quarters of his own.

He would miss the valley with its serene hills but he could not risk more attacks. Theo and the others must see he was not mad.

Chapter Thirty-Eight

I gave Sally the day off and the phone rang as Wes and I were closing up.

Jennings wasn't waiting for me to contact him. A radio or TV blared in the background. I could barely hear him. "You know," he began, "I was thinking. We need to talk about this other person who's after the Van Gogh. My old mother said too many chefs screw up the stew." Rap music thumped louder. I heard him cover the receiver and yell, "Lamar! Turn that crap off!" He waited until the music stopped. "Let me buy you and Wes a drink tonight. The bar at the Drake. Always loved that classy old place. We'll dress up and pretend we're legit."

"I'm busy."

"Lamar checked and your social calendar's open tonight."

"Wes doesn't drink anymore."

"You wouldn't want to disappoint Lamar. Eight o'clock."

Click.

Wes gave me a perplexed look. "Call Barbara," I said. "Tell her we have a business meeting tonight."

***

If nothing else, Jennings was right about the Drake Hotel. Located off Lake Michigan on the Magnificent Mile, the Coq D'Or bar was legendary, a popular watering hole since Prohibition days. The street-level bar never lost its appeal despite the city's tumultuous history. Subdued lighting. Polished mahogany walls. Sumptuous red leather seating. The staff glided around patrons, while a piano player unfurled classics from the thirties and forties. The place overflowed with chic outfits and business suits. Executives and traders from the Mercantile Exchange mixed with Rush Street players trying to score upscale female company. A tall dark-complexioned man leaned on the bar, his back to us, chatting up a waitress as she loaded a drink tray. For no discernible reason, something about the way he stood set off bells. A former friend? Gallery client? A girlfriend once told me such moments were butterflies that never landed.

I forgot about him when I spotted Jennings at a table in the far corner. Dressed in a beige silk suit and black tee shirt, he missed the mark on looking legit. The heap of black stone at his side wore a white tee-shirt and baggy khakis sans jacket, not exactly Chicago's uptown dress code. He spared a cursory glance at Wes and me, scowling at the piano player's renditions of Johnny Mercer. We pulled up chairs and Jennings drew stares when he yelled at the waitress.

"Hey, sugar, how about some service over here?"

I ordered a Dewars and Wes settled for coffee, our host reloading his vodka rocks. As we waited for our drinks, Jennings turned to Lamar. "Hey, Lamar, let me tell you a story about their old man. You'll like this." Arthur swirled the ice cubes in his glass, off on a flight of nostalgia.

"Okay, this was way back when." He pointed at Wes and me. "These two were in knee pants when their father and me ran across this mark with more money than brains. A nouveau riche prick who wanted to impress people who didn't accept him." He laughed. "Robert Barrow told this numb-nuts he could get his hands on a Jackson Pollack." He turned to me. "Jack the Dripper, your father called him. He made up this bullshit story about a bankrupt real estate guy who needed to sell off his collection." The waitress arrived with our drinks and placed a large cup of coffee in front of Wes. Jennings winked at her and waited until she returned to bar before turning back at me.

"Anyway, this guy went wild at the thought of owning a Pollack, so one night, me and your father got drunk as hell and punched little holes in paint cans. Spent two nights dripping paint on this humongous canvas, drinking and laughing our asses off, trying to outdo each other." Jennings slapped the table and almost choked on a chunk of ice, disappointing me when the ice cube failed to do its job. "One of my buddies owned a pizza joint, so we slow bake this thing in his brick oven to dry it. I swear to God it smelled like pepperoni when we delivered it to the schmuck."

He wiped his eyes with a cocktail napkin. "Damn, those were fun times. We made a pile of dough and the guy never caught on. For all I know, the piece of crap's still hanging in his living room." Arthur downed half his drink. "Never had another friend like Barrow, the crazy bastard."

I smiled in spite of myself. Despite his status, I considered Pollack an insider joke. Even modern-day experts hesitated to authenticate his ostentatious drips. The mark in my humble opinion got what he deserved.

Wes took a swallow of coffee and frowned at his cup. "Yeah, our father was a riot. Adam and I grew up running from lawyers and angry victims, hiding out in cheap motels. He scammed people and never looked back at the damage. "

Jennings settled back in his chair with a lopsided grin. "Hey, we all got our sad stories. You think I grew up sucking on a silver spoon? Or Lamar here?"

Wes sipped his coffee and grimaced again, eying my scotch as he stirred more cream into his cup.

"You didn't invite us here to relive old times," I said to Jennings.

Arthur waved at the waitress and pointed at our glasses for another round. "In a way, I did. Your father would've wanted us to work together. Come to an agreement of sorts."

"I told you, Arthur. I'm not interested."

Jennings nudged the behemoth beside him. "See, Lamar? I told you he wouldn't understand what we're offering." He looked at us. "Okay, here's the deal. We provide protection and special benefits. Painting's worth millions, right? So, there's gonna be big arguments over how your old man got his hands on it. Who actually owns the thing and all that. Lots of people are going to claim it. Tie up the whole megillah in court for years. There'll be trains of lawyers lining up and no one will see a dollar except those blood-sucking bastards." He pointed his empty glass at me. "You know I'm right. Robert Barrow didn't fit the profile of someone who legally owned a Van Gogh."

I kept my mouth shut. With Lamar at his elbow I let Jennings make his pitch.

"Anyhow," he said, "I'll find you a big-time buyer, quiet-like. An overseas collector who'll pay top dollar and never asks questions. Take it off your hands before anyone knows it exists. I get a hefty commission and you make more money than you've ever seen."

"That's big of you, Arthur," I said, "but like I told you, I have a backer."

He paused and leaned back, nodding at the piano player. "Always liked the old stuff. Dorsey, Miller, Harry James. Not like the shit Lamar listens to."

"I don't think we've got anything else to talk about."

Jennings's eyes speared me. "You know, I could have Lamar talk to your little blond assistant." He grinned at Wes. "Or pay a visit to your wife. He has a way with pretty women."

Wes started to stand. Sweat glistened on his forehead, his features pale as a new moon. I grabbed his arm and he fell back into the chair, trembling as he caught his breath.

"You okay?" I asked.

He coughed as though trying to clear his throat and stared at his empty coffee cup, his face ashen. "I think she brought me bad coffee."

I raised my hand at the waitress but he pulled my arm down, his breathing shallow. "No, don't."

"Get him some ice water," Jennings said, "He don't look so good."

Wes gagged and doubled over with a convulsive jerk, his head almost hitting the tabletop. He straightened with a grimace, breathing hard. "Dizzy," he muttered. "I think I'm going to be sick."

I pulled him out of his chair and steered him toward the men's room. Heads turned as he stumbled against a table. I grabbed him under his arms and we lurched into the john, pushing several men aside. Wes reached for a stall door but didn't make it. Falling to his knees, he vomited like a fire hose across the tile floor, toppling onto his side.

I knelt beside him. "Wes?"

Jennings stepped inside the restroom and peered down at him. "Hell, he wasn't even drinking." He stooped and turned Wes's head. "Passed out. Better get a doctor."

Five minutes later an ambulance hauled away my brother for the second time in a month.

***

Medicinal alcohol and hospital fumes always made me queasy. The nauseous odors seeped from the waiting room's institutional green walls, repelling all but the most catatonic patients. A young female resident led me to a corner beneath banks of buzzing overhead fluorescents and we sat facing one another.

"Your brother will live," she began, wiping her hands on stained, wrinkled scrubs.

"How is he?"

"We pumped his stomach. His vital signs leveled off and we got an IV running. His wife's with him now."

"What happened to him?"

Her dark-rimmed eyes mirrored the seen-everything trauma of emergency rooms. She pushed back a wayward lock of lank hair. "It appears your brother was poisoned." The words were soft spoken, attempted murder an everyday occurrence in her chaotic universe. "We haven't determined the toxin, but the symptoms point to a poison of some kind."

I stared at her. "He was drinking coffee at the Drake. He was fine before we got there."

She drew a patient breath, shadows beneath her eyes suggesting she was thirty or forty hours beyond a full night's sleep. "It could be food poisoning, but people don't normally lose consciousness from bad shrimp. I can't tell you what he ingested, but initial tests indicate poison. Have you spoken to the police?"

"Police?"

She sighed. "I can't prove anything until the tests are back, but you might want to involve them. This wasn't accidental or self-induced unless your brother's suicidal."

"No, no, nothing like that."

It didn't make sense. Wes had stopped a bullet once, and now lay on a gurney with a tube down his throat. Why would someone poison him? If there was a target in someone's sights, it was me.

Barbara pushed through the swinging doors from the treatment area. Her eyes darted around the waiting room until they rested on me. The doctor rose but Barbara stepped past her and confronted me with tears in her eyes.

"Wes keeps ending up in the hospital," she grated, "while you waltz away. What the hell's happening, Adam? How come you're Teflon, while Wes almost dies?"

I wanted to tell her Wes had started the dance but she was beyond reasoning. The doctor pulled her aside and tried to calm her as heads rotated in our direction. I wondered about Jennings and Lamar. Either one could have slipped something into Wes's coffee as a warning. Before I could explore the possibility, Barbara shot

212 *The Last Van Gogh*

me a lethal look and marched back into the treatment area.

I thanked the nurse and walked from the ER. The lobby of the new Northwestern Hospital promised hope for those who passed through its doors, but the illusion vanished the moment I stepped into the bitter cold, recalling Wes on the men's room floor. An arrogant sewer rat waddled across the almost deserted street and I wondered how many of the human variety were stalking Wes and me. His near death joined the others who weren't so lucky, the dead piling up around me like plowed street snow. I had to find the Van Gogh, if only to stop the madness.

Chapter Thirty-Nine

I went back to the Drake. Jennings was long gone but I needed answers. The bar staff blew me off, believing I was sniffing out a lawsuit against the hotel. After two wasted hours, I headed home. The phone rang when I walked in the door.

Viktor. A perfect ending of my day. "You will be home tonight?"

"Yeah. I'm in for the night."

"Stay there. We pick you up in a few minutes."

He hung up before I could protest. I went to the kitchen and poured a large scotch, sans any sacrilegious hint of water or ice. Alcohol never brought clarity, but it sanded off edges; facing Viktor required a certain amount of shoring up. I needed a drink to fully grasp that I'd become a pawn for someone other than the Russian, knowing pawns were sacrificed for higher objectives. Few ever reached the other side of the chess board to be reborn.

Arby knocked on my door exactly thirty minutes later. He waited without speaking as I grabbed the coat Kat had given me, the pistol's weight a vague comfort. Drink in hand I followed Arby downstairs to the black SUV that resembled a hearse each time I opened the rear door. Viktor sat in the passenger seat and ignored me as I climbed in. Arby pulled away and I took a long swallow of scotch. Neither man commented that I'd come armed with a drink.

"I'm guessing you want a progress report." I said to Viktor.

Instead of answering, he flung the Tribune onto the seat beside me. The front section was folded to an article. "Read shit they write about me," he said.

The story opened with a photo of gawkers lining the Chicago River bank. A brigade of police cars sat in the background. Three bodies, the article began, had been found in the river near the newspaper's plant and presses. The story said a search was underway for 'missing body parts'. It seems the men had been pulled from the water minus their heads, hands bound with wire. Two were said to be known drug dealers, the third unidentified. The article continued with details about the vicious war for control of drug trafficking, speculating the murders might be connected to the Russian mob's fight for controlling the city's heroin trade

Viktor reached over the seat and snatched the article from my hands. "How they write this?" He buzzed down his window and tossed out the paper. "Criminals stick their noses where they don't belong. Is not my fault they end up in river. These people, as you say, have no heads for business. Arby, he is also shocked." Arby grinned without taking his eyes off the street. I tried not to envision Viktor's basement.

We drove to Wheaton, me swilling scotch, wishing I'd filled a larger glass. Arby parked in the garage and I left my empty glass in the car, hoping I'd see it again. I followed Viktor into the house, Arby at my heels. Inside the front door he patted me down, something he'd never done before. He removed the Glock Kat gave me. I hoped Kat was there but the house appeared empty except for the three of us. The odor of boiled cabbage persisted but Viktor's doughty wife was nowhere in sight. He pointed to a chair and I sat. He loomed over me, then pulled up a chair and leaned close, art books scattered on the dining room table.

Viktor massaged his temples. "Katia says trip is waste, that you spend my money for nothing."

"We didn't find the painting if that's what you mean."

"What the fuck you think I mean?" he yelled.

I jumped despite my resolve to remain calm. Kat obviously had told her version, and I wondered if she included the murder in Paris. Combined with the morning newspaper article, whatever she'd said wasn't working in my favor. And if she admitted to sleeping with me, all bets were off.

"I told you my father…"

Viktor slammed his hand on the chair arm. "Do not tell me old stories. You find nothing!"

I clammed up, buying a few seconds. Recovering my breath, I told him about the easel and Marguerite Bouchet's photo. I left out the encounters with Dansby and McMinnis, wondering if Kat told him they'd joined our search.

"You have this photo?" Viktor asked.

"No."

"So, you come back with nothing. How you explain that?"

"I think we discussed what might happen."

Arby picked up my pistol and walked behind me.

"Viktor, the letters indicated the painting reached America. Katia and I tried to learn if this Dejean left clues about its location. He told his daughter about it before he died. Her photo proved its existence."

Viktor's stubby fingers caressed the chair arm. "You say this but maybe I waste good money. Maybe there is no Van Gogh."

Behind me, I heard Arby flick off my pistol's safety. It was time to convince Viktor I believed in the painting more than the sun, moon, and stars.

"Look, I found evidence. You yourself told me these people believe the painting exists. If finding it was simple, someone would have been uncovered it years ago. I think the woman was murdered for the photo. Like you said, whoever killed Vasily wanted Wes and me out of the way."

Viktor stood and it dawned on me he was moving out of the line of fire.

I closed my eyes. Please, God. Grant me forgiveness for all my many sins, past and present. When nothing happened, I opened my eyes. "This wasn't my idea but we're in this together now." My shoulders involuntarily tightened against the bullet. "I want the Van Gogh as much as you."

Viktor made a curt gesture at Arby.

"You are lucky man today," he said. "Vasily like you, so you and brother will keep looking."

"And Katia?"

Viktor gave me an unreadable smile. "She stays with you until you find it."

I nodded, not trusting my voice. "There's something else," I finally managed. "Someone tried to kill Wes tonight."

Viktor's eyes widened. "Again?"

"Someone poisoned him but he's alive." I left out meeting with Arthur Jennings. I didn't need fresh corpses swimming past the *Tribune* building looking for their heads.

"These bastards fuck with the wrong people," Viktor said.

Hoping to end our discussion on a subject to his liking, I said, "A major dealer in New York offered to sell Vasily's remaining paintings. He knows collectors who'll pay top dollar, more than I can get."

Viktor nodded as though granting benevolent dispensation to the dead. "This would make Vasily happy."

"It's up to you. As his closest relative, you own the paintings now." It was a guess but a light came up in his eyes.

He grunted. "I let this person sell them, but I first choose one to keep. To remember Vasily."

"Same agreement on the split?" I asked, steering the conversation further from the Van Gogh. "70/30 on the sales?" I hated talking business with Wes lying in the hospital, but I also wanted to walk back into my gallery one day and pay the rent.

Viktor shook his head. "We argue about this before, you and me. Vasily, he is young and too generous. He like you, but I am not Vasily." He held up nine fingers, then one. "Ninety percent me, ten percent you. If rich people buy paintings, there is more money."

I wasn't in a position to negotiate. I didn't like being Viktor's spaniel but he left me little choice with Arby still holding my pistol.

Riding back to the city I leaned my head against the rear headrest and closed my eyes. Arby retreated into his monk's silence and I counted my luck if you wanted to call it that. Whatever else had happened, the day's score ended on my side: I'd escaped Viktor's house again and Wes and I were alive. Not a landslide victory but I'd take the win. I still stood on the bottom rung but I was standing.

Jennings saw a winning lottery ticket, while Dansby and McMinnis regarded the painting as an opportunity to add zeros to their net worth. For Viktor, it was just money. If it materialized, I wouldn't donate my share to the Red Cross but my future was pure speculation at this point. What I most wanted now was to keep Wes alive and hold onto Kat, finding absolution for our father, and getting myself free of the madness in one piece.

I opened my eyes as the SUV veered onto Wells. Arby dropped me at my condo and I watched it turn the corner, wondering how to climb out of the hole the two letters had dug so long ago. If the Van Gogh existed, I might own it for a few hours and maybe, just maybe, that would be enough to redeem our father's miserable life.

Chapter Forty

I couldn't sleep. Each time I drifted off, my dreams were interrupted by the image of Arby standing behind me, the pistol pointed at my head. I gave up at dawn and padded half asleep to the kitchen. Glancing around I saw the edge of an envelope beneath my front door. I opened the door and found the hall empty. I tossed the envelope on the counter and heaped ground coffee into my old-fashioned maker, closing my eyes in anticipation as caffeine vapors filled the kitchen. Juan Valdez and his donkey were two of my heroes.

Waiting out the machine's cycle, I looked at the envelope again, the front blank except for my name in block letters. Tearing it open I found a color print of Van Gogh's famous portrait of Doctor Gachet. Stapled to the print was a grainy Xeroxed copy of Marguerite Bouchet's photograph. Someone else now owned it and that someone had killed Marguerite Bouchet. I picked up my mobile to check on Wes and jumped when it rang before I punched the hospital number.

"Did you get my envelope?" a male voice said.

What the hell?

"I thought Wes might benefit from another doctor," the voice said. I tightened my grip on the iPhone. Vasily. Wes. Bouchet. The plastic-encased body in Viktor's cellar. The languid voice connected all of them. I tried to picture the caller, the voice almost solicitous, an old friend asking me to join him for a drink.

"There wasn't enough poison in his coffee to kill him," the voice said. "Not this time anyway. That's the good thing about methanol. So easy to acquire and control."

"What do you want?"

"Oh, come now, Adam."

Measured breathing from the other end. Whoever my caller was, he was responsible for Vasily's death and Marguerite Bouchet's murder. The line remained silent as though he was willing to wait me out.

"Who the hell are you?"

"Someone like you who wants the same prize at the bottom of the Crackerjack box. I'm only a messenger. Your supervisor if you like. The job's not so bad, though. You and Miss Veranova provided a fascinating trip through the low countries although I preferred Paris."

There'd been eyes on Kat and me from the beginning. How close had he been? Frustrated, I gripped the phone until my fingers ached, trying to put a face to the assured voice.

"If you can't find the painting, what makes you think I can?"

"Let me explain it another way," the caller said. "You ever watch the NFL football draft on TV, Adam? That big clock that forces teams to make a choice before time runs out?"

I didn't answer.

"I asked you a question."

"Yeah, I've seen it."

"Then play a game with me, okay?"

"I'm listening."

"Look on the back of the old woman's photo I sent you."

I turned over the copy. Written on the back were two words in block letters: Tick Tock.

"You're on the clock. One more week. Find the goddam Van Gogh."

"Very cute but the painting isn't a football game, asshole," I said. "Threatening me won't make me find it any faster. Are you so stupid you can't see that?"

"Sticks and stones," he sighed. For a moment I thought he'd hung up. "I could have killed you and your Russian girlfriend a dozen times over, but we're partners, you and me. My interest is the painting. Don't quit on me and end up like your artist friend."

Jeez, the bastard was crazy.

"Why are you doing this?"

"Now you're being stupid again."

I was standing in my kitchen talking to a killer, a sub-species that walked on two legs. My hand sweated on the plastic casing but I couldn't hang up. But what choice did I have but to hear him out? Kat and I were scrambling in the dark, living on planes, not knowing where to turn next, while this crazy bastard watched and waited.

"How do you justify killing strangers?"

A pause. "Let me ask you something else. You a college grad, Adam?"

"Yes."

"How many degrees?"

I played the game. "Two."

"Two degrees. How much money did you make last year?

"That's none of…"

"I made six million, all expenses included as they say in the corporate world, and I didn't pay a dime in taxes. It's a good living." He waited for me to disagree, to debate him on murder. "I made more money than ninety-nine percent of people in the world. I'm not smarter, just willing to do what they won't do. It's a skill without the tiresome rules and morals."

"Is that how you rationalize it?"

"Oh, I admit there are times when I feel a twinge, but not everyone I encounter is an innocent lamb. They're just part of the job. But you're wasting time. You're not required to agree with how I make my living. You just need to understand I do what's needed."

"This is all bullshit if the painting doesn't exist."

"You think so? The painting's the stuff dreams are made of. You need to find it."

"Did you kill Marguerite Bouchet?"

A sigh. "She's no longer a part of the equation. By the way, your California friend squiring around the big black guy needs to go home. Tell him to stick to hustling fools in LA. You wouldn't want him in the hospital beside Wes."

"You're crazy."

"Remember the clock, Adam, and make me happy."

He was gone

I now had a voice but no face. How had he learned of the Van Gogh? Another of my father's former associates who arrived after I left home, or someone who knew about the letters? Whoever he was, he wouldn't hesitate to kill all of us. I filled my coffee cup and looked at the two photos, resisting the temptation to begin the countdown.

Chapter Forty-One

Afternoon skies spawned a late afternoon tempest off the lake. Temperatures plummeted, flinty ice bouncing off the streets. Art buyers didn't like foul weather and there was no way I could work up the required smile if some hardy shopper braved the storm.

I turned off the lights and pulled a chair into the center of the gallery, facing the dismal street, surrounded by my art as I considered the options. Streetlights came on and I watched the storm escalate, waiting for a bolt of lightning to reveal a plausible means of escape. The mocking voice on the phone measured my future in hours, my life span measured by a painting few people had ever seen.

The door buzzer interrupted my thoughts. Huddled beneath a ruined umbrella, Kat pressed one palm against the plate glass, holding a floppy-brimmed hat in place. I let her in and she collapsed the umbrella, leaning the skeletal remains in a corner. She removed a lined navy-blue raincoat and draped it over my chair.

"You look like the village outcast sitting here alone," she said, pulling off leather gloves. She kissed me, her warm body defying the wintry blast that followed her from the street. "You deserve a written apology, but this may suffice." She kissed me again, her tongue insistent.

I slipped my hands beneath her loose white turtleneck, wishing we were standing in my bedroom. She jumped away, laughing. "Your hands. Turn up the heat and maybe I'll consider a next step."

I kissed her until she pulled back.

"How is Wes?" she asked, catching her breath.

She must have talked with Viktor. "Recovering."

"I know you talked with Viktor. You and I cannot be at war with one another."

"I was a jerk in New York."

"A confusing night. Stupid." She used the Russian word, then slowly repeated it as though enjoying her native language. "In New York, I was a little girl invited to the ball I always dreamed of. Two princes desired me."

I managed a smile. "Horny prince charmings."

I led her to my desk, afraid she might disappear back into the storm. I recapped Wes's second trip to hospital and the phone call. Removing the print and photo from the envelope, I laid them on the desk and told her about my caller and our new time limit.

"A professional," she said. "He's been there all the time. I should have seen him."

"He killed Marguerite Bouchet and poisoned Wes. Warnings, he said."

As she studied the pictures, a white limo made a U-turn on Huron Street and pulled to the curb. A figure emerged and the door buzzer sounded. Surprised a customer would brave the weather, I flipped on the lights.

Phillip Dansby stood erect beneath the awning as though the storm were a spring shower. Ice pellets bounced off his shoulders. his London Fog collar turned up, whipcord khaki trousers sharp with cutting creases. Ignoring the silver coating of sleet in his gray hair, he slipped inside and I locked the door behind him. Slapping at the sleeves he pulled off the bulky coat. He draped it over my chair and ran his hands through his wet hair, tugging down his olive military sweater.

"Bloody awful out there," he said. "If I'm ever elected official scorer, there's no contest. Chicago's unbearable weather defeats New York in a landslide." He walked to Kat. "Katia, my dear. A lovely surprise." He looked around the gallery.

"Quite nice. Very appealing to young collectors."

"Your approval means the world to me, Phillip."

He ignored my jibe and sat at my desk as though he paid the rent. "Don't get your knickers in a wad, dear boy. I'm here on a mission of mercy."

"I didn't think you were in Chicago to enjoy the Oak Street Beach."

He smiled. "Actually, I'm in the city to speak with a new trader. A young man who knows his way around municipal bonds."

A lie by any reckoning. Dansby kept multiple traders at his beck and call. Any young trader would pawn his soul to meet with Phillip Dansby anywhere in the world. I started to say as much when something he said unlocked a memory.

A trader. Stockbroker. The Drake with Wes and Jennings. *That's* what I'd been trying to recall. The man flirting with our waitress at the bar. His back had been toward me, and I'd been too focused on Jennings to examine him closely. The way he held his head and leaned against the bar. I'd seen him in Europe. New York. At odd moments everywhere. No face but I'd recognize him next time—if there was one. Anxious to tell Kat, I heard Dansby's voice again.

"… and together, we're stronger than one."

"Tell me again how you know about the Van Gogh," I said.

Dansby screwed up his face and studied the ceiling as though he'd written the answer on the acoustical tiles. "As I recall, someone in my European network mentioned it, but quite frankly, I could be wrong." Another lie. "I receive alerts about the best art that may be within my reach. Your Van Gogh certainly filled the bill."

"And you chased the rumor, knowing my father as you did?"

"The source is always a consideration, dear boy, but my position permits me to indulge whims, no matter how farfetched. You'd be surprised how many whispers turn up jewels simply because my competition lacked initiative." Dansby looked more closely at me. "And let's not forget you're also sufficiently intrigued to ride to the hounds."

"Did you send me the photo?"

"Photo?" He was either an exceptional actor or genuinely surprised, His expression indicated I'd presented him with an unexpected tactical problem, but if he was behind the phone call, he was playing us again.

I tacked a different course. "Someone almost killed Wes yesterday. He's in the hospital. Again."

Dansby didn't appear fazed. But would a near-death experience concern a professional soldier? It was entirely possible he was behind the warnings. "I'm distressed to hear that. He certainly doesn't need more complications in his life."

"People are dying for this fairy-tale painting," I said. "Whatever you've heard, do you actually believe a huge Van Gogh survived without any record to prove its existence?"

"Belief is a rather strong word. Let's instead say I'm intrigued. An inveterate gambler as it were. You're making a bet yourself. If we win, we'll both rake in a great many chips."

"Then you trust my father's story."

Dansby snorted. "Trust him? Did *you* trust him? Trust is not the issue here.

We're talking about a lost masterpiece, the true chalice from the Last Supper. Would I trust your father if he stood here today and told me he possessed the largest Van Gogh ever seen? Not likely, but he did put pen to paper and that means something." He shook his head with a pensive smile. "Do you know he once attempted to sell me a missing Shakespeare play? Me, like I was some East End dolt. If nothing else, he had quite a set of bollocks on him." He folded his hands on my desk. "No, I'm willing to invest in your little venture because Robert Everham Barrow wrote a dying confession. That's not a matter taken lightly."

The same conclusion Wes had reached. "I have a backer, Phillip. I don't need your money."

"Yes, I know." He looked at Kat. "Comrade Krushenko, our Russian entrepreneur."

"Then you made the trip for nothing," I said.

"Possibly not."

Dansby removed an envelope from his coat and laid it on the desk. A burst of sleet clawed at the front window, trying to warn me. He tapped the envelope with his forefinger.

"This is an agreement with the Chase. A line of credit in your name for $1,000,000. Let's call it a starter fund. Use it your discretion and keep whatever remains when we've successfully concluded our partnership." He locked eyes with Kat. "I'll worry about Mr. Krushenko."

I'd begged and scrounged every dollar I could find to open the gallery, and now a million dollars sat on my desk. Before I could protest, Dansby stood and buttoned his coat. Kat, envelope in hand, followed him to the front door. Ignoring the envelope Kat held out to him, he went to the window and signaled his driver.

"As I said, my dear, I'm a gambler. To the smartest player go the spoils, as the cliché insists. I prefer to think the victor takes risks others avoid. In the end, only the number of chips in your possession determines the winner." He opened the door, wind rattling the nearest picture frames. He turned back to me. "I'm betting on you."

The limo driver trotted to the door with a striped golf umbrella. Dansby ducked inside the car and wind swept away the haze of exhaust, leaving the street empty except only a forlorn garbage truck, yellow-garbed trashmen hanging off the rear.

Kat and I huddled beneath the canvas canopy and watched the limo merge into traffic.

"I understand how he became so rich," she said. "Had he been born Russian, he would be sitting in the Kremlin."

Across the street a gust of wind toppled an empty trash bin, rattling the barrel along the concrete. The storm brought back the old house outside Krefeld and the easel in the barn. Dubinsky had called to certify the paint chips were indeed painter's oils, their composition mixed before the era of Grumbacher and Winsor and Newton. Based on his findings, I saw my father in a gentler light, a damaged human being with a passion he never let the world see, a treasure worth hiding. I recalled touching the easel frame, thinking of the immense painting it may have supported. Whatever his flaws, my father would never have destroyed lives to possess the Van Gogh. He loved great art, even if alcohol and his weaknesses drove him to run con games on the unsuspecting. I saw him in different light now, understanding that he loved the Van Gogh more than dreams of wealth and fame.

Chapter Forty-Two

Eight blocks north of the gallery, the Contractor picked up his pace along Oak Street. The intermittent flurries of sleet subsided, replaced by cold rain that ricocheted off his shoulders and black felt Stetson.

Browsing shops along Armitage Avenue a week earlier, he found himself in a Western store. The sprawling interior smelled of denim and leather, offering everything from blue jeans to pricey Concho belts. He'd spotted the dark blue coat and bought it on an impulse, now congratulating himself on his decision. A contemporary version of the Old West duster, the heavy ankle-length garment shed water like waxed paper. The cowboy boots were a last second indulgence that paid dividends in weather determined to destroy his best shoes. Enjoying the fantasy of having stepped out of a Western movie, he took pleasure from pedestrians' glances. People would remember the clothes, not his face.

Hat brim lowered against the rain, he almost missed the gem in the shop window. The nondescript store sold curiosities and estate jewelry, a forlorn survivor among trendier shops, and if he hadn't glanced to his right, he'd have missed the treasure on the bottom shelf: a tiny grey elephant, a mahout astride its head, the rider dark-skinned enough to warrant a place in his collection. He walked down two steps from the sidewalk, brushing moisture from his sleeves as he stepped inside the overheated interior. The cramped space teemed with odd pieces of bric-a-brac: mismatched china, crystal bowls, antique memorabilia. The air smelled Old World, musty with coatings of dust on glass shelves.

The white-haired man behind the counter wore rimless pince-nez glasses. Ferret-faced with a trim white moustache and goatee, he went to the window and returned with the bronze. He placed the miniature figure in the customer's palm.

The Contractor laid his Stetson on the counter and turned the figure over, inspecting the maker's mark. A hundred years old and unmarred.

"How much?"

"Oh, it's on reserve for a customer, I'm afraid," the man said.

The assertion was an old ploy designed to jack up the price. Why else was it still in the window?

"How much?" the Contractor asked again.

"I'm asking seven hundred," the old man said. "These older ones are extremely rare, especially in this condition and depicting African Americans." A conspiratorial wink and grin made uglier by the snowdrift of dandruff on his coat collar. "Not politically correct as they say nowadays."

"I'll pay seven hundred. Tell your buyer you made a mistake. That it was already sold. I don't have the cash on me but I'll be back in an hour."

The owner nodded and slipped the bronze beneath the register.

Outside, the sky remained asphalt gray, spitting a persistent drizzle at the figure who kept his eyes on the sidewalk. The Contractor adjusted the Stetson and lengthened his stride, fed up with the city's weather as he walked up Oak Street to Michigan Avenue.

The Whitehall Hotel occupied its decades-old niche on Delaware Place. The rain slackened as he crossed the street, clouds rolling toward Indiana. Pausing under the hotel awning, he inhaled a thumbnail of snuff. Inside, he removed a gaily-wrapped package from the duster's deep pocket and made his way to the front desk. Collar turned up against his neck, he tugged down the hat and dredged up his best Clint Eastwood imitation as he expelled his breath.

"Freakin' nasty out there today," he said to the desk clerk.

The clerk, a fastidious young man, gaped at the hat and long coat. "Don't you just *love* February?" he said, enthralled by the rugged face.

For a brief moment, the Contractor worried the little fop might later identify him, but there were no photos of him at Interpol or police files anywhere, and he'd soon be long gone from Chicago.

He held up the gift-wrapped liquor box and pushed a fifty-dollar bill across the counter. "I have a personal delivery for one of your guests, a Mr. Arthur Jennings. A gift from Councilman O'Shaunnesy."

"I'd like to help you, I really would," the clerk gushed, "but it's against hotel rules to give out room numbers. Leave it with the concierge and I'll make certain he takes it up."

The Contractor shook his head dolefully and leaned over the check-in desk. "Look, I can appreciate your rules but this is top of the line booze. O'Shaunnesy will have my ass if it gets misplaced."

The desk clerk admired the tall man's brown eyes. Room numbers were sacrosanct but he knew pissing off a Chicago pol never boded well. He palmed the bill and clicked computer keys.

"Room 1720," he whispered.

The Contractor winked and headed for the elevators. His luck held and he rode alone to the seventeenth-floor, attaching the silencer. Outside the door, he removed the hat and mussed his hair, facing away from the peephole before he knocked. A ghetto voice boomed behind the door.

"Yeah?"

"Delivery for Mister Arthur Jennings."

"Who from?"

"The Adam Barrow Gallery." The Contractor held the wrapped package in front of the peephole, hearing a muffled conversation inside.

He checked the hall again and raised the Browning. The door chain rattled and a one-eyed black man opened the door. The Contractor shot him in the forehead and closed the door. He leaned down and placed a second shot in the temple, the thump no louder than a guest slamming a bathroom door.

Arthur Jennings sat on the side of the bed in his underwear, the room phone in one hand. He stared at the intruder who wore some kind of Western garb that dripped rainwater on Lamar's body. More alarming, the man pointed a long-barreled pistol at him. He touched the heavy gold crucifix dangling against his wife-beater undershirt.

"Who are you?"

"Hang up," the intruder said.

Jennings missed the receiver cradle first try, his eyes on the gun.

"You shot Lamar."

"Regrettable." The Contractor placed the Stetson on a table beside the door. "He would only have interfered with our conversation."

His hand atop the receiver, Jennings could not take his eyes from the gun. He'd seen similar pistols with black cylinders attached to the barrel. Despite the western garb, the man sounded cultured but poor Lamar was deader than a dinosaur.

"Do I know you? Owe someone money?" Jennings wished for the first time he carried a gun but Lamar had always been there.

"Oh, nothing so terrible as that," the Contractor said. He dragged a chair around the body and sat with his legs crossed. He placed the package on the floor, the Browning in his lap.

Jennings hadn't felt the urge to cry since he was a child. Not five minutes earlier he stood at the hotel window admiring the few yachts and sailboats braving the stormy lake. Back in LA he could have bought a boat of his own. Docked it in Santa Monica. Parties. Blow. Chicks. If only Lamar hadn't opened the door.

"I didn't do anything," he said.

"Tell me what I want to know and I'll walk away."

Had Barrow sent the tall man? "Nothing," Jennings stammered. "Barrow won't work with me. I don't know where the painting is. Really, there's nothing I can tell you."

"Then what good are you?"

"For the love of God…"

"Who's He?"

The bullet entered Jennings' left eye. Blood sprayed over the duvet and his body arched backward. The Contractor heaved himself from the chair, walked to the bed, and shot him in the head again. Double taps were insurance. Poor luck or last moment jerk of the head deflected even brass-jacketed slugs.

He looked around the room. Two open suitcases. A half-empty fifth of Jack Daniels beside two water glasses. The Contractor pulled on latex gloves and removed both men's wallets, counting out the contents. A bonus of nine hundred dollars.

Why he'd been ordered him to eliminate the man was his employer's business, but the creature on the bed mentioned the damned painting, and he'd seen him visit Barrow's gallery. Or maybe his employer was settling an old score. He never questioned motives. The way he figured it, his targets had all screwed up one way or the other. Greedy, careless, an unwelcome competitor. He regretted bystanders who showed up at the wrong time, but that was their bad luck.

He collected the spent brass casings, almost missing one under the corner of the bed. Just to be sure, he wiped down the doorknobs and chair arms with a damp handkerchief before he removed a typed sheet of paper from his pocket. He laid the note on Jennings's chest, careful not to smear the paper with blood. If the police discovered it, the message would mean nothing to them, but Barrow possibly finding it was too good a joke to pass up. Using the corner of the sheet he picked up the bedside phone and punched the gallery number with a hotel pen. When the answering machine beeped, he waited for the message and said, "Mr. Jennings and his friend are dying to see you."

Smiling, he hung up and wiped the receiver again. Stripping off the gloves he stuffed the brightly-wrapped package in his coat pocket. He replaced the Stetson and checked the room. Using his coat sleeve, he opened the room door and took the elevator down to the lobby. The desk clerk was nowhere in sight and the Contractor walked out.

***

The owner grinned when the man in the cowboy hat stepped inside. He reached beneath the counter and placed the bronze on a black display mat, his eyes alight. "My buyer changed his mind," he said. "It's yours for seven hundred. Plus, the tax, of course."

The Contractor counted out four hundred taken from Jennings's wallet and smoothed the bills beside the miniature elephant. "I changed my mind too," he said. "Four hundred, including the tax."

The shopkeeper took off his glasses. "The price is seven hundred. I told the other buyer…"

The Contractor removed his hat and laid the Browning beside the miniature, the silencer still attached. Folding his arms on the counter, he hunched over the pistol, shielding it from view. Cars and trucks whispered on wet pavement, and anyone glancing inside the shop saw a buyer and seller in deep negotiation.

Mouth open, the owner glanced at the front door. "You can't…"

"But I am," the Contractor said. He tapped the pistol barrel on the glass countertop. "Is your life worth $300?"

The elderly owner, eyes fixed on the ugly weapon, gawked as though a snake had crawled into the shop.

"Of course, it isn't," the Contractor said. "This is simply a business transaction where you stated a price and we negotiated."

The Contractor dropped the elephant into his pocket atop the latex gloves. The shop owner could identify him if luck turned her face away. A customer could walk in unexpectedly, or the man could run out and find a cop. He lifted the Browning.

The owner grabbed the barrel, twisting it aside. For a few seconds the two men wrestled for the pistol. The younger man twisted the pistol from his grasp. The old man yelled in pain and the Contractor shot him in the chest. The old-fashioned rimless glasses slid from his nose as the frail body collapsed. Stepping behind the counter the Contractor leaned down and fired the second shot.

He pocketed the four hundred dollars, scooped another two hundred from the register, and checked the street. Pedestrians hurried by on the elevated sidewalk but no one glanced inside. The tang of cordite lingered as he turned off the lights and hung the Closed sign in the window, looking back to make certain the body wasn't visible from the window.

He'd made a careless mistake, allowing the old man to grab the gun. He walked back behind the counter and looked down at the body. An unfamiliar stab of guilt brushed him and he hesitated. Lifting the fragile glasses from the counter, he laid them in an outstretched hand. The old bastard made a game effort to avoid the inevitable through fear or courage. Hell, either way, he deserved a modicum of respect for his last seconds on earth.

The Contractor carefully centered his hat and walked to a rear door. He eased it open, checked the alley, and walked away. When the body was discovered, it would be reported as another Chicago murder, a robbery gone bad in this instance. Nothing for the police to get excited about but his carelessness could have proved costly. He could never allow such an error again. The lapse of concentration left him uneasy as he replayed the scene in his head until he regained his composure. Disposing of geriatric shopkeepers was becoming a habit.

Sunlight teased a fissure in the overcast and he turned his face toward the sun. Frigid wind yanked at his hat and snapped his coattails. Damn, he was tired of Chicago. After he took care of the Barrow brothers and disposed of the painting, he'd find a mile of white beach in Tahiti or the south of France. Indulge a woman or two and bask in the sun, anywhere away from the fucking cold. He thought about the note he'd left on Jennings' chest and imagined Barrow's face.

Everything was falling nicely into place.

Chapter Forty-Three

I was relieved when the hospital released Wes next day. He was weak but out of danger, and there was no way the hospital planned to waste a profitable bed on him. Barbara didn't return my calls, so that afternoon Kat and I went to their apartment. I knocked and Barbara answered the door. She eyed Kat and walked back into the living room, her bitterness palatable. Clad in an old flannel bathrobe, Wes raised a hand from the same overstuffed chair he'd occupied during my last visit. He seemed a decade older, years grafted onto his face since they rolled him out of the Drake. The apartment seemed to have aged too as though events were taking a toll on inanimate objects as well.

"This is getting monotonous," Wes said with a sickly grin. "I've become the perpetual patient."

"How're you doing?" I asked.

"I don't think I'll ever trust coffee again," he said, his voice shaky. "Lost ten pounds in two days." He looked up at Barbara with a sickly grin. "Barbara wants the hospital's formula for weight loss."

Barbara clutched the back of his chair and glared at Kat and me. "What I want is for the two of you to get out of here."

"Barbara," Wes said, "if anyone's to blame, it's me. I started all this."

She ignored him. "This is shit, Adam."

I didn't try to defend myself; I'd never heard Barbara utter a profanity.

"You're as much to blame as my starry-eyed husband," she said. "You and your girlfriend traipse around the world looking for this painting, leaving Wes a magnet for killers. Did the hospital tell you some maniac put methanol in his coffee?"

If I had a defense, I couldn't see it at the moment. "The doctor told me someone poisoned him."

"I always took you for half a brain," Barbara continued, "but you went along with this insanity. What happened to you? You know there's no pot of gold waiting for us."

"Okay, I admit I didn't believe the letters. Not at first."

Kat unfolded the Xerox copy of Marguerite Bouchet's photograph and smoothed it on the table next to Wes. "This is what we're looking for," I said. "It proves the Van Gogh exists. Crazy as it sounds, our father may have owned it."

Barbara swiped at the paper, tears in her eyes. "To hell with your painting. In case you overlooked it, money's no good to dead men. My husband's been shot and poisoned. Or do you and your girlfriend even care?"

Kat stooped and retrieved the copy. "Adam could not prevent what happened."

Barbara stepped away from the chair. "Who is this, Adam? Another of your Rush Street bimbos smelling a free ride?"

"Leave it alone, Barbara," Wes said.

Tears ran down her cheeks "Leave it alone? The booze is eating you alive but chasing after this painting is going to get you killed." She pointed at me. "If he dies, I won't be the only one who'll have to live with it." She stalked to their bedroom and slammed the door.

"Sorry, she'll get over it," Wes said. "She hasn't slept since this all started."

Wes's drawn face matched the worst of his bouts with booze and depression. At least they never came close to killing him. He looked around the room with hungry eyes and I saw how badly he wanted a drink. I hoped Barbara had ejected Mister Bushmills and his friends.

"Get well and get your butt back in the gallery," I said. "A tummy ache's no reason to skip work." He smiled weakly and I didn't have the heart to tell him we were on a timetable with less than a week to unearth the Van Gogh. Instead, I pointed at him. "And don't try sneaking out of here. Barbara will have your ass and mine if you take off on a pity-party binge. If the painting's out there, we'll find it."

He nodded but I worried about the boundaries of his endurance. A faceless predator was using him as leverage, stalking all of us. Kat glanced at me. Like Barbara, she knew Wes's limits. People don't merrily skip away after being shot and poisoned.

Outside the apartment building, Kat surveyed the block, inspecting shadows and cars parked along the street. Given what we'd been through, her former habits were good habits.

"What do you think?" I asked.

"About your brother?"

I nodded.

"He is not a bad man. Only weak."

"Weak's the wrong word. It's called dependency."

"In Russia we call it vodka."

"Whatever," I said, avoiding her more accurate label.

We walked north, looking for a cab. Despite his apparent good humor, I couldn't get over Wes's appearance, or Barbara's panicked retreat. They didn't deserve the world falling on them and Barbara was right; I couldn't accept carrying his death for the rest of my life. If I had a reasonable choice, I'd walk away and take my chances with Viktor. Let some maniac have the damned painting. But that wasn't how the game was being played. Not now. Kat had called it correctly. No matter what I did, Wes and I were disposable once the Van Gogh was found. Somehow, I was supposed to overcome a killer no one could see, but I wasn't like the woman beside me. Only in films did gallery owners turn into super heroes.

"Wes and Barbara good people," I said. "The booze will always be part of him, but he believes the Van Gogh will solve their problems. You saw the apartment. It gives you an idea how they live."

Kat didn't break stride. "They would be envied in Russia. You Americans think too much about what you do not own, not what you have."

Three blocks later we lucked into a taxi. I started to give the gallery's address, then said, "The Whitehall on Delaware." Lamar or no Lamar, I needed to get clear of Arthur Jennings. I took Kat's hand, surprised when she clenched mine.

"We need to get Jennings off our backs," I said, "and I need to know what the anonymous phone call to the gallery meant. If Jennings was linked to Wes's poisoning." I thought about Lamar and lowered my voice as we turned off Michigan Avenue. "You still have the gun?" She looked at me as if I'd asked if she was wearing shoes.

Still holding hands, we paraded through the hotel lobby. When the elevator doors opened on the seventeenth floor, a service cart sat at the far end of the hall, the maid nowhere in sight. Kat and I walked quickly to 1720, swiped the entry card Arthur had given me, and let ourselves in.

The room smelled like an abandoned meat locker. Lamar lay face down on the carpet a few feet inside the door, the back of his skull missing. Jennings was sprawled face up across the bed. A huge rust stain on the coverlet framed his ruined face. I forced down the surge of bile and looked closer. His pockets were turned out, a wallet on the floor beside the bed. Kat cracked open the hall door and hung the Do Not Disturb sign on the handle.

A sheet of paper rested on Jennings's chest. I picked it up, looking away from the gory pit of his ruined eye socket.

I handed Kat the Xerox of Marguerite Bouchet's photo. *Six Days* was neatly printed in caps on the back. Kat folded the paper and stuffed it in her pocket.

"I own all this," I said, gesturing at the bodies. "The Van Gogh isn't worth two more lives.

"You no longer believe the painting's a fairy tale."

"People don't get murdered for rumors."

I'd discovered the trouble with boatloads of money: little boats like us got swamped by oceangoing super tankers. I stepped over Lamar's body with a newfound sense of guilt and looked back at Jennings. He'd been a lowlife but never a dangerous antagonist like our pursuer.

Kat opened the room door and checked the hall. The maid's cart was gone. She wiped our fingerprints from both door handles and we walked down two flights before we caught the elevator to the lobby. We stepped onto the sidewalk and I fell in step with her, conscious of the words on the piece of paper in her pocket.

Less than a week remained.

***

She came to my bed that night. I held her until she fell into a restless slumber, her body jerking, fighting her demons with soft Russian cries. As she lay against me, I realized we'd crossed a bridge. Neither of us had the vaguest idea where we were headed, our disparate lives linked only by the Van Gogh. I had few doubts Kat would return to Viktor if anything happened to me. With no family and a fugitive from her native country, she'd have little choice. A childhood without parents or kittens or friendships left her dependent on rigid structures like the KGB and Viktor's empire, no matter how malevolent the organization. And if I survived? There was a part of her I'd never share, doors she'd never allow me to open. I stroked her silken hair and vowed to keep her safe whatever happened in the next six days.

Her arm tightened around my chest. "Are you awake?" she whispered.

"Barely," I lied. "Go to sleep."

"Forget the two dead men," she mumbled. "They won't bother you again."

After a few moments, her breathing deepened, her smooth belly rising and falling against my side. She murmured something in Russian, but it was a contented sound as though we were safe from the future.

Unable to sleep, I squeezed my eyes shut and tried to infuse color into Marguerite Bouchet's photo. I couldn't stop the clock and even if I could, Viktor lingered off stage. He might be my worst nightmare, but was he connected to the voice on the phone? I didn't think so. He had Arby with no need for anonymous threats and cryptic messages. That wasn't his style, but I'd recently misjudged too many people to give him a free ride. Maybe he believed I required a different kind of rebar to intensify the search. With Jennings gone, that left fewer players in the game. And someone I couldn't see.

Chapter Forty-Four

I opened the gallery early next morning and didn't notice the length of rebar. When I opened the door, it fell against the glass and clunked onto the sidewalk. I checked the street. It was empty except for morning traffic. I picked up the bar, went inside, and shut off the alarm system. Viktor was many things, but subtle wasn't one of them. I tossed the shaft into the trash bin. Whatever was happening, Viktor's obsession with the Van Gogh wasn't waning.

The phone rang and I hesitated before picking up, expecting more threats from Viktor.

"Adam, Jack McMinnis here."

I relaxed and sat down. "Jack, I've been meaning to call you. We're working on getting the paintings shipped," I said. "Wes had a set-back." What else was I supposed to call being poisoned? "We're a little behind schedule."

"No problem. I'm thinking about an opening for Vasily's paintings here in New York. Have you fly out and say a few words about him. Buyers like stories. If they buy a painting, the story becomes theirs."

"Vasily would have liked that."

"Look, I've got a favor to ask, and I know you're going to think I've lost my mind. In fact, you may not believe what happened." He gave a half-laugh. "In fact, I don't believe it myself. Dansby called and wants a sit-down. You, me, Wes, and him. He has this idea we can work together to find the Van Gogh. Says there's enough money for all of us. Can you believe that?"

"You're right, I don't believe it," I said, fearing Viktor's reaction if he discovered I was meeting with his competitors. "Dansby doesn't play well with others, and he sure as hell doesn't make alliances unless he believes he'll walk away the winner."

"Or else he thinks the reward is worth the risk," Jack said.

"You don't seem concerned."

Jack was a rich collector but the Englishman was out of his league. It was a stretch but possibly Dansby reasoned a piece of something was better than nothing.

"I wouldn't trust the oily bastard if he let us bring along the Marine Corps," Jack said, "but we'll control where we meet. I'll make certain he's not trying to eliminate the competition."

Viktor's concept of eliminating competition ended with a length of rebar. Jack had no idea about my arrangement with the Russian, although Dansby knew about Viktor and suspected Kat wasn't what she appeared. I didn't believe Jack understood how effectively the Russians removed problems, but we had Dansby to worry about at the moment.

"You think we can control the meeting?" I asked.

"We'll meet in public and I'll ensure protection. Find out what he's got in mind if nothing else."

I didn't like the idea but it had a ring of logic to it. The night in New York had revealed we were at each other's throats, and that didn't bode well for anyone—or the Van Gogh. No matter what came out of the meeting, I couldn't imagine Dansby or Viktor sharing the spoils.

"What do you propose?"

"We come to Chicago," Jack said. "Meet at a major restaurant. I'll make reservations for Thursday night and let Dansby know the location at the last minute."

Thursday was two days away, leaving three days to locate the painting. It wasn't beyond probability that Viktor or someone else might dispose of me whether the Van Gogh surfaced or not. In my favor, Kat might have something to say about the eventual outcome. Tempted to tell him about Jennings, I figured he'd read it in the papers soon enough. I only needed one distraction at a time.

I suggested meeting at Tru, one of the city's most expensive restaurants, thinking I might as well enjoy my last meal. We sure as hell weren't going Dutch, and Dansby could afford the tariff. I hung up and phoned Kat to tell her about the proposed meeting.

"And Viktor?"

"I don't know. I'm just playing this by ear now." She remained silent and I said, "Look, these are powerful men and Viktor can take of himself."

"Viktor doesn't like people who defy him."

"I'll have to risk that."

"What about your brother?"

"I'm on a timetable."

"Am I invited to this meeting?"

"Dansby insisted on just the four of us."

Her voice softened. "You once told me never to walk away. It sounds like you're the one walking away."

"You mean far more than the painting, but I need to buy time. If we find the damned thing, you and I will work things out."

Events were moving fast. When I started to tell her about the rebar at the gallery door, she'd already bung up.

Chapter Forty-Five

Temperatures plummeted again, clouds blurring high rise roof tops along St. Clair Street. During the Uber ride to Tru, I glanced at Wes and wondered what kind of maneuver he'd performed to sneak past Barbara.

McMinnis arrived in a cab a few seconds after us and we entered the restaurant together. It took a few seconds to recognize Kalil who followed us inside. Bundled in a knee-length overcoat long enough to conceal an arsenal, he wore Ray-Bans despite the fading light.

Inside the minimalist vestibule, a bevy of staff helped us out of our coats. Although a favorite among well-heeled diners, Tru's main dining room was best described as Modern Spartan. White tablecloths. White draperies. Plain black chairs. Muted ceiling lighting complemented paintings by Warhol and cutting-edge artists.

The maître d' ushered us to two private tables. The open space around us could have seated another twenty people, our island isolated from other diners. The privacy was costing Dansby a small fortune, but Jack was as good as his word, especially with Kalil seated at a separate table.

"It was only supposed to be the four of us. Your man looks like a Hamas terrorist. You think Dansby will walk out?"

"I doubt it. Too much pride to show he's afraid of anything."

Wes looked from Kalil to Jack. "You don't trust Dansby?"

"I take it your man's armed," I said.

"That's why he's here."

"Wes and I won't be at the top of his list if this thing goes south."

"Kalil is very competent."

Wes looked less than reassured. "You think Dansby might try something here?"

"He's done worse." Jack said.

"You trying to cheer us up?" Wes asked.

"I don't think he's stupid," Jack replied, "but why take chances?"

The wine steward approached and Jack ordered a bottle of French white burgundy which quickly appeared. The label was the evening's first positive. Wes hesitated, then placed his palm over his wine glass, his expression resigned as he regarded the bottle. Kalil did the same and the steward filled the other glasses, waiting until Jack waved him away.

"Too bad Jennings isn't part of our little discussion," I said to Jack.

"Old Arthur? Is he sniffing around the Van Gogh?"

"Not anymore," I said. "Someone shot him and his bodyguard at The Whitehall two nights ago."

Jack shook his head. "Damn, I never liked the little shyster but he didn't deserve that." He sipped his wine. "Arthur was never too smart. Never knew when to quit. I guess he finally pissed off the wrong people."

"He came around the gallery a couple of times. If my father hadn't admitted to owning the Van Gogh, a lot of people would still be alive."

Wes gazed at the wine bottle. "Too late now."

I heard laughter and saw Phillip Dansby weaving his way past occupied tables. Dressed in a blazer with a heraldic crest and sporting a scarlet ascot, he stopped to shake hands with two men, both of whom stood as he graced them with a few words. He said something and the three of them laughed. Waving at another table, he strode up to us with a fulsome grin.

"Hail, hail, the gang's all here," he said, sizing up Kalil.

"Nice quiet arrival," Jack said.

"And I see you ensured us a bit of privacy," Dansby made no move to sit down, assessing Kalil and our isolation. "I believe I said private, old boy, not set apart like a leper colony." His eyes remained on Kalil as he spoke, making a show of shifting his chair to face him before he sat down.

"Tell Mohammed to keep both hands on the table."

"Kalil knows his business," Jack said.

"Just so," Dansby said, unbuttoning his jacket to reveal a shoulder holster, "but tell him anyway."

Jack did as Dansby asked and the table lapsed into an awkward silence. So much for mutual trust. Dansby spread his linen napkin in his lap and raised his eyebrows at me. "The lovely Miss Veranova isn't joining us?"

"Jack's rules," I said.

He grinned at McMinnis. "A dreadful oversight to exclude beauty from our dreary discussion." He turned to Wes. "I understand you've been somewhat under the weather."

"An upset stomach," Wes said.

Dansby suppressed a smile. "I never imagined the art business could be so dangerous, did you, Jack?"

"Depends on who you're dealing with."

This could all fall apart in a heartbeat. The nearest exit was twenty-five feet away and I doubted Wes and I could make it. "We agreed to hear what you have in mind," I said.

"Coordination and cooperation." Dansby plucked the bottle from the wine bucket and examined the label, wiping it dry with his napkin. "Pool our logistics. Attack our objective with maximum force."

"This isn't a half-ass military exercise you dreamed up at Sandhurst," Jack said. "We all know what we're after."

Nonplussed, Dansby regarded him like a subordinate who'd spoken out of turn. The wine steward returned and we fell silent again. Dansby emptied the remainder of the bottle into his glass before the server could assume the arduous task. He ordered a second bottle and shooed away the flustered man. I said nothing and waited to hear whatever plan he'd devised.

"All right, here's what I propose," he said, dabbing at his lips. "Adam, you first share what you know. Jack and I will then do the same. Poor AJ possibly could have added something, but he's no longer among us."

"How'd you know about Jennings?" I asked.

"Dear boy, I read more than the *Wall Street Journal*. Now, if you'll be so kind, tell us what you've learned."

Unable to believe he took me for such a lightweight, I didn't attempt to conceal my laughter. "So, I tell you what I know and then you tell me you've found nothing. Helluva deal, Phillip."

Dansby started to reply but the maître d' returned and recited the menu McMinnis had pre-ordered. When he approached Kalil, Jack's watchdog shook his head, his eyes on Dansby who appeared unconcerned, leaving me to surmise he had sufficient nearby firepower to resolve any difficulties. I could jam all the trust at the table into a shot glass.

We ate in silence. Dansby requested a third bottle of the white burgundy and gave an approving nod to Jack. Refilling our glasses himself he waited until the table was cleared and sat back.

"To business, then," he said. "Given the lack of confidence in one another, shall we all think about my proposal and meet again in two nights? Say at the Four Seasons? I'll make the arrangements this time. And since Adam has reservations about our openness, I'll start the next discussion with what I know if everyone's amenable. And Adam, please ignore Jack's restrictions and invite Miss Veranova. I don't doubt she's privy to your darkest secrets."

Jack tossed his napkin on the table. "And then what, Dansby? Share and share alike? The Four Musketeers? One for all and all that crap?"

"Don't fuck with me, Jack," Dansby said. "I'm trying to be civilized here." The two stared at one another until Dansby refilled his glass. "For all any of us know, we may be chasing a will of the wisp."

"And if it's real," Jack said, "how do I know one of us won't grab the painting and screw the others?"

Dansby stood. "Why, you don't, of course, but that's half the fun, isn't it?"

In the foyer five employees held our coats ready as Dansby tipped each one. Complementary canelés were offered. Everyone declined except Wes. A peace offering for Barbara?

Valets waited outside, holding open taxi doors. Dansby's limo was parked in front of the two cabs, his driver beside the rear door. Dansby gave a cheery wave and I caught sight of female legs as he slipped inside.

Turning my collar up against the lake wind, I saw a familiar figure slip around the corner as Kat disappeared into the night.

Chapter Forty-Six

I was drinking coffee next morning when an express driver delivered a certified letter to my condo. The return address informed me Los Angeles County had rediscovered me. Fearing the window envelope announced some bureaucratic disaster, I ripped it open, surprised to discover our old house in Santa Monica had been designated as 'a home of architectural quality'. My first thought was some faceless civil servant committed a ludicrous mistake, but it seemed the Office of Historical Preservation and Santa Monica's Landmark Commission Trust was certain the battered eyesore typified 'early West Coast cottage design.'

Astonished the grungy little house had any historical significance other than a convenient barroom for my father, I reread the letter. The two-bedroom dwelling barely qualified as a habitable residence, its singular appeal that it sat on the highest bluff along the coast, the Pacific's endless blue panorama breathtaking at sunset… but historically significant?

With all the required legal hoops and snares, the letter required that Wes and I meet a preservation representative on the premises within two days or face a bevy of fines and penalties. All travel at our expense, of course. A short paragraph grudgingly indicated a tax break; two additional paragraphs laid out the penalties for noncompliance.

I tossed the letter on the kitchen counter. With life and death at my heels, the last thing I needed was another deadline. I poured a second cup of coffee and closed my eyes. A day trip to the West Coast left only two days to meet the far deadlier ultimatum, and I absently wondered if the Landmark Commission employed firearms to impose its penalties. The old place exerted more of a warped nostalgic tug than I wanted to admit but requiring it remained intact seemed a travesty. I knew Wes suffered a similar attachment though he never admitted it. To some unfathomable degree, I guess no one outgrows their childhood homes, relegating the worst moments to black holes, keeping the best memories in sunlight. If we complied with the Commission's dictates, it was possible we might become civic benefactors and atone for some of our father's screw-ups whether or not the painting ever surfaced. On the other hand, time spent away from the search might cost our lives.

I called Wes. He'd received the same letter and we agreed to fly out that night. An hour later, I dialed the number on the letterhead and made an appointment to meet the inspector the following day, booking two seats to Los Angeles at nine o'clock that night. I'd justify the outrageous expense of two last-minute flights to Viktor, claiming I didn't want to overlook the house as a possible sanctuary for the Van Gogh, hoping he'd would buy the story.

I packed an overnighter and called Kat to let her know I'd return tomorrow. Wes met me curbside outside his apartment. Barbara was nowhere in sight, a merciful respite for both of us in my brotherly opinion. Our Bahamian Uber driver ignored us, ear buds bobbing to a reggae backbeat berating his eardrums.

"Where's Kat?" Wes asked.

"I didn't invite her." I thought about the automatic I'd left in my condo. In its own way, I'd grown accustomed to its weight and regretted the pistol couldn't accompany me.

"Okay," Wes said, "tell me who the hell she is."

I leaned closer and told Wes everything after making him swear not to tell Barbara or anyone else.

He managed a skewed grin. "KGB? You gotta be kidding me. How would she…" He stopped and his eyebrows shot up. "Holy shit, you really can pick 'em."

"I didn't *pick* her. It was your bright idea to involve Viktor. He assigned her as a bodyguard, and she's damned effective." The street mugger and our interrupted lunch in Paris had proven that.

Five hours later we checked into a Santa Monica motel an hour before midnight, glad of the time change. Our appointment with the Los Angeles official wasn't scheduled until 11:00AM next morning, allowing us to catch a few hours of sleep.

***

The drive to the house was filled with memories we'd worked hard to forget. Wes stared out the car window, most likely reliving the year he'd spent in the house after marrying Barbara. Neither of us said much as I turned off into the hills north of Santa Monica, the roadside canyons and parched outcrops of dry brush little changed since our childhoods. We'd both made the drive countless times but without life-threatening baggage clinging to us. The trip became overpowering as we drew near the house. Wes fixated on the road ahead, afraid he'd discover our father passed out in the back seat if he turned his head.

We crested a precipitous bluff and the house loomed over the car's hood. The miniscule front yard still sported a concrete birdbath my mother purchased before my birth, a tangle of weeds obscuring the chipped base. Luxurious homes sat at respectable distances from the 1940's relic, swimming pools and colorful patio umbrellas glimmering in the sunlight. Our shop-worn homestead looked like second-rate quarters for domestic help, an uninvited squatter among rich kids' playhouses. I couldn't count how many lawsuits failed to expel the blight from their midst, the last eyesore of Ocean Heights as the area was once called. Currently unrented, the exterior showed little surprising change except for the faded stucco exterior and unkept yard. Sunlight had bleached the textured walls to a shade of spoiled cream, the louvered windows streaked with several years of grime. The red-tiled roof at least assured a dry interior.

"I have a set of keys," I said. "Want to go inside before he gets here?"

"No. I hated the place when Barbara and I were forced to live here after dad's death." He looked around. "It's still a dump."

We sat in the car and rolled down the car windows, staring at the ocean below us. Property on the Heights now sold for outrageous prices. Wes and I didn't get along but somehow, we couldn't bring ourselves to let the place go; bulldozers and backhoes erased good and bad memories alike. We'd always been too busy trying to repair our lives, realizing at a subliminal level the place was a bank account accruing usurious interest as California real estate soared to ridiculous heights. I'd often regretted not selling the place although we had multiple offers. Wes always needed money, and I could have used start-up capital for the gallery, but the old place held sway over us. I hired a management company and we broke even from the rents, using the rationale that childhood homes sometimes remained outside the obscene realm of profit. The reasoning sounded crazy, but Wes and I had made worse decisions over the years.

A white Lexus convertible pulled up behind us Wes grumbled about being on time but I cut our benefactor some slack, given that Los Angeles traffic resembled chariot races.

Attired in a chalk-striped black suit our contact wore a blue striped button-down and yellow tie. A tooled leather folio jammed beneath one arm, he shook our hands with genuine enthusiasm as if we'd agreed to sell him the property at a giveaway price.

"The Brothers Barrow, I presume?" he grinned. "Nice to meet people who genuinely care about salvaging our heritage. A pleasure indeed, gentlemen."

Franklin Bonnings was an authentic California specimen, middle-aged with a Malibu tan and perfect capped teeth. He removed tinted sunglasses that accentuated blue eyes—tinted contacts?—and wiped them with a pristine handkerchief, surveying the view as though he'd arranged it for our benefit. I surmised his position was honorary or he was a board member whose civic duty required he occasionally rub shoulders with the middle class. Neither his demeanor nor clothes reflected an underpaid public servant, and I wished I'd worn something other than jeans and a windbreaker over my black tee shirt.

"You work for the Preservation Division in LA?" I asked.

"Actually, no. I'm with LALC. The Los Angeles Landmark Commission. Quite a mouthful but we do good work. We're a volunteer organization that coordinates preservation efforts with the county and state." He looked at us, waiting for tacit approval of his good work. "Members work with owners such as yourselves to ensure the area's history is not lost or overlooked." He swept his hand along the ridge and down the hillside, raising his heels in pleasure as he took in the vista. "Breathtaking, isn't it, but so much of its original charm has been lost. Redevelopment destroyed so much. Your house is the last remaining example of West Coast Bungalow Design."

Wes lit a cigarette and looked at me, strangling a laugh.

Bonnings retained his smile and rummaged through the folio as though about to offer us a wad of bearer bonds. "In case you're interested, I brought copies of the original house plans. Luckily, the architectural drawings were still on file in the County Records Department. Quite a find in their own right since so much history has been lost or thrown out. Records show your parents were the original occupants in 1941."

Wes laughed out loud, drawing a confused look from Bonnings. I nudged my brother, remembering the tax break. Bonnings unfolded the blueprints and I flipped through the faded blue sheets, recognizing the floorplan. The architect's name and signature adorned the bottom left corner, and I wondered if our father had somehow conned him too. The county's legal work waiting for our signatures was paperclipped to the blueprints.

"For your family records. A historic survivor with documentation," he said as if he'd discovered the Magna Carta in a Liverpool basement.

"*Historic*?" Wes said. "Hell, it barely qualifies as a dump."

Bonnings looked genuinely hurt, and I couldn't tell if it was Wes's disparaging remark or the cigarette. "Nevertheless, it's a rare survivor," he said, giving the impression that he was holding his breath as smoke drifted over him. "If you and your brother agree to a few innocuous terms, the Society will guarantee preservation and assume the majority of maintenance. Plus, I'm sure you noted there's an attractive tax concession."

Anxious to keep Wes at bay, I said, "I'd like to take a look inside. We haven't inspected it in quite a while."

Bonnings' good humor reappeared. "Take your time."

I unlocked the front door and the three of us went inside. My breathing constricted as the melancholy staleness greeted us. Years of strangers couldn't erase the memories and familiar odors. I avoided looking at Wes, knowing he was battling his devils.

A single aluminum lawn chair sat in the center of the empty living room, its once colorful plastic webbing frayed and shredded like a bleached rainbow. The room looked somehow larger, almost spacious without furniture. A startled roach scuttled from beneath scattered newspapers, heading for a headless doll propped in a corner of the adjoining dining room. Scars and scrapes from tenants' furniture marred the hardwood floors but I recognized indentations left by my father's springless sofa. Bonnings pretended not to hear when Wes reminded me our father spent most of his final days on the couch, a bottle within easy reach.

Bonnings trailed us through the house, each room reviving a newsreel of nightmares. Bonnings worked hard to praise the 1940's house, insisting on seeing distinctive features. I glanced at the washed out blueprints a final time and tossed them in a kitchen drawer. Despite Bonnings' enthusiasm, I didn't need a map of my broken life as we walked from room to deserted room. Wes trailed behind me and I wondered if assuring the house's immortality only prolonged our defective childhoods.

No longer listening to Bonnings, I walked from the house and stood at the edge of the property staring over the bluff, hands buried in the back pockets of my jeans. Wes toed a clump of weeds without looking back. Bonnings waited near the front door, uncomfortable and embarrassed by the family dynamics he'd blundered into. Maybe it was better to demolish the place and sell the property. Forget everything it represented. I walked back to Bonnings.

"I'd like a few days to consider your proposal," I said.

Ever hopeful, he said, "I would imagine that's possible. We've just approved the house as a preservation candidate and there are several more hurdles we need to clear."

"We'll let you know within the week."

Bonnings slipped on his dark glasses and I sensed he was passionate about his role, a crusading zealot who could afford charitable impulses. "Please consider this carefully, Mr. Barrow," he said. "As I'm sure you realize, not everything is measured in money." We shook hands. His philosophy was particularly useful for those with large portfolios. He got in his car and rolled away, waving as the $80,000 convertible wound down the canyon road.

Wes walked over and looked at the disappearing car. "What'd you tell him?"

"That we'd let him know."

He looked over his shoulder at the house. "We ought to fight do-gooders like him. Tear it down and let some Hollywood bigwig pay us major bucks so he can turn this piece of crap into party town. Build a big manse up here with a fire pit and Olympic swimming pool to entertain naked starlets. Include a clause in the sale that guarantees weekend invitations."

"Barbara would like that," I said.

If the painting existed, I wondered if it had crossed the yard where we stood. Or had dad dreamed up the entertaining tale with a cocktail in hand as he gazed at the ocean? Something to replace mom, while he anticipated the next drink.

"This place is still the pits," Wes said.

I remembered the voice on the phone and pictured the ticking clock he'd described with relish.

"Let's go back inside. I want to check something."

He followed me and I stopped inside the front door. The living and dining rooms were ridiculously undersized by today's standards, barely larger than mud rooms in today's track houses. Wedded to a barely-turn-around kitchen and two cramped bedrooms, the house belonged in Bonnings' proposed museum. Not one pleasant memory emerged from dirty walls and I suddenly felt sick.

"What're we doing?" Wes asked. "Reliving an Ozzie and Harriet episode? The Cleaver boys return home for a family reunion?"

"You started all this. Dad might have found a way to hide it here."

"Right, there's tons of space here to hide something that big."

I walked to the nearest corner and studied the floor boards, the foot-worn varnish curled from wear and heat. Had our father found a way to bury something beneath them? I tapped the boards along the wall with the heel of my loafer, rewarded with solid thumps from the concrete foundation. Wes did the same until we'd covered the living and dining rooms. It took another hour to check out flooring in the halls, kitchen, bedrooms, tiny closets, and the single bathroom, every seam tight as the day the boards were laid down.

We ran our palms along smudged walls without finding the secret panel revealed in old movies. Wes pulled down a rickety ceiling ladder and we climbed into the sweltering attic, ducking overhead rafters and mindful of exposed joists. The space was bare except for cancerous yellow insulation and two rotting cardboard boxes. Nothing indicated anyone had climbed the wooden pulldown in years. I flipped through the boxes' mildewed contents and found nothing related to a 19th century Dutch artist. Wisps of yellow asbestos drifted in the heat and we retreated down the ladder, holding our breath and brushing our clothes.

Defeated, we walked outside and I locked the front door We dusted our hands and avoided looking at one another. A dead-end. I shut my eyes against the sunlight and mentally retraced our steps from room to room. Hell, there hadn't been *that* much to explore. I swore and kicked a cigarette butt in the yard.

"Okay, now we know it's not here," Wes said.

"You lived with him the longest. Any other place he could have hidden it? Did he ever leave the house without explaining where he was going?"

"Only a thousand times," Wes replied. "Usually it was a frantic ride to the liquor store or meeting with a mark. He never said anything about visiting a painting."

"If he stored it in Los Angeles, it's gone forever," I said. My anger rekindled at the thought, recalling the unfinished letter, a few sentences short of unraveling the puzzle. The well had run dry and I hadn't told Wes about the caller or deadline.

I wanted to confide in him but decided I'd call Jack instead.

"You know dad's sitting somewhere in the great beyond with a drink in his hand, laughing his ass off," Wes said. "He thought it'd be a great joke to watch us scramble after something he dreamed up." He spit in the yard. "You and Barbara were right. I know I was a fool but the letters were a way out. A chance to start over." He looked at the house as though he could hear our father's laughter inside. "Too good to be true is always the rule, right?"

I shrugged. If we managed to survive, he was guaranteed a job in the gallery, down to the last dollar. I owed him that.

"What are you going to tell Viktor?" he asked.

"I have no idea."

"Maybe your girlfriend can talk with him."

I wasn't counting on Kat's persuasive skills. Not with Viktor. I had no idea where his patience ended, or how deep his disappointment ran when denied something he wanted. It wasn't beyond the realm of possibility he'd employ Arby's talents and write me off as a bad debt.

The late afternoon flight back to Chicago was mercifully half-full. Wes dozed and I was left thinking about my last flight with Kat. Her involvement with me connected her whatever waited for Wes and me. She had ample cause to resume her association with Viktor who could offer money and security, both of which I lacked. I couldn't protect her if something or someone appeared out of her past. Whatever was left of it, my life was collapsing around me.

I rested my head against the Boeing's scratched window. The sun fled behind the tail as I stared over the wing toward the eastern skies where the gathering gloom waited in Chicago. If I survived and Kat walked away, chances were I'd end up with a clingy art major in love with the idea of marrying a struggling gallery owner, a long way from the dream I envisioned.

The drone of the engines eventually lulled me into an uneasy sleep. My last thought was something Bonnings had said. I tried to force it to the surface but it slipped away each time I closed my eyes. I didn't want to think about the alternatives that remained, but in all likelihood, I was probably going to need the gun hidden in my closet.

Chapter Forty-Seven

July 1890 Ravoux Inn Auvers France

The smudged window in the canted ceiling blurred the stars. A straw-bottomed wooden chair and scarred desk struggled to make the cramped bedroom habitable, unframed paintings haphazardly arranged on the walls and stacked in corners. A trio of sputtering oil lamps illuminated the low bed where a distraught figure loomed above Vincent, the morose features painfully coalescing into his brother's troubled face.

"Theo?"

"I'm here, Vincent. Are you in pain?"

"No, no, I'm alright."

Theo turned away. Doctor Gachet took his arm and led him to the far side of the room.

"Does he remember what happened?" Gachet asked quietly.

"He insists it was an accident, then claims he can't remember." Theo looked at the pale figure on the bed. "It's all very confusing."

What had happened, Vincent thought? He lifted his head from the sweat-damp pillow and picked up the hand mirror to inspect his lower abdomen. The movement produced sharp pain and he saw the small hole was weeping blood again, the wound ringed by an angry red circle. He squeezed his eyes shut against the pain and tried to recall what happened. He'd taken the easel, his paint box, and a freshly stretched canvas into a field of new harvest and then... nothing. A blank. Where was the canvas, his brushes? Theo told him he'd staggered back to the inn empty-handed, his smock drenched in blood.

Gachet walked to the bed and inspected the bullet wound. "Bleeding again."

He gingerly applied a fresh gauze pad and beckoned Theo away from the bed once more. They retreated to the corner, voices too low for Vincent to make out the words. The burning sensation returned, a white-hot iron spike probing his stomach. He must have groaned because Theo was there again, a hand on his bare arm. Gachet reached past Theo and lifted the bloody bandage, inspecting the wound.

Vincent looked at the bearded physician. He'd painted the morose eyes more than once. Did the good doctor carry a burden hidden from his patients? He wasn't a very good doctor, but he was kind and that had been a comfort in the worst of times. Gachet laid another fresh gauze on the wound, frowning when the bleeding quickly soaked the bandage.

Poor Gachet, Vincent thought, his hooded eyes so gloomy and saddened with despair, troubled by the fresh surge of blood. Vincent's mind drifted as boisterous laughter erupted from the inn downstairs, the cries and voices of late night drinkers unaware of his condition. The sounds meant business continued as usual. Bourgeois commerce trumped all, he thought, but it was better that way; the unsolvable universe would continue spinning without him. A drop of warm blood crawled down his side like an inquisitive insect. If only he could recall what happened.

A pistol. That was it. A small revolver. But where had the weapon come from, and who wielded it? He never owned a gun. Did it belong to a friend? Someone at the inn? Or one of the village boys who taunted him? He wanted to ask Theo but the question flew away, spurred by the pain. What had happened to his breath? Theo was saying something and the light was fading. With relief and barest touch of fear, Vincent knew he'd never again hold a worn brush, never again flow creamy greens and yellows onto unblemished canvas. In the hands of others, color would be reduced to mediocrity.

Brightness filled the room as though morning had hurried its passage and found him still in bed. He squeezed his eyes shut against the light, and when he opened them, the girl stood at the foot of the bed, her blue dress radiant just as he'd repainted her. She smiled and he started to apologize for leaving her a second time, but she floated away before the words formed. Content that he'd returned to Holland to repaint her in the colors she deserved, the guilt of deserting her never left him. His sorrow returned with astonishing clarity and he silently wept. She was gone forever but that was not an altogether bad ending. If his critics never saw her, it would be only a just ending for both of them. The high-brows would find ways to deride her, blissfully unaware she deserved more adoration than any woman of flesh and blood.

The pain released him, grayness consuming the light. Where was the light going? He always wondered what happened in the last moments, imagining some grandiose revelation. His thoughts returned to the girl abandoned in the Dutch countryside. Just as well, he sighed. He'd acted as God, creating her with his brush. A blasphemous act, but it mattered little since no one would ever see her again.

Chapter Forty-Eight

I was out of time.

Checking the street, I unlocked the gallery door and stepped inside. Punching off the security code I saw Viktor at my desk. He didn't look up, his fur-collared coat open, the Tokarev under his belt. Standing at his side, Arby Bolkov grinned at me, his unshaven face stubbled with three days growth of beard, hands in the black leather coat pockets. Viktor held a small oil painting on his lap and rubbed a calloused thumb over the gold frame. Pursing his lips, he frowned at the small landscape.

"Not good like Vasily," he declared, tossing the picture on the desk.

I picked it up and rehung it on the wall, angry they'd broken into the gallery. "How'd you get in here?"

Viktor swiveled toward me. "Not to worry. Arby find someone to fix your back door." He spread his hands on the desk and sighed. "You have not called me."

"There's nothing to tell you."

"Nothing? You and Katia go to Europe, spend my money, and you have nothing to tell me?"

"We talked about that. The trip was your idea. I warned you we might not find anything."

"But yesterday, she does not go to California with you. Why is that? Maybe she is no longer welcome in your bed, or you play games with me, you and her?"

Surprised he knew about us and the trip, I said, "Wes and I had family business. Nothing to do with the painting."

"Then why you spend my money to fly there?"

He didn't miss much. "As long as we were there, I wanted to check my father's house one last time."

"You go to your old house?"

"Yeah, but we didn't find anything. The painting's not there."

He shook his head before I finished, eyes half-closed.

"I do not think you me tell me the truth." He glanced at Arby. "What you think, Arby?"

Arby wagged his head with a hungry grin.

"I think maybe you find something and not tell me," Viktor said, stones in his voice.

"I want the painting as much as you."

"Also, you do not tell me about these other men looking for the painting." He exhaled noisily through his nostrils. "You meet with them, then fly to California. Why you do this? You think you fool old Russian like me, but I think *you* are the foolish man. You and me, we have business agreement, but these other people… they will kill you and steal painting."

Kat had told him everything. Whatever happened between us, a portion of her loyalty remained with Viktor, a bond deeper than whatever we shared. Had she grown fearful of gambling on his loyalty, of putting her life at risk? He'd saved her life and I could do nothing to rebalance that fact in my favor.

"A man threatened to kill Wes and me unless I find the painting by tomorrow," I said. "I need to find it, Viktor." The truth might save me if Viktor believed his competition would do whatever was necessary.

"Who is this person?"

"A professional who tried to kill Wes and me. I don't know his name or how to find him. He wants the Van Gogh as much as you."

Viktor looked up at Arby. "What you think, Arby? Maybe this other man has right idea. Adam, he disappears and we find this picture without him."

"Kill me and the Van Gogh's gone forever," I said with as much confidence as I could muster. "You and Kat know nothing about my father. Wes and I are the only ones who can find it." The words were a half-truth that I hoped bought time and maybe my life. If Viktor or the killer considered me disposable, I had no control over who pulled the trigger, so I had to convince Viktor to let me keep looking.

Or I could go to the police and… tell them what? That I was working with the most vicious crime boss in the city? That Kat and I had visited Marguerite Bouchet the day she was killed? That we discovered Arthur's and Lamar's bodies and not reported the murders? All because of a painting none of us had ever seen? Crazy as it appeared, Viktor offered our only safety net against a psychotic killer. I was locked in a pitch-black room with snakes, any one of which might kill me. Two weeks ago, I craved little more than a successful gallery, wanting only my fair share of the king's deer, not an entire dukedom. Now...

Viktor folded his arms and gnawed at the corner of his mouth with the look of a man who survived the worst Moscow had thrown at him. The smartest fox didn't grow old in the swamps of Moscow and Chicago without a sixth sense. Whatever cleverness I possessed had caught up to me and he detected the change, something that wasn't there when I first denied the Van Gogh's existence. Viktor had spent his life weighing profit against the prospect of sudden death, balancing payback with little thought of the means required to attain it. I hoped the rewards promised by the Van Gogh tempted him not to risk a mistake. If I misjudged his greed, I was meat for Arby.

Viktor lifted his hand and started to speak when the door buzzer sounded. A couple peered through the front door glass, shopping bags in hand. The woman smiled and waved. Arby strode to the center of the gallery and motioned them away, staring them down until they hurried down Huron to find another gallery.

Viktor grunted and adjusted the pistol jammed under his waistband. Sucking at his teeth, he studied me. "I think we go to this house in California."

I managed a shrug. "Why? There's nothing there."

"I think there is something you not tell me."

"Wes and I had combed every inch of the place." I could hear my father's laughter as two Russians tromped around the place.

"We go with you," Viktor said. "Make sure this other man does not bother you." He grinned at me. "We take Katia too. She tells me you know about her, why she is good associate like Arby."

Arby looked at me as if something unpleasant clung to his shoe.

"You stay at my house tonight." Viktor made a wry face at Arby, unable to suppress another grin. "Not to worry," he said. "If I kill you, Vasily tells God not to forgive me, that I kill his friend. But Arby, he is not afraid of God. If you do not tell truth, Arby kills you and goes to hell. It does not matter to him."

Arby displayed his industrial dental work and Viktor got to his feet, the discussion ended. He clapped me on the shoulder and tightened his grip. "You and Katia stay at house tonight. Then we go to California tomorrow. Look at this house."

Chapter Forty-Nine

Viktor's grim-faced wife directed me to a narrow bed in a cluttered back room. That night I tossed on rough linens that smelled of harsh soap, staring at a water stain on the old plaster ceiling. The house still smelled of boiled cabbage, and I had no idea where Arby slept, imagining he had no qualms sleeping in the basement. Viktor's suspicions reverberated until the door cracked open and Kat slipped into the room. I heard the rustle of clothes and she slipped naked into bed, erasing any thought of Viktor.

"Hold me," she whispered, her breath a heady mixture of cigarettes and something sweeter as she pressed against me. The house was too small to risk normal conversation and we whispered like teenagers risking pleasure next to our parents' bedroom.

"I thought you'd walked away," I murmured, burying my face in her hair.

I felt her head shake. "You once asked me not to leave you. I should have told you I would never do that. Not now."

I kissed her and she tugged my boxers down. Our hands explored each other and she moaned as I moved on top of her, struggling to stifle her cries in the little room. I remembered our first night when her urgency bordered on desperation. She tested my stamina once again, pushing me to my limit until I collapsed onto my side, our breathing uneven. When Viktor didn't crash through the door, I wrapped one arm around her.

"We'll find a way through this," I whispered. "Painting or no painting, there's no way I'll lose you. No one will ever harm you."

"It's not Viktor that frightens me. I'm tired of looking into strangers' faces, imagining they want my life."

"But you haven't told the American authorities anything."

"You still don't understand," she said. "Fleeing the state is treason. Nothing is left to chance where desertion concerned. Paranoia is more than a mental condition. In Russia, it's guarantees survival."

I wanted to pull the blanket over our heads and tell her she was safe. That I'd never let anyone harm her. It was more than the instinct to protect her. I'd wound my way through a succession of lovers to find the only one who now mattered.

"Don't leave me," she whispered.

"Never."

***

Early next morning, Viktor sat at the small kitchen table, the white enamel surface chipped and stained, his wife nowhere in sight. The Tokarev rested beside his mug of black tea. Arby sat next to me as though breakfast had arrived and I could see Viktor was more agitated than the previous night. Maybe he'd changed his mind about Vasily ratting him out to God.

"What are our plans today?" I asked, willing to sell my soul for a cup of coffee that no one offered.

Viktor didn't look up and Arby flashed a feral smile. I did my best to ignore the golem, my eyes fixed on Viktor. "Last night you said—"

Viktor raised his hand. "We talk when Katia is here."

I did as ordered and leaned away from Arby who did not believe in the time-honored ritual of daily or weekly bathing. No one spoke until Katia joined us, dressed for travel. Aware of the tension, she poured a cup of the tea from a pot on the stove and sat next to Viktor, ignoring the pistol. Dressed in tan slacks and a green pullover, her hair was pulled back in a sleek ponytail. Ignoring the automatic, she pulled her chair to the table, the pistol within easy reach.

Viktor mirrored her movement and moved his hand toward the gun.

"We talk now," he said, pulling the Tokarev closer.

I didn't move, aware the dynamics of our little group had taken an unhealthy detour. I studied Viktor as he looked at Kat, aware the Van Gogh and I had rotted away years of trust, certain she did not feel the calmness she displayed. She lit a cigarette, waved out the match, and squinted through the smoke at her benefactor, her eyes more sorrowful than frightened.

"What is it, Viktor?" she asked.

He drummed his thick fingers on the tabletop. Looking into his mug for an answer, he began shaking his head as though saddened by the death of a friend.

Arby had dismissed me as a threat and watched Kat. Viktor walked his fingers to the automatic in a childlike gesture until his index finger stroked the black plastic grip.

"I think about you after Adam and I talk last night," he said. "Something is not right. I do not think you tell me the truth. You spend my money and do not tell me what is going on."

"There's nothing to tell," I interrupted.

Arby's heavy boot kicked my chair, almost toppling me onto the linoleum floor. I started to my feet but Arby was quicker, pinning me in the chair.

Viktor pointed at me. "You do not talk now. Is bad enough what you and Katia do."

"We've done nothing," I said.

Arby grabbed my shirt collar.

"Yes, you do nothing!" Viktor exploded. "Spend my money. Make love. Go to fancy parties. You think I do not know these things?"

Kat interrupted, "Everything we did was to find the painting."

"You sleep with him and this helps you find painting?" he yelled.

Kat ignored the hurt in his voice. "Adam found Van Gogh's easel and a photograph of the painting. Someone killed an old woman who owned the photo. We talked to another man in France who *told* us the Van Gogh exists." She dropped her cigarette in the tea cup. "Have I ever lied to you, Viktor?"

Viktor shifted in his chair. "I have only your word for what you say."

"I asked if I ever lied to you."

He waved her away. "There is first time for every betrayal."

Kat held his gaze, the next few seconds deciding our fate.

"There is a man trying to kill Adam," she said.

"You already tell me that. What do I care about this man?"

"If he kills Adam, the painting is gone," she said.

Viktor picked up the Tokarev.

I jumped to my feet and snatched a butter knife off the table, feeling ridiculous.

"Sit down," Viktor said. Then to Arby, "I tell you when."

Viktor put down the pistol and I tossed the knife on the table, praying my voice didn't break. "We're close, Viktor. If we find the painting, you'll be there to see it. You and I will make more money that you can imagine." I was buying time and knew he recognized the tactic; desperate ploys were nothing new to him. He'd killed people and forgotten their names next day.

"Ah, but you tell me painting does not exist when your brother comes to me. You were not lying to me then. I should have listened and saved my money."

"I'm not lying to you now."

I shut up and resisted looking at Kat, afraid to say anything that might set Viktor off. Arby sat forward on the edge of his chair as if restrained by an invisible choke leash. Viktor tapped the gun butt on the table, digging more valleys into the surface until he stood and tucked the gun beneath his belt.

"We make new arrangement," he said. "Like I tell you last night, we go to this house in California. All of us."

Chapter Fifty

Tasso sat on the hotel bed and dialed the embassy in Washington. His cheap cell phone crackled with static before a woman answered.

"Give me Ambassador Korinkin," he said in Russian.

"He is not here. Could I connect you with someone else?"

"Find him."

"I'm sorry but that's not possible. He's—"

"Find him now if you value your head."

The line went dead and Tasso thought the woman had hung up. He heard a muffled conversation and several clicks. Angry at being cut off, he started to redial when a man's disembodied voice came on the line.

"Do you have a weather report for me?"

"The weather in Vladivostok is very severe this year."

"Just a moment," the voice said.

Tasso leaned against the headboard and waited.

Korinkin came on the phone, slightly out of breath. "The line is now secure," he said,

"The woman is not in Chicago," Tasso said. "Her landlady said she went to California. I need an address."

"We have no way of knowing where she went," Korinkin bleated.

"Use your magical telecommunication powers. I need an address."

"It may take a while. There are—"

Tasso suddenly remembered Dansby. "Never mind."

Chapter Fifty-One

I called Wes from Viktor's house and told him I'd be away for several days. I wanted to tell him to take Barbara and run, but Arby stood at my shoulder.

At the airport, I was the last one to board United's mid-morning flight to Los Angeles. Viktor sat in First Class watching as our luggage was loaded, ignoring me. In the seat beside him, Arby's collarless shirt bulged over his seat belt, beefy forearms testing the armrests. He glanced up as I lugged my overnight bag into Economy. My unlimited expense account had met its end.

I shoved my canvas bag in the overhead on the last row and plopped down beside Kat who shared my banishment from First Class. She managed a tentative smile. "Viktor is not happy," she said softly.

"I know."

"He does not make threats he does not keep."

My anger rekindled, I leaned closer to her. "If he wants to kill me, tell him the line forms at the rear." Viktor and my unseen shadow expected miracles I couldn't produce. I struggled to recall what I'd almost remembered at the house. Escape lay in something I'd missed, something Bonnings had said. I'd tried to connect the dots but no revelation materialized.

"Viktor believes I lied to him," she whispered.

"You didn't. You only left out a few details."

"One of his associates has arranged a car for him and Arby."

"What about you?"

She removed an airline magazine from the seat pocket in front of her. "I made my own arrangements."

"A car or gun?"

"Both."

The morning sun from the oval window softened her face. If the past thirty years had ordained different fates for us, we might be flying to a Hawaiian or

Caribbean beach to drink rum and make love. Much as I wanted the fantasy, I never found a way to correct might-have-beens.

"I can't change what Viktor believes," I said.

"He has been very patient because he sees a great deal of money."

"He exiled you back here?"

"He believes I am not telling him the entire truth. To him, that is worse than incompetence."

"Did you request a gun for me?"

She concentrated on her magazine and a tear appeared. "No. Arby will search you at the house but Viktor may not let him touch me."

I leaned over and kissed her cheek. Around us, seat belts clicked as late passengers squirmed into cramped seats and the engines whined to life. Eyes closed, Kat took my hand in hers and we blocked out the noise, conserving our strength for what lay ahead.

***

The Contractor's mobile buzzed and he saw the caller's number. Savoring the last bites of his ham omelet he took his time and wiped his mouth before he turned his back to the crowds and pushed the answer button.

"Where are you?" his employer asked.

"Good morning to you, too."

"Cut the crap. I asked where you are."

"Sitting in the magnificent airport restaurant at LAX, watching my fellow citizens run for the gates like sprayed roaches, pulling screaming little roaches after them."

The line went silent.

"Got ahead of you, didn't I?" the Contractor said.

"How'd you know they were headed to Los Angeles?"

"I watched Barrow and the Russian entourage came out of the little house in Wheaton with suitcases. My superb deductive reasoning kicked in and I took a chance. Turns out I was right. My sources revealed their flight and rental car agency. I got an earlier plane and beat them here by an hour. They're due to land in fifteen minutes." He gave a small burp. "You know, the food in this dump isn't half bad. My breakfast…"

"Find out where they're going, then…"

The Contractor interrupted him. "I know my job. I gave Barrow a deadline and I'll make sure he keeps it."

"I don't give a damn about your plan. I'm in Denver, almost ready to board my plane. American Flight 455. I'll call you when I land. Pick me up outside Baggage and don't do anything until I get there." The Contractor pictured his employer staring into space, out of his element as the deadline drew nearer. "Krushenko and his goon could be a problem."

"They won't be a problem," the Contractor said.

"My guess is they're all headed to Barrow's old house."

"You think the painting's there?"

"How the hell should I know? I hired you to find it and we're stumbling around in the dark."

"It's time to get answers."

Silence again. "Possibly. I'm through playing games."

"Then let me do it my way." Questioning the Russian woman in private was especially appealing.

"Pick me up and we'll talk."

The Contractor returned the phone to his pocket. The man treated him like a canker, but he'd soon change all that. Once he possessed the Van Gogh, he'd never deal with his kind again. He checked his watch. Plenty of time to take care of the first order of business, a detail his employer didn't need to know. Not that he'd care once he was out of the way. A waitress approached and he declined a third cup of coffee. No need to load up on caffeine. The endorphins were already kicking in, promising an interesting day.

***

Thirty minutes later the Contractor sat in a mid-size SUV rental near the Hertz exit gate. He hadn't yet figured out how to get close to the Russians but something always presented itself. He often surprised himself when simple answers appeared from nowhere. Patience was hard-earned but trumped impulsiveness, the results adding to the moment. A string of cars exited the lot and he glanced at his watch. More than two hours before his employer arrived at Baggage. He let his window down and leaned back against the head rest, enjoying the sixty-degree breeze.

Chicago would soon be a memory.

A white compact pulled out of the gate and he recognized Barrow behind the wheel, the Russian woman beside him. Five minutes later, Krushenko and Bolkov followed in a Buick sedan and swung northbound onto US 405 toward Santa Monica. The Contractor waited until several cars to passed and followed the Buick onto the expressway, concealed in traffic.

LA traffic was lighter than usual and he switched on the radio, finding a classical station to accompany the half hour drive to the coastal highway. Surprised when the Buick exited the freeway after several miles, he switched lanes, ignoring the horns. The Buick slowed and rambled into a seedy commercial district. Two traffic signals slowed him but he kept the Buick in sight, a plan forming as he noted the timing of the traffic lights. Another quarter mile and he spotted the Buick in front of a small restaurant, hand-printed Russian signs in the window. The Contractor drove past the diner as the two men got out and entered.

The surrounding area boasted tire outlets, payday loan shops, and liquor stores surrounded by trash strewn lots and boarded-up stores. Three blocks from the restaurant, he spotted what he sought and parked in front of a Goodwill store. Inside, no one noticed him as he scavenged the scabbiest bins, the stench of unwashed old sweat gagging him until he turned his head. Holding his breath, he pulled out a pair of filthy sneakers, torn trousers, and a shirt missing several buttons. The sales clerk attempted to steer him to more serviceable clothes, but he handed over a ten-dollar bill and left without taking his change or making eye contact.

A service station across the street provided the changing room. He stripped off his slacks and golf shirt and changed into the reeking clothes, the odor barely endurable. He mussed his hair with both hands, checked his appearance in the mirror, and emerged a street person. He bought a bottle of water from a bored clerk and stole the windshield squeegee from the service island before driving away.

It would work, he told himself. In fact, it would be amusing if he played his part well.

He parked on a side street a block away from the second intersection and got out. Bending down he smeared gutter dirt on his cheeks and hands. The Browning beneath his shirttail he re-checked his appearance in the car's side mirror. He walked back to the traffic light, the reek of a stranger's sweat nauseating as the sun found him. Squeegee and water bottle in hand, he waited on the corner, standing on one foot, then the other, mimicking the dance of street crazies. A few cars zoomed past as he aimlessly shambled back and forth along the sidewalk, muttering to himself as drivers looked away. The traffic light turned red, then green.

Forty seconds. Plenty of time.

Ten minutes later, the Buick appeared and his luck held. There were no other cars in sight as the light changed to red. The Contractor weaved toward the idling car, waving the bottle and scraper, yelling incoherently. In the passenger seat, Krushenko watched his approach. Staggering around the hood to the driver's window, the Contractor lifted the water bottle and squeegee with a stupid grin. Krushenko said something and Arby lowered the driver's window. The Contractor walked to window and shot him point blank.

Bone and brain matter splattered Viktor. The Contractor deftly reached inside, cut the engine, and jammed the gear lever into Park before he shot Krushenko in the face. Two shots finished the job.

Making certain the street remained empty, he opened the car's rear door, found the ejected casings, and dropped them in his pocket before he trotted back to his car, ignoring an impatient horn behind the stalled Buick. He drove around the block to make certain he wasn't followed and pulled behind another service station. In the Men's Room, he stuffed the filthy clothes and shoes in a trash can. Clad only in his shorts and socks he wiped himself down with wet paper towels. The Browning reloaded, he changed back into his clothes and checked his appearance in the fly-specked mirror before he smiled.

God, he loved improvisation.

Chapter Fifty-Two

"One of Viktor's favorite restaurants is near the airport," Kat said as I turned onto I-10 toward the coast. "It is what you call a dump but they serve good Russian food. They will meet us at the house."

Glad to be alone with her, I looked forward to showing her the house where it all started. I couldn't explain my motives but it seemed essential she understand where it all began, why finding the Van Gogh meant more than money. Maybe the house would whisper its secrets to her and she'd understand.

We drove along Pacific Coast Highway past Santa Monica. On our left, the expanse of blue water stretched across the horizon, the day miraculously free of smog. I didn't bother to point out development along the beach, indulging an old dislike for the ramshackle houses that masqueraded as California chic. To me they'd always been eyesores, most of them flat-roofed structures with nothing to distinguish them except outlandish price tags.

North of the city, I turned east onto San Vincente Boulevard and began the familiar ascent toward the bluffs. Brushy canyons and steep drop-offs hemmed in the road as we climbed into the hills. Kat lowered her window and the wind swirled her hair, recalling an engraving I'd seen of a mounted Scythian princess racing across the steppes. She peered into the desolate ravines below the road and I kept my eyes on the blind curves, wondering how seriously she took Viktor's threat.

"I dreamed of Russia and my grandmother last night," she said. "I was in the car with the two men who took me from the orphanage. They drove us to Chicago. At the lake they pushed me in the water as my grandmother watched. The water was freezing and I couldn't scream for help."

"Dreams mean nothing."

She rested her head against door frame and searched the canyons' deaths. "An old Gypsy told me they open doors for us. She said dreams take us to places we can never visit."

I didn't reply until my mother's birdbath greeted us like children come to visit. I pulled onto the broken concrete pad and turned off the engine. What, I wondered, might the mother I'd never known, have thought about the Russian woman beside me and the painting her husband loved and hoarded? Was she complicit in his deception, or tolerant about his passion to own something he never dreamed of? I preferred to think of her involvement as a benign concession to her husband's failures that trailed him like wayward kites.

Kat got out, mesmerized by the boundless blue extending north and south below the ridge. Spellbound, she pulled her coat closer as wind scoured the bluff.

"You grew up here?" she asked.

I nodded, perhaps appreciating the view for the first time. It didn't seem right I'd grown up with such beauty, fighting small battles in the little house, while she struggled daily to stay alive. The feeling grew stronger as I tried to imagine what Kat was feeling, comparing the panorama to the orphanage. None of it was fair, but as my father was fond of saying, "the fair comes in August." It was a stupid saying, but I learned from it, appreciating work without waiting for miracles or a gullible victim to appear. It was a lesson he never learned.

"I was born here," I said. "We never lived anywhere else."

She gazed over the ocean and I imagined she saw a fairy land.

"Viktor will be here soon," she said.

"Did someone bring you a gun?"

She patted her topcoat pocket without taking her eyes from the vista. "While we waited for our luggage."

From where we stood, I saw whitecaps and lines of foam along the beach far below. I checked the road leading to the house and took her hand. I hadn't lived here since I was a boy, but now stood outside the old house for the second time in four days.

"It's too nice a day to talk about guns. Come see the palace where I was raised."

"You believe the painting could be here?" she asked.

A current passed through me again as we stepped inside. I'd seen or heard something to do with the papers Franklin Bonnings showed Wes and me. I waited for the epiphany to solve the riddle, but the fragments refused to mesh.

"Wes and I didn't find anything," I said. "There're memories here but no painting."

"New eyes see new things," she said.

She looked around of the living room, absorbing the dregs of my youth. Removing her coat, she laid it over the frayed lawn chair. Together, we scoured the house, retracing my earlier inspection. She ran her hands over each wall, feeling for out-of-place seams and bulges beneath the paint. We examined the ceilings and crawled along the floors like beggars, checking for uneven boards. She pounded closet walls and paced off each room, looking for construction anomalies. Watching her, it was easy to imagine her searching apartments of KGB suspects.

"What's beneath the floors?" she asked.

"Concrete."

There'd been no alterations to the house that I could see, nothing that indicated my father altered the original plans. Wes and I had replayed our search on the flight back to Chicago until we gave up in disgust. Every room was as we remembered. Neither of us believed we could have lived with a gigantic masterpiece, oblivious of its presence.

Kat looked at the ceiling. "The attic?"

"Nothing. Wes and I checked."

"Could your father have buried it?"

I considered the possibility and shook my head. "If he owned the painting, he loved it too much to hide the girl in a grave. He wouldn't have exposed a Van Gogh to the elements."

We walked outside and circled the house, inspecting the eaves and exterior walls, my frustration at the edge of despair. What in hell had he done with the damned thing? Intelligent wasn't the word to describe Robert Barrow, but he possessed shrewdness like all competent con men.

"There is nothing here," Kat said.

She checked the road for Viktor and Arby and we climbed in the car to wait for them. Kat lowered the window and lit a cigarette, gazing out the windshield at the bluff. "I wanted you to find the painting. Not just for Viktor or the money but for your father. I think you needed to show the world he preserved something of great value. That he was not all bad."

She was right, but I'd failed. Against my better judgment, I bummed a cigarette and lit it, sucking in smoke with a heady rush. If ever I deserved a treat, it was today. Kat continued talking but I knew the quest was over. Abetted by the nicotine and self-pity, I sat numbly and waited for Viktor and Arby. Few people got a shot at redemption and I'd blown mine. My father did his part to hinder my efforts to salvage him, but no stroke of luck or divine involvement intervened to let me to play the avenging hero. All I'd done was sharpen the appetite of people willing to kill me. Better for everyone if the eccentric Dutchman never lived.

I looked at the deserted house as something struggled toward the surface again. Something to do with Bonnings. Something flawed like a cracked pane of glass that became evident only when light struck it at a certain angle. The fragment teased and ran away every time I reached for it. Kat saw my anguish and leaned her head on my shoulder.

"You cannot take the blame," she said. "Your father built walls you can never tear down."

I lost my breath.

Walls.

A stone broke loose and I *knew*. Grinning like a madman, I tossed the cigarette away and opened the car door.

"Come on."

Inside the house I rushed to the kitchen. Copies of the original blueprints were still in the drawer where I'd tossed them. Yanking out the faded pages, I unfurled them and walked into the living room, my hands trembling. The fifth sheet showed interior construction details, a layout of every room, and there it was. Right in front of me.

The original plan showed a combined living room and dining room, but the space had been altered. A wall had been constructed to form a separate living and dining room. Had my mother insisted on a separate dining room after construction was completed? A final change? I didn't think so. Standing at the exposed end of the wall, I saw what we'd all missed. Under the dividing wall, the color and length of hardwood boards extended from the living room floor into the dining room—another wall had been built on top of the original floor.

I paced off the distance, running my hand along the smooth surface. Fifteen feet long with a nine-foot ceiling. Every room in the house had been repainted countless times, layers of paint becoming uniform over the years, concealing the additional wall. Had my father bought hammer and nails, I wondered. Purchased lath strips and bags of plaster? Had he read a book on home improvement, my mother helping him as he constructed the wall? Wes and I had lived with the painting all those years, walking past it every day. We unknowingly breathed the same air that kept the girl safe and warm in my father's improvised cocoon.

"I know where the painting is."

Kat stared at me.

"Here," I said, laying my palm against the wall. "The Van Gogh's right here."

Kat looked at me as if I'd spoken in Greek.

I patted the plaster, grinning. How many times had my father caressed the wall as he walked around the corner?

I pointed to the blueprint. "My father built this wall to hide the Van Gogh. He loved the girl, and even more, I think he loved keeping her close, so much so that he never cashed in. The painting stayed next to him while he drank away his life. It was the last trick he played on the world."

Kat and I never heard the car roll into the drive. No car door, no footsteps. About to explain my father's cleverness, a tall man appeared in the doorway holding a long-barreled automatic at his side. He leaned against the jamb, clad in a Polo shirt and sport coat and as though late for his tee time. It didn't take much imagination to match the assured face with the voice on the phone.

"We've never been introduced," he said.

Chapter Fifty-Three

I started to reply when Jack McMinnis brushed past him. I stared at the confident face and knew my mistake would cost Kat and me our lives.

I'd been a fool, overlooking him, seeing only Dansby and Viktor as threats. Jack saw the Van Gogh as real from the start, the stolen letters whetting his appetite. I'd confided in him, strengthening his belief, while he stayed close to Dansby and me, keeping a step ahead, watching as Kat and I blundered around Europe.

He walked to the center of the room and looked around, reliving his memories, Kat and I forgotten for the moment. How many years had passed since he'd passed through the same door to be greeted by the reek of Gordon's Gin. When he spoke, his voice linked triumph with regret.

"Adam, Adam, Adam," he said, testing the ragged chair before he sat down. "You should have listened to my associate here. Now you've run out of time and I'll have to find the Van Gogh without you."

His companion appraised Kat and me with the expression of an executive dismissing two wayward employees. "Don't be too hard on him," the man said. "He made it interesting. Lots of travel."

I stared at him, every synapse clicking. He'd been outside the hotel in Amsterdam. On the plane. At the bar in the Drake. He'd worn different outfits, a universal presence in every crowd. Even Kat had looked past him.

Settled in the chair, Jack said, "You made things so much easier when you called me but I misread you. I always thought you were the smart one. That you'd find the painting. Now I can't take the chance you'll stumble on it and find a way to keep it." He scanned the room again, blind to what I'd overlooked. "Dansby was a great diversion," he said. "The perfect stalking horse. For all his money and connections, he never got close." He cocked his head, the note of disappointment returning. "Now, I'll have to look for it on my own." He looked around. "I'll start by taking this old place apart."

Kat glanced out the window and the tall man intercepted her glance.

"The Russian cavalry isn't coming, Miss Veranova," he said. "I'm afraid they were detained at a traffic light."

"They're dead?"

"Unless resurrection is back in style."

The gun was in her coat pocket, draped over the chair where McMinnis sat. Afraid she'd lunge for the pistol, I took a step toward McMinnis, blocking the killer's line of fire.

"Why all this, Jack? I would have worked with you. No need to involve this maniac."

McMinnis looked at me with the face of someone I'd misjudged my entire life. "I guess I don't play well with others. Never very good at sharing my toys. You see, I discovered having a long memory is a curse. You and Wes of all people should know that. Bad memories collect resentment like a sewer. Careless hurts turn into bitterness. Sadness becomes hate before you know it. Your father was good at making sure I hated him."

"We need to finish up and leave," the other man said. "Look for your frickin' painting."

McMinnis pointed at him. "Shut the hell up. He deserves the whole story."

It registered they hadn't heard me tell Kat about my discovery. If they'd arrived ten seconds earlier, we'd already be dead. I still held the blueprints in one hand but McMinnis ignored them. Even if I gave him the painting, he'd kill us. Buying time, I said, "I thought you didn't like Van Gogh. You told my father he was a hack."

Slumped forward, Jack shook his head, aiming for benign tolerance. "Whether I like his work isn't the point. This is about money, Adam, nothing more. I would have thought you'd learned that from Robert Barrow if nothing else." He crossed his legs and Kat's coat swayed. I prayed the PPK wouldn't bump the aluminum chair leg. "You know," he said, "you look like him, but I guess people tell you that."

The humor gone, he said, "You want to know what really happened between him and me? To put it in the simplest terms, the old fraud screwed me over. He probably told you I deserted him. That was bullshit. When the mark found us out, he put on a pity show for him and copped a sympathy plea. Told the moron it was all my idea. I went into hiding but got lucky when the mark died in a car accident. I changed my name a couple of times before I became Jack McMinnis again. Robert Barrow cost me ten years on the run, but he taught me how to get what I wanted, and I didn't waste my second chance."

"And the people you killed?" I asked.

He gestured at the tall man. "I never killed anyone. That's why I made an arrangement with him."

"And Wes and me? Kat?"

"In this instance, I'm afraid money rules. After a while, it's like a designer drug. You can't get enough. Finding the painting will put me in Dansby's league. Even if I never sell it, I'll be top dog in art circles. Nothing personal against either of you, and I think you'll agree I'll be doing Wes a favor."

Jack brought it all together in a few sentences. Everything that mattered. Kat. Wes. My father. I didn't care any longer who ended up with the Van Gogh. I wanted only Kat.

"How many lives is the painting worth, Jack?"

"I hope you're not including Jennings. You can't really believe we lost anything of value."

The person I'd once known had coiled into something I couldn't comprehend. Sooner or later he'd sell the Van Gogh. Everything was about money. His kind didn't care about bringing a lost masterpiece into the light of the world. He'd take the credit but cared less about the discovery. No matter what my father may have done, he surpassed McMinnis as a human being.

"You know what's really funny about all this?" Jack said. "Your father was talking crazy one night. Told me this wild tale about a Van Gogh before he passed out." He warmed to the memory. "Next day, he told me that he and some French guy smuggled a huge painting out of France before the Nazis invaded. Claimed it was like nothing the world had ever seen. I dismissed the story as another of his wild tales but it turned out he was telling the truth for once. He was a crafty old bastard, I'll give him that."

Kat shifted her weight and I braced myself.

"Did you believe him?"

"Hell, no. I probably laughed and told him to have another drink. But then Wes contacted me before he called your Russian friend. I wasn't about to chase after some drunk's fantasy, but I had my friend here acquire the letters. I knew then the old bastard hadn't been crazy." He looked around the room frowning at the dirty walls. "I never got a crack at the really big stuff because of him, the kind museums and major auction houses salivate over. Wherever he hid it, he must've had one helluva lucid moment."

He got up and walked into the dining room, frowning at the broken doll before resuming his seat. Kat tensed but he ignored her coat. "Still a dump." He looked at her. "Both of you were after the money, right?"

When neither of us answered, he tossed back his head and laughed. "Oh, God, tell me you didn't do all this to rescue Robert Barrow's soiled name. Please tell me you're not moral crusaders, the bereaved son seeking mercy for his father's soul."

"You've got the letters," I said. "Kat won't say anything with Krushenko gone. She can't afford the notoriety. If you find the painting, no one will ever know she was involved. There's no other proof my father owned a Van Gogh. If you find it, you can destroy the letters and concoct any story you like. Wes and I won't contest your ownership.

"We might work out something," he said, glancing at the man by the door. "Where'd he hide the damn thing?"

I looked at him, my anger building. Did he think I'd believe him? If I had a guardian angel or there was justice, now was the time for the fates to rescue us. But no angel was coming to our rescue, not even Viktor or Arby. It didn't matter if I told him about the wall. Kat and I were dead but he wasn't going to walk away with my father's Van Gogh.

I shrugged. "I guess neither of us lucked out. Why not call it a draw and we all walk away."

"Can't do it, Adam. Too much money's involved. I can't risk it."

For old times' sake, Jack, let her go."

The man killer raised the Browning. "Enough. It's time to go."

McMinnis looked regretfully at Kat. "I'm afraid we've had our last dance, my dear."

I started to speak when a bearded man stepped through the doorway and aimed a revolver at the killer's head.

"Place the pistol on the floor,' he said, his Russian thick. "Slowly, please."

The killer did not move, his pistol aimed at me. He turned his head and looked at the intruder who wore an outdated wool suit. For several long moments, no one moved, the room crowded with people pointing guns.

Puzzled, McMinnis crossed his legs and studied the new arrival. "It's obvious you have more than one guardian, Miss Veranova. It seems I'll have to change my plans to accommodate our new Russian friend."

Kat stood with her arms at her side, her eyes on the man in the doorway. As though acknowledging defeat, she looked at me with heart-rending resignation, aware the reckoning for her past stood a few feet away, retribution in the form of a bearded man dressed in a baggy suit. She glanced at her coat and gave me the barest shrug with a hopeless smile.

The killer looked toward the Russian again and I lunged for his pistol. The taller man staggered back and fired, the bullet hissing past my shoulder. His second shot struck the wall near the ceiling and the Russian clubbed him to the floor. The Russian picked up the Browning and shot him in the forehead. I stumbled away and tripped over Kat, a lake of blood pooling beneath her body.

. Frozen, I watched McMinnis start to speak. The Russian's bullet knocked him from the chair onto the floor. Making certain both men were dead, the intruder wiped the Browning clean and dropped it in McMinnis' hand.

Kneeling beside Kat I knew she was dead. The Russian knelt beside me and laid a finger against her neck.

"Don't touch her!" I yelled.

Sprawled on her back, her lifeless eyes stared on the makeshift wall where a large chunk of plaster had broken away. The Russian stood and I waited for the final shot. Instead, he unscrewed the tubular silencer and tucked the revolver in his waistband. He buttoned his coat and surveyed the three bodies.

"Who are you?" I managed.

"Someone you will never see again."

Kneeling by Kat's body, I looked up at him and I realized I would live. "But why? The painting?"

"Your painting does not concern me."

"Then why?"

"It was old business, as you Americans say."

"Who hired you? At least tell me that."

He walked to the door and looked back. "I am sorry about the woman."

Still on my knees I watched him walk out. A car started up somewhere down the hill a few minutes later. The room buzzed with silence and my breathing

276 The Last Van Gogh

slowed. I tenderly placed my hand on Kat's arm, knowing part of me died with her. I closed my eyes, unable to imagine the rest of my life. When I opened them, I followed her dead gaze to the gaping hole beneath the ceiling.

Gold leaf frame glowed in the jagged cavity. A patch of blue sky lighted the opening, buttery sunlight restoring life to the room. I stared at the familiar brushstrokes and delicate strands of flaxen hair floating in a long-ago breeze.

"There you are," I sobbed, tears in my eyes.

Chapter Fifty-Four

They titled the work *Young Dutch Girl*.

Kat was gone but the girl in the painting lived again. I gradually accepted Kat's loss, remembering the old adage that you never know how much you love someone until you realize you'll never see them again. Kat had known her past would find her one day, that there was still a price to pay. I replayed the disaster at the old house again and again, but no matter how I shuffled events, I never came up with an alternative that let her live. Every hour from my first glimpse of her at Tatiana's to the house on the bluff played out in a way only she could have foreseen. None of us know if love or loss hurts most.

The maelstrom that followed the killings and painting's discovery resulted in hours with California's legal system and art experts who descended on Los Angeles. The police employed every device to prove I was the killer, interrogating me for a week, testing my hands twice for powder residue, subjecting me to multiple detector tests. Forensics and ballistics eventually connected the killer to an unidentified man whom the police suspected of being involved in multiple murders. After a week, they bought my story that the unknown man and McMinnis had argued over the painting before they killed one another, Kat an innocent bystander. No one considered the possibility of a fourth man and I saw no reason to muddy the water. Publicly, I expressed sorrow over McMinnis' demise who I explained was an old friend of my father. Kat was described as my companion, an unfortunate victim in the wrong place at the worst time. No one seemed interested in her background, the media too fixated on any scrap of information they could dig up on the newly discovered masterpiece.

Dansby vouched for my sterling character, fending off buyers and museums and reporters. I suspected he also wielded significant influence with the California authorities who downgraded me to relative insignificance once I was cleared, thrilled the Van Gogh had turned up in their venue. With the hoopla and publicity focused on the discovery, the three deaths quickly became old news, submerged beneath the international storm that raged around the painting

Two weeks later I met Dansby at the Getty Museum high in the hills above the City of Angels. He'd negotiated a deal to have the painting exhibited in the lofty setting before its final fate was decided. Situated a short distance from my father's house, the museum created a fitting mountaintop throne for the newly crowned queen to rule over her admirers.

Dansby, resplendent in a custom suit and flaunting the regimental tie, rubbed shoulders with the art literati and CEO's as though he already owned the painting. In his mind the cat had gotten the canary, at least temporarily. One morning after endless meetings with the museum's board of directors, he and I sat drinking coffee in the director's office, our shoes propped on a glass coffee table. Dansby removed a sterling flask from his jacket and spiked our coffees.

"You found it," he said, leaning back.

"Kat and I both found it." The Van Gogh would always be partly hers. Dansby lowered his head in what passed for regret. "I'm truly sorry, Adam. She was the loveliest of women."

We didn't speak for several minutes, sipping our coffee before I looked up. "Was the Van Gogh worth it, Phillip? All the lives?"

He exhaled heavily. "Katia was what the military labels collateral damage, but there's a balance to everything." Ever the pragmatist, he held his hand up before I could disagree. "Some very bad people were eliminated and your father will be honored for rescuing a great work of art. You're going to be wealthy beyond your wildest imagination, you and Wes both." He poured more whiskey in our cups and checked to make certain the door remained closed.

"Did you tell the police everything that happened at the house?" he asked.

"Most of it."

"Just so. We'll leave it at that."

"One question," I said. "Did you know McMinnis hired a killer to find the painting?"

"The details are in the past now. Better to not ask embarrassing questions."

"And the Russian, if that's what he was, who happened to show up?"

He regarded me with a trace of amusement. "Again, best to leave all that behind you."

He was right, of course. Sleeping dogs never bit you. "Naturally, you'll bid on the painting when it comes to auction."

"Of course! And you'll learn deep pockets win out. You and your brother are famous now, and frankly, I prefer seeing the two of you spend my money."

"You may well end up with the Van Gogh because you're the last one standing, Phillip. You lucked out this time."

He smiled like a roulette player who knows the wheel is rigged. "Luck has nothing to do with winners. And besides, you also had luck, you know. You're still here to enjoy the benefits."

"Did you send the Russian to the house?" I persisted.

His smile fell away. "Leave it alone, Adam."

Dansby and I listened to the hum of the museum's finely-tuned humidifier as I observed him, his coffee cup cradled in both hands, satisfied with whatever machinations he'd engineered. If I was indeed lucky, I had a lot of years left and I'd learn to live with unanswered questions.

"Have you noticed most people are already referring to the painting as 'her'?" he said. "It's as though you rescued a damsel in distress."

"I appreciate you convincing the Getty to give her a temporary home."

"Temporary's the correct word, I assure you. She'll grace my new museum when the proper time arrives."

I stood but Dansby gestured for me to keep my seat a moment longer.

"The girl is only one painting," he said. "Despite the naysayers, there are more masterpieces waiting to be discovered. Lost, stolen, misattributed. I think we'd make a superb team if you want more than your little gallery. I have some capital people at my disposal that I think you'd appreciate. Your brother could run the gallery if you like. We'll make it larger and give him a purpose in life."

"I'll think about it, Phillip."

We rose and shook hands. I had little doubt he'd eventually possess the Van Gogh one way or the other, but only after writing an immense check to Wes and me.

Walking from the conference room, a sense of hollow bewilderment descended on me. It took a few seconds to realize the feeling centered around Kat. She was gone and the chase was over. Head down, my heels echoed in the empty hall as I thought about Dansby's proposition, knowing it entailed a new direction in my life.

I headed toward the east wing where the painting hung, barely glancing at legendary paintings on the walls. The area where the Van Gogh hung was closed off for the week, the staff fashioning a proper tribute to Van Gogh as they finalized security measures. The Getty, it appeared. was doing everything in its considerable power to compete for ownership of the painting.

Two armed guards at the temporary barrier recognized me and waved me inside. A discreet bronze plate beside the double doors proclaimed I was entering the Robert E. Barrow Room. Was he laughing again? Feeling I'd entered a church, I was conscious of my footsteps on the immaculate wooden floor, fearing I might startle the girl who watched me from the opposite end of the room.

Alone on a wall the color of the moon, she appeared to glow within the refurbished antique frame, her isolated setting designed to enrapture those stood before the immense canvas. The painting dominated the minimalist room, exuding a hushed majesty for experts and novices alike. The massive work would shock most who saw it for the first time, the expanse of color unlike any known Van Gogh. He'd surpassed his genius, the unknown girl captured in a single sun-drenched moment. Ten feet away, she appeared eager to step onto the polished floor to inquire who had disturbed her solitude. The gossamer blue dress moved in rhythm with swaying stalks of ripe wheat stirred by a breeze from her left. Hands at her sides, her palms were turned outward as though grasping the wind. The thirsty landscape appeared to drink in the sunlight, shaming the museum lights artfully positioned to show every brushstroke.

I imagined her breathing fresh air for the first time in 80 years, never aging since her creation. Did she plead with me to help her escape the bare room and seek the man who created her? Was she a simple farm girl, or had Van Gogh polished one of his whores? Perhaps she was simply a longing captured in a gilded world of his own making. The question would remain the crux of serious debate for the next millennium. Dansby claimed money trumped good intentions, but this time he was wrong. Luck and justice triumphed over force and avarice. Kat and the unknown girl in the painting were dead but they left behind a legacy of beauty.

***

I met Wes next afternoon at Gladstones in Santa Monica. The restaurant was one of my favorites, the sprawling beachfront icon never able to decide if it was a tourist trap or watering hole for locals.

Wes was waiting for me in the bar. Dressed in a white Boss blazer, khaki shorts, and flip flops, a club soda and lime sat in front of him. Two laughing beach bunnies in bikinis flanked him, his grin far too large for a married man. Pretend drink in hand, he reluctantly disengaged from his admirers and followed me to a table on the cedar sundeck. Colonized by white beach umbrellas, the deck offered some the best celebrity gazing in Santa Monica. Serious mid-afternoon drinkers and tourists crowded the bar, so Wes and I had the deck to ourselves. A mild surf curled onto stretches of sand and I ordered a beer as we watched lethargic waves slide onto the beach.

"I see you made new friends," I said.

He lifted his palms and raised his eyebrows. "Me? I'm just enjoying Left Coast ambiance and its more attractive inhabitants"

"Don't enjoy them too much. I'd hate to rat you out to Barbara."

He laughed and I joined him, my spirits lifted by my future prospects and my brother's tanned face. By God, I'd done it and survived, and it appeared he'd made it too. We looked at one another, reading each other's thoughts. He sipped his club soda, his new persona no doubt abetted by the fact he'd soon be an extremely wealthy man.

"How's the gut and leg?" I asked.

He removed a plastic vial from his jackets pocket, rattling the contents. "The leg's still sore, but these help."

"Just don't get used to them."

Maybe it was the pain pills, but he emitted different aura as though our ordeal purged his torments. I hoped it was more than the promise of money.

"Did the police learn the name of the man with McMinnis?" he asked.

"They have no idea who he was."

Wes sat back in his chair. "You know Viktor and Arby were found dead in their car. The cops say it was a professional hit."

I nodded.

"Want to tell me what really happened at the house?"

I looked around the deck. "I can tell you they didn't kill one another like the papers reported."

"Who then?"

"Someone I've never seen."

"A friend of Dansby, you think?"

I shrugged. "He was east European, most likely a Russian. I think he may have been KGB sent to dispose of Kat, but I guess I'll never know."

"Could have been a pal of Viktor and Arby," Wes said, "although they've gone to their greater or lesser rewards."

"But why leave me alive? Or you?" We were still swimming in waters far out of our depth.

Wes's expression softened. "I'm sorry about Kat."

"I owe her my life." It was all I could think to say. She'd been so close to escaping her past. Maybe I could have helped her. God knows, I would have tried.

We talked for a few minutes about the painting's upcoming unveiling and what would happen afterwards, how our lives would never be the same. A few miles away, an unknown Dutch girl ruled her new home, ready to spawn renewed adulation for her tortured creator. Separated by more than a hundred years, Vincent Van Gogh and my father had shared a secret lover. Emerging from the past, they returned a lovely young girl to life.

End

About the Author

Will Ottinger spent his early life in Savannah, Georgia. A graduate of Emory University with a BA in history and literature, he is also a graduate of Northwestern Graduate Trust School in Chicago.

He published his first novel, *A Season for Ravens*, in 2014. It was named by *Reader Views* as one of its top-three Historical Fiction works of 2014-2015. His second novel, *The Savannah Betrayals*, was published in March 2018. Windrow and Greene Publishers in Great Britain published his non-fiction work on the art of historical miniatures, an art form in which he gained national and international recognition as a Grand Master painter. He authored a magazine column for seven years, trained and lectured extensively in the financial field, wrote articles for trust and investment publications, and has spoken to large and small audiences. He served as president of *Scribbler's Ink*, a Houston writers' group.

Former founder and owner of a wealth management training/consulting firm, he and his wife also owned an art gallery in downtown Chicago. An inveterate fly fisherman, they now live in Atlanta Georgia.

Thank you so much for reading one of our **Crime Fiction** novels.
If you enjoyed the experience, please check out our recommended title for your next great read!

Caught in a Web by Joseph Lewis

"This important, nail-biting crime thriller about MS-13 sets the bar very high. One of the year's best thrillers." *–BEST THRILLERS*

View other Black Rose Writing titles at www.blackrosewriting.com/books and use promo code **PRINT** to receive a **20% discount** when purchasing.

BLACK ROSE writing™

APR 1 8 2019

CPSIA information can be obtained
at www.ICGtesting.com
Printed in the USA
LVHW041518210219
608325LV00002B/414/P

9 781684 331932